OUR

VIOLENT

ENDS

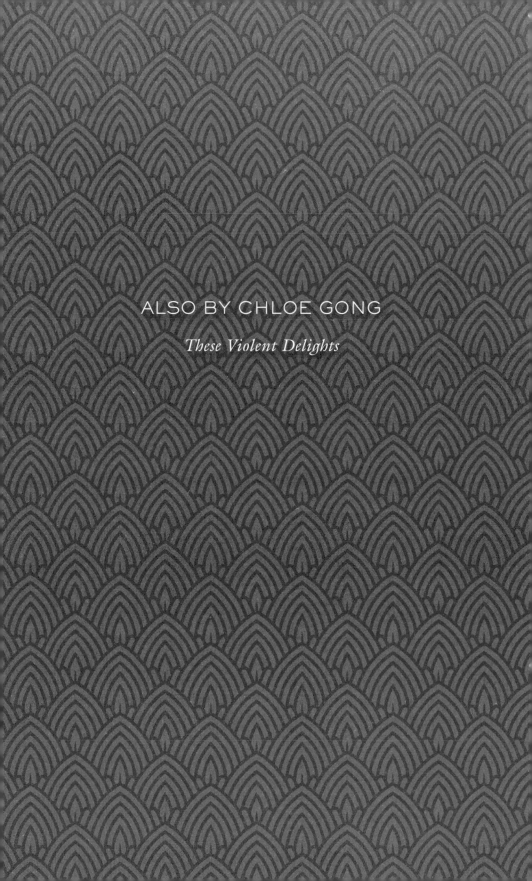

ALSO BY CHLOE GONG

These Violent Delights

OUR

VIOLENT

ENDS

CHLOE GONG

HODDER &
STOUGHTON

First published in Great Britain in 2021 by Hodder & Stoughton
An Hachette UK company

1

Copyright © Chloe Gong 2021

The right of Chloe Gong to be identified as the Author of the Work has been
asserted by her in accordance with the Copyright, Designs and Patents Act 1988.

A CIP catalogue record for this title is available from the British Library

Hardback ISBN 978 1 529 34456 1
Trade Paperback ISBN 978 1 529 34457 8
eBook ISBN 978 1 529 34459 2

Printed and bound in Great Britain by Clays Ltd, Elcograf S.p.A.

Hodder & Stoughton policy is to use papers that are natural, renewable
and recyclable products and made from wood grown in sustainable
forests. The logging and manufacturing processes are expected to
conform to the environmental regulations of the country of origin.

Hodder & Stoughton Ltd
Carmelite House
50 Victoria Embankment
London EC4Y 0DZ

www.hodder.co.uk

For my parents,
who told the stories I needed
to write this book.

"Eyes, look your last!
Arms, take your last embrace! and, lips, O you
The doors of breath, seal with a righteous kiss
A dateless bargain to engrossing death!"
—Shakespeare, *Romeo and Juliet*

One

The New Year in Shanghai passed with such fanfare that a sense of party still permeated the city a week later. It was the way the people moved about—the extra bounce in their toes and the twinkle in their eye as they leaned over the seats of the Grand Theatre to whisper to their companion. It was loud jazz music audible from the cabaret across the street, the cool air of handheld bamboo fans waving about in rapid color, the smell of something fried smuggled into the viewing room despite Screen One's strict rules. Marking the first day of the Gregorian calendar as a time for celebration was a Western matter, but the West had long stuck its roots into this city.

The madness in Shanghai was gone. The streets had been lulled back into uproarious decadence and nights that went on and on—like this one, where theatergoers could watch a picture and then saunter along the Huangpu River until sunrise. After all, there was no monster lurking in the waters anymore. It had been four months since the monster of Shanghai died, shot to death and left to rot on a wharf by the Bund. Now the only thing civilians needed to worry about were gangsters . . . and the increasing number of bullet-hole-ridden corpses showing up on the streets.

Juliette Cai peered over the railing, squinting down at the ground level of Screen One. From her vantage point, she could see almost everything below, could pick out every minuscule detail among the chaos broiling under the golden light fixtures. Unfortunately, it would have been more useful if she were actually down there herself, mingling with the merchant she had been sent here for, rather than staring at him from high above. Their seats tonight were the best that she could do; the assignment had been given far too last minute for Juliette to finagle something good in the thick of the socializing sphere.

"Are you going to be pulling that face all night?"

Juliette swiveled around, narrowing her eyes at her cousin. Kathleen Lang was trailing close, her mouth set in a grimace while the people around them searched for their seats before the picture started.

"Yes," Juliette grumbled. "I have so many better things to be doing right now."

Kathleen rolled her eyes, then wordlessly pointed ahead, having spotted the seats marked on their tickets. The stubs in her hands were ripped poorly after the uniformed ticket boy at the door got his top hat knocked into his eyes by the crowd surging into the portico. He had hardly a moment to recover before more tickets were waved in his face, foreigners and rich Chinese alike sniffing their noses at the slow speed. In places like these, better service was expected. Ticket prices were sky-high to make the Grand Theatre an *experience*, what with its arched ceiling beams and wrought-iron railings, its Italian marble and delicate doorway lettering—only in English, no Chinese to be found.

"What could possibly be more important than this?" Kathleen asked. They took their seats: the front-most row by the second-level railing, a perfect view of both the screen and all the people beneath. "Staring angrily at your bedroom wall, as you have been doing these few months?"

Juliette frowned. "I have *not* been doing merely that."

"Oh, pardon me. How could I forget screaming at politicians?"

Huffing, Juliette leaned back into her seat. She crossed her arms tightly over her chest, the beads along her sleeves clinking loudly against the beads dangling from her front. Grating as the sound was, it contributed only a small fraction to the general bedlam of the theater.

"Bàba is already giving me enough grief for upsetting that Nationalist," Juliette grumbled. She started to take inventory of the crowd below, mentally assigning names to faces and keeping track of who might notice that she was here. "Don't you get on my case too."

Kathleen tutted, setting her elbow onto the armrest between them. "I'm only concerned, biǎomèi."

"Concerned about what? I'm always screaming at people."

"Lord Cai doesn't reprimand you often. I think that might be an indicator of—"

Juliette lurched forward. Out of sheer instinct, a gasp rose in her throat, but she refused to let it out, and instead the sound lodged itself tightly in place, an ice-cold sensation pressed up against the back of her tongue. Kathleen immediately jerked to attention too, searching the floor below for whatever it was that had drained Juliette's face utterly of blood.

"What?" Kathleen demanded. "What is it? Do I call for backup?"

"No," Juliette whispered, swallowing hard. The theater dimmed. Taking their cue, the ticket boys started to walk the aisles, forcing the crowd to settle for the picture. "It is only a small hiccup."

Her cousin's brows were furrowed, still searching. "What *is* it?" Kathleen repeated.

Juliette simply pointed. She watched as Kathleen followed the direction in which she was indicating, watched as the realization set in when they were both looking at one figure pushing his way through the crowd.

"It would appear we were not the only ones sent here for a task."

Because down on the ground level, looking like he had not a care in the world, Roma Montagov smiled and stopped in front of the merchant

3

they were after, extending his hand for the merchant to shake.

Juliette curled her fists tightly into her lap.

She had not seen Roma since October, since the first protests in Nanshi shook the city and set the precedent for those that were to follow when winter swept into Shanghai. She had not seen his physical person, but she had felt his presence everywhere: in the corpses littered across the city with lily-white flowers clutched in their stiff hands; in the business partners disappearing out of the blue with nary a message or explanation; in the blood feud making its mark. Ever since the city caught wind of a confrontation between Roma Montagov and Tyler Cai, the blood feud had shot back into its most terrible heights. Neither gang needed to worry about their numbers being picked off by the madness anymore. Instead their thoughts circled retribution, and honor, and as different mouths ran different accounts of what had happened between the inner circles of the Scarlet Gang and the White Flowers that day, the only definitive truths that came out were this: in a tiny hospital along the edges of Shanghai, Roma Montagov had shot at Tyler Cai, and to protect her cousin, Juliette Cai had killed Marshall Seo in cold blood.

Now both sides were vengeful. Now the White Flowers were pressing down on the Scarlet Gang with a renewed urgency, and the Scarlet Gang were fighting back just as hard. They had to. No matter how carefully the Scarlets cooperated with the Nationalists, every single person in this city could feel something shifting, could see the gatherings grow larger and larger each time the Communists attempted a strike. The political landscape was soon to change, soon to swallow up this way of lawlessness, and for both gangs currently ruling this city with an iron fist, it was either to be violent now and secure their holdings, or regret it later should a greater power swoop in when there was no way to win territory back.

"Juliette," Kathleen said softly. Her cousin's eyes shifted back and forth between her and Roma. "What happened between you two?"

Juliette didn't have an answer to give, just as she hadn't had an answer all the other times she was asked this question. Kathleen deserved a better explanation, deserved to know why the city was saying Juliette had shot Marshall Seo point-blank when she had once been so friendly with him, why Roma Montagov was dropping flowers everywhere he went in mockery of the feud's victims when he had once been so gentle with Juliette. But one more person in on the secret was one more person dragged down into the mess. One more target for Tyler's scrutiny—one more target for Tyler's gun.

Better to speak none of it. Better to pretend and pretend until maybe, just maybe, there came some chance to salvage the fractured state this city had fallen into.

"The picture is starting," Juliette said in lieu of a reply.

"*Juliette,*" Kathleen insisted.

Juliette gritted her teeth hard. She wondered if her tone still fooled anyone. In New York, she had been so good at lying, so good at playing pretend as an utterly different person. These last months had been wearing her down until there was nothing left of her but . . . her.

"He's not doing anything. Look, he's taking his seat."

Indeed, Roma appeared to be walking away from the merchant after a mere greeting, settling into an end seat two rows behind. This did not have to be a big deal. They did not need to engage in a confrontation. Juliette could quietly keep an eye on him from where she sat and make sure she approached the merchant first when intermission came. It was a surprise that she had even been sent after a merchant. The Scarlet Gang rarely chased after new clientele; they waited for clientele to come to *them*. But this merchant did not dabble in drugs like the rest of them. He had sailed into Shanghai last week carrying British technology—heavens knew what kind; her parents had not been specific in their briefing, save that it was some sort of weaponry and the Scarlet Gang wanted to acquire his inventory.

If the White Flowers were trying to get in on it too, then it had to be something big. Juliette made a note to ask for details as soon as she got home.

The lights went dark. Kathleen glanced over her shoulder, fingers twisting into the loose sleeves of her coat.

"Relax," Juliette whispered. "What you're about to watch came directly from its premiere in Manhattan. Quality entertainment."

The picture started. Screen One was the largest viewing room in the whole Grand Theatre, its orchestral sound booming from all sides. Each seat was equipped with its own translation system, reading out the text that appeared alongside the silent film. The couple to Juliette's left were wearing their earpieces, murmuring excitedly to each other as the lines filtered through in Chinese. Juliette didn't need her earpiece, not just because she could read English, but because she wasn't really watching the film. Her eyes, no matter how much she tried, kept wandering down.

Don't be a fool, Juliette scolded herself. She had tipped herself into this situation at full speed. She would not regret it. It was what had needed to be done.

But still, she couldn't stop looking.

It had been only three months, but Roma had changed. She already knew that, of course, from the reports that came back to her about dead gangsters with Korean characters slashed in blood beside them. From the bodies piling up farther and farther inward into Scarlet territory lines, as if the White Flowers were testing the limits they could encroach upon. It was unlikely that Roma had sought out Scarlets specifically for vengeance killings—he didn't have it in him to go *that* far—but each time a conflict erupted, the message left behind was clear: *This is your doing, Juliette.*

It was Juliette who had escalated the feud, who had pulled the trigger on Marshall Seo and told Roma to his face that whatever happened between them had been nothing but a lie. So now all the blood left in his wake was his revenge.

He looked the part too. At some point, he had traded his dark suits for lighter colors: for a cream jacket and a golden tie, for cuff links that caught the light each time the screen flashed white. His posture was sharp, no more slouching to feign casual, no more stretching his legs long so he could slump into the chair and avoid being seen by anyone giving the room a cursory glance.

Roma Montagov wasn't the heir scheming in the shadows anymore. It seemed that he was sick of the city seeing him as the one slitting throats in the dark, the one with a heart of coal and the clothing to match.

He looked like a White Flower. He looked like his father.

A flash of movement blurred in Juliette's peripheral vision. She blinked, pulling her gaze away from Roma and searching the seats across his aisle. For a moment, she was certain she had merely been mistaken, that perhaps a lock of hair had come undone from her front curl and fallen into her eyes. Then the screen flashed white again as a shrieking train derailed in the Wild West, and Juliette saw the figure in the audience rise.

The man's face was cast in shadow, but the gun in his hand was very, very illuminated.

And it was pointed right at the merchant in the front row, who Juliette still needed to speak to.

"Absolutely *not*," she muttered angrily, reaching for the pistol strapped to her thigh.

The screen dropped into shadows, but Juliette took aim anyway. In the second before the man could act, she pulled the trigger first with a loud *bang*.

Her pistol kicked. Juliette pressed back into her seat, her jaw hard as the man below dropped his weapon, his shoulder wounded. Her gunshot had hardly drawn any notice, not when there was a shootout going on in the picture, too, drowning out the scream coming from the man's mouth and covering up the smoke wafting from the barrel of her pistol. Though the picture had no dialogue sound, the orchestral backing track had an uproarious cymbal banging in the background, and the theatergoers all assumed the gunshot a product of the film.

All except for Roma, who immediately swiveled around and looked up, eyes searching for the source of the gunshot.

And he found it.

Their gazes locked, the *click* of mutual recognition so forceful that Juliette felt a physical shift in her spine, like her body was finally righting itself into alignment after months out of configuration. She was frozen, breath caught in her throat, eyes pulled wide.

Until Roma reached into his jacket pocket and drew his gun, and Juliette had no choice but to jolt herself out of her daze. Instead of combating the would-be assassin, he had decided to shoot at *her.*

Three bullets whizzed by her ear. Gasping, Juliette struck the floor, her knees grazing the carpet hard as she threw herself down. The couple to her left started screaming.

The theatergoers had realized the gunshots were not a part of the soundtrack.

"Okay," Juliette said under her breath. "He's still mad at me."

"What *was* that?" Kathleen demanded. Her cousin dropped quickly too, using the railing of the second level for cover. "Did you shoot into the seats? Was that Roma Montagov shooting back?"

Juliette grimaced. "Yes."

It sounded like a stampede was starting on the floor below. The people on the upper level were certainly starting to panic too, hurtling out of their seats and rushing for the exit, but the two doors on either side of the theater—marked EVEN and ODD for the seat arrangements—were rather thin, and all they managed to achieve was a bottleneck situation.

Kathleen made an indecipherable noise. *"He's not doing anything . . . he's taking his seat!"*

"Oh, don't mock me!" Juliette hissed.

This situation was not ideal. But she would salvage it.

She scrambled to her feet.

"Someone was trying to shoot the merchant." Juliette made a quick glance over the railing. She didn't see Roma anymore. She did see the merchant pulling his suit jacket tightly around his middle and securing his straw hat, trying to follow the crowds out of the theater.

"Go find who it was," Kathleen huffed. "Your father will have your head if the merchant is killed."

"I know you're joking," Juliette muttered, "but you might be right." She pressed her pistol into her cousin's hand and took off, calling over her shoulder, "Talk to the merchant for me! Merci!"

By now the bottleneck at the door had thinned enough that Juliette could push through, merging into the main anteroom outside the second floor of Screen One. Ladies dressed in silk qipao were screaming inconsolably at one another, and British officers were clumped together in the corner to hiss hysterics about what was going on. Juliette ignored it all, pushing and pushing to get to the stairs, to get down to the ground floor, where the merchant would be emerging.

She skidded to a stop. The main staircase was far too crowded. Her eyes darted to the side, to the maintenance stairs, and she tore the door open without a second thought, barreling right through. Juliette was familiar with this theater; it was Scarlet territory, and she had spent parts of her early childhood wandering around this building, peering into the different screening rooms when Nurse was distracted. Where the main staircase was a grandiose structure of polished flooring and arched, wooden banisters, the maintenance stairs were made of cement and void of natural light, relying on naught but a small bulb dangling at the middle landing.

Her heels clacked loudly, turning the corner of the landing. She stopped short.

Waiting there, by the door into the main lobby, was Roma, his gun raised.

Juliette supposed she had grown predictable.

"You were three paces away from the merchant," she said. She was surprised her voice remained level. Tā mā de. There was one knife strapped to her leg, but in the time it would take to reach for it, she would be giving Roma plenty of time to shoot. "You left him just to find me? I'm flattered—"

Juliette swerved with a hiss. Her cheek radiated heat, swelling from the harrowingly close contact of the bullets that flew by her head. Before Roma could think to aim again, Juliette ran the quickest survey of her options, then dove through the door behind her, surging into the storage unit.

She wasn't trying to escape. This was a dead end, a thin room crowded with stacked chairs and cobwebs. She only needed . . .

Another bullet whizzed by her arm.

"You're going to blow this place up," Juliette snapped, spinning around. She had come to the very end of the storage space, her back pressed to the thick pipes that ran along the walls. "Some of these pipes carry gas—put a hole in one and the whole theater bursts into flames."

Roma was hardly threatened. It was as if he could not hear her. His eyes were narrowed, his expression scrunched. He looked unfamiliar—properly foreign, like a boy who had pulled on a costume and hadn't expected how well it would fit. Even under the dim lights, the gold of his clothes glimmered, as bright as the twinkling billboards outside the theater.

Juliette wanted to scream, seeing what he had been made into. She could hardly catch her breath, and she would be lying if she said it was only because of her current physical exertion.

"Did you hear what I said?" Juliette eyed the distance between them. "Put that gun away—"

"Do you hear *yourself*?" Roma interrupted. In three strides, he was close enough to point his gun right in Juliette's face. She could feel the heat of the barrel, hot steel an inch away from her skin. "You killed Marshall. You killed him, and it's been months, and I haven't heard a word of explanation from you—"

"There is no explanation."

He thought her a monster. He thought she had hated him the whole time, so viciously that she would destroy everything he loved, and he *had* to think that if he was to keep his life. Juliette refused to drag him down just because *she* was weak-willed.

"I killed him because he needed to die," Juliette said. Her arm whipped up. She twisted Roma's gun away, letting it clatter at their feet. "Just as I will kill you. Just as I will not stop until you kill me—"

He slammed her into the pipes.

The effort was so forceful that Juliette tasted blood inside her lip, sliced by her own sharp teeth. She stifled a gasp and then another when Roma's hand tightened around her throat, his eyes murderous.

Juliette was not frightened. If anything, she was only resentful—not at Roma, but at herself. At wanting to lean in even while Roma was actively trying to kill her. At this distance between them that she had willingly manufactured, because they had been born into two families at war, and she would rather die at Roma's hand than be the cause of his death.

No one else is dying to protect me. Roma had blown up a whole house of people to keep Juliette safe. Tyler and his Scarlet men would go on a rampage in the name of defending Juliette, even if they too wanted her dead. It was all one and the same. It was this city, divided by names and colors and turfs, but somehow bleeding the exact same shade of violence.

"Go on," Juliette said with effort.

She didn't mean it. She knew Roma Montagov. He thought he wanted her dead, but the fact of the matter was that he never missed, and yet he had—all those bullets, embedded into the walls instead of Juliette's head. The fact of the matter was that he had his hands around her throat and yet she could still breathe, could still inhale past the rot and the hate that his fingers tried to press into her skin.

Juliette finally reached for her blade. Just as Roma shifted forward, perhaps intent on his kill, her hand closed around the sheath beneath her dress and she pulled the weapon free, slicing down on whatever she came in contact with first. Roma hissed, releasing his hold. It was only a surface cut, but he cradled his arm to his chest, and Juliette followed close, leveling the blade to his throat.

"This is Scarlet territory." Her words were even, but it took everything in her to keep them that way. "You forget yourself."

Roma grew still. He stared at her, utterly unreadable as the moment drew long—long enough that Juliette almost thought he would surrender.

Only then Roma leaned into the blade instead, until the metal was pressed right into his neck, one hairsbreadth away from breaking skin and drawing blood.

"Then do it," Roma hissed. He sounded angry. . . . He sounded *pained*. "Kill me."

Juliette did not move. She must have hesitated for a fraction too long, because Roma's expression morphed into a sneer.

"Why do you pause?" he taunted.

The taste of blood was still pungent inside her mouth. In a blur, Juliette flipped the blade onto its blunt end and slammed the handle to Roma's temple. He blinked and dropped like a rock, but Juliette threw the weapon away and lunged to break his fall. As soon as her hands slid around him, she let out a small exhale of relief, stopping Roma just before his head could hit the hard floor.

Juliette sighed. In her arms, he felt so solid, more real than ever. His safety was an abstract concept when he was at a distance, far from the threats that her Scarlets posed to him. But here, with his pulse thudding through his chest and beating an even rhythm onto hers, he was just a boy, just a bloody, beating heart that could be cut out at any moment by any blade sharp enough.

"Why do you pause?" Juliette mimicked bitterly. Softly, she set him down, brushing his mussed hair out of his face. "Because even if you hate me, Roma Montagov, I still love you."

Two

Roma felt the prodding sensation on his shoulder first. Then the stiffness in his bones. Then the terrible, terrible pain shooting through his head.

"Christ," he hissed, jerking awake. As soon as his vision cleared, he sighted the black boot responsible for the prodding, attached to the last person he wanted to encounter while slumped on the floor.

"What the hell happened?" Dimitri Voronin demanded, his arms crossed over his chest. Behind him stood three other White Flowers. They were inspecting the storage unit with particular attention, eyeing the bullet holes studded into the walls.

"Juliette Cai happened," Roma muttered, hobbling to his feet. "She knocked me out."

"It looks like you're lucky she didn't kill you," Dimitri said. He smacked his hand on the wall, rubbing charred grit and dust onto his palm. Roma didn't bother saying that all those bullets were his. It was not as if Dimitri were actually here to help. He had probably gathered his reinforcements as soon as he heard about the Grand Theatre rocking with gunshots, frantic to be where the chaos was. Dimitri Voronin had been everywhere these few months, ever since he missed the showdown at the hospital and had to piece together afterward what had gone on between the White Flowers and the Scarlet Gang, like everyone else. Dimitri Voronin would not be left out of the next big showdown. At the sound of any disturbance in the city—no matter how slight—so long as it involved the blood feud, he was now the first on the scene.

"What are you doing here?" Roma asked. He touched his cheek, wincing at the bruising that had spread. "My father sent *me*."

"Yes, well, that was not a great decision, was it? We saw the merchant outside having a nice chat with Kathleen Lang."

Roma bit back his curse. He wanted to spit it to the ground, but Dimitri was watching, so he only turned away, picking up his fallen pistol. "No matter. Tomorrow is a new day. It's time to go."

"You will give up like that?"

"This is *Scarlet*—"

A whistle blew outside, echoing up and down the maintenance stairs. This time Roma did curse aloud, tucking his pistol away before the garde municipale barged into the storage unit, their batons out. For whatever reason, the enforcement saw the White Flowers and decided to direct their attention to Dimitri, eyes pinned on his weapons.

"Lâche le pistolet," the man at the front demanded. His belt glinted, metal handcuffs catching the low light. "Lâche-moi ça et lève les mains."

Dimitri did not do as he was told, did not drop the gun dangling casually in his grip nor put his hands up. His refusal seemed to be insolence, but Roma knew better. Dimitri did not speak French.

"You don't control us," Dimitri snapped in Russian. "So why don't you go on and—"

"Ça va maintenant," Roma interrupted. "J'ai entendu une dispute dehors du théâtre. Allez l'investiguer."

The garde municipale officers narrowed their eyes, unsure if they should follow Roma's instruction—if there was truly an incident outside to tend to or if Roma was only making up lies. It was indeed a lie, but Roma only had to snap "Go!" again and the garde municipale scattered.

That was who he had worked so hard to turn into. That was who he was doing everything in his power to stay as. Someone who was listened to even when the officers were Scarlets.

"Impressive," Dimitri said when it was just the White Flowers again. "Really, Roma, it is most—"

"Shut up," Roma snapped. The effect was immediate. He wished he could feel some satisfaction at the red that rose up Dimitri's neck, at the amused smirking from the men that Dimitri had brought along, but all he felt was empty. "Next time don't come prancing into foreign-controlled territory if you don't know how to deal with the foreigners."

Roma marched out, overly aggressive in his stride as he took the maintenance stairs back down to the ground floor. It was hard to say what exactly had him this worked up; there was so much boiling beneath his skin—the merchant slipping away, the strange assassin in the stalls, Juliette being here.

Juliette. He stomped extra hard coming out of the theater, squinting up at the gray clouds. A jolt of pain came from his arm then, and his hand flew to the cut that Juliette had made, thinking he would find a clump of blood, as rancid and dead as his feelings for her. Instead, as he rolled his sleeve up gingerly, his fingers came upon only smooth fabric.

With a start, Roma stopped at the side of the pavement. He peered at his arm. It had been finely wrapped, secured with a bow.

"Is this *silk*?" he muttered, frowning. It looked like silk. It looked like the silk of Juliette's dress, torn from the hem, but *why would she do that?*

A horn blew from the road, drawing his attention. The car idling there flashed its headlights, before the chauffeur at the driver's seat stuck his arm out and waved at Roma. Roma remained unmoving, his brow furrowed.

"Mr. Montagov!" the White Flower finally hollered after a long minute. "Can we go yet?"

Roma sighed, hurrying to the car.

There were twenty-two vases scattered around the Cai mansion, all of them filled with red roses. Juliette reached out to cup one bud in her palm, her finger sliding along the delicate petal's edge. Nightfall had long passed outside. The hour was late enough that most of the servants had gone to sleep, shuffling to their rooms in their nightgowns, bidding Juliette a good rest when they passed her in the hallway. She figured they had spoken only because it would have been strange not to acknowledge the Scarlet heir lying on the floor, arms splayed and legs propped upright on the walls as she waited outside her father's office. The last servant had bidden her well more than half an hour ago. Since then she had stood up and started pacing, much to Kathleen's annoyance. Her cousin had remained seated primly on an actual chair the whole time, a folder waiting on her lap.

"What could they possibly be talking about?" Juliette grumbled, releasing the rose in her hand. "It's been *hours*. Move it to another day—"

Lord Cai's office door finally opened, revealing a Nationalist taking his leave. Months ago, Juliette would have been curious about the meeting, would have asked for a briefing. Now the sight of Nationalists coming and going in this house was so common that she hardly cared. It was always the same—squash the Communists, whatever the cost. Riddle them with bullets, break up their labor unions: the Nationalists didn't mind how the Scarlets did it, so long as they achieved their objectives.

The Nationalist hovered at the doorway, then turned back, as if he had one more thing he forgot to say. Juliette narrowed her eyes. The sight of Nationalists had grown familiar to her, true, but this one . . . There were stars and badges galore decorating his uniform. A general, perhaps.

Testing her limits, Juliette held out her hand for Kathleen to take. Kathleen, albeit confused, accepted and picked up her folder, both of them walking toward the Nationalist.

"No more warlords." The Nationalist flicked an imaginary piece of lint off his military uniform. "And no more foreigners. We enter a new world, and whether the Scarlet Gang enters with us is a matter of loyalty—"

"Yes, yes," Juliette interrupted, squeezing past him and pulling Kathleen along. "Blessed be the Kuomintang, wàn suì wàn suì wàn wàn suì . . ." She started to push at the door.

"Juliette," Lord Cai snapped.

Juliette stopped. A glint had entered her eye. The same sort that came about when the cooks brought out her favorite meal. The same sort when she spotted a diamond necklace she wanted in the window of a department store.

"Present and reporting," she said.

Lord Cai leaned back in his large chair, folding his hands over his stomach. "Apologize, please."

Juliette bobbed an unbothered curtsy. When she looked at the Nationalist, he was observing her carefully, but it was not the leer of men on the streets. It was something far more strategic.

"Please accept my apologies. I trust you can find your way to the door?"

The Nationalist tipped his hat. Though he offered her a smile, as was polite, the expression stopped entirely before reaching his eyes, merely crinkling his crow's feet without any sign of warmth.

"Of course. Pleased to make your acquaintance, Miss Cai."

He had not been introduced to her, so they had not made an acquaintance at all. Juliette did not say this; she merely closed the door, then rolled her eyes in Kathleen's direction.

"So *tiresome*. When you're on your way out, then *leave*."

"Juliette," Lord Cai said again, with less bite now that the Nationalist was no longer present for Juliette to be a pest in front of. "That was Shu Yang. General Shu. Do you know who he is? Have you been following the papers and the advancement of the Northern Expedition at all?"

Juliette winced. "Bàba," she started. She dropped into a seat opposite her father's desk. Kathleen silently followed suit. "The Northern Expedition is so terribly boring—"

"It will determine the fate of our country—"

"Okay, fine, fine—the *reports* are so boring. General so-and-so took this segment of land. Army division so-and-so moved this far up. I practically cry in excitement when you send me to strangle someone instead." Juliette clasped her hands together. "Please, just let me do the strangling."

Her father shook his head, not bothering to entertain her theatrics. His eyes only swiveled toward the door thoughtfully.

"Pay attention to this," Lord Cai said slowly. "The Kuomintang is changing shape. Heaven knows they are no longer pretending to cooperate with the Communists. We can afford carelessness no longer."

Juliette thinned her lips but did not get smart with her response. Revolution was coming; she couldn't deny that. The Northern Expedition, that was what they called it: Nationalist troops marching north through the country, fighting the warlords that ruled regions and fragments, seizing territories in an attempt to piece China back together. Shanghai would be the stronghold, the last piece before the current poor excuse of a national government was utterly ousted, and when the armies came, there were no warlords here to defeat. . . . There were only gangs and foreigners.

So the Scarlet Gang needed to get on the right side before they arrived.

"Of course," Juliette said. "Now—" She gestured for Kathleen to go on. Almost hesitantly, her cousin leaned toward Lord Cai's desk, gingerly passing the folder in her hands.

"You were successful?" Lord Cai asked, still speaking to Juliette even as he took the folder from Kathleen.

"You'd better frame that contract," Juliette replied. "Kathleen almost got in a fistfight for it."

Kathleen nudged a subtle elbow into Juliette's side, a warning in her expression. By normal circumstances, Kathleen couldn't look stern even if she tried, but the room's low light helped. The miniature chandelier dangling from the ceiling was dialed to the dimmest setting, casting long shadows up against the walls. The curtains behind Lord Cai's desk were undrawn, blowing faintly because the window was open the smallest crack. Juliette knew her father's old tricks. In the dead of winter, as it was now, the open window kept the office chilly, kept every visitor on their toes when they took off their coat to be polite and ended up shivering.

Juliette and Kathleen kept their coats on.

"A fistfight?" Lord Cai echoed. "Lang Selin, that's not like you."

"There was no fistfight, Gūfù," Kathleen said quickly, shooting another sharp glance at Juliette, who only grinned in response. "Merely a scuffle between some people outside the Grand Theatre. I managed to extricate the merchant, and he was thankful enough that he was willing to sit down at the hotel next door for a cup of tea."

Lord Cai nodded. While he scanned the handwritten terms, he made a few noises of approval here and there, which from a man of silence meant the business deal had lifted his mood.

"I didn't know the specifics on what we wanted him for," Kathleen hurried to supply when Lord Cai closed the folder. "So the language is rather vague."

"Oh, no bother," Lord Cai replied. "The Kuomintang are after his weaponry. I do not know the specifics either."

Juliette blinked. "We're entering a business partnership where we don't even know what we're dealing?"

By all means, it was not any big matter. The Scarlet Gang was used to trading in human labor and drugs. One more illicit item only added an inch to what was already an infinitely long scroll, but to trust the Nationalists so wholeheartedly . . .

"And on that matter," Juliette said suddenly, before her father could answer her question, "Bàba, there was an *assassin* after the merchant."

Lord Cai did not react for a long moment, which meant he had already heard. Of course he had. Juliette may have had to wait hours before she could see her own father, slotted at the bottom of a waiting list filled with Nationalists and foreigners and businessmen, but messengers could come and go at a whim, slinking into the office and whispering a quick report into Lord Cai's ear.

"Yes," he finally said. "It was likely a White Flower."

"No."

Lord Cai frowned, his gaze darting up. Juliette had jumped in with her disagreement rather quickly and empathetically.

"There was . . . a White Flower present who was also trying to make an acquaintance with the merchant," Juliette explained. Her eyes darted to the window unwittingly, eyeing the golden lamps humming in the gardens below. Their light made the rosebushes glow with warmth, a far cry from the real biting temperature at this time of night. "Roma Montagov."

Her eyes flicked back, swallowing hard. If her father had been paying attention, the speed at which she sought his reaction would have given away her guilt immediately, but her father was gazing off into space.

Juliette let out her exhale slowly.

"A curious matter on why the White Flower heir was after the merchant too," Lord Cai muttered, half to himself. He waved his hand then. "Nevertheless, we need not worry about an amateur assassin. Likely a Communist, or any faction opposing the Nationalist Army. We'll have Scarlet men protect the merchant from now onward. No one would dare another attempt."

He sounded certain. Still, Juliette chewed her lip, not so convinced. A few months ago, perhaps no one would dare upset the Scarlets. But today?

"Has there been another letter?"

Lord Cai sighed, lacing his fingers together. He said, "Selin, you must be tired."

"It is my bedtime, yes," Kathleen replied easily, taking the cue to leave. She was out in seconds, the office door closing behind her before Juliette could say good night. Her father must know that she would merely fill Kathleen in afterward about what was going on. She supposed it made him feel better to think the rest of the family wasn't getting involved in this, that the fewer people knew, the less likely it was to explode into a troublesome matter.

"The blackmailer strikes again," Lord Cai said, finally retrieving an envelope from his desk drawer and passing it to Juliette. "The largest sum yet."

Juliette reached forward, first examining not the letter inside but the envelope itself. It was the same each time. Utterly plain and remarkable, save for one detail: they were all postmarked from the French Concession.

"Tiān nǎ," she breathed, pulling out the letter and reading its contents. A truly outrageous amount. But they had to send it. They *had* to.

She tossed the letter back onto her father's desk, letting out a tight breath. Back in October, she thought she had killed the monster of Shanghai. She had shot Qi Ren, watched as the bullet studded into his heart and the old man seemed to crumple in *relief,* freed from the curse that Paul Dexter had set on him. His throat had split open and the mother insect had flown out, landing on the wharf of the Bund with finality.

Then Kathleen found Paul Dexter's letter—

In the event of my death, release them all.

—and the screaming followed immediately. Juliette had never run faster. All the worst-case scenarios flashed through her mind: five, ten, fifty monsters, ravaging the streets of Shanghai. Each and every one of them a starting point of infection, their insects flying from civilian to civilian until the whole city was dead in the gutters, throats torn to shreds and hands bloody to the wrist. Instead, Juliette found only one dead man—a beggar, by the looks of him—slumped up against the exterior of a police bureau. The screaming had been the shopper who'd spotted him, and by the time Juliette arrived, the small, panicked crowd had already dispersed, wanting to avoid interrogation if the Scarlet Gang became involved.

Dead men on the streets of Shanghai were as common as starving men, desperate men, violent men. But this one had been murdered, his throat slit right down the middle, and next to him, pinned to the wall with the bloody knife that did it, was the insect that had flown out of Qi Ren.

To any other observer, or to the police detective who would later examine the scene, it was nonsensical. To Juliette, the message was clear. Someone was out there, holding on to the other insects that Paul Dexter created. They knew what the insects did and the damage they could wreak if released.

The first blackmail letter, demanding a sum of money in exchange for the city's safety, came a week later. They had been coming ever since.

"Your thoughts, daughter?" Lord Cai said now, his arms relaxed on either side of his chair. He was watching Juliette carefully, cataloging her reaction to the demand. He asked for her thoughts, but it was plain that her father had already made up his mind. This was merely a test to ensure that Juliette's judgment aligned with the correct course of action. To ensure that she was a good heir, fit for leading the Scarlet Gang.

"Send it," Juliette replied, swallowing the tremor in her voice before it could escape. "Until our spies figure out where the hell these letters are coming from and I can put the blackmailer six feet underground, we keep them happy."

Lord Cai remained quiet for a second, then another. He reached for the letter, let it dangle between his fingers.

"Very well," her father said. "We send it."

Alisa had fallen back into her old habits, eavesdropping in the rafters. She was crammed inside that ceiling space above her father's office again, having crawled down from a broken crevasse between the drywall in the sitting room of the third floor.

"Ouch," she muttered, moving the weight of her body off her knee. Either she had grown taller in these last few months, or she still wasn't fully recovered from lying in a coma for weeks. She used to be able to squeeze herself small enough that she could squirm along these rafters, then drop into the hallway outside her father's office when she wanted to leave. Now her limbs felt awkward, too stiff. She tried to lean down, but her balance tilted immediately.

"Shit," Alisa whispered, gripping the rafter hard. She was thirteen now. She was allowed to curse.

Below, her father was deep in discussion with Dimitri: him behind his desk, Dimitri seated with his feet up. Their voices, unfortunately, were soft. But Alisa had sharp hearing.

"Curious, is it not?" Lord Montagov asked. He had something in his hands—perhaps a notecard, perhaps an invitation. "No threat, nor violent action. Merely a demand for a sum of money."

"My lord," Dimitri said evenly. "If I may, I would argue that the message is rather threatening."

Lord Montagov scoffed. "What? This old line?" He flipped the paper over, and Alisa confirmed that it was indeed a notecard—thick and cream-colored. Expensive. "*Pay up, or the monster of Shanghai resurrects*. It is tomfoolery. Roma destroyed that wretched monster."

Alisa swore she saw Dimitri's jaw twitch.

"I hear that the Scarlets have already received multiple threats, starting from months prior," Dimitri insisted. "They have paid the amount demanded each time."

"Ha!" Lord Montagov turned toward his window, opting to observe the street below. "How are we to know it is not the Scarlets pulling this, a scheme to loosen the gold in our pockets?"

"It is not," Dimitri replied surely. A beat passed. Then he added, "My source reports that Lord Cai believes the threat to be real."

"Interesting," Lord Montagov said.

"Interesting," Alisa echoed up in the rafters, so quietly that she was audible only to the dust motes. How would Dimitri know what *Lord Cai* believed?

"Then the Scarlet Gang are merely made up of fools, which we have known all along." Lord Montagov threw the card to the floor. "Forget it. We are not paying an anonymous blackmailer. Let them do their worst."

"I—"

"It is marked from the French Concession," Lord Montagov interrupted, before Dimitri could get another word in edgewise. "What are the French to do? Will they walk themselves here and intimidate us in their ironed suits?"

Dimitri had no further leeway to argue. He merely leaned back into his seat, lips pursed, thinking for a long moment.

"Indeed," he said eventually. "Whatever you believe to be correct, then."

The conversation turned to the White Flower clientele lists, and Alisa frowned, wriggling along the rafter. Once she was far enough from her father's office not to be overhead, she slowly eased herself down a thin gap in the wall to emerge in the hallway. This house was a Frankenstein-esque experiment in architecture: multiple apartment blocks mashed together with barely finished stitching. There were so many nooks and crannies above and below various rooms that Alisa was surprised only she alone used them to get from place to place. At the very least, she was surprised no White Flower had accidentally pressed up too close to a wall and fallen through the floorboards when they trod upon a loose tiling.

Alisa started up the main stairs, taking them two at a time in her hurry. The plain necklace dangling at her clavicle jumped up and down with each of her hard steps, cool against her flushed skin.

"Benedikt!" Alisa exclaimed, coming to a stop on the fourth floor.

Her cousin hardly paused. He pretended not see her, which was ridiculous because he was walking right for the staircase, and Alisa was still standing at the head of it. Benedikt Montagov was a wholly different person these days, all gloom and dark frowns. He may not have been the happiest person a few months ago, either, but he lacked a certain light in his eyes now that made him seem like a complete marionette, moving through the world at command. Mourning periods in this city were often short affairs. They came in rapid succession, like cinema showings ushered in and out of the theater to make room for the new.

Benedikt was not only in mourning. He was half-dead himself.

"Benedikt," Alisa tried again. She stepped in his path so he couldn't wind past her. "There are honey cakes downstairs. You like honey cakes, right?"

"Let me through, Alisa," he said.

Alisa stood firm. "It is only that I haven't really seen you eat, and I know you no longer live here so maybe it occurs outside of my sight, but the human body needs nourishment or else—"

"Alisa!" Benedikt snapped. "Get out of my way."

"But—"

"Now!"

A door flew open. "Don't yell at my sister."

Roma was calm when he stepped into the hallway, hands behind his back like he had been patiently waiting at his door. Benedikt made a noise deep in his throat; he spun to face Roma with such menace that Alisa would have thought the two to be enemies, not cousins of the same blood.

"Don't tell me what to do," Benedikt said. "But wait—you seem to only have something to say when it doesn't matter, don't you?"

Roma's hand jerked up to his hair on instinct before his fingers halted an inch away from his newfound style, unwilling to mess up the gel and the effort. Roma had not broken as Benedikt had, had not shattered into a thousand sharp pieces to cut anybody who got too close . . . only because Roma Montagov had swallowed it all inward instead. Now Alisa looked at her older brother—her only brother— and it was like he was being corrupted from the inside out, turning into this boy who wore his hair like a foreigner, who acted like Dimitri Voronin. Each time their father lavished praise on him, clapping his shoulder solidly, Alisa flinched, knowing it was because another dead Scarlet had been discovered on the streets with scrawls of vengeance beside the body.

"That's unfair," Roma said plainly. He had little else to counter.

"Whatever," Benedikt muttered, pushing past Alisa. She stumbled ever so slightly, and Roma rushed forward, calling after their cousin, refusing to let him have the last word. But Benedikt did not so much as glance back while he took the stairs down. His footsteps were already thudding along the second floor by the time Roma neared Alisa and took her elbow.

"Benedikt Ivanovich Montagov," Roma yelled down. "You—"

His frustrated insult was drowned out by the slam of the front door.

Silence.

"I just wanted to cheer him up," Alisa said quietly.

Roma sighed. "I know. It's not your fault. He's . . . having some difficulties."

"Because Marshall is dead."

Alisa's words were heavy, thick—a terrible weight sliding across her tongue. Hard truths tended to be that way, she supposed.

"Yes," Roma managed. "Because Marshall is . . ." Her brother could not finish his sentence. He merely looked away and cleared his throat, blinking rapidly. "I must go, Alisa. Papa is expecting me."

"Wait," Alisa said, her hand snaking out and snatching the back of Roma's suit jacket before he could start down the stairs. "I heard Papa's meeting with Dimitri. He—" Alisa looked around, making sure no one else was nearby. She lowered her voice further. "Dimitri has a mole in the Scarlet Gang. Maybe even their inner circle. He's been siphoning information from a source direct to Lord Cai."

Roma was shaking his head. He had started shaking his head before Alisa had even finished speaking.

"Little good that will do us now," he said. "Be careful, Alisa. Stop eavesdropping on Dimitri."

Alisa's jaw slackened. As soon as Roma tried to ease his jacket out of her grip, she only tightened her hold, not letting him leave.

"You're not curious?" she asked. "How did *Dimitri* put a spy into the inner circle of the Scarlet Gang—"

"Maybe he is simply more intelligent than I am," Roma interrupted dryly. "He knows how to sight when someone is a liar and can establish *his* lie first—"

Alisa stomped her feet. "Don't mope!" she said.

"I am not moping!"

"You *mope*," Alisa insisted. She looked over her shoulder again, hearing a rustling on the third floor and waiting for whoever it was to retreat to their room before speaking again. "Another thing I thought you would want to know: Papa received a threat. Someone claims to have the ability to resurrect the monster."

Roma lifted a single dark brow. This time, when he eased his jacket out of Alisa's grip, she let go, seeing no point in accosting her brother any longer.

"The monster is dead, Alisa," he said. "I'll see you later, yes?"

Roma walked away, his saunter casual. He could have fooled any-one, in that tailored suit and cold stare. But Alisa saw his fingers tremble, saw the muscle in his jaw twitch when he bit down too hard to keep his expression steady.

He was still her brother. He wasn't gone entirely.

Three

One cabaret in White Flower territory is particularly loud tonight.

Business at the Podsolnukh is usually booming anyway, tables full and raucous for the antics that the showgirls pull onstage, overspilling with people and alcohol bottles and every combination of the two. The only place that may compete with its noise and vigor is the fight club next door, the one tucked underneath an otherwise unassuming bar, unknown to the city if not for the constant stream of visitors.

When the door to the Podsolnukh opens at the exact stroke of midnight, a gust of the winter wind blows in, but not a soul in the establishment feels it. Out there, when the day breaks, they are garbage collectors and beggars and gangsters, barely scraping by. In here, crammed shoulder to shoulder at every table, they are invincible so long as the jazz continues playing, so long as the lights don't drop, so long as the night lives on and on and on.

The visitor who entered at midnight sits down. He watches White Flowers throw coins into the air, frivolous with their unending excess, grabbing showgirls adorned in white like they are brides, not runaways from Moscow with smiles as cracked as their hands.

Everyone is here for the exact same reason. Some chance it with drunken stupor, pouring gasoline into their veins so that maybe, just maybe, something will ignite in an otherwise empty chest. Some are more roundabout, collecting and collecting and robbing drunk boys dry when they look the other way, a nimble finger dipping into a pocket and hooking out three crisp notes with her sharply filed nails. Maybe one day she can quit this place. Open her own little shop, put her name up on a sign.

Everyone in this room . . . they all want to feel something, make something, be something—be real, real, real and not just another cog driving the money and mania of this city.

Everyone except the visitor.

He takes a sip of his drink. Huángjiǔ—nothing too strong. He eyes the showgirl coming toward him. Young—fourteen, maybe fifteen. He smooths his tie down, loosening the knot.

Then he knocks his drink over, the smell of alcohol soaking his clothes, and he *changes*.

The showgirl halts in her steps, her hands flying to her mouth. She is already drowsy from the shots she has taken with the patrons, and she almost thinks that she is imagining it, that she is mistaken under the low, flashing lights. But his shirt rips and then his spine grows tall, and it is no longer a man seated at the center of the Podsolnukh but a monster, hunched over and ghastly, green-blue muscles flexing at the ready.

"RUN!" the girl screams. *"Chudovishche!"*

It's too late.

The insects come: they burst from the holes studded into the monster's back, thousands of tiny, frantic critters, crawling onto the tables, the floors, over and under one another until they find sweaty skin and screaming mouths, until they burrow into eyes and noses and hair, sinking in deep and finding a nerve. The cabaret becomes enswathed in black, an ever-moving blanket of infection, and in seconds, the first succumbs, hands flying to throats and clutching, clutching, clutching, trying to squeeze the insects out.

31

Nails break into skin, skin splits for muscle, muscle parts for bone.

As soon as blood spurts from one victim, inner flesh exposed and veins pumping red, the next is already tearing before they have a moment to feel the visceral disgust that comes with being soaked in hot, sticky gore.

It takes one minute. One minute before the cabaret goes still: a battlefield of bodies on the floor, legs overlapped with awry arms. The dancing has stopped, the musicians are unmoving, but a tinny tune continues playing from a gramophone in the corner, pushing on even when not a body stirs any longer, all empty-eyed, staring blankly at the ceiling.

The monster straightens slowly. It breathes in—a ragged, heaving suck of air. Blood soaks the floorboards, dripping through the cracks to line the ground beneath the building.

Only this time the madness does not spread. This time the insects crawl out from their burrowed skin, vacating the corpses, and rather than skittering outward in search for another host, each of them returns to the monster, recedes back whence it came.

No longer is the madness a contagious matter. The madness strikes at will now, at the whims and mercy of whoever controls the monster. And as the monster takes in the last of its insects, it rolls its head in a slow circle, shrinking until he is merely a man again, undirtied by the scene around him, unsullied by his conscience.

Five minutes after midnight, the man walks out of the Podsolnukh.

The news spreads like wildfire. Whether Scarlet Gang or White Flower, this city holds itself upright by the power of information, and its messengers work frantically, whisper passing whisper until it reaches the ears of its rival darlings.

The Scarlet heir slams a door closed; her White Flower counterpart flings one wide open. The Cai mansion falls to a hush, frantically conferring how this could have happened. The White Flower headquarters trembles with confrontation, demands and accusations thrown over and over until finally, so loudly that the whole building shakes: *"Then why didn't you just pay the damn blackmail money?"*

Soon the gangsters will all know. The shopkeepers will know. The workers will know.

The Scarlet Gang and the White Flowers have failed. They promised to rein Shanghai into order, promised that *their* rule, not the Communists, was the one to trust.

But now havoc is loose once more.

"A letter has arrived," a messenger gasps, coming to a stop outside Lord Cai's office.

"Found outside, by the gates," another says elsewhere, entering through the White Flower front door.

The letters are received at once, unfolded in tandem. They reveal the same message, typed in ink, the sign-off still bleeding with black as fresh as spilled blood.

Paul Dexter only had one monster. I have five. Do as I say, or everyone dies.

Roma Montagov kicks a chair. "God—"

"—dammit," Juliette Cai finishes with a whisper, far across the city.

Paul Dexter had thought himself to be a puppeteering god commanding the city. But he knew nothing. He controlled little save for coincidences and terror. He was the hand gripping a barely controlled mass of chaos.

This time the chaos will take shape, grow jaws and sharp teeth, prowl the corners for any opportunity to attack.

And it will have this city dance on its strings.

Four

W ord of the attack spread through the city so quickly that by morning it was on the lips of every servant in the house. They murmured to one another while they dusted the living room, not daring to discuss White Flower casualties with any sense of pity, but moving the volume control on the radio as high as it would go, captivated by the reports coming through.

All morning, everyone waited for the inevitable, waited to hear about rising numbers. But it didn't come. The White Flowers of the Podsolnukh had all dropped dead like this was merely the work of an assassin, not a monster bearing contagion.

Juliette ran her blade over the flat of the bowl again. She was sharpening her knives because they were as blunt as a well-fed beast, each metallic strike echoing through the house. No one seemed particularly bothered; Rosalind was sitting in the living room, blowing on the nib of a pen while she leafed through the giant tome of a French-to-English dictionary on the table.

"I'm not disturbing you, am I?" Juliette called over.

Her cousin glanced up briefly. "With your loud blade-whacking? Why, Juliette, who could possibly be disturbed?"

Juliette pretended to scowl. One of her great-aunts wandered in from the hallway at that moment, hovering between the kitchen and the living room, catching sight of Juliette just as she struck the bowl again. When Juliette switched quickly to a grin, the aunt only eyed Juliette with absolute apprehension before sidling into the living room and hurrying away.

"Now look what you did," Rosalind remarked, arching a brow. The aunt's footsteps faded up the staircase. "Your knives are already too sharp."

"You take that back." Juliette set her weapons down. "There is no such thing as too sharp."

Rosalind rolled her eyes but didn't say more, opting to resume her task. Curious now, Juliette turned the bowl right side up and walked over, peering at what Rosalind was writing.

Stock Report on Commercial and Economic Conditions in Shanghai Following Anti-British Boycott of 1925

"For your father?" Juliette asked.

Rosalind made an affirmative noise, her finger scanning down the page of the dictionary in front of her. Mr. Lang was a businessman located in the central city, delegated to handle the smaller Scarlet merchant trade that wasn't important enough for Lord and Lady Cai but still important enough to keep within the family. For the last few years, he had quietly done his job, to the point where Juliette would downright forget Rosalind and Kathleen still had a father until he showed up to a family dinner as a reminder. It wasn't as though Rosalind and Kathleen interacted with him often either, given their residence at the Cai house, and as far as Juliette knew, her two cousins didn't *want* to reside with their grouchy father.

But he was still their father. And about a week ago, when he had proposed taking them out of the city to move into the countryside instead, Rosalind and Kathleen had hated the idea immediately.

"I'm trying to get as much of his affairs in order as possible," Rosalind explained absently, flipping to the next page of the dictionary.

"He's using the excuse of politics to get out, but I also think he is sick of work. I will not be made to leave simply because my father won't write up a few reports."

Juliette squinted at the paper. "What on earth is a hog casing, and why are we exporting them to America?"

"Je sais pas," Rosalind grumbled. "But prices dropped last February, so that's all we care about."

In truth, Juliette wasn't quite sure she cared about that either. Her father certainly didn't. That was the very reason why Mr. Lang was off chasing merchants about hog casings, and the inner circle of the Scarlet Gang busied itself with funneling opium and torturing police chiefs who wouldn't fall into line with gangster rule.

Juliette came around the other side of the sofa, sinking in next to Rosalind. The cushions bounced up and down, cold leather squeaking against the beads of her dress.

"Have you seen Kathleen?"

"Not since this morning," Rosalind answered. Her tone had turned colder, but Juliette pretended not to notice. Kathleen and Rosalind kept having little fights. If it wasn't Kathleen getting on Rosalind's nerves, telling her to quit doing their father's work, it was Rosalind getting on Kathleen's nerves, telling her to quit running around with Communists when she wasn't on a task. There was something lurking under the surface, something that Juliette suspected neither sister was telling her, but she had no business trying to push. At the end of the day, Kathleen and Rosalind couldn't stay mad at each other for long.

"Well, if you see her before I do," Juliette said, "let her know there's dinner tomorrow night. At Cheng—"

The front door of the house flew open, interrupting Juliette midsentence. A commotion stirred through the house, relatives poking their heads into the hall. When it was Tyler who hobbled in, his nose bloody and his arm looped over one of his men, Juliette only rolled her eyes. He wasn't putting any weight on his left leg. A knife wound, perhaps.

"Cai Tailei, what in heavens happened?" an aunt asked, bustling into the foyer. Behind her, a crowd of Scarlets followed, half of them Tyler's usual men.

"No matter," Tyler replied, grinning even while blood dripped down his face, staining the lines between his sparkling white teeth. "Only a small skirmish with a few White Flowers. Andong, send for cleanup on Lloyd Road."

Andong ran off immediately. The Scarlets were always fast when it came to summoning others ready for dirty work.

"What were you doing picking fights on Lloyd Road?"

Tyler's gaze snapped in Juliette's direction. She rose from the sofa, leaving Rosalind to her writing. Suddenly, the relatives gathering near the foyer were much more interested, heads turning back and forth between Juliette and Tyler like they were spectators in a game.

"Some of us don't fear the foreigners, Juliette."

"You are not showing bravery against the foreigners," Juliette shot back, coming to a stop in front of him. "You are performing for them like a horse at the Shanghai Racecourse."

Tyler did not rise to her bait. It was infuriating how at ease he looked, like he saw nothing wrong with the situation—with heightening the blood feud at the very center of the International Settlement, where men who knew nothing about this city governed it. The blood feud ravaged the whole city, true, but the worst of the fighting was always contained within gangster-controlled territory lines, kept out of the foreign concessions as much as they could help it. The British and the French did not need to see firsthand how wickedly the Scarlets and the White Flowers hated each other, especially now. Give them a reason—any reason—and they would try their luck with *fixing* the blood feud by rolling in their tanks and colonizing the land they hadn't already taken.

"Speaking of the foreigners," Tyler said. "There's a visitor outside for you. I told him to wait by the gates."

Juliette's eyes widened for a fraction of a second before she furrowed her expression in irritation. It was too late; Tyler had already caught it, and he grinned wider, disappearing up the stairs and disappointing all the relatives who had gathered around to fawn.

"A foreign visitor?" Juliette muttered beneath her breath. She pushed to the front door and slipped out, forgoing her coat with the thought that she would quickly dismiss whoever it was. Suppressing a shiver, she hopped over the awry plant that had drooped onto the mansion footpath and trekked down the driveway to the front gates.

Juliette stopped dead in her tracks. "Good God," she said aloud. "I must be hallucinating."

The visitor looked up at the sound of her voice and, from the other side of the gate, scrambled back a few steps. It wasn't for several delayed seconds that Juliette realized the only reason Walter Dexter had reacted in such a way was because she still clutched the knife she had been sharpening.

"Oh." She slid the knife into her sleeve. "My apologies."

"Not to worry," Walter Dexter replied, rather shakily. His gaze darted left and right to the Scarlets who guarded the gate. They were pretending not to notice the conversation taking place, staring straight ahead. "I hope you have been well since we last met, Miss Cai."

Juliette almost snorted. She had been the opposite of well, in fact, and it all started with her meeting with Walter Dexter. It was almost eerie to look upon the middle-aged man now, his pallor as gray as the thick winter sky above them. She wondered briefly if she ought to invite him in, as would be the polite thing to do, so the both of them could stop shivering in the cold, but that reminded her too much of when Paul Dexter came calling on behalf of his father. It reminded her of when she had willingly let a monster into her house before she knew of the literal monster he controlled, before she put a bullet right through his forehead.

Juliette didn't regret it. She had made a pact with herself long ago not to despair over the people she killed. Not when they were so often men who had forfeited their lives to greed or hate. Still, she saw Paul Dexter in her nightmares sometimes. It was always his eyes—that pale green stare, looking directly at her. They had been dull when she killed him.

Walter Dexter had the same eyes.

"How can I help you, Mr. Dexter?" Juliette asked. She folded her arms. There was no point keeping up small talk when it was unlikely Walter Dexter truly cared. It did not seem like he had fared well either. He had no briefcase; nor was he wearing a suit. His dress shirt was too big, the collar loose around his neck, and his pants pockets were practically fraying into threads.

"I've come with something of value," Walter Dexter said, reaching into his coat. "I'd like to sell you the remains of my son's research."

Juliette's pulse jumped, each *thud* inside her chest suddenly picking up in pace. Archibald Welch—the middleman who ran Paul's shipments—had said that Paul burned his notebooks after making the vaccine.

"I heard that he destroyed it all," Juliette said carefully.

"Indeed, it is likely he would have thought to discard his primary findings." Walter pulled a bundle of papers from his coat, neatly clipped together. "But I found these in his bookshelves. It is possible they were so unimportant that he had not the idle thought to even deal with them."

Juliette folded her arms. "So why do you think we would want them?"

"Because I heard he passed on his chaos," Walter replied darkly. "And before you ask, I have nothing to do with any of it. I am boarding the first ship out of here tomorrow for England." He shook his head then, an exhale rattling his lungs. "If the madness starts again, I will not remain to see how this one plays out. But I figure you, Miss

Cai, may want to counter it. Make a new vaccine, protect your people against its spread."

Juliette eyed the merchant warily. It sounded like Walter Dexter didn't know this madness was a targeted matter, dropped on its victims like a bomb.

"He claimed to have done it for you," Juliette said quietly. "He took you into a period of riches, but now you are here, back where you began, and your son is dead."

"I didn't ask for him to do it, Miss Cai," Walter rasped. All his age shuttered down on him, weariness sagging every line and wrinkle on his face. "I didn't even know what he was doing until he was dead and I was paying back his debts, cursing him for trying to act the savior."

Juliette looked away. She didn't want to feel pity for Walter Dexter, but it twinged at her anyway. For whatever reason, her mind flashed to Tyler. At the heart of the matter, he and Paul were not so different, were they? Boys who tried to do the best for the people they cared about, not concerned for the collateral damage they might wreak in the process. The difference was that Paul had been given real power—Paul had been given a whole system that bowed at his feet—and that made him so much more dangerous than Tyler could ever be.

Slowly, Walter Dexter extended his arm through two of the bars in the gate. He almost looked like an animal at the zoo, foolishly reaching out in hopes of some food. Or perhaps Juliette was the animal inside the cage, taking poison being fed to her.

"Take a look and see if it may be useful," Walter Dexter said, clearing his throat. "My starting price is written at the top left corner of the first page."

Juliette received the papers, then unfolded the dog-eared corner, revealing the price. She lifted her brows. "I could buy a house with that amount."

Walter shrugged. "Buy it or not," he said simply. "It is not my city that is soon to suffer."

Five

By all technicalities, Benedikt Montagov was grocery shopping. In reality, he was more or less collecting items to destroy, trading money for fresh pears, then taking one bite before squeezing the rest into oblivion, throwing the mushed core onto the pavement.

Benedikt was a terrible cook. He burned eggs and underprepared meat. In the first month, he attempted it at least, resolute not to waste away like a pathetic ghoul of a person. Then, as if a shutter had come down, he couldn't step into the kitchen at all. Every meal he made was one that Marshall hadn't. Every flicker of the gas, every puddle growing by the sink—the more that Benedikt took notice of the space that Marshall had once constantly lounged around, the emptier it grew.

It was bizarre that *that* was what had broken the dam, pushing through every wall Benedikt had put up to suppress his mourning. Not the absence of sound in the morning, not the absence of movement by his side. One day he had been operating in numbness, shoving aside the art supplies abandoned on the floor and going through each step of his routine with hardly any trouble. The next moment, he entered the kitchen and could not stop staring at the stovetop. The water started boiling and still he could not look away, until he merely crumpled to the floor, sobbing into his hands as the water evaporated into nothingness.

Benedikt put a stick of gānzhè in his mouth, chewing slowly. Now he could hardly eat. He didn't know why, but things wouldn't stay down, and things that did stay down felt wrong. The only loophole around the instinct was to take a bite out of everything he could get his hands on and throw it away before his thoughts could catch up. It kept him fed and kept his head quiet. That was what mattered.

"Hey!"

At the sudden shout, he spat out the raw sugarcane clumps. There was a commotion erupting by the far side of the market, and Benedikt started over immediately, wiping his mouth. Any commotion would have been harder to discern if this were a busier market, but the stalls here barely extended past two streets, and the vendors hardly had the energy to shout their wares. This was one of the poorer parts of the city, where people were near starving and would do whatever it took to survive, which included pledging devout loyalty to the closest available power. It was a bad idea to draw attention to himself, especially here, where territories shifted and changed at a moment's notice. Benedikt knew this, yet he turned the corner anyway, dashing into the alleyway where the shout was heard.

He found a whole crowd of Scarlets, and one White Flower messenger.

"Benedikt Montagov!" the boy screeched immediately.

Of all times to be identified. Benedikt had nowhere near the level of recognition that Roma received on the streets, yet here he was, pinned for a Montagov, pinned for the enemy. A tear streaked down the boy's face, running a wet trail that caught the midday light before hitting the concrete.

Benedikt inhaled fast, assessing the situation. The White Flower was Chinese—he shouldn't have been identified at all for his allegiance, if not for that white thread he'd twined around his own wrist.

Foolish. The blood feud had gotten horrific these last few months. If he had the ability to blend in, why not do it? How old was he? Ten? Eleven?

"Montagov?" one of the Scarlets echoed.

Benedikt reached for his gun. The smarter move would have been to run when he was vastly outnumbered, but he cared little. He had no reason to care, to *live*—

He didn't even have the chance to pull a weapon. A blow came to the side of his face out of nowhere, then Benedikt was reeling, crushed to the ground amid shouting and cursing and someone calling for the death of his whole family. His arms were bent back and his head was pushed hard into the cement, before something ice cold, something that felt like the butt of a gun, jammed up against his temple.

No, he thought suddenly, his eyes squeezing shut. *Wait, I didn't actually want to die, not* yet, *not really . . .*

A deafening sound shook the alleyway. His ears rang, but other than the bruises forming all over his body, he felt no pain, no white-hot bullet pressed into his skull. Maybe this was death. Maybe death was nothing.

Then the sound came again, and again, and again. Gunshots. Not from the alleyway. From *above*.

Benedikt's eyes flew open at the exact moment a spray of blood landed across his face, tinting his vision red. He gasped, jerking upright and scurrying up against the wall, unable to comprehend anything past his disbelief as the Scarlets around him dropped one by one, studded in bullets. Only as the shooting almost stopped did he think to look up, trying to find where the bullets were coming from.

He caught the barest flash of movement. There—at the edge of the rooftop—then gone with the last bullet, the last Scarlet dropping dead.

Benedikt was breathing hard enough to be heaving. Only one other person remained standing in the alleyway: the messenger, fully crying now, his fists clenched so tightly that they were white and bloodless. He didn't look injured. He was only bloody, as splattered as Benedikt was.

"Go," Benedikt managed. "Run, in case there are more of them."

The boy faltered. Perhaps it was a *thank you* that hovered on his tongue. But then there was a shout from the market, and Benedikt snapped, "Kuài gǔn! Before they come!" The boy took off, not needing to be told another time. Quickly, Benedikt staggered to his feet, following his own advice, knowing that those shots had been loud, and any Scarlets nearby would arrive immediately to investigate the cause.

But as he stood there, his whole body trembling, it struck him that with the speed those bullets had come, whoever had saved him had been waiting, poised to enter in rescue. He eyed the buildings, the evenly constructed rooftops separated only by alleyways that were narrow enough to leap from one to the other. Someone had been watching—perhaps for a while, tailing him through the market.

"Who would bother?" Benedikt whispered aloud.

Six

The second floor of the teahouse had been booked out tonight for the Scarlet inner circle meeting. All its square tables were pushed to the wall, making way for the large round one installed right in the center of the space.

Juliette thought it looked a little like a barricade. She took a sip of her tea, peering over the rim while she eyed the setup, wary that some poor waiter was going to trek up the stairs to check on the Scarlets only to ram right into the table that was blocking the end of the stairs. All the windows had been left untouched—though for teahouses like this, "window" was hardly the right word when they never installed glass. They were merely closed using wooden shutters, drawn when the teahouse went dark for the night and pulled open during its operating hours. The frigid cold blew in every so often, but alcohol was flowing at the table, and the oil lamps in the corner were buzzing with warmth.

Still, for whatever reason, Juliette's eyes kept being pulled back to the barricade of tables pressed to the walls, and then up, where the walls gave way for the rectangular cutouts that let in the night. In here, there was the illusion of comfort and safety. But all that stood between them and the lurking unknown was a thin teahouse wall. All that stood between them and five monsters prowling the city was . . . well, nothing, really.

"Juliette."

Lord Cai's summons drew Juliette's attention back to the Scarlet dinner, to the cigar smoke that wafted in gray plumes above them and the clinking of chopsticks upon porcelain bowls. Her father tipped his chin at her, indicating that he was finished with his agenda and she could speak now, as she had requested earlier today.

Juliette set her teacup down and stood. The tablecloth stirred, but before it could get caught on her dress, Rosalind reached over and yanked it down.

"Thanks," Juliette whispered.

Rosalind responded by flicking a single grain of rice off the table-cloth, aiming it at the seats directly across from them. She almost hit Tyler, although he wouldn't have noticed a puny piece of rice landing in his lap when he was eyeing Juliette so intently. Perhaps it was only his bruised nose causing the scrunch in his expression. Perhaps he was already preparing himself for a fight, and the distaste was showing through.

"Here." From Rosalind's other side, Kathleen passed the stack of papers she had been holding on to. Juliette received the papers, then set them carefully onto the spinning glass, on an empty spot right between the sauce-soaked crabs and smoked fish.

"I'm sure by now you have all heard about the attack on the White Flowers." The table hushed at the mention of the White Flowers. "And I'm sure you've wondered if we are to be next, again at the mercy of another monster."

Juliette spun the glass. The feast swirled under the lights: shimmering green qīngcài, deep brown hóngshāo ròu, and the plain black-and-white ink of what could save them.

"This is the last vestige of research that Paul Dexter left behind. You might also know him as the former Larkspur—now dead from my bullet." Juliette drew herself taller, though her spine was already as straight as a blade. "It may be some time before we can stop whoever has resurrected his work. But in the meantime, I propose *we* use his work. We allocate our resources toward research, mass-produce a vaccine, and distribute it through the whole city. . . ." Now came the part where Juliette actually needed support, past merely making a case with her father. *"For free."*

Eyebrows shot up immediately, teacups freezing halfway to mouths as Scarlets stalled and blinked, wondering if they had misheard her.

"It is a preemptive measure before the Scarlet Gang can be attacked," Juliette hurried to explain. "Regardless of who you are—Scarlet or White Flower, Nationalist or Communist or nonaffiliated—if we all stand immune to the madness, then whichever fool is trying to play at the new Larkspur loses every shred of power. In one fell swoop, we protect the city and keep everything the way it is, at no threat from a destroyer."

"I have an alternate proposal." Tyler stood. He rested his knuckles on the table before him, his body relaxed, an utterly casual picture compared to Juliette's stiff composure.

Rosalind leaned forward. "Why don't you—"

"Rosalind, don't," Kathleen hissed, closing a hand on her sister's shoulder. Lips thinning, Rosalind sat back again, and Tyler went on as if nothing had happened.

"If we can truly create a vaccine, it is in our best interest to charge anyone who is not a Scarlet. The Larkspur was a fool in many things, but in this, he was not. The people are scared. They will do anything for a solution."

"Absolutely not," Juliette snapped, before any of the Scarlets could decide that Tyler's interruption meant their opinion should be heard by the whole table too. "This is not a show ticket. This is a vaccine that decides between life and death."

"And what about it?" Tyler asked. "You wish for us to protect the White Flowers? Protect the foreigners who do not even see us as people? The last time the madness went around, Juliette, they did not care until it was them who were dying, because a Chinese collapsing on the streets may as well be an *animal*—"

"I *know*!"

Juliette inhaled sharply, regaining her poise. She had to get her points in quick. Her mother's jaw was tight, watching the argument spiral, and if it deteriorated any further, Lady Cai was going to shut this down.

Juliette breathed out. Let the brief silence ebb around her, so that she was in control of the conversation and not desperately chasing the end of it.

"It is not about extending our kindness to those in the city who don't deserve it," she said. "It is about mass protection."

Tyler pushed off from the table and plopped back onto his seat. He hung an arm along the back of his chair while Juliette remained standing.

"Why do we need mass protection?" Tyler asked, scoffing. "Let us make *money*. Let us rise so impenetrably to the top that we are untouchable, and then, as we have always done, we extend protection to our people. To the Scarlets. Everyone else falling away matters not. Everyone else dying out is to our advantage."

"You would be risking Scarlet lives in the process. You cannot guarantee their safety like that."

Despite her unflinching insistence, Juliette could feel her credibility slipping away. She was trying to stake her logic on the sanctity of one life saved as something worthy of all sacrifice, but this was the Scarlet Gang, and the Scarlet Gang did not care for such sentimental notions.

One of the Scarlets seated beside Lord Cai cleared his throat. Seeing that it was Mr. Ping, who Juliette usually liked, she looked to him and nodded, prompting him to go on.

"Where is the funding going to come from?" Mr. Ping asked. He winced. "Surely not us?"

Juliette threw her arms up. Why else would she bother to stand here, bleating the advantages of a free vaccine, if not for the funds of the Scarlet Gang's inner circle? "We can *afford* it."

Mr. Ping's eyes darted about the table. He mopped his damp forehead. "We are not a charity for the weak and poor."

"This is a city built on labor," Juliette said coldly. "If madness tears through the streets once again, *we* are only as safe as the weakest and poorest. They fall, and we fall too. Do you forget who runs your factories? Do you forget how your shops open every morning?"

The table fell silent, but nobody jumped to put in their acknowledgment of her point. They merely shifted their gazes away and remained mum, until the silence extended for long enough that Lady Cai was forced to tap her fingers on the spinning glass and say, "Juliette, take a seat, would you? Perhaps this would be a better discussion once we actually make a vaccine."

A beat later, Lord Cai nodded his agreement. "Yes. We shall decide if this research proves useful. Run it to the lab in Chenghuangmiao tomorrow and see what we can find."

Begrudgingly, Juliette nodded her acceptance of the decision and eased back into her seat. Her mother was quick to change the topic and put the Scarlets at ease again. As Juliette reached for the teapot, her eyes met Tyler's across the table, and he grinned.

"Allez, souris!" he said. His fast switch into French was to prevent the other Scarlets from understanding him, save for Rosalind and Kathleen, but even without knowing what he was saying, anyone could tell by his manner, his expression, his tone that he was goading Juliette and announcing his victory in a tug-of-war for favor. The simple fact that he had not been shot down on an idea that went starkly against Juliette's, that her parents seemed to consider it on equal basis—indeed, Tyler had won.

"Je t'avertis . . . ," Juliette snapped.

"What?" Tyler shot back, still in French. "You're warning me of what, dearest cousin?"

It took everything in Juliette not to pick up her teacup and throw it right at him. "Stop playing god upon my plans. Stop intruding upon matters that have naught to do with you—"

"Your plans are always flawed. I am trying to help you out," Tyler interrupted. His smile fell, and Juliette tensed, reading immediately what was coming next. "Look at how your last one turned out. In your whole time *tricking* the White Flower heir, what information did you gather from him?"

Under the table, Juliette dug her long nails hard into her palms, releasing all her tension through her hands so that her expression would not give her away. He suspected. He had always suspected, long before she told her lie in that hospital, but then Juliette had shot Marshall Seo, and Tyler had had to reevaluate his instincts, unable to align why she would have killed Marshall if she was truly Roma Montagov's lover.

Except Marshall was alive. And all along, Tyler had been right. But if he knew this, then Juliette's role as the heiress was over, and Tyler would not even have to lead a coup. He only had to tell the truth, and the Scarlets would fall in line behind him.

"You ruined my plan, Tyler," Juliette said evenly. "You forced me to give myself away too early. I worked so hard to gain his trust, and I had to throw it away lest you misunderstood me. You're lucky I haven't tattled to my parents about your uselessness."

Tyler's eyes narrowed. His gaze flickered to Lord and Lady Cai, realizing that her parents did not have the full picture of the hospital, just like the rest of the city. It would have been impossible to keep the rumors away from them, but as far as they knew, Juliette and Tyler had shown up to that White Flower confrontation as a united force.

The thought was almost laughable. But it didn't raise questions.

"Lucky," Tyler echoed. "Sure, Juliette." With a brief shake of his head, he turned away, engaging with the aunt beside him in Shanghainese.

Juliette, however, couldn't lapse back into the casual socializing at the table. Her ears were a roar of noise, head buzzing with the threat lining every word of that conversation. There were goose bumps all along her neck, and even as she pulled her dress tighter around herself, clutching at the fur around her throat, she could not fool herself into thinking that it was merely the cold blowing in.

It was fear. She was deathly afraid of the power Tyler held over her after what he had witnessed at that hospital. Because he was right: he really did have reason to uproot her. Tyler would do all in his power to ensure the survival of the Scarlet Gang, while Juliette no longer had a single desire to be fighting the blood feud, not when it was so damn *pointless*. Let them both voice their truths to Lord Cai, and who would he choose to be heir?

Juliette reached for the liquor bottle passing on the spinning glass and poured a splash into her teacup. Without caring who was watching her, she choked it down.

"You're hitting too high."

Roma jabbed Alisa in the armpit, and she yelped, darting back several steps. Her scowl was half-hearted, shoulders coming up to her ears as she hunched into herself. Roma resisted his sigh, only because he knew Alisa would be annoyed if he seemed irritated by her slow progress.

"You said you were teaching me self-defense," she grumbled, smoothing down her hair.

"I am."

"You're just—" Alisa waved around her hands, trying to imitate Roma's fast movements. "It's not very helpful."

A breeze floated in from Alisa's window, and Roma walked toward it, pulling down the pane to keep the cold out. He didn't say anything as he huffed a breath onto the glass. He only blew until there was considerable mist, and then with his finger, he drew a little face that was smiling.

"Is that supposed to be motivating?" Alisa asked, watching over his shoulder.

He reached over to pinch her cheeks. "It's supposed to be you. Tiny and annoying."

Alisa smacked his hands away. *"Roma."*

It wasn't that he didn't like spending time with his sister, but he had a suspicion she was asking for these lessons only to distract him from his other tasks. And it wasn't that he didn't like hanging around with his sister instead of tending to his other tasks, but he was also sure the little scamp had schemed this up only to prevent him from guarding their territory lines, not because she actually wanted to learn how to punch an attacker.

"This is very important, you know," Alisa said now, as if she could sense where his train of thought was going. "I was in a coma for so *long*. I cannot be weak! I must know how to punch bad men!"

A thump came through the floor. It was either a sitting room in the house growing too raucous, or someone on the level below throwing knives at the wall. Roma heaved an exhale, then positioned Alisa, making her hold her arms out.

"Okay. Try again then. Keep your fist tight."

Alisa tried again. And again. And again. No matter what she did, her blocks were flimsy and her efforts at striking Roma when he pretended to grab her were soft and wobbly.

"Why don't we stop here?" Roma said eventually.

"No!" Alisa exclaimed. She stamped her foot down. "You haven't taught me how to hit. Or shoot! Or catch a knife!"

"Catch a . . ." Roma trailed off, flabbergasted. "Why do you want to—you know what, never mind." He shook his head. "Alisochka, no one learns how to fight in one day."

Alisa folded her arms, storming over to her bed and collapsing in a flurry of movement. Her sheets flew up and settled down around her like a white aura.

"I bet Juliette learned to fight in one day," she grumbled.

Roma froze. He felt his blood flash hot, then cold, then somehow both at once—a simultaneous broiling fury paired with a frozen fear just at the mere sound of her name.

"You shouldn't want to be *anything* like Juliette," he snapped. He wanted to believe it. If he said it enough times, maybe he would. Maybe he could look past the illusions she glimmered with, look underneath the wide eyes she blinked at him even as she spilled blood at his feet. No matter how brightly she shone, Juliette's heart had turned as charred as coal.

"I know," Alisa muttered, matching Roma's tone. She was grumpy now because it sounded like Roma was grumpy at her, and Roma swallowed his anger, knowing it was misdirected. It prickled at him that he had become so easily irritable, and yet he couldn't stop himself. The red-hot urge to be terrible was always pulling at his skin, easier to slip into than ignore.

Roma rolled up his sleeves, checking the clock on her mantel. Alisa seemed content to have a little brooding moment, so he walked over and poked her belly. "I'm needed elsewhere. We can pick up another time."

"Okay." Another low grumble, her arms folded tightly. "Don't die."

His brow lifted. He'd expected Alisa to protest, to ask again why he needed to be on the streets and watching their territory lines. But all these months singing the same tune had tired her out.

"I won't." He prodded her again. "Practice your stances."

Roma left her room, closing the door behind himself. The fourth floor was quieter than usual, void of the thumping that had been heard earlier. Perhaps they too had tired of trying to learn to throw a knife.

I bet Juliette learned to fight in one day.

Damn Juliette. It wasn't enough that she had to occupy his

thoughts, sunken into his very bones. It wasn't enough that she had to appear in the city everywhere he needed to go, trailing him like a shadow. She had to come into his home as well, graced across White Flower lips like the final frontier of her invasion.

"Where are you off to?"

Roma's stride didn't stop as he came off the stairs. "That would be none of your business."

"Wait," Dimitri demanded.

Roma didn't need to. Nothing was preventing him from treating Dimitri Voronin however he wished, turning the tables until the whole house was dizzy, because Dimitri Voronin had gotten comfortable as the favorite, and now Roma had decided he wanted the whole Scarlet Gang dead after all. So many years spent trying to balance being the heir and being good, and with one snap of his fingers, the goodness gave way for violence, and Lord Montagov had liked the look of it. Being a White Flower was about playing the game. And Roma was finally playing.

"What is it?" Roma asked dully, making an exaggerated show of slowing down and turning around.

Dimitri, who was sitting on one of the plush green couches, stared forward curiously, his fingers tapping on the back of the couch, one foot resting against his other knee.

"Your father wants your audience," Dimitri reported. He flashed an easy smile. A lock of black hair fell forward into his face. "Whenever you're ready. He has some matters to discuss."

Roma's eyes darted up, following another outburst of sound from within the house, the ceiling shifting and trembling from some second-floor commotion. It might even be coming from his father's office.

"He can be patient," Roma said.

With Dimitri's gaze still pinned on him, Roma pulled the front door open and swept outside.

Seven

H ere, here, and here."

Kathleen circled parts of the map, slashing the fountain pen hard. The city map was practically fraying, one of the many coarser copies that Juliette owned, so she only eyed the markings thoughtfully as they bled red, soaking through the thin paper and onto her vanity table beneath. She and Kathleen were both jammed on one backless velvet seat, trying to peer at the map together. This was her own fault for never installing a proper desk in this bedroom. She only ever splayed herself on her bed. How often had she needed to use an actual hard surface?

Kathleen made a final marking. Just as she set her pen down, one of the map corners started to curl upward, but before the paper could roll into itself and smear the ink, Juliette snatched one of her lipsticks from a box on her vanity and set it on the corner to keep the map down.

"Really?" Kathleen asked immediately.

"What?" Juliette shot back. "I needed something heavy."

Kathleen simply shook her head. "The fate of the city rests upon your lipstick. The irony is not lost on me, Juliette. Now—" She shifted back into business mode. "I don't know if it's worth shutting down operations in these parts just to prevent a strike, but the next one will hit somewhere here. The labor unions are only going to keep blowing things bigger and bigger."

"We'll warn the factory foremen," Juliette confirmed. She lifted a thumb to the map, trying to gauge how far away the locations were from one another. As her hand hovered over the southern part of the city, over Nanshi, she faltered, sighting the road where a certain hospital was.

If the protesters that day hadn't stormed the hospital, Juliette wondered if there could have been another way out.

Wishful thinking. Even if they had all backed away without a fight, Tyler would have shot her in the head the moment she reached for Roma's hand.

"Juliette."

The bedroom door flew open. Juliette jerked in surprise, ramming her knee hard against the vanity table. Kathleen, too, sucked in a fast inhale, her hand flying up to the jade pendant around her throat as if to check if it was in place.

"Māma," Juliette breathed when she turned to face the doorway. "Are you trying to scare the living daylights out of me?"

Lady Cai gave a small smile, opting not to respond. Instead, she said, "I'm off to stroll Nanjing Road. Would you like anything? New fabric?"

"I'll pass."

Her mother pressed on. "You could get a new qipao. Last I checked, you only fit two in your wardrobe."

Juliette barely refrained from rolling her eyes. Some things never changed. Lady Cai might voice it rarely now that Juliette was at the ripe age of nineteen, but she still detested those flashy, loose Western dresses her daughter so loved.

"I'll truly pass," Juliette replied. "I love the two in my wardrobe far too dearly to acquire a third."

It was her mother's turn to resist an eye roll. "Very well. Selin? Are you eyeing any fabric you'd like me to snatch up for you?"

Kathleen smiled, and though Juliette had been flippant through this whole conversation, her cousin seemed genuinely touched to be asked.

"That's kind of you, Niángniang, but I have enough garments in my wardrobe as it is."

Lady Cai sighed. "All right, then. If that is how you ladies choose to live." She turned on her heel and was on her merry way, brisk and quick. Except she had left Juliette's door wide open.

"I swear my mother does this on purpose," Juliette said, rising to close the door. "She's far too smart to actually forget that—"

A disturbance wafted into the hallway. Juliette stopped, inclining her ear out.

"What is it?" Kathleen asked.

"Sounds like yelling," Juliette replied. "Perhaps from my father's office."

Right on cue, Lord Cai's office door flew open. The volume grew infinitely louder, and Juliette frowned, digesting what the argument was actually about.

"Oh, wonderful." She reached into the back of her dress, feeling around amid the fabric at her shoulder blades. There, where the loose stitching dipped into a little hollow to accommodate a sash of black that trailed to her legs, she dug out her pistol. "I've just been dying to thwack a Nationalist lately."

"Juliette . . . ," Kathleen warned.

"I'm *kidding*." But she didn't put the pistol away. She merely waited by the doorway, watching the Nationalist march out with her father closely behind him. This was a different Nationalist from the many she had already seen coming and going from the office. A lesser-known officer with fewer medals pinned to his chest.

"You have free rein because you're supposed to keep this city in check," he shouted. "Until the National Revolutionary Army comes and swallows the Beiyang government for the Kuomintang, there is only you. Until we may install a central force so that power in Shanghai is not a game of bribing police officers and militia forces, then there"—he started punctuating each word with a stab of his finger into the wall—"is—only—you."

Juliette's grip twitched. Again, Kathleen gestured furiously for her to put the gun down, but Juliette only pretended not to see. How foolish of the Nationalist to put the Scarlets in their place by reminding them of what was coming. The Scarlet Gang wouldn't possibly cooperate with a future where they bent to the will of a government . . .

. . . Would they?

Juliette looked at her father. He did not appear offended or otherwise irritated.

"Yes, you have made that point very clearly," Lord Cai said, his voice wry. "The front door is that way."

The Nationalist ignored him. "What am I supposed to report to my superiors about the state of this city? When Chiang Kai-shek asks why Shanghai is under attack *again*, what am I supposed to say?"

"It is no concern," Lord Cai said evenly. "This is no longer an epidemic; this is one blackmailer. Once we figure out who is responsible, we can stop this."

"And how are you to do that? By paying the blackmailer more and more each time? I'll say this, Lord Cai: on behest of the government, you are not to grant this last request."

Juliette was ready, her mouth already half-open to jump in with outrage, but her father was faster.

"We will not fulfill this demand. But you must know there will be an attack."

"So put a stop to it." The Nationalist pulled at his jacket, huffing out an angry breath. He took his leave, hurrying down the stairs in rapid motion. With each step, his badges and medals glimmered under the overhead lights, soft golden light reflecting off the edges of decoration that spoke of such valor and bravery in battle—but Juliette had only witnessed today a frightened foot soldier.

"What did he mean?" Juliette called over.

Lord Cai turned suddenly, his jaw twitching the smallest fraction. That was the closest Juliette would ever get to startling her father.

"You didn't want to go shopping with your mother?" he remarked, peering over the banister one last time before returning to his office.

Juliette made a disgruntled noise, shoving her pistol back into her dress and mouthing to Kathleen that she would not be gone for long. Before her father could close the office door again, Juliette sprinted down the hallway, sliding in just as he was pushing at the handle.

"You didn't tell me there was another demand," Juliette accused. It had hardly been three days since the last. The previous ones had had weeks in between.

"And you are eerily fast for someone who never gets any exercise." Lord Cai sat down at his desk. "A few walks in the park would be good for your health, Juliette. Otherwise you will be like me and have clogged arteries at old age."

Juliette thinned her lips. If her father was diverting the topic this outrageously, it had to be something bad. He had a letter in front of him on his desk, and when she reached for it, Lord Cai moved it out of the way, shooting her a look of warning.

"It is not from the blackmailer," he said.

"Then why can't I see it?"

"That's enough, Juliette." Lord Cai folded the letter in half. Something in her gaze must have looked ready to argue, because her father did not bother taking on a stern tone; nor did he try ordering her out of his office by command. He simply relinquished and said, "Weapons. They want military weapons this time."

Whatever Juliette had been expecting, it wasn't that. She blinked, dropping into the seat opposite her father. These few months, they had been fulfilling the demands, hoping that the blackmailer would go away once they had siphoned enough and could run. But it was clear as day now that they weren't in it for the money. They were here to stay, for whatever endgame.

Why military weapons? Why so much money?

"That's why the Nationalist was so stoutly against giving in to the demand this time," Juliette said aloud, connecting the dots. "The blackmailer is building something. They're gathering forces."

It didn't make sense. Why gather guns when you had *monsters*?

"It could be for a militia," Lord Cai said. "Perhaps to aid a workers' rebellion."

Juliette wasn't so sure. She chewed on the inside of her cheeks, focusing on the harsh sting of her teeth biting down.

"It just doesn't seem to add up," she said. "The letters are coming from the French Concession, but beyond that, this is Paul Dexter's work. Whoever has control of the monsters now, whoever had the mother insects, which began the infection, he *gave* them over." Juliette thought back to the letter Kathleen had found. *Release them all.* That was the hurdle she simply could not cross. If Paul Dexter had had a partner in this all along, how did she not know? She may not have paid him that much attention while he pursued her, but surely for someone as important as a mission partner, he would have dropped a name at some point.

"Therein lies the rub," her father remarked evenly.

Juliette slammed her hands down on the desk.

"Send me into the French Concession," she said. "Whoever this is, I can find them. I know it."

For a long moment, Lord Cai said nothing. He only stared at her, like he was waiting for her to say she was kidding. Then, when Juliette did not offer an alternative, he reached into a side drawer by his desk and pulled out a series of photographs. The black-and-white images were grainy and too dark, but when her father set them down, Juliette felt her stomach turn, a rolling sensation tightening her gut.

"These are from the White Flower club," Lord Cai said. "The . . . what was it? Xiàngrìkuí?"

"Yes," Juliette whispered, her eyes still latched on the photos. Her father hadn't actually forgotten the name of the club, of course. It was only that he refused to speak Russian, even if it was so easy to lapse into the language from Shanghainese with the sounds so similar— perhaps even more so than Shanghainese and the actual Chinese common tongue. "Podsolnukh."

Lord Cai pushed the photographs even closer. "Take a good look, Juliette."

The victims of the madness in September had gouged their own throats out, clawing and clawing until their hands were gloved in blood. These photos did not only show torn throats. Of the faces that Juliette could catch, they no longer resembled *faces* at all. They were eyes and mouths torn until they were no longer circular in shape, fore-heads with golf-ball-sized holes, ears dangling from the thinnest inch of a lobe. If it were possible to photograph in color, the whole scene would have been drenched in red.

"I am not going to send you into *this* alone," Lord Cai said quietly. "You are my daughter, not my lackey. Whoever is doing this, this is what they are capable of."

Juliette breathed out through her nose, the sound loud and grat-ing. "We have one lead," she said. "One lead, and it says this mess is coming out of foreign territory. Who else is able? Tyler? He'll be killed with a knife to the throat before the insects get him."

"You've missed the point, Juliette."

"I haven't!" Juliette screeched, though she suspected she had. "If this blackmailer came out of the French Concession, then I will find them by merging right into their high society. Their rules, their customs. Someone will know. Someone will have information. And I will get it out of them." She lifted her chin. "Send me in. Send Kathleen and Rosalind as accompaniment if you must. But no entourage. No protection. Once they trust me, then they will talk."

Lord Cai shook his head slowly, but the motion wasn't one that indicated refusal. It was more or less an action to digest Juliette's words, his hands absently reaching for that mysterious letter again, folding it further into quarters, then eighths.

"How about this?" her father said quietly. "Let me think about what we shall do next. Then we figure out if you are to enter the French Concession like a covert operative."

Juliette mocked a salute. Her father shooed her, and she skittered off. As she was closing the door after herself, she peered through one last time and found that he was still staring at the letter in his hands.

"Careful, Miss Cai!"

Juliette squealed, narrowly stopping herself from stepping right onto a maid crouching in the hallway.

"What are you doing there?" she exclaimed, her hand pressed to her heart.

The maid grimaced. "There is just a bit of mud. Don't mind me. It'll soon be clean."

Juliette nodded her thanks, turning to go. Then, for whatever reason, she squinted at the clump of mud the maid was working at, and sighted, stuck inside the clump that had been smeared into the threads of the carpeting, a single pink petal.

"Hold on," Juliette said. She got to her knees, and before the maid could protest too loudly, she stuck her finger into the mud and dug the petal out, dirtying her nails. The maid winced more than Juliette did; Juliette only wrinkled her nose, looking at what she had unearthed.

"Miss Cai, it's just a petal," the maid said. "There have been a few clumps here and there these past months. Someone is not wiping their shoes properly before coming in."

Juliette's eyes shot up immediately. "You've found these over *months*?"

The maid looked confused. "I—yes? Mud, mostly."

A rumble of noise erupted in the living room below: distant cousins, arriving for a social call over the mahjong tables. Juliette sucked in a breath and held it. The mud was smeared right near the wall, a splotch small enough that truly nobody but an eagle-eyed maid looking for places to clean could have spotted it. It was also near enough to the wall that it could have been left by someone pressed up against her father's office door, listening in.

"The next time you see something like this," Juliette said slowly, "find me, understand?"

The maid's confusion only grew. "May I ask why?"

Juliette stood, still holding the petal. Its natural color was a pale pink, but in this light, with so much mud, it almost looked entirely black.

"No particular reason," she answered, flashing a smile. "Don't work too hard, hmm?"

Juliette hurried away, almost short of breath. It was a stretch. There were plenty of peony plants across the city and even more patches of mud where those plants grew.

Then she remembered her father at that dinner so many months ago, when he had claimed there was a spy: no ordinary spy, but someone who had been invited into the room, someone who lived in this house. And she knew—she just *knew*—that this particular petal came from the peonies at the Montagov residence, from the back of the house where the petals shed from the high windowsills and settled into the muddy ground.

Because five years ago, Juliette was the one tracking these all over the house.

Kathleen was in *another* Communist meeting.

It wasn't that Juliette kept sending her to them, but rather that the

Communists kept meeting up, and if Kathleen was going to maintain appearances and get invited back to the next ones through the contacts she had painstakingly cultivated, then she had to keep showing up, as if she were another worker and not the right hand of the Scarlet heiress.

At last Kathleen finished pinning down her hair, having adjusted her whole style in the last five minutes while the speaker at the front talked about unionizing. She had learned by now that the initial speakers never had much of a point to them: they were there to ramble until the important people arrived and the seats filled well enough to avoid rustling when latecomers shifted into the open gaps. No one was paying attention to Kathleen while she tuned out and squinted into a handheld mirror from her pocket, determining that the complicated plaits Rosalind had made earlier were a little too bourgeois for this meeting.

"Excuse me."

Kathleen startled, turning at the soft voice behind her. A little girl, missing two front teeth, was holding one of Kathleen's pins.

"You dropped this."

"Oh," Kathleen whispered back. "Thank you."

"That's okay," the girl lisped. She was swinging her legs, glancing momentarily at the woman seated to her left—her mother, perhaps—to check whether she would be told off for talking to a stranger. "But I liked your hair better before."

Kathleen swallowed a smile, reaching up to touch the pinned curls. Rosalind had said the same, lavishing praise on herself as she was plaiting. Her sister was rarely in the mood to sit around and chat these days. She likely would not refuse if Kathleen caught her around the house and asked for a moment of her time, but the trouble was precisely that she was never around.

"I liked it too," Kathleen replied quietly, and turned back in her seat. She almost wished she hadn't taken it out now, ruining her sister's handiwork.

The room suddenly broke into applause, and Kathleen hurried to follow suit. As the speakers changed, she sat up in her seat and tried to shift her attention back to listening, but her thoughts kept wandering, her hands idly reaching up to touch her hair. Their father had visited again last week, more insistent on their move out to the countryside. Rosalind had rolled her eyes and stormed off, which their father hadn't taken very well, and Kathleen had been the one left behind to entertain his theatrics about the state of the city and where its politics were taking it. Maybe that was the way the two of them split their duties. Rosalind talked back and pushed all his buttons, but when their father wasn't watching, she stuck her nose into his work and did his business for him. Kathleen smiled and nodded, and when their father needed the assurance, she did everything expected of the thoughtful, demure Kathleen Lang that this city knew. She had always known that adopting this name would mean taking a part of her sister's personality, if not for the sake of appearances, then purely for the sake of ease. Sometimes her father spoke to her as if he had truly forgotten that the real Kathleen was dead. Sometimes she wondered what would happen if she spoke the name "Celia" before him again.

Kathleen shifted in her seat. Nevertheless, she was more worried about Rosalind than she was worried about herself. If she was being honest, she was a little miffed that Rosalind had stopped her from going to Juliette's aid so many months ago, yet found no problem hanging around the cabarets on neutral territory, socializing with Frenchmen in the city's trade network.

How can we be on the same side when they will never fall? Rosalind had said. *They are invulnerable. We are not!*

Nothing had changed. Rosalind and Kathleen were still set apart from the rest of the Scarlet Gang carrying the Cai name, but suddenly let it be a task that gave Rosalind a sense of self-decided purpose, and here she was, uncaring about vulnerability. Maybe it was inevitable in a city like this. Each and every one of them, taking on a path of destruction, even if they knew better, even if they would warn someone else off it. Rosalind didn't like Kathleen's involvement with the Communists; Kathleen thought it was utterly foolish for Rosalind to play diplomat. Who cared if their father threatened to move them? He had no true power over them, not anymore, not in Shanghai. Filial piety be damned. One word from Juliette, and he would have to tuck tail and turn away, pack his bags and depart the city alone.

"We are absolutely not leaving," Kathleen muttered to herself as another round of applause swept the room, drowning her out. She sat back, resolute to pay attention as debate began, as one Communist argued that it was the foreigners causing the problems in this city, not the gangsters, and another rebutting that the only solution was to kick them all out. The planning started—the very reason why Kathleen was here, leaning forward in her seat as probable strike locations were determined and timelines constructed for the ultimate destruction of foreign imperialism.

It was at that moment her gaze wandered—only for the briefest scan of the room. She didn't know what it was that had inspired her to do so, but her attention snagged on a foreign face. When she blinked once more, Kathleen realized by his clothing that it was no foreigner at all but a Russian White Flower.

Kathleen frowned. She returned her attention to the front, but pulled up the collar of her coat, hiding as much of her face as she could.

Dimitri Voronin, she thought, her mind racing. *What are* you *doing here?*

Eight

Let me guess," Juliette said, pulling the car door after herself. "You've discovered that I am a secret revolutionary and now you are taking me to the outskirts of the city for execution."

From the driver's seat, Lord Cai glanced over at her with a furrow of his brow. Then he pushed a button on the dashboard, letting the engine rumble to life.

"I am begging you to stop watching the Wild West films coming from America," he said. For someone who likely had not driven a car in years, her father spun the steering wheel and pulled out of the driveway with expert maneuvering. "They're rotting your brain."

Juliette twisted in her seat and peered out the back window, waiting for other cars to follow behind them. When none came, she turned to the front again and put her hands in her lap, pursing her lips.

This was mightily strange. She couldn't remember the last time they'd gone anywhere without an entourage—or at least *one* other Scarlet for backup. It wasn't that her father needed protection, not when he was the one who had taught her how to use a blade at three years old, but having a group of men clustered around him at all times was about posture, and she didn't think he ever went into public without that protection.

"So," Juliette tried, "where are we going?"

"You managed to get into this car without asking questions," her father replied plainly. "Now refrain until we arrive."

Juliette pursed her lips further and sank into her seat. By the time they were easing down Avenue Edward VII in the thick of the city, Lord Cai's driving had grown more erratic, starting and stopping when people walked onto the road with none of the smoothness of their chauffeurs. Just when Juliette thought they were close to running over an elderly woman, her father pulled into a wide alleyway and parked, reaching into the back seat for his hat.

"Come on, Juliette," he chided, already climbing out.

Juliette followed slowly. She took in the alleyway, still trying to gauge the situation as she rubbed her hands together to keep them warm. There was one door here, the back entrance of what Juliette would guess to be a restaurant, if the noise coming from inside was any indication. Lord Cai called for her again. Juliette hurried over just as the door opened and the serving boy silently gestured for them to enter.

"If we're here to eat food that Māma hates, you only had to say so," she whispered.

"Quiet."

The serving boy led them through the back corridors of the restaurant, bypassing the rumble of the kitchen. Juliette had been jesting about eating a meal, but she still frowned when they also walked past the doors into the main restaurant without a second glance. Had her father booked a private room? For just the two of them? Maybe Juliette shouldn't have joked about a revolutionary execution after all.

Don't be ridiculous, she told herself.

The serving boy turned a corner and stopped in front of a nondescript door. Everything was dim and damp back here, looking like it hadn't been cleaned in years, never mind used to serve customers.

"If you need anything, I'll be outside." The serving boy opened the door.

Lord Cai walked in promptly, Juliette close on his heels. A part of her had already decided that this was going to be a quaint teaching lesson. Perhaps a sparse meal laid out to show how quickly they could lose everything they had.

The last thing she had expected to find inside the room, seated at a round table, was Lord Montagov and Roma.

Juliette's eyes bugged, her hand fumbling at her sleeve for a weapon, more out of shock and automatic instinct than any real preparation for a fight. While she clutched at air, however, Roma bolted to his feet and actually drew his pistol, ready to shoot.

Until his father said, "Hold on, boy."

Roma blinked, his arm receding back an inch. The gray light streaming in from the filmy windows gave him an eerie appearance, or perhaps that was just him now, his mouth an angry slash, his jaw tight enough to resemble stone. "What—"

"I sent an invitation to meet," Lord Montagov said. Then he switched from Russian to Chinese. "Sit, Roma."

Slowly, Roma sat.

"Bàba," Juliette hissed. "What is the meaning of this?"

"Sit, Juliette," Lord Cai simply echoed. When Juliette didn't move, he closed a hand over her elbow and gently guided her to the table, leaning close to his daughter and whispering, "The perimeter is secure. It is not an ambush."

"If it were, it is not like they would declare it," Juliette whispered back. She plopped ungraciously into a seat, resting only half her thigh so she could leap up at a moment's notice.

"Yes, you mustn't worry, Miss Cai," Lord Montagov declared. "There are only so many times you can ambush someone before they come to expect it."

Juliette felt her chest go cold. Lord Montagov, meanwhile, was smiling, and the sight itself would have been terrible enough, but it was rendered even more abhorrent because . . . it looked so much like Roma's smile.

How dare he.

"You—"

Juliette lunged over the table, knife out, but Roma was quicker. His pistol pressed into her forehead, and Juliette froze, her breath escaping in a quick sound through her clenched teeth.

When Juliette dared meet Roma's eyes, she found only loathing. It shouldn't have hurt so badly when this was her fault. The image was only right, only fitting. Who else would he hold a gun to but his enemy? Who else should he defend save his own father?

It shouldn't have hurt so badly, and yet it did.

I did this, Juliette thought numbly. *You told me you would choose me above all else, and then I did this to us.*

She had put him back on the side of his own father, who had caused Nurse's death, who had threatened to kill *him* if Roma couldn't kill *her.* It almost didn't seem worth it. Almost, almost—but Juliette was making the exact same choice Roma had. At least he would be alive, whatever the consequences she had to swallow.

"Juliette," Lord Cai warned again, though his command was soft. "Knife away, please."

With her teeth gritted even harder, Juliette pushed the blade back into her sleeve. Roma, in courteous response, set the pistol down on the table within reaching distance.

"It is much nicer to be civil, is it not?" Lord Montagov said. "I have a proposition. And it involves you, Miss Cai."

Juliette narrowed her eyes. She didn't prompt him to go ahead. She only waited.

"I would like you to cooperate with my son."

Juliette immediately jerked against her seat, her head snapping in Roma's direction. He did not react. He had known already—had agreed.

"I do beg your pardon," Juliette managed. "Why would I do that?"

"Don't you wish to find who is sending the threats?" Lord Montagov asked. "The two of you have the foreign language skills to socialize into the French Concession. Sending a gangster in alone is asking for trouble, but pairing enemies together . . . oh, the foreigners would not know what to do."

What game is he playing at? Juliette remained quiet. Something was afoot here, and she didn't like it.

"It is a good idea, Juliette," Lord Cai said, finally speaking up. His voice was even, almost bored. "If both gangs are receiving threats, then nothing will scare the blackmailer more than us teaming up, however momentarily. Both Scarlet Gang and White Flowers walk out of this with a third enemy defeated."

But you don't understand, she wanted to say. Juliette stared at Lord Montagov, stared down the hard glint in his dark eyes. This was not merely a way to combine their forces. Lord Montagov knew exactly what past she and Roma had—this was a scheme to gather Scarlet information, to have Roma do what he refused five years ago: win her trust, act the spy. The moment they started working together, Juliette wouldn't be able to shake him. Anything the Scarlets discovered, the White Flowers would have too.

Only Juliette couldn't vocalize any of this, could she? She was trapped, and Lord Montagov knew it. Cooperate, and there would be no questions asked. Refuse and rebel, and her father would ask why, and she would have to tell the truth: the first time, her romance with Roma caused an explosion at the Scarlet house; the second time, Tyler almost took all their lives.

"A fine idea indeed," Juliette said dully.

Lord Montagov clapped his hands together, making one, thunderous sound. "What ease! If only the rest of our men were as friendly as we were." He turned to Roma. "Have the two of you formally met? I imagine not."

Roma and Juliette looked at each other. Roma's jaw tightened even further. Juliette's fists grew deathly white under the table. All the while, Lord Cai was unconcerned, the only one in the room whom this whole show was for.

"We have not," Roma lied, his gaze steady. He stood. Extended his hand across the table. "Roman Nikolaevich Montagov. Pleased to make your acquaintance."

Roman. She almost said it aloud like an echo, almost passed it through her lips simply out of the urge to commit it to memory.

There was a part of her that had always known that that was his true name, but the city had long forgotten it just like they had forgotten that hers was Cai Junli. The city only knew him as Roma. It was easier to pronounce in Chinese; it was what everyone who knew him called him.

She supposed she didn't know him anymore—not this boy who stood with his arm outstretched, his fingers steady like they had never before pressed into her skin as gently as a kiss. Lovers turned to strangers, and it cut deep enough to bleed.

"The pleasure is mine." Juliette stood and reached to shake. Their palms touched, and she did not flinch—she *would not* flinch. "May I invite you on a walk around the perimeter? There are some details I would like to work out."

Lord Cai raised his eyebrows. "Juliette, perhaps not—"

"The perimeter is secure, isn't it?" she interrupted.

He could hardly argue against that. So long as there wasn't a chance of ambush, it wasn't as if Juliette couldn't handle the White Flower heir. Lord Cai gestured for her to go on.

"I will wait for you in the car."

Juliette marched out of the private room, counting on Roma to follow her. She strolled through the corridors so briskly that wisps of her hair had come undone by the time she shoved out the back door and emerged into the alley, her shoes stepping into soggy sheets of newspaper. *Deep inhale, deep exhale.* Her breath clouded in front of her, fogging her vision with white when Roma emerged too and she turned to face him, meeting his glower.

"Walk," Roma commanded, starting in the other direction of the alley.

"Don't tell me what to do," Juliette muttered. Nevertheless, she marched after him and followed along, keeping pace beside Roma with a carefully placed distance between them. If the alleys here were any busier, she would not have suggested this—opting to forgo a private conversation rather than be seen having one—but the passageways were tight and dark, and they could circle around the restaurant for however long they needed without approaching any main road.

"So what is this supposed to be?" Juliette asked outright. Overhead, a rusty pipe dripped a bead of water onto her neck.

"My father sprang it on me as well," Roma answered, sounding like he was speaking through shards of glass in his throat. "This whole thing was Dimitri's idea. I'm supposed to win back your trust and siphon information."

Juliette bit down on the inside of her cheeks. Her guess was right. It was an attempt to finish what they had started five years ago, only Lord Montagov didn't know that Juliette had already finished it.

"Does he know about—"

"The hospital?" Roma interrupted. "No. It hasn't gotten back to them. They know about the . . ." He paused. Swallowed hard. "The *confrontation*, but as far as your role in it goes . . . your cousin kept the information contained."

Which meant the White Flowers knew that Tyler had ambushed Alisa, that Juliette had killed Marshall, but they did not know why. They did not know that Tyler had accused Juliette of being a traitor, because as far as Tyler knew, he was wrong, and he did not want to be made a fool.

"Win back my trust and siphon information," Juliette repeated softly. "Except I beat you to that game."

The alley narrowed. Instinctively, Juliette swerved to avoid a rubbish bag, losing her careful distance with Roma as her fingers brushed up against his. The contact was brief, barely an event in the hubbub of the city, entirely infinitesimal when it came to a measurable length of time. All the same, her whole arm flexed like she had been shocked by an electric line. In her periphery, she caught Roma jolt, his expression hardening.

Neither of them said anything. They let the sound of distant tram lines and yelling paperboys ebb and flow around them. They let the silence run, because Juliette could hardly *think* when Roma was so close, and Roma didn't seem too eager to loosen the anger in his eyes.

"It is clear why my father put me up to this," he managed eventually. They turned into a wider alley. "But why did yours agree?"

Juliette pulled at one of the beads on her dress. It wasn't a real question. She could hear it in his tone.

"You have a spy," Roma went on when she remained unspeaking. "One of ours has infiltrated your inner circle. And whoever it is has talked your father into this."

"I know," she said, though she hadn't been certain. Better to sound confident than have Roma think he was offering her new information. "Call them off if you're so concerned."

Roma snorted. The sound was uncharacteristic enough that Juliette glanced over sharply, catching him just as he ran a hand through his hair. It messed up the style, but he did not need to fix it to look perfect. It was something about the tilt of his chin, the blankness in his stare. He had changed more in these few months than he had in those years while she was away.

"I have nothing to do with it," Roma replied sharply. "I suspect Dimitri sent them in. He's planning something—something to hurt you and overthrow me at the same time." There was a pause as he hopped in his step, avoiding a muddy puddle. "I think it'll serve both of us to be wary of this situation. Let us not invite more plotting by defying this arrangement."

He was right. That was logical. But *God*—was everything she had done for nothing? She had faked Marshall Seo's death to remove Roma from her side, to quash any chance that she would cave and draw him back, and now they were to work together anyway? How unfeeling was she expected to be? There was only so much strength she could summon.

"If we are to collaborate," Juliette said, "it must be public information. The White Flowers must agree that this is not a secret."

Roma frowned. He had caught the tightness in her voice. "Of course. Why would it be?"

"I am only checking. Not a worry." It was a colossal worry. If they were spotted together once more and suspected of being lovers, Tyler would destroy them—and then climb to the top and rule the Scarlets himself. Juliette could not let that happen.

She would rather die.

Juliette slowed her pace. They were fast approaching the restaurant again, having circled the buildings once over. "How does a week to collect our sources sound? Then we merge right into the French Concession."

"Sounds fair," Roma said, just as dryly. He came to an abrupt halt. Clearly he had no interest in accompanying her back to the restaurant, nor walking any farther when their conversation was finished.

With a shaky exhale, Juliette stopped too, smoothing her expression down until it was blank. She turned to face Roma, a polite goodbye poised on her tongue.

"But don't be mistaken, Juliette."

His eyes swiveled to her slowly. That once-familiar stare was now fathomless, and Juliette's breath caught in her throat, stilling like a creature in the headlights. She was ready. She knew what he would say. But it still tore into her, it still stung as mightily as razor wire wrapped around her heart, both ends pulled until it could wrap no tighter.

"When this is over, I will have my revenge. You will answer to me for what you did."

Juliette swallowed. She said nothing. She waited lest he had more to say, but when there was silence, she simply turned on her heel and walked away, her shoes clicking on the hard gravel.

Lord Cai was already in the car by the time Juliette returned to the alley behind the restaurant. She slapped her hands onto the hood of the car, huffing so vigorously into the cold that her breath was visible in a shroud around her.

"It's not too late," she said. "We can call an ambush. Lord Montagov remains yet in the vicinity."

By now Roma had to have long left. An opportunity was an opportunity.

"Darling daughter"—Lord Cai pinched the bridge of his nose—"get in the car please."

"Father," Juliette shot back, "I crave violence."

"Get in the car. Now."

Juliette huffed again, then pushed off the car hood. "They are the *enemy*," she snapped when she slammed the passenger door after herself. A loose bit of hair blew into her eyes, and she yanked it back. "If they have suggested a seemingly great idea, it is obviously with an ulterior motive, so why are we playing along—"

"The blood feud is a thoughtless notion, Juliette," Lord Cai cut in, adjusting the rearview mirror. "What have I taught you?"

Juliette drummed her fingers against her knee. She wished he wouldn't make some lesson out of this *now*, when the boundaries were evidently black and white. Once, she would have been rather pleased to see a lessened hatred for the White Flowers, but at present it didn't seem like her father was ignoring the blood feud. It seemed like . . . like he didn't *care*. Like something else was more important.

"We hate those who harm us," Juliette said, an echo of the words her father had given her long ago. "We do not hate senselessly." She shook her head. "It is a pretty idea, but the White Flowers *do* want to hurt us."

"Needs and desires change as fast as the breeze." Lord Cai rolled down a window, and the cold flooded in. She was starting to think he had gotten too accustomed to the biting temperatures of his office. "So long as we do not lose face, if the leadership of the White Flowers requests a quiet cooperation so that both gangs *survive* a second monster reckoning, what is the issue?"

There was more to it. It could not be that simple, because her father was not that easily swayed.

"What are we getting out of it?" she asked directly.

Lord Cai's response was to start the engine. Slowly, they reversed from the alleyway, merging back into the pandemonium that rumbled ever constant in the hub of the city. Through the open window, the aroma of deep-fried street food wafted in, a decent companion to the frigid cold.

Minutes later, when they stopped at the signal of a police officer running traffic control, Lord Cai said: "Keep them distracted."

Juliette blinked. A rickshaw halted to a stop outside her window, and from the corner of her eye, she watched the runner of the rickshaw let go of the poles, mop his forehead free of sweat, and eat a whole meat bun—all within seconds.

The officer signaled for them to move. The car crept forward.

"Distracted?" Juliette repeated. *You have a spy. One of ours has infiltrated your inner circle. And whoever it is has talked your father into this.* "From what?"

But Lord Cai only drove onward, giving a nod to the officer as they passed. It was another bout of silence, entirely typical for her father, before he said, "Some things you do not yet understand. Tīng huà. Do as you're told."

Juliette could hardly argue.

Nine

When the last of the maids closed their doors to retire for the night, Juliette slipped out from her bedroom, clutching her basket to her chest. She made good time tiptoeing down the hallway—her mind singularly focused on making it out of the house—only then she passed Rosalind's bedroom and noted the glow of light underneath the door.

Juliette paused. This was strange. "Rosalind?"

A rustling came from within the room. "Juliette? Is that you? You can come in."

Juliette set her basket down against the wall and opened Rosalind's door before her cousin could change her mind, letting the gold light of the bedroom flood out into the hallway. When Juliette remained at the threshold for a long moment, taking in the scene, Rosalind looked up from her desk, her thin brow arching smoothly. Her face was still made up despite the late hour. The curtains of her windows were left undrawn, the half-peeking moon shining through the clouds and upon the bed.

"It's so late," Juliette said. "You haven't retired yet?"

Rosalind set her pen down. "I could say the same to you. Your hair is still done up as neatly as mine."

"Yes, well . . ." Juliette did not quite know how to finish that sentence. She hardly wanted to say it was because she was on her way out. Instead, she zeroed in on Rosalind's desk and changed the subject. "What has your attention?"

"What has your curiosity?" Rosalind replied just as quickly.

Juliette folded her arms. Rosalind smiled, indicating her tone to be a joke. The moonlight dimmed, passing entirely behind a cloud, and the room's lamp bulb seemed to hesitate along with it.

"Your sister wanted me to speak with you, actually." Juliette inched a few steps into the room, her eyes scanning the desk. She caught sight of flyers from the burlesque club, as well as one or two pieces of notepaper torn from whatever ledger it had come from. "She's worried about you."

"About *me*?" Rosalind echoed. "Whatever for?" She leaned back, eyes wide. As she did so, there was a glint from her collar—metal catching light. *A new necklace*, Juliette noted. Kathleen always wore her pendant, but Rosalind had never been one for jewelry. She said it was dangerous to wear valuables on the streets of Shanghai. Too many pickpockets, too many eyes.

"No concrete reason; call it intuition." Whip-quick, Juliette strolled closer, then pinched her fingers around a slip of paper, pulling before Rosalind could stop her. Juliette pivoted on her heel, turning her arms the other way in case Rosalind was to snatch it away, but her cousin only rolled her eyes, letting Juliette look.

> Pierre Moreau
> Alfred Delaunay
> Edmond Lefeuvre
> Gervais Carrell
> Simon Clair

Juliette scrunched her nose, then turned back, asking without words what the list was.

Rosalind held her hand out. "Patrons at the club I'm to accost for funds. Would you like an in-depth explanation about how I drug their drinks? A chronological order of who pulls out their coins first?"

"Oh, hush," Juliette chided lightly, returning the slip to Rosalind's hand. She ran her gaze across the other papers for a brief while before determining that there wasn't much to scrutinize. Kathleen had been concerned about Rosalind's involvement with foreigners, but to live in this city was to be involved with foreigners.

"Don't tell me you're getting on my case too."

"Who, me?" Juliette asked innocently. Rosalind's bed jangled with noise when Juliette plopped onto the mattress for a makeshift seat, all the pearls and feathers from Rosalind's dance costumes tangling together atop the deep blue sheets. "Whatever about?"

Rosalind rolled her eyes, getting up from her desk. Juliette thought her cousin was coming to join her, but Rosalind pivoted the other way and wandered over to her window instead.

"Kathleen cannot go two seconds without trying to trail me across the city. I'm on neutral territory, not operating on White Flower ground."

"I think she's more concerned about the foreigners than the blood feud."

Rosalind leaned up against the windowsill, propping her chin into her hand.

"The foreigners see this country as an unborn child to keep in line," she said. "No matter how they threaten us with their tanks, they will not harm us. They watch us split internally like embryos in the womb, twins and triplets eating each other until there is no one left, and they want nothing more than to stop it so we can come out whole for them to sell."

Juliette was grimacing when Rosalind turned back around. "Okay, first of all, that's a disgusting metaphor and not how biology works."

Rosalind jazzed her hands around. "Ooh, look at me. I studied with Americans and I know how biology works."

"Ooh, look at me," Juliette imitated, her hands doing the same. "I'm a triplet and yet my French tutors forgot to tell me I can't eat another sibling in the womb."

Rosalind couldn't hold back her laugh. It spluttered out in a short and loud sound, and Juliette grinned too, her shoulders lightening for the first time that week. Unfortunately, it didn't last long.

"My point," Rosalind said, sobering, "is that the danger in this city is its politics. Forget the foreigners. It's the Nationalists and the Communists, tearing at each other's throats then working together for revolution in the same breath. No one should be messing with them. Not you. Not Kathleen."

If only it were that simple. If only one thing could be to blame. As if they didn't all ripple off each other like the world's most cursed game of falling domino tiles. Whether they wanted it or not, revolution would come. Whether they ignored it or not, it would come. And whether they carried on business as usual or shut down every operation before they could be hurt, it would still come.

"Your necklace," Juliette blurted suddenly, "it's new."

Rosalind blinked, taken aback by the switch in topic. "This?" She pulled at the chain, and out came the silver, dangling with a plain strip of metal at the end. "It's nothing special."

A feeling prickled the hairs at the back of Juliette's neck—a peculiar anxiety that she couldn't quite place.

"I just never see you with jewelry." She scanned her cousin's desk again, then the shelf space above, where Rosalind's loose knickknacks sat. Short of a few earrings, she sighted little else. "Imperial women used to own mounds upon mounds of jewelry, you know. They were seen as vain, but it wasn't that. It was because it was easier to run with jewelry than it was with money."

The clock on the mantel gave a loud chime. Juliette almost jumped, but Rosalind only quirked her left eyebrow.

"Biǎomèi," Rosalind sighed. "I'm not a merchant that you need to speak in metaphors with. I'm not going to run. The whole reason I'm picking up after my father is because I have no interest in leaving." She splayed her hands. "Where would I even go?"

There were plenty of places to go. Juliette could list them, by distance or by English alphabet. By safety or by likelihood of being found. If Rosalind had never considered it, then she was the more righteous person here. Because Juliette had, even if she could never actually carry it out.

"I don't know" was all Juliette said, her voice faint. The clock chimed again to mark the first minute of the hour passing, and noting the time, Juliette quickly stood, feigning a yawn. "Anyway, good talk. I will retire now. Don't stay up too late, all right?"

Rosalind waved her off, casual. "I can sleep in tomorrow morning. Bonne nuit."

Juliette slipped out from the room and, after closing her cousin's door, retrieved her basket. Rosalind's words had left her uneasy, but she tried to push the apprehension down, to swallow and repress it as she did with all things in this city that needed to be dealt with, for otherwise one might implode with all that rested on their shoulders. With a quick pitter-patter, Juliette hurried through the rest of the house and out the front door, easing it shut with a quiet click.

"The things I do," she muttered to herself. The moon glowed overhead, lighting the driveway. "And for what? To get a gun held to my head, that's what."

She slid into the car, waking the chauffeur, who had been snoozing at the driver's seat.

"Hold out for a little longer, could you?" Juliette said. "I would really prefer not to crash."

"Don't worry, Miss Cai," the chauffeur chirped, immediately sounding more awake. "I'll get you to the burlesque club safely."

That's where the chauffeur thought she went when she took these midnight trips every week. He would idle in front of the burlesque club, and Juliette would slip in then out through the back, trekking the rest of the distance to the safe house. It usually took her no longer than half an hour before she would return, sliding into the car again. The chauffeur would drop her home, and then he was off to his own apartment so he could take his rest before his next early-morning shift, and everyone in the Scarlet Gang would be none the wiser to what Juliette was up to.

Juliette poked her head into the front seats. "Have you eaten?"

The chauffeur hesitated. "There was a short break at six—"

There was already a bun floating beside him, dangling in its bag. Juliette had extra from the many she'd bought off the street cart earlier, and unless Marshall Seo could eat five in two days, they would go bad.

"It's a little cold," Juliette said when he took it gingerly. "But it'll go colder the longer it takes for us to reach our destination, where you can eat it."

The chauffeur hooted a laugh and pressed the car faster. They rumbled through the streets—busy as ever, even at such an hour. Each building they passed was flooded with light, women in qipao ignoring the winter cold and leaning out their second-floor windows, waving their silk handkerchiefs into the breeze. Juliette's coat, meanwhile, was long enough to completely cover the dress she had on beneath, thick enough to hide the shapelessness of those American designs.

At last they arrived a distance away from the burlesque club, where they always parked to avoid the stream of men coming and going from the front doors. The first time, the chauffeur had offered to walk Juliette, but his offer dried up as soon as Juliette removed a gun from her shoe and set it in the passenger seat, telling him to shoot if he was ambushed. It was easy to forget who Juliette was when she was lounging in the back seat, inspecting her nails. It was harder when she clambered out and put on her heiress face to combat the night.

"Lock the doors," Juliette ordered, holding her basket with one hand and rapping on the window with the other. The chauffeur did so, already biting into the bun.

Juliette started forward, keeping as close to the shadows as she could. The fortunate part of the winter season was a lack of observers: people did not like looking up for too long with the wind prickling at their eyes, so they walked staring at their shoes. Juliette never had much trouble making her way to the safe house, but tonight she was on edge, glancing over her shoulder once every few seconds, paranoid that the noise she heard some street over was not the last tram rumbling to its stop but a car trailing her just out of sight.

She blamed all that talk about spies.

"It's me," Juliette said quietly, finally arriving at the safe house and knocking twice. Before her fist had even finished coming down the second time, the door was opening, and instead of welcoming her in, Marshall leaned out.

"Fresh air!" he said, dripping with theatrics. "How I thought I would never experience it again!"

"Hajima!" Juliette snapped, pushing him back inside.

"Oh, we're speaking Korean now?" Marshall stumbled from Juliette's shove, but he recovered fast, shuffling into the apartment. "Just for me? I'm so honored."

"You are so *annoying.*" Juliette shut the door, pulling the three locks. She set the basket down onto the table and hurried to the window, peering through the thin crack between the boards nailed to the glass. She didn't see anything outside. No one was coming for them. "I'm going to kill you a second time just to see how you like it."

"It might be fun. Make sure to shoot me so it's symmetrical with the other bullet scar."

Juliette spun around, putting her hands on her hips. She glared at him for a long moment, but then she couldn't help it. The smile slipped out.

"Ah!" Marshall shrieked. Before Juliette could shush him, he was already lunging at her, picking her lithe frame off the ground and spinning her around until her head was dizzy. "She shows emotion!"

"Cease immediately!" Juliette screeched. "My hair!"

Marshall set her down with a steady thump. He held on to her even once she was on her own feet again, his arms splayed along her shoulders. Poor, touch-starved Marshall Seo. Maybe Juliette could find him a stray cat.

"Did you bring me alcohol this time?"

Juliette rolled her eyes. Finding the room to be too dark, she wordlessly tossed Marshall her lighter so he could light an extra candle while she brought out the food, unwrapping fruits and vegetables at rapid speed. In the weeks that Marshall had been hunkered down here, they had worked together to get the water running again without horrendous rumbling in the pipes and the gas connected so that Marshall could cook. In honesty, Juliette didn't think this was a bad living situation. Disregarding the whole legally dead situation, that was.

"I am never bringing you alcohol," Juliette said. "I fear I would find this place in flames."

Marshall responded by hurrying to the other side of the table and inspecting the bottom of Juliette's basket. He hardly heard her biting remark; after all this time, Juliette and Marshall had grown familiar enough with the other that they could tell what was intended to be sharp and what was not. They were incredibly alike, and that was too eerie a thought for Juliette to mull on it long.

Marshall retrieved one of the newspapers lining the bottom of the basket, his eyes scanning the headline. "A vigilante, huh?"

Juliette frowned, peering at the page. "You know you can never trust the papers to report on feud business."

"But you've heard about him too?"

"Indeed a few whispers here and there, but . . ." Juliette trailed off, her gaze narrowing upon a bag on the floor, one that she knew hadn't been in this apartment the last time she was here.

Then, some few inches away, there was a leaf.

Now, how would Marshall Seo have heard about a vigilante in the city?

Juliette folded her arms. "You've been outside, haven't you?"

"I—" Marshall's mouth opened and closed. He tried his best. "No! Of course not."

"Oh?" Juliette reached for the paper and turned it her way, reading aloud. "*The masked figure has intervened on multiple counts to knock both sides out before shots can be fired. Anyone with information should—* Marshall!"

"Fine, fine!" Marshall sat upon the rickety seat with a heavy sigh, his energy depleting. A long moment passed, which was rare in any room with Marshall Seo. When he did speak again, he was quiet, his voice pushed out with effort. "I'm only trying to keep an eye on him. I step in on other feud business if I happen to see something while I'm lurking."

Him. Marshall didn't say his name, but he was evidently talking about Benedikt. There were no other contenders to be the subject of such carefulness. She should have chided him immediately, but she couldn't find it in herself. She had a heart, after all. She was the one who had put him here, away from everything—every*one*—he loved.

"Has Benedikt Montagov seen you?" she asked tightly.

Marshall shook his head. "The one time he actually got himself in trouble, I shot everyone around him and ran." At that, his eyes shifted up, a brief flicker of guilt appearing when he remembered who he was talking to. "It was quick—"

"Best not to think too deeply about it," Juliette said, cutting him off. He had killed Scarlets; she would kill White Flowers. For as long as they lived, so long as the city remained divided, they would kill, and kill, and kill. In the end, would it matter? When the choice was between protecting those you loved and sparing the lives of strangers, who would ever think that to be a hard decision?

Juliette shifted to the window again, peering into the night. It was better lit out there than it was in here, the streetlamps humming happily in harmony with the wind. This safe house had been strategically chosen, after all: as far out as Juliette's eye could see, there were no particular corners or nooks where anybody could be hiding, watching her as she looked out. Nevertheless, she surveyed the scene warily.

"Just be careful," Juliette finally said, dropping the curtain. "If anyone sees you . . ."

"No one will," Marshall replied. His voice had grown firm again. "I promise, darling."

Juliette nodded, but there was a tightening sensation gripping her chest even as she tried for a smile. During these few months, she had expected Marshall to start resenting her. She had promised she would figure something out soon, but she still had Tyler breathing down her neck and no concrete way around it. Yet she hadn't heard a word of complaint from Marshall. He had taken it in stride, even though she knew it ate him up inside to be stuck here.

She wished he would yell at her. Get angry. Tell her that she was useless, because that certainly seemed to be true.

But he only welcomed her in every visit like he had missed her dearly.

Juliette turned away, blinking rapidly. "There are rumors that there will be Communist-led riots on the streets tonight," she said when she had her tear ducts under control. "Don't go outside."

"Understood."

"Stay *safe*."

"When am I not?"

Juliette reached for the now empty basket with a glare, but her malice at Marshall—even when feigned—was always half-hearted. Marshall grinned and sent her off with two big, swooping air kisses, still making the faintest noises even as Juliette closed the door after her and heard the locks bolt again on the other side.

She had to stop growing so fond of White Flowers. It would be the death of her.

Lord Montagov pushed the file right to the edge of his desk, giving Roma no choice but to reach out quickly and grab it lest the papers inside flutter to the floor. From the other corner of the desk, leaning upon the outside edge in an ever-so-casual slouch, Dimitri squinted, trying to read upside down as Roma flipped open the folder.

Roma doubted that Dimitri could pick out anything. Dimitri needed glasses, and the bulb light on Lord Montagov's desk was not doing him any favors. It flooded the room in a cold, off-white color that treated their electric bills kindly but hurt the eyes to be near for long, casting a deathlike tinge on their skin.

"Comb through carefully, memorize the names of the clients we seek," Lord Montagov instructed. "But that is your secondary goal. First and foremost, you are to keep track of the Scarlet effort with this blackmailer. Don't let them gain an advantage. Don't let them shove it on us. If the Scarlet Gang manage to rid themselves of the threat, the White Flowers should too."

"It will come around to how they achieve it," Roma replied evenly. "Whether we find the perpetrator or find a new vaccine."

Finding the perpetrator would be a done and dusted deal. It didn't matter which side shot the bullet or slashed their blade. A dead blackmailer was no blackmailer. But if the solution to the madness was a new vaccine, then it was a game of who could hold on to the secret and save themselves first.

Dimitri leaned forward, about to say something. Before he could, Roma slapped the file closed.

"Either way, I have it handled."

A knock came on Lord Montagov's office then, and the White Flower outside announced an incoming phone call. Roma pushed his chair back, making way for his father as Lord Montagov stood from behind his desk and exited the room. As soon as the door clicked, Dimitri wandered over to the other side of the desk and dropped into Lord Montagov's chair.

"First of all, you're welcome," he said.

Roma could feel an immediate headache starting up at his temples.

"All the clientele in that folder, all these Scarlet merchants on the edge of defection to the White Flowers—that is my doing, Roma. All you have to do is make the killing blow. Should be easy enough."

"Congratulations," Roma said, resting his arm on the back of his chair. "You did your job."

Dimitri shook his head. The gesture was drenched with feigned pity, accompanied by an unspoken *tut-tut-tut* in the air.

"It is not enough to see the merchants as a job," Dimitri urged. "You must accept them. Respect them. Only then will they listen."

Roma did not have the time for this.

"They are colonialists." He took the folder into his hands, crinkling the edges mercilessly. "They deserve to be robbed and looted, as they have done to others. We work with them to gain what we can. We do not work with them because we love them. Get it together."

Dimitri didn't appear chastised. It was hard to tell how much he actually believed in the words he was saying and how much he was saying them only to rile Roma up.

"So that's how it is?" Dimitri asked. He brought his feet up to the desk. "All this hostility to your allies. But taking an enemy as your lover."

The room had already been cold. Now it felt chilled like ice.

"You must be mistaken." Roma stood up, releasing the folder. "I work with Juliette Cai until I can take a knife to her throat."

"Then why haven't you done so?" Dimitri countered. He kicked at the desk and tipped Lord Montagov's whole chair back, letting it teeter dangerously on its hind legs. "In these prior months, before your father wanted to keep her alive for information, why did you never hunt her down?"

Roma stood up, fire stirring beneath his skin. Dimitri did not protest when he stormed out of the office. Dimitri was probably trying to drive him into storming off anyway, all the better to make him look bad when his father returned to find him missing. Uncaring about his father's irritation, Roma swerved into the nearest empty room and dropped into a settee in the dark, biting back the curses he wanted to let loose.

The dust around him stirred in disturbance. When the room settled again, Roma felt covered by a grimy veneer. Three paces away, the windows had broken blinds, casting irregular silver shapes onto the opposite wall. He couldn't see it, but he could hear a heavy clock in the corner ticking too, counting down his time in this abandoned room before someone inevitably found him.

Roma exhaled, then slumped ungraciously onto the armrest. He was exhausted by this; he was exhausted by Dimitri's accusations. Yes—Roma had wet his hands with blood at fifteen years old for Juliette. For what it mattered, he might as well have lit the fuse that tore through a whole household of Scarlets. All to save Juliette, all to protect her, though she had never asked for such protection. Once, he would have burned the damn city to the ground just to keep her unharmed. *Of course* it was hard for him to hurt her now. It went against every fiber of his being. Every cell, every nerve—they had grown into place with one mantra: *protect her, protect her.* Even after knowing she had become someone else, even after hearing all the terrible things she had done in New York . . . she was still Juliette. His Juliette.

And now she was not. She had made that abundantly clear. He kept waiting, and waiting, and waiting. Much as he loathed Dimitri, one point was true—Roma kept refusing to commit to vengeance because some part of him screamed that he knew Juliette better than this. That something was up her sleeve, that she could never betray him.

But Marshall was dead. She'd made her choice. Just as Roma had chosen Juliette's life over her Nurse's. Just as Roma had done what he did to send her back to America, send her far, far away. Even if she lied about her coldness, even if she hadn't feigned her weeping, soft eyes that day behind the Communist stronghold—it didn't matter. Marshall was unforgivable.

Answer me something first. Do you still love me?

"Why wouldn't you *fight*?" Roma whispered into the empty room. His head was light. He could almost imagine Juliette sitting next to him, the smell of her flowery hair gel dancing beneath his nose. "Why would you give up and give in to the blood feud in the most despicable way?"

Unless he was wrong. Unless this wasn't a hard choice at all, and there was no love anywhere to be found in Juliette Cai.

Enough was enough. Roma jerked upright, his fists tightening. They were to work together at present, but that arrangement would end sooner or later. If Juliette wanted to play the route of the blood feud, she would get blood for blood. It would wound him just as deep, but he would plunge in the knife.

He *had* to.

The door to the sitting room opened then, and Lord Montagov poked his head in, frowning when he sighted Roma on the settee. Roma had half a mind to wipe at his eyes just in case, but that would have looked more odd than staring ahead blankly, not letting his father see his full expression.

"Dimitri said you might have wandered in here," his father said. "Can you not sit still for a single minute?"

"Are we to resume the meeting?" Roma asked, diverting the question.

"We covered enough." Lord Montagov frowned in distaste. "Stay inside. There's a riot tonight." He closed the door.

Ten

A revolution is never pretty. Nor is it clean, quiet, peaceful.

The city watches the crowds gather that night, clustering for an uprising that might finally be heard. Whispers travel about monsters and madness, and it hits a breaking point—how much *misery* can the streets hold before there is spillover? The unions flock together in effort. They threaten all who listen with what will happen if the gangsters and imperialists are not removed. The starving will wilt into nothing. The poor will blow away with the wind. And in Shanghai, where the factory workers number up to the hundreds and thousands, they are listening.

The people march, throngs coming upon police stations and garrison posts. They enter foreign concessions and swarm through Chinese territory alike. The foreigners bolt their doors with trembling hands; the gangsters step out onto the streets, adding numbers to the troops sent to break the crowds.

"Is this a good idea?" one worker among the crowd asks.

His friend casts him a glance askew, shivering. It is freezing cold in Shanghai. Ice crystals remain on the streets, and when a bird caws from somewhere afar, the sound hardly echoes because a gust blows fiercely enough to drown it out.

"What does it matter?" his friend replies. "The city can only get worse. We may as well try."

They approach the station. From above, one might admire the way the crowd fans out, flaming torches raised to the sky, blots of orange running a perfect semicircle in formation, blocking off all paths of escape. It almost looks like warfare, and the wind leans forward.

"This is your first and only warning," an officer bellows through a megaphone. "Those causing civil unrest will be beheaded on sight!"

It is not an empty threat. Here, at the outskirts of the city, where gangster royalty and foreigners would rarely go, there have already been sightings upon sightings of decapitated heads impaled upon lampposts. They decorate street corners like mere shop signs, used as a warning to other dissidents who dare attempt to overthrow the territory they live in. It has come to this; it is not enough to expect loyalty, not enough to scare by force.

The Scarlets have long known that the people are no longer afraid of them. And that is something for the Scarlets to be afraid of.

"No gangster rule!" the crowd demands at once. "No foreign rule!"

The officers ready in formation. Broadswords glimmer under the silver moonlight—an option far messier than bullets, but rifles are short on supply. The Nationalist armies have their pick of the weaponry, and they have taken the guns to fight a real war elsewhere.

The city sniffs, and the clouds grow dense, blocking the shine of the moon. Shanghai fights a war too. The soldiers in uniform have not arrived yet, but it is a war, nonetheless.

"Your numbers mean nothing," the megaphone tries once more. "Disperse, or—"

The officer steps back abruptly, seeing something in the crowd. It is a chain effect, and all the workers turn to look too, one after the other, raising the gas lamps in their hands and lighting the dark night.

And they see a monster standing in the crowd.

At once the masses fall loose in fear. Police officers and gangsters on the other side of the line rush for shelter. By now this city knows how to react. Its people have gone through this play enough times that they have memorized their lines and they remember which exit to take. They pick up children and haul them to their shoulders, they offer the elderly their arms, and they *run*.

But . . . the monster does not do anything. Even when the workers have dispersed, it stands there, one lone entity in the middle of the road. When it blinks, its eyelids come together from the left and right, and at once a collective shudder shakes the city from all who look upon it. They wish not to see how the monster's blue skin grows murky under the light, but the moon shines on anyway, and the officers in the station must turn away from the window, breathing shallowly with fear.

In this part of Shanghai, the uprising pauses. Other places—other fringe districts and dirt roads—burn and become awash in blood, but here there is no movement from within the station, no slash of a broadsword nor heads atop pikes, so long as the monster remains.

It tilts its head up, looking at the moon.

Almost like the monster is smiling.

Eleven

T he sun was out today, burning above the city as if it were a large diamond studded into the sky. It seemed most suitable, Juliette thought as she stepped out of the car, breathing in the crisp air. There were parts of Shanghai that she could not look at directly because it glimmered too harshly, so overwrought with the strength of its own extravagance that it could not be appreciated for any of it.

Particularly here, at the heart of the city. This was technically International Settlement territory, but the French Concession was only some streets over, and the overlap in jurisdiction was messy enough that Juliette never cared much about the border that existed along Avenue Edward VII. Neither did its inhabitants, so this was where they were starting their work in the French Concession: outside of it.

Juliette ducked into the shadow of a building, slinking around its exterior. Here lay all the fanciest hotels, so close in succession, and Juliette didn't want to get trapped into conversation with any overeager foreign ladies out to experience the local culture. Quick as she could, she stepped into the alley and stopped, steeling herself.

He was wearing white again. She had never seen so much goddamn white on him.

"Alors, quelle surprise te voir ici."

Roma turned at the sound of her voice, unamused by her false astonishment. Both his hands were in his trouser pockets, and it may have been Juliette's imagination, but she swore one hand twitched like it was clutching a weapon.

"Where else would I have been waiting, Juliette?"

Juliette merely shrugged, having no energy to continue being a nuisance. It didn't make her feel any better; nor did it improve Roma's default scowl. When his hand came out of his pocket, she was almost surprised to find that it was a golden pocket watch he retrieved, flipping its cover to check the time.

Juliette was late. They had agreed to meet at noon behind the Grand Theatre because their destination was across the road at the Recreation Ground, where the foreign race club was. The race club was always at high capacity, but especially at these hours, when socialites and ministers threw bets like it was their full-time job.

"I was running errands," Juliette said as Roma put the watch away.

Roma started off in the direction of the racecourse. "I didn't ask."

Ouch. Juliette physically flinched, a throbbing hot sensation starting in her heart. But she could handle it. What was a small bout of meanness? At least he wasn't trying to shoot her.

"You don't want to know what errands I was running?" Juliette pressed, following his brisk walk. "I offer you information on a platter and you do not even take it. I was checking the postmarks on the letters, Roma Montagov. Did you think to do that?"

Roma glanced over his shoulder momentarily, then turned back around as soon as Juliette had caught up at his side. "Why would I need to?"

"They could have been fake if the blackmailer hadn't truly sent them out of the French Concession."

"And were they?"

Juliette blinked. Roma had stopped suddenly, and it took her a second to realize it wasn't because he was enraptured with their conversation. He was simply waiting to cross the road.

Roma waved for them to cross.

"No," she finally answered when they were on the sidewalk again. From here, she could already hear the thundering of hooves. "They indeed came from various post offices across the Concession."

What Juliette didn't understand was why someone would go through the labor. It was harder to make stamps talk than people . . . Juliette could accept that. No one would be foolish enough to hire help for delivering the messages, because then Juliette could catch the help and torture a name out of them. But to use the postage system? Could they not have left letters around the city for any old gangster to pick up and bring to Lord Cai? It was as if they *wanted* Juliette to storm into the French Concession, given how obvious the postmarks were.

She didn't say any of this aloud. Roma didn't look like he cared.

"You're giving this blackmailer too much credit," he said. "They come from the French Concession because, as expected, it is someone around these parts of the city who took on Paul's legacy." A sigh. "So here we are."

At once, Roma and Juliette lifted their heads, looking upon the race club's central building. The clubhouse stood on the western side of the racetrack, spilling outward with its grandstand and climbing skyward with its ten-story tower. A collective roar sounded from the track to signal some race finishing, and activity inside the clubhouse rumbled with excitement, awaiting the next round of bets.

This was a different face of the city. Each time Juliette walked into a Settlement establishment, she left behind the parts that juggled crime and party in the same hand, and instead entered a world of pearls and etiquette. Of rules and dazzling games only maneuverable by the fluent. One wrong move, and those who did not belong were immediately ousted.

"I hate this place," Roma whispered. His sudden admission would have taken Juliette by surprise if she, too, weren't so simultaneously captivated by awe and revulsion—by the marble staircases and oak parquet flooring, by the betting hall within glimpse of the open doors, loud enough to compete with the grandstand cheering.

Roma, despite what his words were saying, could not look away from what he was seeing.

"Me too," Juliette replied quietly.

Maybe one day, a history museum could stand where the clubhouse was instead, boxing within its walls the pain and beauty that somehow always existed at once in this city. But for now, *today*, it was a clubhouse, and Roma and Juliette needed to get to the third floor, where the members' stand was.

"Ready?" Roma's voice returned to normal, like the previous moment had been erased from memory. Rather reluctantly, he offered his arm.

Juliette took it before he could have second thoughts, wrapping her fingers around his sleeve. Her hands were gloved, but still her skin jumped upon contact.

"There were sightings yesterday. In the outskirts of the city where workers were striking. They said a monster was present."

Roma cleared his throat. He shook his head like he didn't want to discuss it, though monsters stalking their city were precisely why they were here. "Unless people are dying, I don't care," he muttered. "Civilians make up sightings all the time."

Juliette dropped the topic. They had stepped inside the clubhouse, and the double takes started almost immediately. It would have been impossible to go entirely under the radar, not when Roma Montagov and Juliette Cai were wholly recognizable, but Juliette had thought at least there would be a delayed reaction. There was no delay at all. Frenchmen in suits and women twirling their pearls were positively craning their heads with outright curiosity.

"None of them are going to be helpful," Roma said under his breath. "Keep moving."

The onlookers thinned out as they climbed upward, passing a bowling game happening on the mezzanine level. The second floor rang loud with a billiards game clacking across the space, almost in tune with the hooves clamoring just outside.

On the third floor, there was a booth installed outside the closed double doors, standing sentry to the long lines of dark timber and glazed panels that made up the domineering entranceway. A fireplace roared close by, keeping the floor warm enough that an immediate sweat broke out under Juliette's coat, prompting her to undo a few buttons until the fur hung open.

"Hello," Juliette said, waiting for the woman behind the booth to look up. By her hair, she appeared to be American. "This is the members' stand, yes?"

A collective outburst of laughter wafted from the doors, accompanied by the sound of glasses clinking, and Juliette immediately knew that it was. In there were all the well-to-dos and must-knows of the French Concession. In a city that teemed with people, *someone* had to be aware of *something*. All it took was to find the right people.

"Are you members?" the woman asked dryly, sparing the briefest glance up. Her accent came out clearly. American.

"No—"

"Grandstand for Chinese is outside."

Juliette let go of Roma's arm. He reached out as if to pull her back, but thought better of it at the last moment, his hand floating inanely in the air as Juliette walked forward, her heels clicking on the smooth flooring. She approached the booth, then slapped her two hands right onto it. Just as the woman was finally startled into looking up properly, Juliette leaned in.

"Say that again," she said, "but actually look at my face this time."

Juliette started to count to three in her head. *One. Two—*

"M-miss Cai," the woman stammered. "I didn't see you on our expected visitor list—"

"Stop talking." Juliette pointed to the door. "Open it, would you?"

The woman's already wide eyes flickered to the door and then to Roma, before widening even farther, at risk of popping right out. Some dark part of Juliette reveled in it, in the rush that surged through her veins each time her name was spoken with fear. Some darker part still was more rapt at the sight that she gave, looming while Roma waited at her side. They would rule this city one day, wouldn't they? One half each, fists over empires. And here they stood, together.

The woman hurried to open the door. Juliette offered a smile that was nothing but bared teeth as she passed.

"You embarrassed her so deeply that she'll be looking over her shoulder for the next three years in fear," Roma remarked inside. He inspected a passing tray of drinks.

"It means little that I managed to embarrass her," Juliette grumbled. "Every other Chinese person in Shanghai doesn't have the same privilege."

Roma picked up a drink, giving it a sip. For a moment, it almost seemed like he was going to say something more. But whatever it was, he clearly decided against it, because all that came out was "Let's get to work."

For that next hour, they mingled in and out of the crowds, shaking hands and exchanging pleasantries. Foreigners who moved into this city long-term liked to call themselves Shanghailanders, and though that term gave Juliette such nausea she preferred to permanently block out its existence from her mind, it was the only acceptable one that she could think to use to describe every person in this room.

How dare they claim such a title. Juliette clutched her fists tight as she let a couple pass in front of her. *How dare they label themselves the people of this city, as if they did not sail in with cannons and forced entry, as if they are not here now only because they come from those who lit the first fires.*

But it was either the wretched Shanghailander or *imperialist*, and she doubted her father would be very happy if she went around the room addressing merchants and bankers as such. She simply had to swallow it. She had to laugh with one Shanghailander after the other in hopes that they had information to give when she casually mentioned the new deaths.

So far nothing had turned up. So far they were more interested in why Juliette and Roma were working together.

"I thought y'all didn't get on," one remarked. "I was warned that if I did business in this city, I oughta pick a side or get shanked."

"Our fathers tasked us together," Roma said. He flashed a quick grin, looking debonair enough that the foreigner visibly swooned—though she was old enough to be his mother. "We're on a mission so vital that the White Flowers and Scarlet Gang must collaborate, even if it means placing . . . *business* aside for the meanwhile."

Juliette wondered if Roma had practiced those words and the way he was to deliver them. He spoke like the perfect glimmering prodigy, because no one could hear the bitterness but her. All the foreigners took in was his easy beauty and smooth speech. Juliette listened to the words. To the resentment that they were *tasked* to this, for otherwise he would be far, far across the city.

She hoped the blackmailer would hear about this, or better yet, could see them right this moment. She hoped they would observe the cold cooperation and have terror strike their heart. Once the Scarlets and the White Flowers joined together, it was only a matter of time before their mutual enemy collapsed.

"Why, I don't know if I should be offended that I have waited so long still without a greeting!"

Roma and Juliette both turned at the voice, coming from a short, booming man. He tipped his newsboy cap, and in return, Roma inclined his boater hat, looking the picture of sophistication in comparison to the man's huffing, red face. It was an unfair competition. Juliette eyed the two women who accompanied the man and knew that they saw it too.

"Forgive us," Juliette said. The man reached for her hand, and she let him take it to press a kiss to her gloved fingers. "If we have met before, you will need to remind me."

Ever so faintly, the man's grip tightened on her fingers. He let go in the next second, so it could have been played off as a mere slip of his grip, but Juliette knew that he had acknowledged her slight.

"Ah, we remain strangers, Miss Cai," the man said. "Call me Robert Clifford." His eyes flickered back and forth between Juliette and Roma before gesturing at the two women with him. "We were having a delightful conversation before our curiosity simply got the best of us. And I thought—well, why not ask? The member applications usually come through me, but I have not seen yours. So . . ." Robert Clifford lifted his arms and gestured all around the room, like he was reminding them where they presently stood. "When did they start letting gangsters into the Club?"

Ah—there it was.

Juliette smiled in response, biting down hard until her molars made a sound at the back of her mouth. The red-faced man's tone was jovial, but there was a certain sneer in the word "gangsters" that made it clear he did not mean only that. He meant "Chinese" and "Russians." He had much more nerve than the American outside. He thought he could look them head-on and walk away with a victory.

Juliette leaned in and plucked the handkerchief out of Robert Clifford's pocket. She held it up to the light, inspecting the fabric quality.

She gestured for Roma to take a look, using the opportunity to turn away from the man and mouth, *Is he British?* The two women with him were French, if the Coco Chanel sportswear was any indication. But Juliette did not have the same eye for men's fashion, and accents were hard to parse when people learned all the European languages as a sign of wealth.

Yes, Roma responded.

Juliette released an airy laugh, returning the handkerchief with a harsh shove into his pocket. She flicked Robert Clifford's hat, hard enough that it almost came right off his head, then turned to the two women and said in French, "Mon Dieu, when did they start letting English newspaper boys into this city? Maman is calling him home for dinner."

The women hooted in sudden laughter, and Robert frowned, not understanding what Juliette had said. His hands darted up to his hat, fixing it back in position. A single bead of sweat came down his face.

"All right, Juliette," Roma cut in. It sounded like he was starting a scolding, but he had switched to French too, so she knew he was playing along. "You mustn't expect too much of him. His newspaper runs must have tired him out. Poor soul might need a towel."

That, at least, seemed to ring some comprehension in the man's expression. *Serviette.* He quickly mopped his face again and caught on. It was too hot in the room. He was wearing a suit too expensive, its thick fabric suited for the cold winter outside.

"Please, excuse me for a moment," he said tightly. Robert Clifford pivoted on his heel for the washroom.

"And I thought he would never leave," one of the women remarked, visibly relaxing while she adjusted the belt on her wide-flared trousers. "All he does is yap—yap yap finances yap yap horses yap yap monsters."

Roma and Juliette exchanged a look, the passing glance lasting an incredibly brief moment with only the blankest of expressions—but still, they knew how to read each other. Perhaps they were finally onto something.

Juliette extended a hand. "I don't believe I've had the pleasure . . . ?"

"Gisèle Fabron," the woman in the trousers supplied, shaking firmly. "And my companion is Ernestine de Donadieu."

"Enchanté," Ernestine offered primly.

Roma and Juliette returned the introductions with poise and grace and flattery. Because these were the roles they had been raised to play. These were the games they knew how to win.

"Of course we know *you*," Gisèle said. "Juliette. Lovely name. My parents almost named me so too."

Juliette placed her hands to her chest, feigning amazement. "Oh, but a fortune that they did not when Gisèle is so beautiful!" As she spoke, she nudged her shoe out, stepping her heel down so it would graze Roma's ankle.

Roma took the hint. He pretended to search through the members' room. "Funny, has Robert Clifford left us permanently?"

Ernestine wrinkled her nose, smoothing her short hair with nonchalance. "He may have wandered out into the members' stands. I suspect he placed some rather large bets while we were downstairs."

"Is that so?" Roma replied. "Or perhaps he has roped another poor soul into a riveting discussion about monsters."

The two women broke into chuckles again, and Juliette had to resist patting Roma on the shoulder to congratulate him on the fantastic segue.

"For shame!" Juliette said with mock admonishment. "Do you not hear that the city stirs awake once more?"

Roma pretended to pause and consider. "Indeed. But I hear it is not a monster this time. I hear it is a puppet master, controlling creatures who do his bidding."

"Oh, bof." Gisèle waved a flippant hand. "Is it not the same as before? Swindlers and raving con men, using the opportunity to sell their wares."

Juliette tilted her head. By "swindlers," Gisèle surely meant the Larkspur and his vaccine; she meant Paul Dexter, who had distributed saline solutions for profit even though he possessed the true cure. Only there was no Larkspur anymore hawking his wares on the streets. So who was she speaking about?

"Yes," Juliette said, trying to hide her confusion. "They are quieter this time, I admit."

"Quieter?" Ernestine repeated with some disbelief. "My, they have been cramming flyers under my door for the past week. Just this morning"—she patted around her pockets, and her eyes lit up when there was the sound of crunching—"ah, I thought I still had it. Ici."

From her pocket, she retrieved a terribly thin flyer, half-transparent when it was held to the light. Roma took it first, his brow furrowed deeply, and Juliette hovered her chin over his shoulder, reading alongside him.

The French was riddled with errors. But the sentiment was clear enough.

THE MADNESS ARRIVES AGAIN!
GET VACCINATED!

At the bottom of the flyer, there was an address, just like last time. Only now the address wasn't even in the city. It was in Kunshan, which was a whole other city in a whole other *province*. Despite the railways making it a relatively short journey, to go so far from Shanghai was to leave its protective bubble and enter a whole new battleground of warlords and militias. Shanghai was its own unique mess, but out there, rulers and rule shifted at a moment's notice.

No matter. It was better than nothing.

"May we keep this?" Juliette asked, flashing a grin.

The rest of their time at the clubhouse provided nothing of particular importance, and Roma suggested they leave before the afternoon turned dark. Juliette was still mulling over the flyer as they exited the racecourse ground, returning onto Nanjing Road. The city roared back to life around her, rumbling trams and honking cars replacing the rhythmic beating of hooves. Juliette almost felt herself relax.

Almost.

"Why advertise in French?" she mused aloud. "Why *only* advertise to the French? I have seen nothing of the sort anywhere else. It is rather selective to only slide such flyers beneath the doors of residential buildings."

"Think it through," Roma said roughly. Now that they were no longer playacting for the foreigners, he had returned to his coolness and detachment. "The blackmailer seeks resources from us, meaning if we fail, it is only our people who will suffer for it." His gaze slid to her, then slid away in the same second, like a mere glimpse of eye contact was too nauseating. "But it is not as if the foreigners know this. It is two birds with one stone. Feed off foreign fear and take their money. Let the gangsters remain vulnerable so they may die when they are selected to die."

Juliette thinned her lips. So it was indeed the Larkspur all over again. Only this one was smarter. Hardly any of the Chinese or Russians in the busiest parts of the city had the money for such vaccines anyway, so why waste the effort?

Roma muttered something beneath his breath, as if he had heard her thoughts.

"What?" Juliette prompted, startled.

"I said—" Roma stopped in his tracks. The sudden halt forced civilians walking behind him to jolt and go around with a slight glare cast back, only the glare morphed into fear when they recognized Roma and then astonishment when Juliette was sighted too. The two heirs ignored the goggling. They were used to it, even if the attention magnified tenfold now that they were together.

"—we always end up here, don't we?" Roma waved the flyer that was still in his hands, crumpling the paper so roughly that it started to tear. "Chasing lead after lead and inevitably circling back to where we started. We will continue asking around the French Concession, and when all roads lead to this vaccine facility, we will go, only to be pushed right back into the Concession. I can see it already. How easy it would be if we could just cut right to the end."

His eyes met hers, and this time he did not flinch away. In that moment, Juliette knew they were both sifting through the very same memories, through the events that had transpired months past. Roma was right. It felt like the exact same path. Zhang Gutai's office. The address of the Larkspur's facility. The testing of the vaccine. Mantua. *Mantua.*

Juliette blinked hard, trying to shake out of it, but the memories were gelled to her mind like glue.

"If it were that easy," she said quietly, "it would not be us who needed to do it."

She had thought that would perhaps earn her an affirmative response, but Roma remained stony. He merely looked away, then checked his pocket watch. "We resume tomorrow."

And off he walked.

Juliette remained on the sidewalk for some time until she snapped out of her stupor. Before she could stop herself, she was chasing after him, pushing through the swaths of window-shoppers. Nanjing Road was eternally busy, and the cold did nothing to deter them. As Juliette exhaled in a hurry, her breath clouded all around her, blurring her vision. She almost lost sight of Roma before he turned into a smaller road, and Juliette hurried to follow, squeezing by a strolling couple.

"Roma," she said. She finally caught up to him, yanking off one of her gloves and grabbing his wrist. "Roma!"

He whirled around, eyeing the hand she had clasped around his wrist like it was a live wire.

Juliette swallowed hard. "For what it's worth . . . ," she said. "I'm sorry."

"Why should you be?" Roma replied, like the words had already been waiting on his tongue. "You returned the hurt I gave you, after all. We are the faces of two sides in a blood feud, so why not revel in the death and the misery—"

"Stop," Juliette spat. She was shaking. Her whole body had started trembling without her noticing, and she didn't know if it was anger toward Roma, or anger toward his accusation.

Roma made a noise of disbelief. "Why do you react like this?" he asked harshly. He scanned her up and down, at her barely contained outrage. "It was false to you. I mean nothing to you. *Marshall* meant nothing to you."

This was a test. He was goading her. For as long as Roma was Roma, there would be a part of him that could not fully believe Juliette would betray him, and he was *right*, but he could not *know*. She could not be a foolish girl, and though she was, though that was exactly what she was and what she wanted to be, she needed to be something bigger. Everything that unfolded between the two of them was bigger than them, bigger than two children trying to fight a war with their bare hands.

Juliette smoothed her expression over, choked back the emotion that soured her throat to the point of pain.

"I understand if you want your revenge," Juliette said. Her voice had leveled, sounding almost fatigued. "But do so after our city is safe. I am what this city made me. If we are to cooperate once more, you cannot hate me while we're on a task. Our people will be the sacrifice of such carelessness."

Do not do this to me, she wanted to say instead. *I cannot stand seeing you like this. It will break me faster than the city ever could if it tried to cut us down together.*

Roma yanked his wrist away. With everything and nothing hidden in his cold gaze, he only said, "I know," and walked away. It was not forgiveness. It was far from it. But at least it wasn't open, unadulterated hatred.

Juliette turned and started to move in the other direction, her ears faintly ringing. These past few months, she might have thought herself to be living in a dream if it weren't for the heaviness that constantly dragged in her chest. She put her hand there now and imagined reaching in and *tearing* out whatever was weighing her down: the feeling of tenderness blossoming as physical flowers in her lungs, her relentless love curling in and out of her rib cage like climbing vines.

She could not succumb to it. She could not let it grow so thickly inside her that she knew of nothing else. She was a girl of stone, unfeeling—*that* was who she had always been.

Juliette scrubbed at her eyes. When her sight was clear again, Nanjing Road was half-swathed in the falling dark, its neon signs flickering to life and bathing her in red, red, red.

"These violent delights have violent ends," Juliette whispered to herself. She tilted her head up to the clouds, to the light sea breeze blowing in from the Bund and stinging her nose with salt. "You have always known this."

Twelve

Benedikt was tiring of the city's talk, tiring of the fear that a new madness had erupted.

It had. There *was* a new madness—that was already certain. What good was jabbering on about it, as if discussing the matter would increase one's immunity? If it was supposed to be a coping mechanism, then Benedikt supposed he had never been much good at taking advantage of coping mechanisms anyway. He only knew how to swallow, and swallow, and swallow, until a black hole had grown in his stomach to suck everything away. Until it was all pushed somewhere else, and then he could forget that he never knew what to do with himself in the daylight hours anymore. He could forget the argument with Roma this morning, about the rumors that he was working with Juliette Cai, and then his confirmation that they were not mere rumors but truth, that Lord Montagov had set them to become allies.

Benedikt wanted to break something. He hadn't touched his art supplies in months, but recently he had been entertaining the urge to destroy it all. Stab his paintbrush right through his canvas and hope that the damage would be enough to make him feel better.

For all that they had done, the Scarlet Gang didn't deserve clemency even in the face of a new madness. But then who was Benedikt to have any say in this?

"Benedikt Ivanovich."

Benedikt looked up at the summons, his hands stilling around the pocketknife he was testing. He wasn't in the main Montagov head-quarters often, dropping by only to swipe a few new weapons and rummage about the cupboards a little. Even so, in all the times he had been here previously, he had caught incensed discussions from Lord Montagov's office, usually about the new threat of madness and what they were to do if an assassin let loose monsters on the city. It always ended the same way. Ever since the Podsolnukh, they paid the demands that came.

Today was the first time in a while that the floor above was silent; instead of voices wafting down, a White Flower was leaning on the handrail of the staircase, waving for his attention.

"We need extra hands to install a wardrobe," the White Flower said. Benedikt didn't know his name, but he recognized the other boy's face, knew that he was one of the many occupants in this laby-rinth of a house. "Do you have a moment?"

Benedikt shrugged. "Why not?"

He stood and slipped the pocketknife away, following the White Flower up the stairs. If Benedikt continued climbing, he would approach the fourth floor, where his former bedroom used to be, where Roma and Alisa still resided. It was the core wing of the house, but instead of continuing up in that direction, the White Flower he was following pivoted left and ventured deeper into the middle rooms and hallways, squeezing by bustling kitchens and ducking under poorly installed ceiling beams. Once one walked farther away from the main wing of the headquarters and into the parts that used to be different apartments, the architecture became a fever dream, more nonsensical than logical.

They came upon a small room where three other White Flowers were already waiting, holding up various panels of wood. The boy who had summoned Benedikt quickly grabbed hold of a hammer, securing one of the panels from a White Flower who was visibly sweating.

"If you—ow! Sorry, if you could get the last few panels over there?"

The first boy pointed, then put the thumb of his other hand to his mouth. He had accidentally caught it in the path of his hammer.

Benedikt did as he was told. The White Flowers working on this wardrobe seemed a rumbling cauldron of activity, throwing instructions at each other until their voices overlapped, comfortable in their routine. Benedikt had not lived in this house for years, and so he recognized none of the faces around him. There weren't many Montagovs left in this household, only White Flowers who paid rent.

Really, there weren't many Montagovs at all. Benedikt, Roma, and Alisa were the last of the line.

"Hey."

Benedikt's eyes flickered up. The White Flower closest to him—while the others were arguing about which way the nail went in—offered a wan smile.

"You have my condolences," he said quietly. "I heard about your friend."

His *friend*. Benedikt bit his tongue. He knew little of those in this household, but he supposed they knew of him. The curse of the Montagov name. What was it that Marshall had said? *There's a plague on both your damn houses.* A plague that ate away at everything they were.

"It is the way of the blood feud," Benedikt managed.

"Yes," the White Flower said. "I suppose it is."

Another panel was hammered in. They tightened the hinges, jiggled about the boards. As soon as the wardrobe was standing on its own, Benedikt excused himself, letting the others continue with their task. He backed out from the room and wound along the floor, walking until he found himself in a vacant sitting room. Only there did he lean against the fraying wallpaper, his head going light, his vision flooding with absolute white. His breath came out in one long wheeze.

I heard about your friend.

Your friend.

Friend.

So why couldn't he mourn his friend like others had? Why couldn't he keep going like Roma had? Why was he still so *stuck*?

Benedikt thudded his fist hard against the wall.

Sometimes, Benedikt was half-convinced there was someone else's voice in his head: a miniature invader relentless against his ear. Poets spoke of internal monologues, but they were supposed to be nothing save metaphors, so why was his so loud? Why could he not shut himself up when it was just *him*?

". . . non?"

An unfamiliar murmur floated along the hallway then, and Benedikt's eyes snapped open, his mind silencing at once. It seemed *he* couldn't shut *himself* up, but oddities in his surroundings certainly could.

Benedikt surged out from the sitting room, his brow furrowing. The murmur had sounded feminine . . . and nervous. He knew he was out of touch with the White Flowers, but who in the gang fit *that* description?

"Alisa?" he called hesitantly.

His footsteps padded down the hallway, hands trailing across the banisters erected along an awkward staircase that went into a half story between the second and third. Benedikt kept walking, until he came upon a door that had been left slightly ajar. If memory proved correct, there was another sitting room on the other side.

He pressed his ear to the wood. He had not misheard. There was a Frenchwoman in there, mumbling incoherently, as if she were in tears.

"Hello?" he called, knocking on the door.

Immediately, the door slammed closed.

Benedikt jolted back, his eyes wide. "Hey! What gives?"

"Mind your business, Montagov. This does not concern you."

That voice was familiar. Benedikt pounded his fist on the door for a few seconds more before a name clicked in place.

"Dimitri Petrovich Voronin!" he called. "Open this door right now."

"For the last time—"

"I will kick it down. So help me, I swear I will!"

The door flung open. Benedikt barged in, looking around for the source of the mystery. He found only a table of European men playing poker. They all stared at him with annoyance, some putting their cards down. Others folded their arms, sleeves crossed over the white handkerchiefs poking from the chest pocket of their suit jackets. Merchants, or bankers, or ministers—it didn't matter; they were allied with the White Flowers.

Benedikt blinked, puzzled. "I heard crying," he said.

"You misheard," Dimitri replied, in English. Perhaps it was for the benefit of the foreigners at the table.

"There was a woman," Benedikt insisted, his jaw clenching hard, remaining in Russian. "A crying Frenchwoman."

Dimitri, lifting the corner of his mouth, pointed to the radio in the corner. His shock of black hair whipped after him as he spun and adjusted the volume, until the speakers were loudly running a program in the middle of a play. Indeed, there was a Frenchwoman reading her lines.

"You misheard," he said again, walking toward Benedikt. He didn't stop until he was right in front of him, placing his hands on his shoulders. Benedikt was about as close to Dimitri as Roma was: not very. This manhandling was hardly fitting for a fellow White Flower, and yet Dimitri had no qualms about pushing Benedikt toward the door.

"I don't know what you have going on," Benedikt warned, staggering to the entranceway, "but I am monitoring your funny business."

Dimitri dropped his smile. When he finally switched to Russian for his response, it was as if a change had come over him, a look of complete scorn marring his expression.

"The only funny business," he hissed, "is that I am maintaining our connections. So do *not* butt in."

Fast as the fury came, it was gone again. Dimitri leaned in suddenly and feigned placing an exaggerated kiss on Benedikt's cheek, the way that relatives sent off children. A *chmoc!* echoed through the room before Benedikt grunted in indignation and shoved Dimitri aside, shoved his hands off of him.

Dimitri was hardly fazed. He smiled, and returning to English, commanded, "Now, run along and play."

The door slammed closed.

Tyler Cai was picking at a bāo, rolling up little bits of the dough into mini pellets, and throwing them at the men who were slacking off.

"Come on, no snoozing!" he shouted, aiming another mini bun pellet. It struck one of the assistants right on his forehead, and the boy chortled, opening his mouth so it trailed down his face and dropped in.

"Why don't you help out?" the boy shot back. Despite his tough talk, he quickly straightened out of his nap and ducked to lift a big bag beneath the table, throwing it across the room.

Satisfied, Tyler leaned back in his chair, propping his feet up on the foreman's desk. The foreman was nowhere to be seen. He had run off an hour ago, when Tyler came down into the lab to run inspections, and had yet to return, likely passed out in some brothel. Never mind that it was two in the afternoon.

No matter. That was what Tyler was here for after all—he'd do a much better job of overseeing the vaccine creation than a man with half their drug supply dusted in his beard.

"What does that say?" one of the scientists muttered over the worktable. "I can't read any of this English; the letters are in horrendous shape." He showed it to the man working opposite him, and they both peered at the copied sheet, squinting at the handwriting that some hired Scarlet help had copied over twenty times for every scientist in the facility, down to the flicks and dots.

Tyler wandered over, extending a silent hand. The scientists hurried to pass the sheet to him.

"Cadaverine," Tyler read aloud.

"What does that mean in Chinese?"

He tossed the sheet back, furrowing his brow. "Do I look like a translator to you? Go find it in one of the dictionaries."

"How are we to re-create a vaccine when we can't even read the damn notes?" the second scientist muttered beneath his breath, scribbling something into his notebook.

Tyler continued walking, picking up a ruler and smacking it on the tables when it looked like the assistants were fooling around. It was a habit learned from his father: that ever-constant sound following him when he was young to keep him on task when the tutors were around. It was never supposed to be a threat: it was a reminder, a little shock to the senses whenever he started to doze, staring off into space to wonder what present was coming for his birthday next week. The tutors used to think he was so disciplined, but that was only because his father was always overseeing the lessons.

Until he wasn't anymore.

Tyler halted in his inspection of the room, catching one of the younger assistants waving for him. He almost ignored it, but then the waving turned more frantic, and Tyler approached with a sigh.

"Is something wrong?" He flicked the ruler absently. How much pressure would it take to snap the wooden instrument? A hard thwack over a wrist? A sudden bend down the middle?

"Don't look too fast, shàoyé," the boy said quietly, "but I think we have spies."

Tyler stopped. He dropped the ruler. Slowly, he followed the boy's line of sight, up to the small panel windows at the topmost part of the far walls. Those windows provided the only light for a facility located deep enough underground to stay hidden beneath a restaurant but not so deep that the smells of Chenghuangmiao's food stalls couldn't float in. Where the view was usually only the feet of the shoppers perusing Chenghuangmiao, right then, there were two faces peering in instead, taking inventory of the space.

Tyler retrieved his pistol and shot at the window. The glass fractured immediately, splitting in every direction as the two faces jerked back. All the scientists in the room cried aloud in surprise, but Tyler merely spat, "White Flowers" and ran out, sprinting up the steps into the restaurant and out the main door.

The White Flowers were already some distance away, nearing the Jiuqu Bridge. But in their haste, they had cleared a path through the crowds of shoppers, leaving Tyler a direct shot . . .

He aimed.

"Tyler, *no!*"

The command came too late. By then Tyler had pulled the trigger twice in rapid succession, two White Flower heads cracking with an explosion of red, crashing to the ground. Chenghuangmiao erupted with a wave of screaming, but most shoppers reacted quickly and hurried out of the way, in no mood to be caught in a gangster dispute. They didn't have to worry. This was no dispute; there were no other White Flowers nearby to retaliate.

A hard shove landed on Tyler's back. He whirled around, his hand coming up to block the next hit, arms colliding with Rosalind Lang's clenched fist.

"You have no heart," she spat. "They were retreating. They wanted no fight."

"They were about to take Scarlet information," Tyler shot back, shaking Rosalind off. "Don't get righteous."

"Scarlet information?" Rosalind shrieked in echo. She pointed to the windows, hardly visible from the exterior, if not for the bullet hole now studded into the glass. "I was watching them, Cai Tailei. I already had my eye on them to make sure they weren't going to be trouble, and they cannot *hear anything* from out here. What could they have taken with them?"

Tyler scoffed. "All they need is one leak. And then the White Flowers are on the market before we are."

It was already bad enough that his cousin was messing with the White Flower heir *again*, by Lord Cai's command. Tyler had guffawed when a messenger reported that Juliette had been sighted at the racecourse with Roma Montagov, sure that he had finally caught her this time. Only when Tyler had reported it to Lord Cai, Lord Cai had waved him off, apathetic. *We must make compromises,* Lord Cai had said. It was a fool's task—each and every one of the White Flowers were underhanded and quick, taking and taking, and any lesser Scarlet than Tyler would scarcely notice.

"Do not lie to save your honor." Rosalind pointed a sharp fingernail. "You kill because you enjoy it. I'm warning you. Your name cannot protect you for long."

In a flash, Tyler reached out and grabbed Rosalind by the chin, forcing her to look at him. Rosalind did not flinch, her jaw locked hard, and Tyler did not let go. They were all like this. Rosalind. Juliette. Pretty, loud, *terrible* girls who threw accusations braced knee-deep in the guise of morality, as if they weren't just as guilty of this city's teachings.

"I don't need my name to protect me," Tyler hissed. He eyed the smattering of glitter dancing across Rosalind's cheek. "I protect my name. Just as I protect this gang."

Rosalind managed a choked laugh. Her hand came up around his wrist and squeezed, threatening to claw her nails into his skin. Tyler felt the pain, felt the five sharp points dig in like blades, and then the cool wetness of blood dripping once down his sleeve.

"Do you?" she whispered.

Tyler finally let go, shoving Rosalind away. She regained her balance easily, never off-kilter for more than a flash of a second.

"Don't get righteous, Lang Shalin," he said again.

"It is not righteousness." Rosalind eyed the red spreading on his sleeve. "It is goodness. Of which you have none."

She pivoted fast, sparing one glance at the bodies near the bridge before marching away, her lips thinned in horror. Tyler remained, crossing his arms with a swallowed wince, trying not to touch the throbbing wounds at his wrist.

Goodness. What was goodness at a time like this? Goodness did not keep people fed. Goodness did not win wars.

Tyler leaned over and thudded a fist against the outside of the panel windows, waving for Scarlets to come out. They had to move the bodies. This part of Chenghuangmiao was White Flower territory, and if White Flowers caught wind of their own being gunned down and arrived for a fight, it could put the Scarlet facility at risk.

Goodness. Tyler almost laughed aloud as the Scarlet men came outside and started in the direction of the two dead White Flowers. What was the Scarlet Gang without him? It would crumble, and no one seemed to realize that, least of all Juliette and her miserable cousins. Hell, Juliette herself would be dead without him, from that very first time they were ambushed by White Flowers and she froze, unwilling to shoot.

"Back to work!" one of the assistants shouted from the restaurant door, summoning the Scarlets who weren't needed around the corpses. Tyler watched them trek back, his head humming with sound. They all nodded his way in passing, some throwing a salute.

The Scarlet Gang recognized Juliette across Shanghai because they painted her face on advertisements and creams. The Scarlet Gang recognized Tyler because he *knew* this city, because the people had seen him at work, pushing for their victory at every turn, no matter how brutish his tactics were. Everyone else be damned, his people came first. That was what his father had taught him. That was what his father had died for, raging for the Scarlets in the feud, and for as long as Tyler lived, he would make that spilled blood mean something.

All the Scarlets eventually filtered back into the building. The rest of Chenghuangmiao resumed its bustle, its hawking and its sizzling, its infinite smells.

"You need me," Tyler said, to no one in particular, or perhaps to everyone. "You all need me."

Thirteen

In the weeks that passed, the dance that Roma and Juliette settled into grew almost predictable. In the most literal sense too, given how often they were dropping into the various dance halls across the Concessions. Show up, target a foreigner, get answers.

Juliette didn't mind. Navigating a wǔtīng was far more palatable than navigating places like the Grand Theatre and the racecourse. Here, although it still required the same sharp tongue, although they remained surrounded by pearls and champagne and the knowledge that this was foreign-owned land, there were still Chinese tycoons and gangsters dancing the night away, blowing their cigarette smoke out without caring that it might bother the Frenchman at the next table. A dance hall was no different from a burlesque club in practice. Same showgirls onstage, same smoky interiors, same lowlifes lurking by the doors. The only reason they seemed so much fancier was because they ran on foreign money.

Juliette returned from the bar, offering Roma the second drink in her hand. Meanwhile, the French merchant who had approached them earlier in the evening continued chattering on, following right on her tail. Roma took the drink absently, his gaze remaining elsewhere in inspection. They had spent long enough here at Bailemen—or *Paramount*, to the foreigners—to have spoken with almost every wealthy elite present tonight. By now it was obvious that the flyers were not limited to those in the French Concession but the International Settlement, too, all the occupants of Bubbling Well Road gasping in confirmation when Juliette asked about them.

Funnily enough, though these flyers were the only thing people reported regarding the new monster business, nobody had actually gone to the address. Many had already been vaccinated by the Larkspur and thought it unnecessary, or they didn't believe the flyers to be real. The blackmailer wasn't smarter than Paul Dexter after all. Because they hadn't built any of the reputation that the Larkspur dove into Shanghai with, and now nobody trusted the idea of a new vaccine enough to actually go get it.

"And besides," the merchant behind her was saying once Juliette tuned in again. "Your cousin has said that the Scarlets are close to a breakthrough on their own vaccine. What use is another?"

At this, Roma choked on his drink, managing to suppress his cough before it was too obvious. The man prattling on did not notice because he was Scarlet-affiliated and had been pretending that Roma did not exist. Even if the merchant was happy to speak as if the White Flower heir was not two steps away, he *was*, and he could hear everything that the man did not even realize was sensitive information. Juliette's eyes slid to Roma as the last of his cough died, checking only that he did not need a great big thump on the back. He seemed to recover. A shame.

"My cousin is not to be trusted," Juliette said. She traced her finger around the cool edge of her glass. There was no one that the man could be referring to save for Tyler. She highly doubted Rosalind or Kathleen was going around gossiping with Scarlet-affiliated French merchants. They could—they had the linguistic ability, but not the stomach.

The merchant leaned one shoulder against the wall. This corner of Bailemen was rather empty, hosting one or two tables that had a poor view of the stage. Of course, Roma and Juliette weren't standing here to watch the show; they were here to peruse the crowd and see if there were any more people worthy of approaching.

"Oh?" the merchant said. "If I'm not overstepping, Miss Cai, the city seems to trust your cousin more than they trust you."

Juliette turned around, fixing her eyes on him. The merchant flinched a little, but he did not back down.

"I'll give you two seconds to take that back."

The merchant forced an awkward laugh. He feigned deference, but a certain note of amusement colored his stare. "It is merely an observation," he said. "One that notes how daughters will always have their attention elsewhere. Who could blame you, Miss Cai? You were not born for this like your cousin was, after all."

How dare he—

"Juliette, let it go."

Juliette cast Roma a glare. "Stay out of this."

"Do you even know this merchant's name?" Roma looked the Frenchman once over. Apathy oozed from the gesture. "On any other day, you'd have walked away. He's irrelevant. Let it go."

Her grip tightened on her drink. By all means, it was foolish to make a scene in a dance hall, especially among so many foreigners— among those she needed to respect her if she was going to get any information out of them.

Then the merchant grinned and said, "You take instructions from White Flowers now, do you? Miss Cai, what would your fallen Scarlets say?"

Juliette threw her drink down, the glass shattering into a thousand pieces. "Try me one more *time*." She lunged, pushing the merchant into the wall, so fiercely that his head made a *crack!* against the marble. Juliette reared back, her fist closing for another strike. Only then an iron grip came around her waist, hauling her two steps away.

"Calm down," Roma hissed, his mouth so close to her ear that she could feel the heat of his lips, "before I throw *you* into the wall."

A chill swept down Juliette's neck. In anger or attraction, she wasn't quite sure. It seemed unnecessarily cruel that each time Roma Montagov decided to get so close, it was to make threats, especially when Juliette was hardly in the *wrong* here.

Anger won out. It always did.

"So do it," she said through her teeth.

Roma didn't move. He wouldn't—Juliette had expected that. Threats were easy to make, but they could not be seen fighting with each other, not when their collaboration was supposed to be some big stand against the blackmailer.

"That's what I thought."

By then the merchant had regained his bearings and, without sparing Juliette a second glance, hurried toward the back of the hall, scampering off like a frightened animal. Roma let go, slowly, his arm winding away bit by bit, as if he was afraid the merchant was only going to come running back and Juliette would need to be reined in again.

Juliette eyed the broken glass on the floor.

"Go sit down, would you?" Roma suggested. There was no sympathy in his voice. All his words were level, betraying no emotion. "I'll get you another drink."

Without waiting for her response, he turned and left, and Juliette frowned, supposing she had no choice except to slink up to a table and drop into a chair, putting her head in her hands.

"So—" Roma returned, setting a glass in front of Juliette as he sat down too.

Juliette suppressed a sigh. She knew what was coming.

"—you are working on a vaccine?"

"Yes." Juliette rubbed her forehead, then winced, knowing she was smearing product all over her fingers. She should have snapped for him to mind his business, but she was bone-weary of this dance, this routine of dead ends and useless information. It hardly occurred to her that she needed to stop before she was saying, "We have some papers that Paul left behind."

This was exactly why Lord Montagov had given Roma his task. To pick up all the information Juliette let slip.

"And what will you do," Roma asked, seeming not to notice as Juliette reached right into her drink and took out an ice cube, rubbing it along her fingers to clean the makeup off, "when you re-create the vaccine?"

Juliette barked a harsh laugh. Suddenly she was glad for the darkness of the hall, each bulb of the chandeliers above twinkling dimly, not only to hide the mess she had made of her makeup, but the mania she was sure had entered her expression.

"If it were up to me," she said roughly, "I'd send it through the whole city, put a protective casing on everyone so the blackmailer loses power." A knife materialized between her fingers, and she stabbed the blade into the table, crushing the ice cube into fractions. "But . . . my father may listen to Tyler instead. We may give it only to the Scarlets, then sell it to everyone else, and it will merely be a pity for those who cannot afford it. It is the smart option, after all. The profit-making option."

Roma said nothing.

"You don't have a lot of time left," Juliette went on, only because she knew she had his full attention now. "You should begin a campaign to capture our information so that the White Flowers distribute the vaccine into the market first."

Juliette yanked the knife out of the table, and ice shards flew in all directions, scattering on the small wooden tabletop. It was always going to be hope that ruined her. Hope that she had presented a terrible thing to him on a platter, and he would not do it, hope that he might care enough to keep the information to himself.

Why would he? He had no reason to care for her when she had given him so many reasons to hate her. And yet she was foolish enough to test him anyway.

"It's time," Roma finally said. Juliette looked at him quickly, but he had long moved past the topic at hand. "We need to go to the facility in Kunshan. It may be our very blackmailer."

"Somehow, I doubt it," Juliette muttered. She put her knife away and stood, dropping into a mocking curtsy as if they were nothing more than dance partners taking leave for the night. "I'll see you at the railway station tomorrow."

Without waiting for further retort, Juliette grabbed her coat and exited the dance hall, plunging back out into the night.

From the roof of Bailemen, Marshall leaned into the cold breeze, letting his hair flutter with the wind. It was a precarious drop down to the pavement—one slip of his shoes and he'd plummet over the edge, falling along the straight wall of the dance hall with nothing to grab on his way down. Just at the thought, his grip tightened on the pole beside him, and he clung a little closer to the towered peak at the center of the building.

Movement flashed below. The glimmering lights of Bailemen reflected off the rain puddles that had collected on the streets earlier, spelling PARAMOUNT BALLROOM backward in red and yellow. Marshall was hardly surprised when he watched Juliette storm out from the dance hall and stomp right into one of the puddles, as if ruining her shoes might improve her mood.

"I wonder what Roma did," Marshall said aloud.

He got his answer—in a roundabout way—when Roma emerged from Bailemen a minute later and stopped some distance into the road, ignoring the rickshaw runners calling for his business. Instead, he turned his head skyward and emitted one short yell. Marshall ducked out of view, just in case Roma caught sight of him, but he shouldn't have worried. In seconds, Roma had stormed off too, in the opposite direction of Juliette.

"Tragic," Marshall muttered into the wind. Montagovs were so dramatic.

Yet he missed the dramatics, missed being right in the heart of the city, at the heart of the feud that kept it in halves. If Benedikt were here, he would probably tell Marshall to stop being thickheaded. There was nothing good about a feud. Nothing other than loss. But if nothing else, it was a singular purpose in a place that seemed to ask for too much.

Another gust of wind blew hard into his face, and Marshall shrank back, searching for a better place to sit. He had come out tonight for a breath of fresh air; only then he had sighted Roma and Juliette walking along Avenue Foch and wasted no time following on their tail. They hadn't noticed him trekking a few steps behind, nor when he hurried ahead to get onto the scaffolding at the back of Bailemen when Roma and Juliette disappeared within. Marshall was almost surprised. He expected more from two heirs who could probably hit a fly with a needle if they threw hard enough.

"What have you two descended into?"

There was no reply to come, not unless the night itself had an answer. Marshall needed to stop speaking out loud, but it was the only thing keeping him less lonely. He missed conversation. He missed people.

He missed Benedikt.

The wail of a siren swept the streets some distance away, then the echo of what might have been a gunshot. Marshall pulled his legs up to his chest, resting his chin on his knees. When he first joined the White Flowers, he was just another scrappy kid picked off the streets, thin and hungry and constantly dirty. That was how Benedikt found him that day. Curled up in the alley behind the Montagov house, legs pulled close, arms wrapped in a fetal position. He hadn't yet learned how to fight, how to smile so sharply that it would cut as fast as any blade. And when Benedikt crouched in front of him—looking like a shining cherub with his pressed white shirt and curly combed hair—he didn't remark on any of that. All he did was extend a hand, asking, "Do you have somewhere to go?"

"I do have somewhere to go now," Marshall muttered. "But it was better when you were there with me."

A sudden rustle came from the other side of the rooftop, and Marshall jolted, startling out of his thoughts. He had gotten so caught up in his memories that he had tuned out the world around him. A mistake—one that he couldn't afford to make. This was Scarlet territory.

And indeed, a Scarlet circled around the rooftop tower, coming into view. He froze as he looked up, cigarette dangling from his lips.

Please don't recognize me, Marshall thought, his hands creeping for the pistol in his pocket. *Please don't recognize me.*

"Marshall Seo," the Scarlet croaked. "You're supposed to be dead."

Aish.

The Scarlet threw his cigarette down, but Marshall had readied himself. There was only one way this could end. He drew the pistol from his pocket in one fast motion and fired—fast and first, because that was what mattered.

At the end of the day, that was the only thing that mattered.

The bullet landed true. With a harsh clatter, the Scarlet's weapon fell to the floor. It might have been a gun. It might have been a dagger. It might even have been a throwing star, for all the consequence it held. But in the hazy dark, all Marshall cared about was it being out of reach, and then the Scarlet collapsed too, a hand clasped over the hole studded into his breastbone.

For a few tense seconds, Marshall heard labored breathing, the metallic smell of blood permeating the rooftop. Then, silence. Utter silence.

Marshall kicked the edge of the rooftop, skittering little stones down the side of Bailemen. All this death on his hands. All this death, and in truth, none of it mattered to him so long as it protected him, protected the secrets of those he was hiding for.

"Goddammit," he whispered, scrubbing his face and turning to the breeze, away from the smell. "I hate this city."

Fourteen

Juliette peered at the train platform, eyeing the tracks below. When she felt a presence behind her, she didn't have to turn to know who it was. She recognized him by footfall, by that soft pitter-patter paired with a hard stop, like he had never in his life walked in the wrong direction.

"To the southwest," she said beneath her breath. "White man with the tatty clothing and French novel tucked under his arm. He's been watching me for the past ten minutes."

Out of her periphery, she watched Roma turning slowly, seeking the man in question.

"Perhaps he thinks you are pretty."

Juliette clicked her tongue. "He looks ready to kill me."

"Same concept, really—" Roma stopped, blinking rapidly. He had sighted the man. "He's a White Flower."

Surprised, Juliette shifted her eyes again, straining to get another look. The man had turned his attention to his novel now, so he did not notice.

"Are you . . . certain?" Juliette asked, deflating from her confidence. She had hoped that maybe it was the blackmailer, finally showing up in the open now that Juliette and Roma were on their way toward the possible truth. It was too much to hope that someone would materialize like this just to stop them, but it certainly would have sped the investigation along. "I thought he was French."

"Yes, he *is* French," Roma said. "But loyal to us. I have seen him in the house before. I am certain of it."

The man suddenly looked up again. Juliette swiveled her gaze away, pretending to be inspecting something else, but Roma did not do the same. He stared right back.

"If he is a White Flower," Juliette said without moving her mouth, "then why does he look rather murderous toward you, too?"

Roma pursed his lips and turned back around, facing the tracks just as their train pulled in. Fellow passengers hurried forward, scrambling to the front and pushing right to the edge of the platform so they could secure a good seat.

"Perhaps he thinks I am prettier," he replied easily. "Do you wish to speak to him? With enough effort, the two of us could probably pin him down."

Juliette considered it, then shook her head. Why waste their time with White Flowers?

They boarded, finding seats by the window. With a sigh, Juliette plopped into the hardback chair and undid her coat, dropping it onto the table between her seat and Roma's. By virtue of the train's setup, they were facing each other, and stacking more items onto the table was like she was building a makeshift wall. Sitting face-to-face felt too intimate, even while twenty-odd other passengers occupied the compartment.

"To Kunshan," the compartment loudspeaker emitted in English. "Welcome aboard."

Roma dropped into his seat. He didn't shed the gray coat over his suit. "What's the next language coming?"

"French," Juliette replied immediately, a second before grainy Shanghainese blared over the loudspeaker. Her eyebrows lifted. "Huh. Interesting."

Roma leaned back, the smallest smile playing on his face. "Ye of little faith."

That barest glimpse of humor came and went in a flash, but it was enough to make Juliette go stock-still, her stomach clenching. For the smallest moment, Roma had likely forgotten. And when the train started to move, when Roma turned his gaze to the scene outside and the glass reflected back the sudden hardening of his expression, Juliette knew that he remembered again—who she was, who they were, what she had done, what they were now.

The train rumbled on.

Shanghai to Kunshan was not a long journey, and the window view quickly turned rural, passing dilapidated houses on dirt roads. Swaths of grass stretched on beside the train tracks, flat and even and eternal—more natural green than Juliette had ever seen inside city limits, discounting what the foreigners cultivated in their parks.

Juliette released a soft breath, leaning her cheek upon the window. Roma was doing the same, but she resolved not to look at him any longer than necessary, lest he catch her staring. Her head turned, finding entertainment in the compartment instead, eyeing the dozing passengers as the train continued chugging, chugging, chugging.

When Roma broke the silence, enough time had passed that Juliette startled, doing so well at ignoring him that his voice was a shock.

"Assuming we do find the blackmailer"—no prelude, no overture, merely jumping directly to the point—"I gather we need a plan of attack."

Juliette drummed her fingers on the table. "Shoot to kill?"

Roma rolled his eyes. She was rather aggravated that he looked so beautiful in the midst of the action, the dark shadows of his eyelashes flickering up like a dusting of kohl.

"And after?" he asked. "It is no different from when we thought we were chasing the Larkspur. If we kill the blackmailer, how do we get to the monsters?"

"It *is* different this time," Juliette countered. She felt a chill brush through the train car, running goose bumps up her arm. When she shivered, Roma's frown deepened, his gaze tracing along the dip of her neckline. It was hardly appropriate for winter, she knew. She didn't need his judgment.

"How so?"

Juliette reached for her coat. "There was nothing that linked Paul Dexter to the Communists because he met with Qi Ren once and then chanced the chaos on random transformations. This blackmailer, however"—she stood up so she could swing her coat back on, the long fabric brushing the backs of her knees—"I doubt is many steps removed from their monsters. Not when the monsters are being sent out like little servants doing the blackmailer's bidding. That requires personal instructions. Constant meetings."

"That sounds like a guess," Roma remarked.

"This entire mission is a guess," Juliette replied, popping her collar. "I—" She stopped, her eye catching down the aisle just as she was preparing to sit again. The French White Flower was in this compartment too, sitting some rows away.

And he looked . . . in pain.

"Juliette?" Roma prompted. He ducked his head out into the aisle, trying to spot what she was looking at. "The hell is going on?"

The White Flower grabbed the glass he had in front of him and threw the liquid in his own face.

"Fire!" Juliette screamed suddenly.

The man roared with pain as Juliette yanked Roma by the arm, ignoring his utter confusion while he searched for the nonexistent fire. Others were not as doubting—they shot for the compartment door immediately and hurried into the next one over. This was the trouble with being at the tail of the train. There was only one direction to go.

"What the hell, Juliette?" Roma asked again as she pushed him hard against the bottlenecking passengers, toward the door. "What's—"

Juliette gasped, hearing a *snap!* by the windows, the tearing of clothes. In the next moment there was no man hunching over his seat but a monster, so tall that it crushed against the ceiling, chest heaving, nostrils flaring. Its green color seemed even more grotesque by the clear daylight, faintly transparent and revealing motion just beneath its skin: little black dots, rushing toward its spine.

They were nearing the door, but half the compartment was still behind her. If she tried to usher everyone through, the insects would dive forward into the rest of the train, infecting every soul on board. But if she stopped it now . . .

The insects tore outward from the monster with one colossal burst.

So Juliette pushed Roma across the threshold and slammed the door closed between them.

Roma whirled around with his breath caught in his throat, thudding his fists against the door. Was it a *monster* that had just come to life inside the compartment? Was it the *White Flower* who had just transformed into the monster?

"Juliette!" he roared. "Juliette, what the *hell*?"

All the passengers in front of him had fled, hurrying through the second sliding door that gave way into the next compartment. It was only Roma and Roma alone in this in-between passageway, where the flooring underneath him shifted at every turn and jolt of the train. He pushed at the door this way and that, bruising his knuckles in his effort to shift it, but *something* was holding it solidly closed, keeping it from budging even an inch.

"Juliette!" His fist came down on the door with a shudder. "Open this damn door!"

That was when the screaming started.

Juliette wound the cord around the door handle and pulled it tight, holding the compartment closed. The second she had it secure, the insects started to rain down, skittering black legs upon every surface they could find: body or floor or wall. This wasn't the first time she had experienced such a sensation, yet all the same, it tossed at her stomach, nausea threatening at her throat.

Crawling. So much crawling. Through her hair, into her dress, along the crooks of her elbows, her knees, her fingers. All she could do was squeeze her eyes shut and count on the vaccine she had taken months ago. She didn't even know if it still worked, but there was nothing to do now, nothing except—

With a gasp, Juliette brushed a clump off her neck, desperate to be rid of the feeling as soon as the falling stopped. She whirled around, her eyes flying open. There was no urge to claw at her throat, no urge to incite destruction. The vaccine had held true. As the people around her staggered to a seat or fell to their knees, Juliette remained steadfastly rooted on her feet, her hands braced to her sides. As the people around her hauled their nails up to their skin and started to dig, Juliette could only watch.

Oh my God.

The monster made a noise, an unearthly, carnal shriek. Immediately, Juliette surged forward, pushing past the victims undergoing the madness. She wanted to flinch and she wanted to hide, but there was no time for what she *wanted*, only for what she had to do.

Don't close your eyes, Juliette commanded herself. *Watch the carnage.*

Watch the destruction. Feel the slick of the blood as it paints the carpeting red, and remember what is at stake in this city, all because some foreign merchant wants to play greedy.

Juliette pulled her gun, aiming and shooting the monster in the gut.

The sound of gunshots echoed through the locked compartment. Roma took a horrified step back, so aghast at the noise that he couldn't find the energy to keep pushing at the door. In that moment, he didn't care anymore. The city faded, the blood feud faded, all his anger and rage and retribution crumbled to dust. All he could think about was Juliette—dying, she was dying, and he wouldn't allow it. Some removed part of him determined that it was his job to kill her; the part of him in the present simply couldn't bear it—not here, not now.

"Don't," he whispered, a tremor breaking his voice. "Don't."

The monster dove aside, hardly affected by her bullets. Its flailing limbs were slick with moisture, little beads of water that looked viscous to the touch.

Juliette aimed again, but the sounds behind her—the pained, frightened groans of a victim's last gasp before death—distracted her more than she could bear, and when her bullet only hit the monster's shoulder, it took the chance to squeeze between two seats and dive right at a window, fracturing a web through the glass.

It was trying to escape.

Juliette reached for the knife at her thigh, intent on a throw. What creature could survive a blade through the eye? What creature, no matter how monstrous, could take its whole head carved open?

But she wasn't fast enough. By the time she had struggled through the fallen bodies, the monster had dived against the window once more and shattered it entirely, blasting shards of glass across the compartment. Juliette gasped, throwing a hand over her face. Before she could fully recover, the monster had rolled right out, uncaring of the train's fast speed.

"No!" Juliette exclaimed, spitting a curse. She rushed to the open window, watching the monster land upon the hills and phase back into a man, the transformation as casual as a coat being shed. In seconds he was out of view. The train flew by, leaving him in the countryside, all this blood on his hands and no one wiser to his identity.

Juliette stumbled away from the window, her legs close to giving out. She had believed it already, but seeing it with her own two eyes was another matter entirely. No longer was this Qi Ren and his ill-timed transformations, fighting against himself and leaving sketches of his other form in an effort to uncover what was happening to his body. No longer was this a sickness spread near the water, hitting the gangsters working at the Bund at odd hours. *These* monsters were assassins. Assassins under someone's command, growing to beasts at will and fading back into men when purpose suited it.

This situation was growing more and more dire by the minute.

When the screaming stopped, Roma could hardly move. Every possibility flashed before his eyes, most of them with Juliette's body strewn in pieces on the train floor. If there was a higher power, Roma hoped they were listening. All they would hear was: *Please, please, please.*

Please be okay.

The silence was cut through suddenly by the sound of glass shattering in the compartment. With a trembling breath, Roma surged forward again and pulled at the door as hard as he could.

At last it slammed open.

He smelled blood immediately. Then felt the wind, howling through a shattered window. The monster was nowhere in sight. But

Juliette—there stood Juliette, like some avenging angel surveying her battlefield, the only figure who remained upright in a car full of fallen corpses, her cheek smeared with blood.

She blinked, so slowly it looked as if she were waking up from a dream. When she started toward him and stumbled, Roma lunged out and caught her without thinking, holding her close for one beat, two beats, three. In that drawn-out moment, he pressed his cheek against the hard texture of her hair, against the soft skin of her neck. She exhaled, relaxing against him, and it was that which jolted Roma back to reality. Juliette was okay, so all his panic transformed into fury.

"Why did you *do* that?" Roma demanded, jerking back. He shook her by the shoulders. "Why would you do that?"

Bodies on the floor, throats clawed to shreds, red trails running from eye to ear. But Juliette . . . Juliette looked untouched.

"I took Paul's vaccine," she said shakily. "I am immune."

"That was for the first monster," Roma snapped. "These could have been different."

The very thought that this had been a *White Flower* hiding under their noses as a monster only heightened the heat in his chest. Had he known to stop the White Flower earlier, none of this would have happened. Had he *known* any of this, he could have tortured something out of the man long ago and the absurd blackmailing on their city would be over.

"I figured it would work the same." Juliette brushed his hands off her shoulders. "And it *did*."

"It was a gamble. You gambled with your *life*."

There was a visible twitch in Juliette's jaw, her pointed chin tipping up in aggravation. Roma knew he was being condescending, but he cared little when the air was still permeated with gore, violence soaking into their clothes, sticking to their skin. Noting the same fact, Juliette shoved Roma over the compartment threshold and slammed the sliding door closed again.

"It *worked*," she hissed. Now it was only the two of them occupying the in-between train space, one panel of hardwood keeping them separated from a room full of corpses. "I saved the whole train from infection."

"No," Roma said. "You decided to play hero and got lucky."

Juliette threw her hands into the air, scoffing. A mark of blood yet remained on her cheek. She had another stain across her sleeve, and another down her leg.

"How is that a problem?"

It was. It was a problem, and Roma couldn't explain how. He wanted to pace, to move, to release this frantic, pent-up feeling roaring to a crescendo inside of him, but there was no space here—nothing except walls closing in on them and the unstable train rumbling beneath their feet. He couldn't think, couldn't function, could hardly comprehend this reaction that was happening inside of him.

"Your life," he seethed, "is not a game of luck."

"Since when," Juliette spat, mimicking his emphasis, "did you care about my life?"

Roma marched right toward her. Perhaps he had been intent on intimidation, but they were too similar in height, and where he meant to loom, he and Juliette only ended up standing nose to nose, glaring at one another so fiercely that the world could have gone up in smoke and neither would have noticed.

"I don't." He was trembling with his fury. "I hate you."

And when Juliette didn't recoil, Roma kissed her.

He pressed her right into the door, both his hands coming up to grip her by the sides of her neck, getting as close as he dared to the fiery, candied scent of her skin. A barely stifled gasp parted Juliette's lips, and then she was kissing him back with the same red-hot vexation, as if it were only to get it out of her system, as if this were *nothing*.

They were nothing.

Roma jerked away like he had been burned, heaving for breath and coming to his senses. Juliette appeared equally dazed, but Roma didn't spare her a second glance before he turned on his heel and marched through the next sliding door, slamming it behind him.

By God. What had he done?

The rest of the train was humming away in complete normalcy. No one paid Roma any heed as he remained standing by the compartment entrance, his heart hammering in his ears and his pulse thrumming beneath the thin skin of his wrists. It wasn't until a man wandered up to him, intending to skirt past and get through the door, that Roma finally shook out of his stupor and held out his arm, warning, "Don't. Dead bodies everywhere."

The man blinked, taken aback. Roma didn't stick around to offer an explanation; he pushed past rudely and forged ahead, entering into the next passageway. Only there, boxed in between two new compartments and removed from watchful eyes, did Roma finally shove a hand through his hair and breathe out a long sigh.

"What is wrong with me?" he muttered. He wanted to scream and rage. He wanted to scream at *Juliette* until his lungs grew hoarse. Only he knew that if he screamed *I hate you,* what he really meant was *I love you. I still love you so much that I hate you for it.*

The train rocked under his feet, finding smooth tracks. Its screeching noise became swallowed, and for a suspended moment, all that could be heard in that compartment space was Roma's heavy breathing.

Then the tracks grew rough again, and the floors continued their dull screeching.

Fifteen

I t was late afternoon by the time the train arrived in Kunshan and even later by the time Roma and Juliette finished speaking to the authorities, because what qualified for authorities here was no more than men in flimsy uniforms blanching at the sight of the bodies. What could have taken ten minutes instead took two hours of Juliette making threats and yelling, *"Do you know who I am?"* before they had the bodies removed and a completed list of victims. The bodies went to storage, and messengers were sent in cars to Shanghai, en route to notify both the Scarlet Gang and the White Flowers what had happened. They sent men out along the tracks, too, traipsing through the hills to look for the escaped monster, but Juliette doubted they would find anything. Not with their level of incompetence. By the time she summoned Scarlets to drive out and search with them, she was sure the monster would be long gone.

"Outrageous," Juliette was still grumbling as she and Roma left the railway station. "Utter outrage."

"It is expected," Roma replied evenly. "I imagine they have never before encountered such mass casualties."

Irked, Juliette swiveled her narrowed eyes at him but opted to remain quiet. They had not spoken about whatever it was that had happened between them on the train, and if that was the way Roma wanted to play it, then Juliette was happy to oblige. It seemed that they were to pretend it never happened, even if Juliette could hardly look in Roma's direction now without all the little hairs on her arms sticking up.

She shouldn't have kissed him back.

He hated her, but that didn't override their whole past, nor the instinctive tug that had always drawn them into collision with each other like meteors in orbit. Juliette knew what was going on in his head because it was exactly what *she* had been circling around some few months ago, so why had she become so thoughtless as to give in? Even if he didn't hate her as deeply as he said he did, it was all the more dangerous. The whole *point* of lying to him was to keep him away. The whole *point* was that they couldn't do this again, because the moment he saw through her, then their city of blood would catch up to them, and perhaps they could be together at last if it was together in *death*.

And what was love if all it did was kill?

"—a car?"

With a start, Juliette realized she hadn't been listening, and only now registered Roma's suggestion, glancing upon the road. After handling the bodies, they had asked an officer for the directions to their destination, and the route was a simple, albeit hefty walk. Kunshan itself was classified a city, but it was a far cry from Shanghai. Rather than a living, breathing entity that turned inside out upon itself in an effort to find space, Kunshan was a small lasso on a map: a grouping of ten or so quiet towns that sat side by side with little activity past its day-to-day humdrum energy. This place was easy to navigate because it was quiet and still, but that also meant it was impossible to hide within, should they pick up a tail.

"No, we can't take a car," Juliette replied. She peered over her shoulder, eyeing the few officers that remained standing by the railway station, deep in conversation. "The blackmailer is onto us. We would be too easy to follow."

Roma looked back too, frowning when he saw that Juliette was still watching Kunshan's useless administrative officers. *"Them?"*

"Obviously not."

Juliette hurried along. At this rate, the sun would have set by the time they reached the address. The cold was biting enough already, but once night fell, it would be almost unbearable to stand outside, especially when Juliette's thick coat was a tad more fashionable than it was practical.

"However, I thought about it," she continued. "That man was sent after us in the train car, but he took his damn time transforming. Paul Dexter is the one who vaccinated me, so I cannot imagine that his collaborator does not know I am immune. They weren't trying to kill us. They were trying to scare us, collateral damage be damned."

A bell rang somewhere in the distance. Its echoes bounced down the flat row of buildings erected stoutly on the other side of the road. As Roma and Juliette walked along the footpath, a thin river flowed gently on their left, lapping into the fading evening.

Sometimes Juliette forgot that this was how the rest of the country lived. The farther one receded from the coastal cities, they also receded from coastal control, from power-hungry Nationalists and invading foreigners. They receded away from places where every move felt like life and death, and instead . . .

The river trickled into a wider stream. When a small bird came to perch upon a rock jutting from the riverbed, it barely disturbed the flow of the water.

Instead, they had the space to breathe.

"Believe it or not," Roma said now. "This monster attack was a good thing."

Juliette pulled her attention away from the water, searching for the next street sign. The last thing they needed was to get lost. "I do beg your pardon. The bodies on their way to the morgue would argue otherwise."

"Heaven rest their souls, obviously I do not wish for more death."
Roma's words were edged with a bite. "When we return to Shanghai,
I can root through every White Flower within our ranks until I find
exactly who that Frenchman was. And if our trip here does not prove
useful, then finding whoever that monster was may be the fastest way
to trace back to the blackmailer."

Juliette didn't see a point in arguing. Nothing was stopping Roma
from refusing to share the information with her if their next course of
action was solely down to him, but if she got heated about it, then he
got heated back, and they would start screaming at each other again
because it was too easy to lean into anger just for a split second of
truth. For a sign that Juliette wasn't entirely lost to him, Roma would
pick a fight. In a moment of weakness to glimpse the Roma she loved,
Juliette would entertain it. It was a volatile game. She needed to stop.
She couldn't keep doing this. If she had to turn cold, then so be it.

So all Juliette said aloud was "I hope this trip proves useful, then."

She gestured for them to move along, glancing once more over
her shoulder.

"I suspect we are here," Roma said.

He stopped, looking at the sight ahead with an undisguised puz-
zlement stamped into his expression. Juliette, too, searched along the
row of shops, thinking that they were misunderstanding something.

They were not.

The address for the alleged vaccine center was a wonton shop.

"They advertised this place across the whole French Concession,"
Juliette exclaimed. She couldn't hold back the accusatory tone in her
voice, though she was not quite sure whom she was putting at blame
here. "It cannot possibly be a scheme just to have more customers for
a bowl of húntún tāng."

Roma suddenly pulled two revolvers from the inside of his suit jacket, one tucked on each side. Juliette blinked at his fast handiwork and absently wondered how she had not felt them when she was pressed up against him earlier.

"It cannot be a mere shop," he said. "Let's go, Juliette."

By the time Juliette retrieved her pistol, Roma had already charged ahead and kicked in the shop door. Juliette hurried after him—feeling rather foolish to be storming into a wonton shop of all places—and found Roma by the register, demanding an audience with whoever had the nerve to be distributing a new vaccine. In the far corner, there was one elderly couple in the shop, eyes wide and concerned.

"Please, please!" the man behind the register shrieked, immediately putting his hands up. He was old too, but at the end of middle age, hair long and pulled back with a band. "Don't shoot! I am not who you are looking for!"

Juliette tucked her pistol away, making eye contact with the elderly couple and jabbing a sharp thumb toward the door. Not needing to be prompted twice, they hobbled to their feet and gathered their bags, scuttling out of the shop. The door slammed after them so quickly that the ceiling light flickered.

"Then who is?" Roma asked. "Who owns this place?"

The man's throat bobbed up and down as he swallowed nervously. "I—I do."

While Roma kept his weapons upon the shop owner, Juliette leaned onto the register and peered around the back of the shop. A cursory sweep revealed a table dusted with flour, a lump of dough hardening by the sink, and there, by the chair—

"Well, I see that the flyers originated from here, so no use lying your way out," Juliette said cheerily. "Lǎotóu, how are you making the vaccine?"

The man blinked, his clear terror suddenly morphing into confusion. "Making . . . the vaccine?" he echoed. "I—" His head pivoted back to Roma, eyes crossing to stare down the barrel of the revolver.

"No! I am not making anything! I am auctioning off the last vial that remains from the Larkspur of Shanghai."

Juliette pushed off the register. She exchanged a fast glance with Roma, and then, caring little for social propriety, she climbed right up on the counter in her heels and hopped into the back of the shop, retrieving one of the flyers. It was identical to the one that Ernestine de Donadieu had given them, down to the error-riddled French. Only this time, Juliette realized exactly what mistake they had made.

THE MADNESS ARRIVES AGAIN!
GET VACCINATED!

Where did it say that the location upon the advertisement would be giving out vaccinations? They had merely assumed, because that was what the Larkspur's flyers had said.

"Tā mā de," Juliette cursed, throwing the flyer down. "You have *one?*"

The man nodded eagerly, seeing it was this information getting the two gangsters off his back. "I was hoping to collect offers from foreigners, then sell to the highest bidder. I am low on cash, you see. It is not easy running a húntún shop in Kunshan, and when my cousin from Shanghai passed along this vial he had held on to—"

"Oh, stop talking, I do beg," Juliette interrupted, holding a hand up. This was not a vaccine center at all. This was an auction.

With a sigh, Roma withdrew his revolvers, shoving them back into his jacket. He was visibly annoyed. This had been a waste of time. What could they do with one vial? They had already asked Lourens at the White Flower labs to test the vaccine the last time around in an effort to re-create it, but he had not been successful.

Juliette's eyes widened suddenly.

Lourens had failed in the past . . . but the Scarlets had Paul's papers now.

"I'll take it," Juliette said, her declaration coming so loud and so abrupt that the man jumped. In a smooth motion, Juliette bent and swept up the flyer, then plucked a fountain pen from the side of the register, scribbling down a number. "My offer."

The man peered at the sum, his jaw dropping immediately. "I—I cannot simply agree. I must send telegrams in case there are higher bidders—"

"Double it," Roma cut in. When Juliette's gaze shot to him sharply, he smiled, the expression mocking. "We will share, won't we, Miss Cai?"

"What do you think you're doing?" Juliette demanded in Russian. She pasted on her own smile, so that the shop owner would not realize they had switched to a different language to argue. They didn't need the shop owner deciding his vaccine was in high demand. "You already ran tests, remember? Lourens couldn't reengineer it; he could only determine that it was true."

"Yes," Roma agreed. "That time we did not have materials from Paul Dexter. Remember, we can still steal them from you. And if you want this vial that badly, I am sure you think having it will cause a breakthrough alongside the papers."

Juliette almost started vibrating with her new irritation. He had read her through and through. He always did.

"If shàoyé and xiǎojiě each want their own . . . ," the man supplied, hands wringing in front of him. There was a new nervousness in his air. He had figured it out, then. Connected the dots on Juliette's and Roma's identities, for as soon as Roma had called her Miss Cai, it was not hard to see that the heirs of the Shanghai-native Scarlet Gang and Russian White Flowers stood before him.

"There were two in circulation after the Larkspur went under." He reached for another slip of paper, and with the same fountain pen Juliette had been using, quickly began scribbling. "The second is in Zhouzhuang, so this is the seller and address—"

147

"Forget it," Juliette said. "We only need one, so don't think you can siphon double the money from us. Take it or leave it."

The shop owner paused. Juliette could imagine the cogs turning in his head, calculating the chances that there could be a higher bidder, and the risks he would invite if he turned down Shanghai's gangsters.

Without a word, the man dropped into a crouch and started to enter a combination into a safe under the register, one that Juliette had not even noticed. She frowned, and he seemed to sense it, because as he twirled the combination dial, he said, "People get desperate, and I cannot afford guards."

The safe hissed open. The man reached in, and out came the vial, glistening the same lapis lazuli blue that Juliette remembered. She shuddered.

"I don't suppose you have cash on you, do you?"

"We'll sign IOUs," Roma replied without missing a beat. The shop owner knew who they were, after all. He knew they were big and mighty enough to keep their word; the Scarlet Gang and the White Flowers had the money.

All they had was money, really.

"Well, thank you for your business," the shop owner said gleefully, watching Roma and Juliette scrawl their names on the same sheet Juliette had scribbled her offer on. He was right to be gleeful—he had just become very, very rich. The two gangs would feel the effect of this payment, but it was nothing they couldn't recover from. The Scarlets had recovered time and time again after paying the blackmailer.

"I will be holding on to this," Juliette said, gesturing for the vial and shooting Roma a warning glance.

Roma did not complain. He let the shop owner press the vial into Juliette's hands, and while her palm was out, the man tucked in the slip of paper with the address of the second seller.

"You should take this anyway."

Juliette shoved both into her pocket. Roma only watched the motion warily, his eyes glowering black, like he suspected she would perform a magic trick to make the vial disappear. She wouldn't be surprised if he tried to make a grab for it at some point on their way back into the city.

Don't even think about it, she mouthed.

Wouldn't imagine it, he mouthed back.

"So," the man said into the silence that had fallen. "Would you two like a bowl of wontons?"

Sixteen

The last train back to Shanghai had been canceled.

"What do you *mean* it's been canceled?"

Roma and Juliette jolted and glanced at each other, disturbed by the unison in which they had spoken. The worker behind the ticket booth didn't notice. She was more occupied by the book open on her lap.

"It has been canceled," she repeated. "The train scheduled to arrive at nine o'clock was operating earlier and encountered some trouble. It has been rerouted for maintenance."

Juliette pinched the bridge of her nose. That was the very same train that had brought them *here* then, the one with the last compartment soaked in blood from a monster attack. *Maintenance.* She hoped they had some heavy-duty bleach.

"Don't tell me," Juliette managed tightly, her breath fogging the air around her, "we just missed the previous one?"

The worker peered at the timetable board. Juliette could have sworn she was holding back an amused grin. Rural dwellers were without doubt sadistic when it came to the misfortunes of city folk.

"By ten minutes, xiǎojiě," she confirmed. "Next one is tomorrow morning."

Juliette made a noise at the back of her throat and paced away from the booth, stomping along the platform.

"All the local cars have stopped for the night," Roma said, following after her, "but we can call one from Shanghai."

"By car, the two cities are almost four hours apart . . . *one-way*," Juliette replied. She stopped, observing the empty station. "It would be morning before we return if we call a chauffeur. We may as well remain here until the train comes. At least it is relatively warm."

Roma stopped too, pensive as he turned to face her. His mouth hovered open to speak. Only then his eyes widened at something over her shoulder, his whole expression turning stricken.

"Get down!"

Juliette hardly had a moment to register his command before he had grabbed her arms and yanked her to the ground. Her breath snagged in her throat, her knees scraping hard against the platform. With his hands circling her wrists and her gloved fingers curled up against the edge of his sleeves, the thought that it would be so easy to draw him close whispered through her mind, but that was all: a whisper. Easily quieted, easily snuffed out. Before she could do or say anything preposterous, Juliette shook out of Roma's grip and turned around, trying to catch whatever it was that had incited such a reaction.

"What gives?" she demanded.

Roma's eyes remained narrowed, searching the dark. "A shooter," he said simply. "A shooter who decided not to shoot, it appears."

Juliette saw nothing, but Roma had no reason to lie. There had been a strange, watchful feeling following her all afternoon, and she had thought it to be discomfort—that prickle up and down her spine only natural in a place so quiet. But maybe it had not been in her head. Maybe as she had suspected earlier, someone had been on their tail since they disembarked the train.

"Come on," Juliette said, getting to her feet. "We cannot stay, then. Not in the open."

"Where else is there to go?" Roma hissed. After a delayed beat, he hurried up too, brushing the dust off his trousers before it could stain. "Do you know how early people go to sleep around these parts?"

Juliette shrugged, forging ahead. "We are charming people. We can charm some doors open, I am sure."

But as it turned out, Roma was right. They trekked to the nearest residential block of Kunshan and started to knock on doors, making their way down the narrow streets. By the time they had twisted around and along each building, smacking their palms against every front gate, there was still no answer from anyone.

And it was miserably cold.

And Juliette was getting a prickly feeling again.

She palmed a knife, stopping at the end of the road. When Roma finally trudged over after giving up on the final building, she held out her hand, asking for him to stop too.

"It's freezing, Juliette," he managed, teeth chattering. "This was not a good idea."

"It is still better than the station," she whispered. They were surrounded by darkness, for streetlamps in a city like this were few and far between. Perhaps that was why nobody came out so late, because they had nothing to guide their way save the sliver of the moon peeking through the thick clouds. It was hard to see what was lurking out there.

"We're being followed," Juliette stated.

Roma pulled out one of his revolvers. It almost looked comical— him, aiming at nothing. "Shall I fire?" he asked.

"Don't be ridiculous," she said, pushing his arms down. Her eyes snagged on a blip of light in the distance. "Look—someone is awake over there."

Juliette started off immediately, the knife still clutched in her hand in case anyone was to jump out from the darkness. She didn't understand how they could possibly have a pursuer, though her certainty was growing stronger and stronger. All around them, there was nowhere to hide: the residential street stretched on with another thin stream flowing on one side and a dense cloister of bamboo forestry on the other.

"Do you think," Roma said, catching up with her, "that perhaps ghosts are real?"

Juliette shot him an incredulous look. "Don't be ridiculous."

"Why?" he demanded. "Once, we didn't think monsters were real either."

He had her there, but still, Juliette rolled her eyes and slid her knife into her sleeve, at last coming in view of the illuminated building. She made a tense inventory of the nearby darkness, and when it seemed there was no movement, she hurried up the steps to knock.

Juliette's hand came down once, then froze, hovering an inch away from the folding doors. Its frames were paneled with fabric— the style of buildings from the imperial dynasties. Above the doors, there was an engraving of three characters, usual for places of business to declare their function. Now, with the light beaming out from the doors, Juliette could read it.

"Juliette," Roma said, coming to the same conclusion.

An unbidden snort escaped her. "It's a whorehouse."

She hadn't said it with derision: it was truly the term most suitable. The door swept open, and a woman peered out, her robes flowing for what seemed like miles behind her. This was not like the brothels of Shanghai, not a little back area in someone's fabric shop or the top half of a restaurant. This was a magnificent structure going up at least three floors, varnished wood banisters looping in circles around each level and a fountain pumping at the very center, wafting with the sweetest floral scents.

"Hello," the woman said, tilting her head. "I've never seen you before."

"Oh," Juliette said. "We're, uh—" She cast a glance back at Roma.

He pulled an anxious expression, beseeching Juliette to handle this. "We're not customers. We're stranded overnight and were hoping for a place to stay."

At this, Roma finally cleared his throat. "We have cash to pay, of course."

The woman observed them for a moment longer. Then she swept her arms up, the sleeves of her hanfu billowing with the wind. "Come in, come in! We welcome all wayward travelers, of course."

Roma and Juliette didn't have to be encouraged further; they darted out of the cold and entered, sparing the night a warning glance in case it was watching. Roma shut the door firmly, and Juliette nodded, signaling to him that they were safe now, out of the watchful eyes of whoever—whatever—had been on their tail.

"If you'll follow me, children!" The woman was already walking off, her steps light. There was a dance to the way she moved, exchanging entertainment for attention, making every second captured upon her worthwhile.

"Thank you," Juliette called after her. "How do you prefer to be called?"

There was a sudden burst of giggling from the far corner, and Juliette's eyes landed on a kaleidoscope of colors: of flying silk and lace fans, held by delicate figures dressed in various shades of high-end qipao.

They almost sounded happy.

"Call me Miss Tang," the woman said over her shoulder. She pointed at the staircase. "Shall I put you up high?"

Juliette lifted her head and examined the higher floors, eyeing the men leaning over the banisters, girls on every side of them. Their slouches were casual, looking down and watching the rest of the house as if there were no hurry to their night. She knew that appearances were deceiving. She knew that every place had its dark side, that perhaps these girls were merely better at hiding their bitterness. The girls of Shanghai did their jobs like their life had already been sucked out of them.

But the glamour here was seductive, and nothing was more surprising than making the find in a city not renowned at all for it, not like Shanghai was. Beauty here was an art—something to perfect, and wield, and make a performance out of. In Shanghai, beauty was a transaction for one end or another.

"Whatever you have free," she sighed in reply. "We really don't mind—"

"Ah!"

Juliette whirled around, hearing Roma's yelp. She hadn't noticed that he wasn't beside her anymore. Nor had she noted when exactly he had fallen out of step. Her pulse ratcheted up, fingers immediately twitching for the blade still hidden by her wrist.

Then she caught sight of him and realized there was no need to reveal the weapons under her coat. Roma had merely been snagged off by three of the girls. He was struggling to get freed, by the looks of it, because both his arms were caught and the girls were not going to release their catch so easily, already pleading for an audience. Juliette bit down on her cheeks.

"No, no, it's okay," Roma insisted. "We're only here for lodgings, really—"

Unable to suppress it any longer, Juliette snickered a laugh. Roma's head whipped up, as if the sound had reminded him that Juliette stood three feet away. Only instead of calling for help, he exclaimed, "Lǎopó!"

The girls startled, releasing him for a short moment. Juliette wasn't laughing anymore. Her eyebrows shot straight up. *Who the hell is he calling his wife?*

Roma quickly pulled free, hurrying to Juliette's side. "I'm so sorry!" he called back. His arm came around Juliette's waist, and when Juliette jumped, immediately trying to dart away, he preempted the direction she tried to pivot in and tightened his grip. "My marriage vows forbid such mischief. Maybe in another lifetime!"

"Please forgive me," Juliette muttered under her breath. She could feel the press of his fingers through her coat. She could feel the tension in his arms, the way he was trying to stop himself from settling into the usual hold they had perfected five years ago. *Don't lean in. Whatever you do, don't lean in.* "I don't even remember when we exchanged our vows."

"Play along," Roma said through gritted teeth. "I fear they would kill me in my sleep without a better excuse."

"This isn't Shanghai, qīn'ài de. They will kill you with their kindness, not their blades."

"Speak less, dorogaya."

Juliette shot a sharp look at him, then wondered if she could get away with holding a blade in her hand and *tripping* to slice his beautiful face—just a little, a red nick here and there. She had used a term of endearment sarcastically, but she still bristled to have him do the same. Before she could grab her knife, however, Miss Tang was gesturing ahead to follow her up a winding staircase, onto the second floor.

"Ah, young love," Miss Tang said when they caught up with her at the top of the staircase. She sighed, splaying her arms against the banister theatrically. "I have almost forgotten what it is like."

Torture, Juliette replied silently. They started to walk along the second floor. *Everything hurts, and I'm certain that I am soon to collapse into agony and dust—*

"Same room or separate?" Miss Tang asked, interrupting Juliette's reverie.

"Separate," Juliette snapped, so fast that Miss Tang jumped, peering over her shoulder with wide eyes. Juliette offered an appeasing smile. "My"—she turned to Roma, just daring him to refute her—"*husband* snores extremely loudly."

Miss Tang clucked under her breath. When she came to a stop

near the rooms, it was hard to tell where exactly the doors were, given they opened and closed by a folding mechanism, hinges blending into the wall like merely another part of its elaborate decoration. But Miss Tang, all the while lecturing Juliette on putting up with a husband's flaws, pushed easily, and doors opened in on two rooms, side by side. Juliette hardly heard a word: her eyes were quick at work, searching the interior of the rooms. They looked safe enough. No chance of a waiting attacker inside ready for ambush.

"You are absolutely correct, Miss Tang," Juliette said, lying so easily she hardly registered her own words. "I'll start working on my behavior once we're back in the city."

That seemed to appease the madame. She nodded, appraising Juliette up and down. "Washroom is over there, on the far side of the building. Rest well!"

The moment Miss Tang sashayed off, Roma released Juliette like he had been prodded with an electric shock, down to the sudden flex and clench of his fists.

"Well," Juliette said. "Good night?"

Roma stomped into his room without a word, pulling his door shut. There was another low giggle nearby, and though Juliette knew they were too far away to be giggling at *her*, her hackles still rose, never fond of any chance of mockery.

"What are you getting mad at me for?" she muttered, stepping into her room too. "*You* are the one who married us off."

The burlesque club was quieter than usual tonight, so when Kathleen pulled an apron on, she figured it would be a way to kill time rather than any real work. She hadn't shown up to waitress in so long that she didn't even know who was managing the club anymore, given how quickly they were switched out depending on Scarlet inner circle ongoings.

"Table at the back is free!" one of the other girls, Aimee, shouted from the bar. "Someone go wipe—" She blinked, sighting Kathleen. "Miss Lang, what are you doing here?"

Kathleen rolled her eyes, adjusting her sleeves. She had changed from a qipao into a buttoned shirt. She was attending another Party meeting immediately after this and she needed to look the part, and if she picked up a few stains from waitressing away the few hours beforehand, then so much the better.

"I know everyone forgot," Kathleen answered, "but I do work here."

"Oh, no, that's not what I meant." Aimee wrung her rag cloth, then pushed a tray of freshly washed cups down the bar where Eileen was drying. "Miss Rosalind said she was off to eat dinner with you. She left almost an hour ago."

Kathleen froze. A serving boy brushed by, almost colliding with the elbow she had jutting out. Had she forgotten her plans? Had Rosalind asked to meet? Almost frantically, Kathleen searched through her memory, but all she could conclude was that Rosalind certainly had not made plans to eat with Kathleen, and it was unlikely that the barkeeping girls had misheard for someone else instead, because the only other possible contender was Juliette, and Juliette was out of the city.

"I . . . think she might have misremembered," Kathleen said.

Eileen didn't pick up on Kathleen's confusion. She grinned, making fast work of wiping the glass in her hands. "Or maybe she's off to see her foreigner."

Her . . . *what*? Kathleen felt like she had stepped into a film without watching the first half. Aimee hushed Eileen immediately, but her mouth had a quirk to it, as if the thought itself was amusing.

"Chen Ailing, don't spread rumors."

"About a *foreigner*?" Kathleen asked, finally recovering from her shock. "What are you talking about?"

Eileen and Aimee exchanged a glance. One of their expressions said

Now look what you did. The other said *How does she not already know?*

"Lang Shalin has been sighted with a man who might be a lover," Aimee reported, entirely matter-of-fact. "Only rumors, of course. No one's gotten a good look at his face. They can't even decide if he is a merchant or the son of a governor. If you listen to the messengers running it, the same ones would say that Miss Cai was seen embracing Roma Montagov."

Which was . . . true.

Kathleen didn't let her expression show her continued bewilderment; she merely quirked an eyebrow and turned away, making for the table at the back to begin clearing it. She hardly paid attention to the plates as she stacked them onto her arm, laying them one atop the other until she was balancing them all upon her wrist. Of late, this would be fully in line with Rosalind's peculiar behavior. And Kathleen could not fathom it, could not pinpoint when her sister had changed.

For the longest time, it had been Kathleen and Rosalind against the world. Their antics together constituted some of Kathleen's earliest memories: as toddlers climbing the mansion gates when Juliette's Nurse was not watching; as children trying to hide the bump on Rosalind's head after they failed to slide down the staircase railing; as just the two of them, playing pretend with dried leaves because there was nothing better to use. The Langs had been triplets, but hardly anyone would have known by watching the three of them interact. Even after they were sent to Paris, the dynamic remained the same. Their third sister was an empty seat at the dining table because she was in bed again fighting a cold while Rosalind and Kathleen whispered secrets beneath their napkins, giggling if the tutors asked them to eat properly. Their third sister was the empty middle seat, absent at all the events Rosalind and Kathleen crashed, leaning on each other in the back of the car and laughing louder if the chauffeur glanced back in concern.

And now . . . now Kathleen had known nothing of these rumors, though they had once shared their every secret. Of course, it was possible that there was no lover at all, merely another merchant Rosalind was accommodating for their father. Yet Kathleen still felt a suspicious chill sweep up her spine as she entered the kitchen, dumping the plates in the sink for the kitchen hands to deal with. Had they grown apart? Had Kathleen become too much of a stranger for her sister?

"What are you up to, Rosalind?" she muttered. "What aren't you telling me?"

The kitchen door slammed. Serving boys moved in and out, bustling around her as they got to work. Kathleen stayed near the tables, wiping her hands on a washcloth.

Rosalind had always trusted Celia. Maybe that was the problem here. Maybe Celia was fading, forgotten under the layers of Kathleen that she had taken on.

Kathleen shook her head, picking up a clean stack of trays and hurrying back into the club.

Seventeen

The room was too cold, and Roma couldn't sleep.

With a huff, he turned in his blankets again, eyes opening begrudgingly. The window above him had the slightest crack, and though he had tried his best to patch it up, cold air blew in relentlessly. Once or twice, he almost thought he heard creaking, like the window was being lifted, but each time he jerked his head up and squinted into the dimness, he found only stillness, nothing but the wind trying to get in. Roma turned again and unwittingly thumped his elbow hard on the wall. He winced. A second later, there came a responding thump.

Juliette.

He was going to lose his damn mind, and it would be entirely Juliette Cai's fault.

Their beds were side by side, which he knew because the walls were so thin that any time Juliette *moved*, so too did his bedframe. Every little sound she made was audible, each low, long sigh that Juliette released because she likely could not sleep either, not in a place so strange and foreign, swathed by the scent of perfume.

Roma pulled the blankets up, all the way up, over his head in hopes that it would muffle the sounds.

"Sleep," he commanded himself. "Go to sleep."

But all the same, his mind continued running on a loop, relentless between only two thoughts: *It is so* goddamn *cold,* and then, *Why did she kiss me back?*

Roma smacked the blankets off in frustration. *He* hadn't been thinking. *He* was in over his head working in such close proximity to her, forgetting constantly that she was a liar, that she had bided her time pretending to love him again just to betray him. *He* was a fool.

What was *her* excuse?

Roma shifted to face the wall. Perhaps with enough effort, he could peer right through and see Juliette there, lying next to him. Perhaps with enough effort, he could understand the girl he had been working with these past few weeks, who had killed the people he loved without remorse, yet looked at him like they were still kids playing with marbles on the Bund.

She had pushed him through the compartment door. Roma couldn't rationalize that—no matter how hard he tried. And despite the bravado that Juliette had put on, Roma had seen the horror in her eyes when she stumbled forward into his arms. She hadn't known that she was completely immune. It had been a wager, and if it hadn't worked, she would have spent precious seconds that she could have used saving herself to push him out instead.

Whatever was going on with Juliette, it couldn't have *all* been a lie. Whether it was that she turned cold in New York or she turned cold at some point in their time hunting the Larkspur, someone who had been pretending from the very beginning wouldn't have reacted that way on the train—wouldn't have protected him without a second thought, wouldn't have kissed him with the same longing that still stung his lips.

Something had been real in their past, before she chose her side. Something within her still reached for him, even if it wasn't with her whole heart, even if it was an instinct more than a choice.

Can you have a girl without the heart? Roma blew a puff of air onto his cold hands, scrunching them up against his neck. She cared for him. He could see that now. So, what then? Would he have her even with hatred running through her veins, even if she would betray him when the Scarlets asked? Just to have her near, might he pretend that she wouldn't keep cutting down the people he loved simply because he loved her most?

Roma cursed out loud, horrified by where his thoughts were going.

This wasn't him. This was weakness. Even if they were inexplicably bound to each other, he didn't want the girl without the heart. He didn't want Juliette without the love—love that wouldn't cut. Love that wouldn't destroy.

But in a city like theirs, that was impossible.

His touch feather-soft, Roma set his palm on the wall, pretending it was Juliette instead.

On the other side, in the other room, Juliette felt her bedframe shift. She opened her eyes into the silver moonlight streaming through the windows, tracing the glow that ran along the wall.

For whatever reason, weary with the day, her hand extended out of its own volition, pressing a gentle palm to the wall. She felt something thrum beneath her skin, some feeling of calm, like the whole wide ocean coming to a stop underneath her prayer. In another world, she could reach for Roma instead, but here and now, there was only a barrier, cutting between them without mercy.

Like twin statues reaching for each other, they both fell asleep at last.

Juliette dreamed of burning roses and lilies wilting at the stem. She was dreaming of so much at once that she felt like she was drowning in it, drowning in the fragrance of a thousand gardens and unable to surface.

Until she did.

Juliette stirred awake, although her eyes stayed closed. For a long second, she wasn't sure why she had awoken, and yet she had. For a long second, she did not know why she remained still, and then she did.

Juliette bolted upright. There was a dark figure at the foot of her bed, rummaging through her coat. The window was wide open, the white satin curtain blowing like a second phantom.

Juliette pulled the knife from under her pillow and threw it.

The mysterious intruder immediately grunted. He was masked, clothed in black from head to toe, but her blade had embedded into the side of his arm, a shining thing that reflected the light as the intruder jerked around, trying to pull it out. By then Juliette was already up, launching herself on the intruder and throwing him to the floor. She rammed her elbow into his neck, keeping him down.

"Who the hell are you?" she demanded.

The intruder bucked and kicked her off. He wasn't bothering with the knife in his arm anymore. He was trying to get out.

Juliette's head slammed hard into the bedframe, colliding with such intensity that she was immediately seeing double. Though she recovered fast, pushing herself onto her stomach with a livid cough, the intruder was already up. There was something in his hands. Something blue.

The vaccine.

The intruder ran out.

"No!" Juliette yelled. "No—*goddammit!*" She staggered to her feet, then shoved on her shoes. She pulled her coat around her shoulders so roughly that her weapons almost fell out, but with one hand digging around for her pistol, she kicked open her door and slapped a hand repeatedly on the one next door. The intruder was already out of sight. Downstairs, though the floor was dark and the fountain was switched off, the front door was wide, wide open.

"Roma!" Juliette hissed. "Roma, get outside *now!*"

She took off running. The good thing about having no pajamas to change into was that she was dressed already, her coat billowing after her like a cape in the wind. She charged into the night, searching the streets.

There.

"Juliette!"

Her head whipped back. Roma was coming toward her, his hair disheveled, but otherwise fully dressed too.

"What's going on?"

"Go the other way, circle around the forest patch," Juliette snapped, pointing down the street, where it led into a dense cluster of trees. "He took the vial! Find him!"

Pulling the safety on her pistol, Juliette sprinted directly into the trees. She twisted in and out of the thin bamboo trunks, shoes coming down on the dead leaves underfoot, and spotted a flash of movement: a blur of the intruder swerving sharply left. She didn't hesitate. She aimed and shot, but he ducked, and the bullet missed. Again and again, Juliette shot into the night, sending her bullets upon the briefest flash of movement, but then the intruder dove into a particularly dense grouping of bamboo, and by the time Juliette was there too, she had lost sight of him.

"Tā mā de," she spat, kicking a bamboo stalk. She should have known better; outside the safety of her house, without her usual retinue of Scarlet guards, she should have slept with one eye open, or at least with all her valuables clutched close to her chest. She had known there was someone after them, someone on their tail. But how was she to know that some masked man would climb in through the damn second-story window? And why take the *vaccine?* Why not just kill her?

Juliette smacked the bamboo again. It didn't make her feel any better. It just made her hand throb. She couldn't tell her father about this. He would use it as another reason why Juliette needed backup—needed a group of men watching her surroundings for her, as if they wouldn't have been just as useless in this situation, stationed outside her room. As if they wouldn't have just gotten in her way.

Do better. Juliette's fist closed hard. Never mind her father. If she wanted to prove to *herself* that she didn't need any damn help, she had to stop letting her guard down. She was the heir of the Scarlet Gang. How was she to hold on to an empire when she couldn't hold on to the belongings in her pocket?

Footfalls suddenly sounded off to the side, and Juliette whirled to attention, pointing her pistol. The crunching leaves came to a stop. Juliette relaxed and put her pistol away. "Did you see him?"

"Not a flicker," Roma replied, approaching cautiously. "We lost the vaccine?"

"Yeah," Juliette grumbled. "And my knife."

"That's what you're worried about?"

Roma folded his arms. His gaze was pinned on her, and Juliette suddenly resisted the urge to wipe at her face. It was bare, her cosmetics removed before she slept.

"Convenient, isn't it?" Roma said. "The vaccine we both acquired that you insisted on safekeeping has gone missing to a mysterious bump in the night."

Juliette's eyes widened. "You think I orchestrated this?" she demanded. "Does this *look*"—she whirled around to show him the back of her neck, a hand sweeping her loose hair up—"like something I would orchestrate?"

She felt the winter wind sting her bare skin, prickling against the wet blood that slowly trickled down the base of her skull. Roma gave a sharp intake of breath. Before Juliette could stop him, he had reached out and brushed a gentle finger near the wound.

"Sorry," he whispered. "That was unfair."

Juliette released her hair, stepping away. She thinned her lips, the wound at her neck pulsating with a relentless sensation now that she had focused on it. The bedframe had been as hard as rock. She was lucky it had only sliced a surface wound and not cracked her skull right open.

"It's fine," she grumbled, sticking her cold hands into her pockets. "It's not as if—" Juliette stopped, her hand coming upon a crinkle of paper. With a gasp, she yanked it out, drawing Roma's concern again until he registered what she had retrieved.

"The second vial," he said.

Juliette nodded. "Since we're already in the vicinity, how do you feel about a small trip tomorrow morning before we return?"

Eighteen

For the right amount of money, Miss Tang was more than happy to provide Roma and Juliette with a car, putting one of her men in the driver's seat and instructing him to drive smoothly. Zhouzhuang was, by all technicalities, a town within Kunshan, but it lay much farther south, practically on the same latitudinal line as Shanghai. Still, it was a simple car ride in and out, and then they could catch the next train out of Kunshan's city central.

"In and out," Juliette muttered to herself, watching their misty gray surroundings blur together through the window. No more getting jumped by mysterious figures in the dark. No more getting distracted by White Flowers pretending to be her husband. "In and out."

"Are you talking to me?"

Juliette jumped, her head—still throbbing from the night before—almost colliding with the low ceiling of the car. Said White Flower was staring at her in concern, leaning against the window on his side.

"No," Juliette replied.

"You were muttering something."

Juliette cleared her throat, but she was saved from answering further when the car started to slow, pulling into a cleared patch of hard dirt. Ahead, a canal was running quietly into the morning, its waters glistening despite the light spattering of clouds.

They had already ventured so far from Shanghai that Juliette figured they may as well return with something to show for it. Still, as she weighed the risks in her head and tried to plot a way forward for stopping the blackmailer, she wondered if she was lying to herself—if acquiring a second vaccine was nothing more than a matter she pretended was pressing just so she could sit near Roma for a second longer, her hand resting on the seat inches from his. She could not reach over, but the mere proximity soothed a part of her she didn't want to acknowledge.

The car came to a stop.

"We're here," the driver declared. "You need a guide? I know Zhouzhuang well."

"No need," Roma said, all business. "We'll be out soon." He reached for his door, then glanced at Juliette again, who remained seated. "Come on, get a move on, lǎopó."

Juliette thinned her lips, practically blowing her own door off its hinges as she got out.

"You can let that whole jig go now," she muttered.

Roma had already walked far ahead. With a sigh, Juliette reluctantly followed, dragging her feet as she too ducked under the loose willow tree and entered the canal town.

She had never visited Zhouzhuang before, but it felt familiar in the way that desert roads and snow-capped mountains did: sights that she had never glimpsed with her own eyes but plucked from storybooks and word-spun tales. As she and Roma picked carefully through the narrow footpath, edging along the side of the river canals, they kept track of the street names using small markers along the cornerstone buildings. Every so often, elderly voices would call out from within their shops, selling candy or handheld fans or dried fish, but Roma and Juliette avoided looking into the stores they passed, for they were walking so closely to the entrances that a mere second of eye contact would trap them in conversation.

Juliette suddenly paused. Where Roma swerved around the woman by the canal scrubbing at her laundry, Juliette's gaze latched on to the soap suds running along the concrete and into the water. The woman paid no attention, crouched over her task. The soap suds approached the edge . . .

Juliette dove toward the canal, her knees scraping the ground and her hand closing around the small string of pearls just as they fell over the edge, saving the jewelry before it could be washed into the water. The woman gave a cry of surprise, startled by Juliette's quick rescue.

"I gather that this isn't something you intended to toss into the canal," Juliette said, holding out the soapy pearls.

The woman blinked, realizing what had happened. She gasped, dropping her laundry and waving her hands around with fervor. "Goodness, you are heaven sent! I must have left it in one of the pockets."

Juliette offered a small, amused smile, dropping the string back into the woman's hand. "Not heaven sent; I can just spot pearls from two miles away."

There came the sound of someone clearing their throat, and Juliette looked up to find Roma waiting, brow quirked to ask why she was lingering and chatting. The woman, however, was still turned to Juliette, the crow's feet of her eyes crinkling deeper in kindness.

"Who are your parents? I'll bring some luóbosī cake over later as a thank-you."

Juliette scrambled for an answer. Roma, overhearing the offer, cleared his throat again to urge Juliette to hurry up and extricate herself.

"Oh," Juliette said carefully. "I'm . . . I'm not from around here."

She didn't know why she was being so delicate around the subject. She could have easily said that they had come in from Shanghai. But there was something entirely too genuine about the woman's offer, something untainted by the usual give-and-take exchange of the city. Juliette didn't want to ruin it. She didn't want to pop the illusion.

"Oh?" the woman said. "But you look familiar."

Juliette pulled her coat tighter around herself, then nudged a loose lock of hair behind her ear. She stood up, trying to signal to an impatient Roma that she *was* trying to wrap this up.

"I drop in sometimes," Juliette lied. "To see . . . my grandmother."

"Ah," the woman said, nodding. She turned her head out toward the water, closing her eyes for the wind to blow against her face. "It is a peaceful place to retire, isn't it?"

Yes, Juliette thought without hesitation. *Peace*—that was the all-consuming sensation making the township sound different to her ear and the air smell different to her nose. It was unlike anything she had ever known.

"Dorogaya," Roma prompted suddenly. The only reason was to avoid using her name, Juliette knew. He was playing along with the little act Juliette had put on for the woman, but her gaze jerked up anyway, her heart rabbiting in her chest. She wished he wouldn't throw the word around like that. It used to mean something. It used to be sacred—*moya dorogaya, I love you, I love you* whispered against her lips.

"I must go," Juliette told the woman, taking her leave. She surged a few steps ahead of Roma, not wanting him to see her expression until she had a handle on herself. She would have continued forward aimlessly if Roma hadn't called out again.

"Slow down. It's this way."

Juliette turned around, seeing Roma point across a narrow bridge. As he started to climb, Juliette only stood by the canal, watching the water run languidly beneath the short structure.

"I kept them, you know."

Roma stopped at the top of the bridge. "What?"

All the pearls and diamonds. All the bracelets he had picked for her later in their relationship and that one necklace when they were fifteen—the first gift he had given before he kissed her on the rooftop of that jazz club. She kept them all, took them in a box with her to New York, even though she said she wouldn't.

"Did you say something?" Roma prompted again.

Juliette shook her head. It was for the best that Roma hadn't heard her. What was the point of telling him any of that? This place was making her sentimental.

"Juliette," Roma chided when she remained yet unmoving. "A word of warning that if you fall into the water from there, I will not be coming to your rescue. Come *on*."

"I'm a better swimmer than you are anyway," Juliette shot back darkly, clutching her fists and finally starting her climb. The stone under her feet seemed to sink in and shift around. Once they were on flat ground again, Roma ducked his head to avoid a shop sign and stepped into an alley, his eyes tracing the markings along the wall; Juliette simply trusted that he was navigating correctly, more concerned with where she was stepping in case her shoes caught an uneven brick and she tripped.

They ventured deeper into the alleyway. Juliette tilted her head, listening while she walked. She was trying to decipher what was so strange about what she was hearing, until she realized it was because she could hear very little at all, and that was incredibly unusual. The walls on each side of the alley blocked out the hum and buzz of the townspeople around the canals. They boxed Roma and Juliette in, like every thin alley in this township was in its own bubble, like every twist and turn led into its own world.

"It got so quiet," Juliette remarked.

Roma made a noise of agreement. "I hope we're not going in the wrong direction," he muttered. "This place is a labyrinth."

But it was a beautiful labyrinth, one that felt not like a cage but rather an endless arena. Juliette reached out to brush the bumpy wall of the shop they passed, angling her shoulder to avoid thwacking a protruding alley pipe.

"Zhouzhuang has been standing since the Northern Song Dynasty," she said absently. "Eight hundred long years."

From the corner of her eye, she saw Roma nod. She thought that he would leave it at that, entertain her musings without much interest and think nothing more of it.

Only he replied, "It must feel safe."

Juliette glanced at him properly. "Safe?"

"Don't you think?" Roma shrugged. "There must be a certain comfort here. Cities can fall and countries can go to war, but this"— he raised his arms, gesturing at the rivers and the stone paths and the delicate ceiling tiles that decorated what were once temples—"this is forever."

It was a nice thought. It was a thought Juliette wanted to believe in. But:

"This is a town within a city within a country that is always near war," Juliette said quietly. "Nothing is forever."

Roma shook his head. He looked visibly shaken, though Juliette was not certain if it was because of what she had said or because of what her words had incited within him. Before she had a chance to ask, Roma was already brushing it off. He cleared his throat. "They call this place the Venice of the East."

Juliette scowled. "Just as they call Shanghai the Paris of the East," she said. "When are we going to stop letting the colonizers pick the comparisons? Why don't we ever call Paris the Shanghai of the West?"

A twitch pulled on Roma's lips. It almost looked like a smile, but it was so fast that Juliette might have imagined it. They were emerging from the alley now, nearing an open square with a large bridge on its opposite end. Beyond the bridge, they would find their destination.

But here, in the square, there was a group of men loitering with military weapons slung over their shoulders. Militia soldiers.

Juliette exchanged a glance with Roma. "Keep walking," she warned.

In quiet places like this, it was true warlord rule that continued to thrive. Militias patrolled the streets, utterly loyal to the one general who oversaw the wider district. The generals who had grown into warlords were no mighty figures—they were only men who had managed to seize power when the last imperial dynasty fell. The current government, really, was no more than a warlord installed in Beijing: all they had different from the rest of the warlords was the seal of approval from the international stage, but that did not mean control; it did not mean their power actually stretched any wider than the soldiers they had loyal.

"Juliette," Roma said suddenly. "How far along is the Northern Expedition right now?"

"The Northern Expedition?" Juliette echoed, taken aback by the question. "You mean the Nationalists?" She tried to remember the last update she had heard from her father, searching her memory about their campaign to defeat the warlords and unify the country with a true government. "A telegram some days ago said that they've completely captured Zhejiang."

It would have been a worry. Zhejiang was the province directly below Shanghai, but after all, what had the Scarlet Gang been doing sidling up to the Nationalists this whole time if not to ensure their own survival? The Nationalist fighting armies were edging closer and closer to the city, but it wasn't as if they were truly *defeating* the warlords. Merely placating them. Reaching agreements, so that there was an understanding about the Kuomintang's place as eventual rulers of this country.

"They may have come even closer since then," Roma muttered. He inclined his chin toward the militiamen. "Look."

It was not the men he was gesturing to. It was what the men were looking at, which Juliette saw as soon as one shifted on his feet and moved away: a rising sun, painted crudely on the outside wall of a restaurant. The symbol of the Nationalists.

"Hey, you!"

The militiamen had spotted them.

Juliette immediately stepped forward. "Who, me?"

"Juliette, stop it," Roma hissed, making a grab for her wrist. She jerked her arm out of his reach, and he didn't try again.

"Not you," one of them said with a sneer, approaching. "The Russian. Did you do this?"

"Do I look like I have the time?" Roma retorted.

The man lunged forward. "You sure have a lot of time to talk back—"

Juliette held out her hand. "Not a step closer. Unless you want your ashes scattered into the Huangpu."

Like magic, the soldier immediately halted, a clarity entering his eyes. Juliette's coat was undone now. It was time for her identity to be used, placed in the open like a playing card in a game of offensive maneuvers.

"Let's go," Roma muttered to Juliette.

When she didn't move, he nudged her shoulder. This time, Juliette allowed herself to be led off, sparing one more glance at the men eyeing her warily. Though she was finished, the one at the front of their group clearly wasn't.

"Soon it won't matter who you are, Lady of Shanghai," he called after her. "The Nationalists are coming for all of us who rule by anarchy. They will take us all down."

With one last tug, Roma had Juliette over the bridge and out of sight before she could retort.

"It's supposed to be in and out, Juliette," he muttered.

Juliette's neck gave a little *crick!* with the speed she turned to look at him. "You heard me in the car?"

"I'm a liar—what can I say?" Almost flippantly, Roma stopped and pointed up ahead. It was an old-style residence, built in a way that was utterly untouched by foreign influences and so *spacious*, because all who had once lived there and lived there still could afford it. "How are we going to do this?"

They had arrived. The residence of Huai Hao, owner of the second vial. When Juliette approached the circular entranceway, she stepped through without any care—these residences were built precisely to welcome in visitors. They were void of doors around the facility, allowing wanderers to enter and appreciate the scenery, perhaps write a poem or two as they waited for the host to arrive, if this were eight hundred years ago.

But it was the modern world now.

"I'm flattered you would let me make the decision," Juliette said, running her finger along a bird feeder.

Though she teased, she knew exactly why he was buying time to ask such mundane questions. They had thrown enough money around. The White Flowers *had* the means to pay such outrageous sums, but to keep doing it over and over without approval first was toeing the line. Juliette knew him too well—he couldn't fool her—and she knew him well enough to know that admitting this outright would be a sign of weakness.

In another world, where she was smarter, she would let him suffer, sow discord within the White Flowers. But this was her world, and she only had her present self.

"I wasn't letting you *make* the decision," Roma replied. "I was asking your opinion."

"Since when did you value my opinion?"

"Don't make me regret asking."

"I've a feeling you already do."

Roma rolled his eyes and marched ahead, but then there was the sound of a door sliding, and Juliette grabbed the back of Roma's coat, yanking him back. They ducked behind the bird feeder, hearing two sets of footsteps approach their direction.

"Mr. Huai," a voice called. "Please, slow down. Shall I call for the car, then?"

"Yes, yes, do one thing right, could you?" a gruff voice snapped.

The second pair of footsteps hurried back in the other direction, but another kept walking. Soon, he was in view, and Juliette poked her head out to find a middle-aged man strolling for the exit. He already had so much here. Opulence and luxury on par with the city. It was a far cry from the man in the wonton shop. There was no desperation to survive. There was only greed. And Juliette, too, could play greedy.

"You asked how we are to do this," she whispered to Roma. "How about like this?"

She reached into her coat, and as Mr. Huai walked by, not noticing his intruders despite how exposed they were, Juliette stepped out in front of him and leveled her gun to his forehead.

"Hello," she said. "You have something we would like."

Nineteen

News of a monster attack arrived in Shanghai far before their rival darlings did. Already—regardless that the casualties had occurred out in the countryside—the people of Shanghai were boarding up their windows and locking their doors, finding quarantine to be a better solution than risking madness on the streets. Perhaps they feared the monster, who was said to have crashed out the moving train windows and rolled upon the hillsides. Perhaps they feared that it would soon stumble into city limits, spreading infection.

Benedikt threw half of his sandwich into the trash, strolling under the flapping shop banners. Again and again, no matter how many times the White Flowers said it, no one cared to listen. These monsters were not random hits. So long as the White Flowers behaved, so long as they continued fulfilling demands . . .

It had been a while since the last demand came.

Benedikt stopped. He turned over his shoulder. It felt like he was being watched: from both above and below. Eyes on the rooftops and eyes in the alleys.

It wasn't his imagination. Quickly he spotted a boy on his tail, lingering at the mouth of an alley. When Benedikt locked gazes with him, the boy hurried out, stopping two paces away. He was a whole head shorter than Benedikt, but they looked the same age. There was a white rag tied to his ankle, half-covered by his tattered trousers. A White Flower, then, but not an important one. A messenger, most likely, if he was chasing after Benedikt.

"I'm looking for Roman Nikolaevich," the messenger huffed in Russian. "He is nowhere to be seen."

"You decided to tail me for Roma?" Benedikt replied, his eyes narrowing.

The boy folded his arms. "Well, do you know where he is?"

Benedikt's eyes only narrowed further. "He's not here." All the lower-tiered White Flowers should have known that. It was not difficult to keep attuned with the important members of the gang; it was the messengers' job to keep track of where one was most likely to be in order to find them.

And who still called Roma *Roman*?

Suddenly Benedikt's hand snagged out and grabbed the messenger's wrist. "Who *really* sent you?"

The messenger's jaw dropped. He tried to tug away. "What do you mean?"

In one smooth motion, Benedikt twisted the boy's arm behind his back, then pulled forth a pocketknife and pressed the blade to his neck. It was nowhere near any major artery to act a threat, but the messenger froze, eyeing the blade.

"You're a Scarlet," Benedikt guessed. "So who sent you?"

The messenger remained quiet. Benedikt pressed his knife in, cutting the first layer of skin.

"Lord Cai," the messenger spat quickly. "Lord Cai sent me because we know. We know that the White Flowers are behind the blackmail demands."

Benedikt blinked rapidly. "We are not," he said, confused. "Where did you hear such information from?"

"It is too late now." The messenger tried to writhe about. "Lord Cai wanted confirmation and confession, but Tyler will have you answer for your insolence. You dare threaten the Scarlet Gang, you pay with blood and fire."

Just as Benedikt was about to let go of his hold on the Scarlet messenger's arm, the Scarlet twisted his head and bit down hard on Benedikt's hand. Benedikt hissed, dropping his knife, and the boy bolted, disappearing down the street in record speed. Hardly any of the onlookers by the food stalls even blinked.

Something was wrong.

Benedikt rushed for headquarters, his heart pounding in his ears. By the time he was nearing the residential block, he could already hear the yelling. When he tried to push through the front door, he was almost pushed right out.

"Hey, hey, cut it out," he snapped, fighting through the crowd. At the center of the living room, the same White Flower who had asked Benedikt to help assemble the wardrobe was clutching a slip of paper in his hands, his face practically red as he explained its contents. Benedikt caught bits and pieces as he struggled closer. *Bank statement. Our latest payment. Exact number. Scarlet account. It's them.*

"Order!" Benedikt roared.

The room became still. Benedikt was almost surprised. He had never commanded attention like this before. It was always Marshall jumping on the tables or Roma snapping one directive that swept the room like ice. But now neither Marshall nor Roma was here. Benedikt was the only one left.

"Give me that," he snapped, holding his hand out for the paper. "What are we crowing over?"

"It was sent to us, Mr. Montagov," a voice within the crowd answered. "Proof that we have no blackmailer, and it has been the Scarlets all along."

So why did the Scarlet messenger say the exact opposite?

"Don't move a muscle," Benedikt said without looking up, stop-

180

ping the group near the door in their tracks. They had been on their way out, guns at the ready to find Scarlets to fight. With Benedikt's instruction, they were forced to look as he turned the paper around, tapping the top corner.

"The account is registered to Lord Cai," one insisted, even as he squinted where Benedikt was pointing. "The deposit amount matches the last demand we paid—"

"It's not real," Benedikt interrupted. "I want the Scarlets dead too, but don't be foolish. No bank crest in this city looks like this—it is not even a good inking." He tossed the paper to the table, flicking his hands for the men to disperse. "It is the blackmailer once again. The Scarlets got the same falsified document blaming *us*. Now get back to your jobs."

"Benedikt."

The summons came from above. Benedikt's head snapped up—as did everybody else's in the living room—to find his uncle atop the staircase. Lord Montagov's hands were crowded with silver when he set them on the handrails, rings that glinted by the light of the sunset streaming through the windows.

"Did you say," Lord Montagov said slowly, coming down the steps, taking one at a time like he had to weigh himself on each landing first, "that the Scarlet Gang received the same information?"

Benedikt could feel sweat starting at the back of his neck. "I was accosted by one of their messengers on the streets," he said carefully. "He accused us of sending the threats."

"And still"—Lord Montagov came down the last few steps, the nearest men parting to make way for him, a path clearing toward Benedikt like some miniature Red Sea—"knowing their malicious intent, you stop our own from rushing out?"

An abrupt, scraping sound came from the wall outside, like someone had slipped off and fallen to the ground. Before Benedikt could entertain the possibility of an eavesdropper outside, a White Flower messenger—a true one, this time—scrambled through the door, heaving for breath.

"Come quickly," he gasped. "Tyler Cai is launching an attack."

"I will find the Frenchman," Roma said when the train pulled into Shanghai, the station coming into view. "And as soon as I find him . . . perhaps he will be afraid enough to tell us directly who turned him into a monster."

Juliette nodded absently. Her eyes watched the window, pinned on the approaching platform. The sky was horribly dark, but the hour was also growing late. They had spent longer in Zhouzhuang than Juliette had liked, and the car ride back to Kunshan had been slowed by the potholes on the gravelly roads.

"It will not be that easy," Juliette grumbled. "Not if the blackmailer sent him right after us. He did not even bother hiding his face." She turned away from the window and looked at Roma. "But still—it is better than nothing. We work from there."

Roma rose and reached up to gather his coat from the overhead storage. Before Juliette could stop him, he had hers too, tossing it upon her.

"Careful," she chided. She stuck her hand into the pocket, checking on the vial they had stolen from Mr. Huai. It was fine, the blue liquid sloshing at its half-filled point. She had a sneaking suspicion that Roma had intended for her to worry that he was going to damage it; he was not foolish enough to *forget* it was in her pocket.

Especially not when he had the other half of the vaccine in his pocket, separated into its own vial.

"We have arrived at the destination," the compartment speaker announced as Juliette got to her feet. The train came to a screeching stop, but even after, as the noise faded, there was still a dull roar coming from the misty grayness outside, and Juliette peered

through the window again, searching for the source.

"Do you hear that?" she asked.

She didn't give Roma any time to respond. Juliette was already hurrying off the train, watching her step over the platform gap and surging into the crowds jostling at the station. This wasn't right. There were too many people here. Why were there so many people?

"Juliette!" Roma called. His voice was almost immediately drowned out, and when Juliette glanced back momentarily, she had already lost sight of him.

A sharp police whistle sounded to her right. Juliette whipped her attention to the officer, who had one foot balanced on the base of a column while the rest of him clung to it, putting him a few feet above the masses. He was waving at people to move off the platform and into the station, but only because droves of people were hurrying in from outside.

Juliette grabbed the nearest person. An elderly woman stared up at her with wide eyes, lips tightening in recognition.

"What's going on?" Juliette demanded. "Where are all of these people coming from?"

The woman's gaze darted to the side. In her hands, she was holding today's newspapers, crumpled under her tight grip.

"Smoke outside," she managed. "A gangster safe house is on fire."

Coldness swept down Juliette's spine like a lightning strike. *Marshall*. She let go of the woman so fast that they both stumbled, but then Juliette was moving, her pulse pounding in her chest as she shoved her way through the station.

Maybe it was only a small fire. Maybe it was already well controlled.

With a gasp, Juliette emerged outside, right onto Boundary Road—aptly named given that the Shanghai North railway station sat at the very border of the International Settlement. Juliette needed only to look up, observing the state of the skies above the International Settlement.

The sun was to set within the hour, so there was yet enough light to show great big plumes of smoke, driving those on the streets toward whatever shelter they could find.

"No, no, *no*," Juliette mumbled under her breath, throwing her arm over her nose and breaking into a run. She locked her watering eyes on the plumes, diving forward even as civilians fled in the other direction. Once or twice, she heard sirens in the distance, but the sounds were far enough that Juliette knew she would get to the scene first.

Then a terrifying scream echoed into the air: a sharp and unusual piercing that sounded neither human nor animal. She stopped right in her tracks, waving the smoke out of her eyes. The safe house where she had put Marshall was much farther ahead, but the screaming was coming from the next street over, which meant—

"Oh, thank *God*," Juliette cried. It wasn't hers. It wasn't her safe house. But then . . . what was burning?

Juliette ran the rest of the distance, cutting through a dark alley. She found herself coming onto a wide road, joining the crowd that was gathered before the spectacle. The people here had not run as those farther away had. They were enraptured by the horrific scene, just as someone experiencing the end of the world would stop and stare.

"I have never before seen such a sight," an old man beside her croaked.

"It is the work of the blood feud," his companion replied. "Perhaps they are getting their last hits in before the Nationalists arrive."

Juliette pressed her knuckles to her lips. The smoke plumes flowed from a building entirely swathed in flames, and standing around it, like soldiers guarding an enemy castle, were Tyler and a flock of Scarlet men.

Tyler was laughing. She was too far away to hear what he was saying, but she could see him, holding a plank of wood swirling with flames. Behind him, the building's roaring inferno drowned out the screams, drowned out the whole occupancy burning to death. Juliette heard nothing save that they were *pleading*—women in nightgowns and elderly banging on the closed windows, muffled Russian crying to *stop! Please stop!*

In the third-floor window, there was a little hand reaching through a hole in the glass. Seconds later, a small face appeared, hollow and ghastly and tear-tracked.

And before anyone could do a thing about it, the hand and the child dropped out of view, succumbing to the smoke.

The screams had sounded so strange from the railway station— almost animal—because they had come from *children*.

Juliette fell to her knees, a sob building against her throat. There was a shout from behind her: clear Russian, rather than muffled— White Flower forces, arriving for a fight. She couldn't find it within herself to run. She would be killed if she lingered here, pathetic and brittle on the side of the road, but what did it *matter* when this whole city was so broken? They deserved to die. They all deserved to die.

Juliette choked on her sudden gasp, caught by surprise when a pair of hands closed around her arms. She almost started to struggle before realizing it was only Marshall Seo yanking her into the nearest alleyway, a cloth covering the lower half of his face. As soon as they were in the alley, Marshall ripped off the cloth and raised a finger to shush her, the two of them keeping quiet as a group of White Flowers moved past the mouth of the alley.

Roma was among the group, his face aghast. Seconds later, Bene- dikt ran up to him from the other direction, giving Roma's chest a hard shove as he began to yell.

Roma. Oh God. What was he going to think? Juliette had run off without explanation. Would he suspect that she had a hand in this? Would he think that their trip to Kunshan had been a ploy, an attempt to get him out of the city so the Scarlets could launch their attack?

In his shoes, Juliette would jump to the exact same conclusions. She should have been pleased—wasn't this exactly what she desired? For him to hate her so violently that he wanted nothing to do with her?

Instead, she only burst into tears.

"What has Tyler done?" Juliette rasped. "Who approved this? My father? When has the blood feud ever involved innocent *children*?"

"This isn't just the blood feud," Marshall said softly. He grimaced, then wiped at Juliette's tears. She was letting them run. More and more gangsters on both sides were arriving, and by the sudden gunshot sounds, Juliette guessed a fight to be breaking out. "The blackmailer tricked both gangs. Your Scarlets think the White Flowers are the ones making the demands. They hurried to get the upper hand, desperate to show that they were too strong to be messed with. Tyler led the attack."

Juliette dug her nails into her palms. Her skin throbbed with pain, but it didn't make her feel any better.

"I'm sorry," she managed. "I'm sorry his heart is so wicked."

Marshall frowned. He was trying to hold back his look of distress, but Juliette still saw it in the speed with which he tried to clear her tears. Once, she might have protested, might have feared the weakness she was showing. Now she did not want to pretend that she felt nothing; she would welcome the world's pity if it meant she could just stop *hurting*.

"The wickedest part isn't his heart," Marshall said. He glanced to the end of the alley, jumping ever so slightly when a spray of gunfire came near. "It is that he is truly acting on Scarlet interests, dear Juliette. The wickedest part is that this city is so deeply divided as to allow such atrocity."

Juliette breathed in deeply, steadying herself. Indeed, it always came back to the blood feud. It always came back to the hatred that ran through the very veins of this city, not their hearts.

"What are you doing here?" Juliette asked now, scrubbing the last of the wetness from her face. "I *told* you to stay inside."

"If I hadn't come out, you would be over there getting shot by Roma," Marshall replied. "Nor would I have heard—" He broke off, misery flashing through his expression. "I was too late. I ran faster than the other White Flowers did, but I couldn't stop it."

"It's good that you didn't try." Juliette straightened up, forcing Marshall to look at her. "It is not worth it, do you hear me? I cannot take Tyler down if you just give him more ammunition by revealing yourself to be alive."

But Marshall just stared at the mouth of the alley. For someone who usually could not stop talking, he was eerily silent, his eyes tracking the flashes of violence that came near.

"Mars," Juliette said again.

"Yeah," he replied. "Yeah, I know."

Juliette bit down on the insides of her cheeks, flinching when the yelling got closer.

"I must run back to Scarlet territory and get backup," Juliette said with regret. "No matter how wicked Tyler and his men are, I will not stand by and watch them be outnumbered." She paused, then heaved an exhale. "Go help him, Marshall."

Marshall's eyes swiveled back. "I beg your pardon?"

"Benedikt," Juliette clarified. "Go help Benedikt. You look like you're ready to claw off your own skin in helplessness."

Marshall was already tying the cloth back around his face. When he pulled the hood of his outer jacket up, he was unrecognizable, only another part of the rapidly falling night. "Be careful," he said.

Another spray of gunfire.

"I should be telling you that," Juliette said. "Hurry!"

Marshall ran off, joining the fray, joining yet another fight of the blood feud that was tearing this city into pieces.

And Juliette turned on her heel, retreating to bring more forces to their death.

Benedikt could hardly see past the sheen of red in his vision. He didn't know if the red was from fury or actual blood, splattered along his temple and dripping into his eyes.

"Get over here," Roma hissed from some paces away. His cousin was crouching behind a car, gun in hand. Benedikt, meanwhile, was only standing behind a streetlamp, hardly covered given the thinness of the pole. Up ahead, Scarlets were in a shoot-out with the rest of the White Flowers, and the odds were not looking good for their side. The Scarlet numbers were only growing, though this was White Flower territory. Someone within Scarlet ranks had to have gathered reinforcements the moment this started. The White Flowers were not so lucky.

"What's the use in hiding?" Benedikt asked. From where he stood, he fired off a shot. It hit a Scarlet in the leg.

"I'm not asking you to hide." Roma, making a frustrated sound, stood suddenly, fired a shot, then ducked back down. "I'm asking you to get over here so we can *leave*. This is turning into a slaughter."

Benedikt's vision flashed. The red cleared for blinding white. Night had fallen around them, and their surroundings would have been dark if not for the fire still raging in the safe house, consuming the walls and lives within.

"We cannot just leave the fight," Benedikt snapped.

"You're a damn Montagov," Roma hissed, his words just as sharp. "Know when to concede. That's how we *survive*."

A Montagov. Benedikt's stomach roiled as if he had just ingested something rotten. Being a Montagov was exactly what had gotten him here in the first place—right in the middle of a blood feud, bitter as bone, with only his cousin by his side and no one else.

"No," Benedikt said. "I do not walk away." He charged headfirst into the fight.

"Benedikt!" Roma roared after him.

Roma ran to his side, giving him cover as they both fired, working as fast as they could. But the road had turned to a battleground, soldiers stationed at every strategic place. Though their bullets were running out, gangsters were not afraid to grapple, and before Benedikt could call out a warning, there was a Scarlet diving for Roma, knife in hand.

Roma cursed, narrowly dodging a heavy blow. When the Scarlet tried again, his cousin's fight became a blur in the dark, and Benedikt needed to pay attention to what was coming at *him*—first a bullet that narrowly missed his ear, then a flying blade, slashing him in the arm only when he dove to the concrete.

The ground trembled: the fire had finally eaten up a gas pipe. There was a colossal shrieking sound, and then the upper half of the house burst with an explosion and collapsed in on itself.

Benedikt staggered to his feet. His mother had died to the feud. Nobody had given him the details because he had been five years old, but he had sought them out anyway. He knew that after she was killed—an accidental casualty of a shoot-out—they had burned her body right in an alleyway until only charred smithereens remained.

Maybe this was the way he would join her. The Scarlets would kill him, then throw him right into the raging fire—ashes to ashes, dust to dust.

Benedikt gasped. This time, when the bullet flew at him, he felt it graze his shoulder, sending sparks of pain up and down his arm. Before he could think to raise his weapon again, something hard came down on the back of his head.

And everything went dark.

Marshall winced, catching Benedikt before he fell. Quickly, he nudged his friend over his shoulder, hoping that no Scarlet was watching them, and if they were, that the Scarlet would think Marshall was merely one of their own, dealing with a White Flower. Roma was somewhere in the chaos too, but he could handle himself. If he couldn't, their men would surely jump in front of him. It was only Benedikt who seemed to need forcible removal. Marshall felt bad for having to hit him so hard.

"You got less heavy," Marshall remarked, even though Benedikt was unconscious. It felt less . . . kidnappy when he talked as he ran, as if Benedikt were keeping pace beside him rather than being tossed around. "Have you been eating? You're keeping some strange habits, Ben."

A sudden shout nearby shut Marshall up. He pressed his lips thin, ducking under the cover of a closed restaurant. When the group of Scarlets passed, Marshall continued moving, muttering a quiet prayer up into the heavens that they were already on White Flower territory. Within minutes, he was in front of a very familiar building complex, nudging the door open with his elbow and entering, arms straining.

"Please tell me you haven't started locking up," Marshall whispered. "I'm going to be so mad at you if you only started locking up after I died and never when I told you to before—"

Their front door opened easily under his palm. With a breath of relief, Marshall stumbled in, taking a moment to sniff at the apartment. It seemed different. Losing an occupant would do that to it, he supposed. The air was dusty, as was the kitchen counter, like it had not been wiped in weeks. The blinds were crooked, pulled up once some time ago and then abandoned, allowing half-light to enter in the day and only blocking out the half-dark of the night.

Marshall finally entered Benedikt's room and carefully set him onto his bed. Now that they were safe, the exertion of his kidnapping task caught up at once, and Marshall rested his hands on his knees, breathing hard. He did not move until his heart stopped thudding, tense in fear that the sound was so loud it would stir Benedikt awake, but the other boy remained still, his chest rising and falling in the barest of motions.

Marshall dropped to a crouch. He watched him—resolute just to watch him—like he had done these past few months, a pair of eyes following Benedikt's every move in fear that Benedikt would do something foolish. It was strange to be so close again when he had gotten used to being a shadow. Strange to be near enough that Marshall could reach out with his fingers—and suddenly his hand *was* hovering forward, brushing a blond curl out of Benedikt's face. He shouldn't. Benedikt could wake upon disturbance, and the last thing Marshall needed was to break his most important promise to Juliette.

"How mighty you are," he whispered quietly. "I am grateful that our roles are not switched, for I would have dove headfirst into the Huangpu should I be left in this world without you."

Before the White Flowers, Marshall's childhood had been dreary hallways and snatches of fresh air when he managed to wander out. If his mother grew too occupied with her dressmaking, Marshall was trekking into the fields behind the house, skipping stones on the shallow creeks and scraping moss from the rocks. There was no one else for miles—no neighbors, no kids his age to play with. Only his mother hunched over her sewing machine day after day, her gaze caught out the window, waiting for his father to return.

She was dead now. Marshall had found her body, cold and still one morning, tucked in bed as if she were merely frozen in sleep.

A soft sigh. Marshall's hand stilled, but Benedikt continued breathing evenly, his eyes closed. Abruptly, Marshall stood, tightening his fists in reminder to himself. He was not supposed to be here. A promise was a promise, and Marshall was a man of his word.

"I miss you," he whispered, "but I haven't left you. Don't give up on me, Ben."

His eyes were burning. Staying here a second longer would undo him. Like a curtain being drawn across the stage, Marshall stood up and trailed out from his former apartment, fading back into the darkness of the night.

Twenty

Benedikt awoke in the morning with his head pounding something awful. It was the glare of light in his eyes that had roused him out of sleep, and it was the glare of light now worsening the ache at the base of his skull, the feeling reverberating outward and down his spine like some skeletal menace was pinching at his nerves.

"Christ," he muttered, lifting a hand to block out the sun. Why hadn't he pulled his bedroom blinds before going to sleep?

Benedikt bolted upright. When had he even *gone* to sleep?

The moment he started to move, his shoulder pulled with a sharp discomfort, and he glanced down to find a small pool of blood on his sheets—entirely dried by now, having seeped from the shallow wound. Benedikt rolled his arms around gingerly, testing the extent of his injuries. He was stiff but otherwise fully functioning, at his usual level, anyway. The wound had closed on its own, and he had no clue how long he had even been lying here, letting his body knit itself back together.

Flabbergasted, Benedikt pulled his legs to his chest, resting an arm on his knees and pressing the flat of his hand into his forehead, trying to push the headache back. He tried to visualize the last thing he could remember, and all he saw were bullets in the night, the raging inferno of the safe house in the background. He had been charging toward a Scarlet, pistol in his hand, and then . . .

Nothing. He had no idea what happened next. He didn't even know where his gun had gotten to.

"How is that possible?" he asked aloud. The house did not answer him. The house only stirred with his voice, shifting and exhaling in the way that all small spaces did every once in a while.

Suddenly, so viciously that Benedikt was almost bowled over, he caught the faintest whiff of a scent—of gunpowder and pepper and deep, musky smoke.

Benedikt shot to his feet. *Marshall.* The pain came to him all over again, like the first morning he had awoken and remembered, remembered that this apartment was empty, that Marshall's room was empty, that his body had been left to cool on the floor of an abandoned hospital. Benedikt was losing it. He could *smell* him. As if he had been here. As if he were not *gone.*

With a ragged inhale, Benedikt yanked a new jacket out of his wardrobe and tugged it on, hardly bothering to go easy on his throbbing shoulder. What was the point? What was one more point of pain against the whole smorgasbord? He was a damn walking collection point for grievances and grief.

He closed all the doors in his apartment—three times—then walked the short distance to the main Montagov residence, letting himself in. Before any of the White Flowers in the living room could take notice of him, Benedikt was slinking up the stairs, climbing to the fourth floor. Unprompted, he walked into Roma's bedroom, shutting the door after himself.

Roma jumped, immediately whirling around on his desk chair. He had a cotton pad in his hand and a mirror in the other. There was a wound on his lip, running scarlet red.

"I was looking for you *all* night," Roma snapped, throwing the mirror down. "Where the *hell* did you go? I thought you were dead in a ditch!"

Benedikt slumped onto Roma's bed. "I don't remember."

"You don't"—Roma stood, then rested his hands on his knees, his voice pitching up ten octaves—"*remember?*"

"I guess I hit my head and got myself home."

"You were there one second and nowhere the next! The fight hadn't even dispersed before you were gone. I almost got flayed because I kept looking around and searching—"

Benedikt got to his feet too, cutting his cousin off. "I didn't come here to argue with you."

Roma threw his hands into the air. He was exerting so much energy in that one motion that his cheeks flushed with color. "I am hardly arguing with you."

Silence. Roma's expression shifted from annoyed to thoughtful to grim within the span of seconds as the two Montagovs stared at each other, having a silent conversation with nothing but facial expressions. They had grown up together. No matter how far they were pulled apart, the language of childhood was not one easily forgotten.

"You can't keep working with Juliette," Benedikt finally said, tearing right into the wound of the matter. "Not after this. Not after what they did to us."

Roma turned away, placing his hands behind his back now. He was buying time. He only paced when he couldn't puzzle through his answers.

"This whole thing was orchestrated," Roma said in lieu of an answer. "The blackmailer struck again, had us think the Scarlets were responsible, had the Scarlets think we were—"

"I know it was orchestrated. I'm the one who figured it out," Benedikt cut in, seconds away from giving his cousin a hefty shake. What part of this was hard to understand? What part of this was hard to *see?* "But her people chose to set those fires. Her people burned *children* to death."

Roma swiveled around. "Juliette is not her people."

And Benedikt snapped. "Juliette let your mother die! Juliette killed *Marshall!*"

His voice crashed across the room with the same intensity of a cannon, landing with complete devastation. Roma rocked like he had been physically hit, and Benedikt, too, clutched his stomach, bearing the kickback of his words.

That—that was the central point which they could not forgive. Even mothers could be forgiven, in a city soaked in blood. But Marshall Seo could not be.

"I *know*," Roma spat. The volume came unwillingly, like he hadn't wanted to shout, but that was the only way this conversation could be tolerated. "I know, Benedikt. God, don't you think I know?"

Benedikt laughed. It was the most humorless sound, somehow blunt and bladed at once. "You tell me. Because you sure act like everything can be forgotten, gallivanting off with her like this."

"He was my friend too. I know you two were a hell of a lot closer, but don't act like I didn't care."

"You don't get it." Benedikt couldn't think past the roar in his head. Could hardly breathe past the twist in his throat. "You just don't get it."

"What, Benedikt? What could I possibly not get—"

"*I loved him!*"

Across the room, Roma exhaled out once, letting the rest of his anger go in that short breath. Quick as his surprise came, it was gone in the next beat, like he was kicking himself for being surprised at all. Benedikt, meanwhile, put his hand to his throat, like he could swallow his words, could return them inside his lungs where they once lived undisturbed. He shouldn't have said that. He shouldn't have said anything at all . . . but he *had* said it. And he didn't want to take it back. He meant it.

"I loved him," Benedikt said again, softly this time, only to feel what those words tasted like on his tongue a second time.

He had known all along, hadn't he? It was only that he could not say it.

When Roma looked over, his eyes were glistening. "This city would have destroyed you for that."

"It has destroyed me anyway," Benedikt replied.

It had always taken, and taken, and taken. And this time, it took too much.

Roma strode toward him. For half a second, Benedikt considered that Roma was coming to attack him, but instead, his cousin drew him into a fierce hug, arms as steady as steel.

Slowly, Benedikt returned the embrace. Doing so felt like seizing a gasp of his childhood, plainer days when his biggest worry was the sparring mat and whether he was going to get the wind kicked out of him. It never mattered even if he did. Roma always helped him back up again.

"I'll kill her," Roma whispered into the quiet of the room. "On my life, I swear it."

Twenty-One

Juliette slammed down the telephone receiver, letting out the faintest scream. She sounded so much like a whistling tea-kettle that one of the maids at the end of the hallway peered over her shoulder, checking if the sound had come from the kitchen.

With a sigh, Juliette retreated from the telephone, her fingers red from the excessive cord twirling. At this point the switchboard operators probably recognized her by voice alone, given she was calling so many times a day. She had no choice. What else was she to do? Suffice it to say, after Tyler's arson, their cooperation with the White Flowers had ended, and when Juliette asked her father if it would not be beneficial to meet at least once more, her father had thinned his lips and waved her off. She couldn't comprehend why Lord Cai would be eager to work with the White Flowers one moment, and when Juliette was finally onto something—when she *needed* their resources to find the identity of the Frenchman who had transformed into a monster—suddenly it was no good working with the enemy.

Who was the one whispering into her father's ear? There were too many people coming and going from his office to ever begin making a list. Had they been infiltrated by White Flowers? Was it the Nationalists?

"Hey."

Juliette jumped, her elbow banging against the jamb of her bedroom door. *"Jesus."*

"It's Kathleen, actually, but I appreciate the holiness," Kathleen said from upon Juliette's bed. She flipped her magazine. "You look stressed."

"Yes, I *am* stressed, biǎojiě. How perceptive of you." Juliette pulled her pearl earrings out, setting them onto her vanity and massaging her lobes. It turned out that wearing earrings and pressing a receiver to her ear for hours at a time did not go well together. "Had I known you were home, I would have roped you into helping me."

At this, Kathleen closed her magazine, sitting up quickly. *"Do* you need my help?"

Juliette shook her head. "I jest. I have it handled."

For the past week, since the White Flower safe house burned to the ground and Roma hadn't responded to any of her delivered messages, Juliette had been calling every French hotel in their directory, asking a series of the same questions. Was any guest acting peculiar? Was anyone making a mess in their rooms? Leaving behind what might look like animal tracks? Making too many noises at random hours of the night? Anything—*anything*—that might signal someone keeping control of monsters or turning into a monster themselves, but Juliette had gotten nothing but false leads and drunks.

She heaved a long exhale. At present, gravel was crunching from somewhere outside, beyond Juliette's balcony doors. When Kathleen walked over, peering through the glass, she reported, "That looks like your father coming home."

Seconds later, Juliette identified the sound of tires rolling down the driveway.

"You know what strikes me as strange?" she asked suddenly. The front door opened and closed. A burst of voices downstairs signaled the arrival of visitors accompanying her father's return, interrupting an otherwise leisurely late morning. "There has only been one attack thus far, two if we count the train. And it is awful of me, but I cannot help but feel as though there should be more."

"But there have been sightings," Kathleen said. She leaned up against the balcony glass. "Numerous sightings."

"Largely at the workers' strikes," Juliette countered.

The first time, she had brushed it off. Roma thought it to be a rumor; she had thought the same. Only now the rumors were coming from police officers and gangsters, more and more of them arguing that they were unable to defend their post—defend against the striking workers as they tore down their factories and stormed the streets—because they had spotted a monster in the crowd.

"I don't know," she went on. "I imagine releasing insects would spread fear much faster than mere sightings."

Kathleen shrugged. "We have labeled this person a blackmailer for a reason," she said. "It is not Paul Dexter. The purpose isn't chaos. The purpose is money and resources."

But still, Juliette bit down on the inside of her cheeks. Something did not sit right with her. It was like she was looking directly at a picture and seeing something else because someone had already told her what to look for. Just as she had charged into a wonton shop without thinking about how it didn't make any sense for it to be a vaccine center. She had merely assumed from the beginning—from the moment she laid eyes on that flyer—because that had been the case once before.

So what wasn't she seeing now?

"Miss Cai?"

Juliette tucked a curl behind her ear, turning her attention to the messenger when he stuck his head into her room. "Yes?"

"Lord Cai summons you. His office."

The ruckus of voices drifting down the hallway was growing louder. It sounded like her father had a whole assembly in his office.

Tired as she was, Juliette moved immediately, exchanging a meaningful glance with Kathleen and then hurrying out into the hall. Though she didn't know exactly what she had been summoned for, she could take a guess as soon as she slipped into her father's office and found it filled to the brim with Nationalists.

"Oh boy," Juliette muttered beneath her breath. She had entered late, it appeared, because they were mid-debate, one Kuomintang man already speaking with his arms clasped behind his back. She recognized him—or rather, recognized the fact that his lapels were decorated to every square inch.

General Shu. She had looked into him since her father's warning. Among the Kuomintang, he was powerful enough to be second to Chiang Kai-shek, their commander in chief. He wasn't in Shanghai often—he had an army to lead, after all—but if the expedition finally reached the city, it would be his men who marched in first.

Juliette's dress started to itch at her skin, too long and bright among so many dark suits. Her mother was nowhere in sight. Only her father, behind his desk.

"—it is best to protect those who matter first. What good is there aiding those we want gone?"

Suddenly, Juliette caught sight of another very familiar figure in the corner of the room. Tyler was seated with the slightest of smiles, legs propped wide and something that looked like a chunk of blue dough hanging from his fingers. She squinted closer. It was a familiar blue. Lapis lazuli blue.

Juliette understood now. Her dear cousin had been spending all his time at the Scarlet facility in Chenghuangmiao overseeing their efforts for this reason precisely. The vaccine was ready. And Tyler had brought in the news ahead of anyone else, giving him first access to a room full of Nationalists, letting him set the stage before Juliette even had a chance to say a word.

"We do as Cai Tailei proposed," General Shu said.

"No," Juliette snapped. Heads turned fast in her direction, but she was ready, discomfort fading from her skin. "What kind of government are you going to be if you let your own people die?"

"Even once we are in power," General Shu said, offering her the sort of placating smile that one would give a child, "there are certain people who will never be our *own*."

"It doesn't work like that."

The Nationalists in the room bristled, as did Tyler.

"Juliette," Lord Cai said plainly. There was no reproach in his tone. That was more of Lady Cai's trademark, and she wasn't here to be offended at Juliette's social decorum. Her father was merely reminding her to think carefully about every word coming out of her mouth.

General Shu turned to face Juliette, his eyes narrowing. As a powerful war general, he could surely read a room; Juliette was getting away with saying such things to his face, so Juliette was not a mere girl he could flick away.

Juliette was, perhaps, a threat.

"The Communists are growing out of control," General Shu boomed. He was looking at Juliette, but he spoke to the whole room, capturing their attention like the esteemed guest of a rally. "They are overpowering the Kuomintang party. They are overpowering the city. The moment they rise"—he pointed a finger at Juliette—"you and I are both out of power, little girl. The moment the Communists take over, the Kuomintang and the gangsters die alongside one another."

He might be right. He might be predicting their exact future. And still:

"You'll regret it," Juliette said evenly. "Shanghai is its people. And if you let its people die, it'll come back to bite you."

At last the Nationalist seemed to be reaching the end of his patience. He thinned his lips. "Perhaps you have not heard?" he said. "The Communists have allied with the White Flowers."

The Communists have—what?

Before Juliette could say anything else, General Shu turned his address elsewhere, hands pressed cleanly to his sides. His mind was made. Perhaps everyone else's in the room was too.

"It is the only option, Lord Cai," another Nationalist said. "Our enemies grow in power, and if we protect them, we lose this opportunity. Revolution is coming any day. Before it does, let their numbers be culled. Let their chances of success die a pitiful death."

Juliette took an involuntary step back, hitting the door with her shoulder blades.

"I suppose it is truly the only option," her father said. "Very well. We keep the vaccine within our own circles."

In the corner of the room, Tyler lifted the corner of his mouth in a smirk.

Juliette spat a curse and swung the door open, then pulled it shut after herself with a loud slam. Let the men jump. Let them be afraid of how she moved, like a hurricane intent on destruction. Her father might chide her for leaving so suddenly, but she doubted he had the time for discipline.

Why the hell *would the White Flowers ally with the Communists? There is no benefit at all.*

Juliette stormed back into her bedroom, almost short of breath.

"The Communists and the White Flowers are working together," she said to Kathleen, who startled, not expecting to see her back so soon.

Kathleen's magazine slid right out of her hands. "I beg your pardon?" she said. "Since when?"

Juliette twisted her arms around her middle and sat primly on her bed. Their two enemies had just merged like the head of a reverse hydra. "I don't know. I—" She stopped, blinking at her cousin, who was now sliding off the blankets and getting her shoes on. "Where are you going?"

"Making a phone call," Kathleen answered, already walking out the door. "Give me a minute."

Juliette dove backward, splaying her arms and legs like a five-point star atop her sheets. Roma was supposed to have found the Frenchman by now. They were supposed to have threatened or tortured a name out of him and eradicated the threat of a blackmailer. But in all honesty, it didn't even seem to matter. Who cared about a few dead bodies if revolution was sweeping into Shanghai? What was one blood-soaked nightclub up against a blood-soaked city? This blackmailer was not Paul Dexter. They didn't want the city flooded with monsters and madness; they only wanted . . . well, Juliette didn't know.

"See, this is why we always check our sources."

Juliette bolted upright, her hair crackling with her movements. The pomade in her curls would start to loosen if she kept disturbing it like this. "Is it false?"

"Not false exactly," Kathleen replied. She closed Juliette's bedroom door, leaning up against it like her body was an additional barrier against eavesdroppers. "But it is not Lord Montagov who has allied with them. It is a sect within the White Flowers that the Communists are bragging about having secured. Honestly, with the way Da Nao was talking . . ." Kathleen trailed off, her thin, arched brows furrowing together in thought. "I wonder if the Montagovs even know about it."

The intrigue only seemed to thicken. Juliette shuffled back on her bed, drawing her leg up and pressing her chin to her knee. For three long seconds, she stared into space, trying to make sense of what Kathleen was saying.

If he is a White Flower, Juliette had asked on that train platform, *then why does he look rather murderous toward you, too?*

"What do you mean by a sect?"

Kathleen shrugged. "I mean exactly what I think Da Nao meant. A group within the White Flowers seems to have enough power and influence to be making agreements with the Communists on their own. They may have been working together for quite some time now—it is only that the information has recently slipped to the Nationalists."

And just like that, the connection snapped in place.

"Huh."

Kathleen blinked. "Huh?" she echoed, mimicking Juliette's casual tone. "What's that supposed to mean?"

Juliette drew her other leg onto the bed too. If any of her relatives saw her right at this moment, they would surely chastise her for sitting in such an appalling manner.

"The blackmailer was asking for money and money and more money, and then suddenly *weapons*? Why weapons?" She inspected her fingers, the varnish on her nails and the barely visible chip on her pinkie. "What if it's the Communists? They need weapons for revolution. They need money *and* weapons to break from the Nationalists and take the city."

The Communists working with a sect of the White Flowers who did not heel to Lord Montagov's nor Roma's word. It made perfect sense. It was why, for months, the monetary demands had only come to the Scarlet Gang before ever approaching the White Flowers. Because they were *already* siphoning resources out of the White Flowers.

"Slow down," Kathleen said, though Juliette was speaking plenty slow. "Remember what happened the last time you accused a Communist of the madness."

She remembered. She had accused Zhang Gutai and killed the wrong man. She had been led astray by Paul Dexter.

But this time . . .

"It makes sense, does it not?" Juliette asked. "Even if the Communists have their revolution, even if they get rid of us gangsters, they cannot overthrow their Nationalist *allies*. The only way they can win this revolution without the Nationalists swooping in afterward and claiming that Shanghai has been taken for the entire Kuomintang to enjoy"—Juliette splayed her hands out—"is by preparing to fight a war."

Silence swept into the room. All that could be heard were the sprinklers outside watering the gardens.

Then Kathleen sighed. "You better pray it is not. You may be able to kill a monster, Juliette. You may purge all the insects that a foreign man has brought in. But you cannot put yourself in the middle of a war."

Juliette was already scrambling up, opening her wardrobe. "If the Communists are using these monsters to start the war, then I sure can."

"I fear you will kill *yourself* trying."

"Kathleen, please." Juliette poked her head into her hangers, searching the floor of the wardrobe. She caught sight of a few revolvers, discarded necklaces, and a shoebox—which contained a grenade, if she was remembering correctly. At the back of the mess, her lightest coat had fallen into a bundle. She retrieved it and shook it out, then held the garment in the crook of her elbow. "I'm not that easy to kill."

Kathleen was trying her best to pull an angry face. It wasn't as effective when she was smoothing a hand along her softly curled hair, twisting a strand along her finger.

"A secret White Flower working with the Communists still doesn't add up," she argued. "This all began with Paul Dexter's note. *In the event of my death, release them all.* He wrote to someone he knew. He wrote into the French Concession."

"A French White Flower," Juliette replied in answer. "It still tracks."

"But—"

"I have someone who might know something. I've got to go now so I can get back before our trip with Māma this afternoon."

"Hold on, hold on, hold on."

Juliette halted, the door half-open under her hand. Quickly, Kathleen hurried over and pressed the door closed again, waiting a second after the soft click to ensure no one was outside.

"It's about Rosalind."

Oh. Juliette wasn't expecting that.

"She's coming later, isn't she? To the temple?"

Lady Cai had insisted upon it. She needed an entourage, and her usual crowd couldn't offer accompaniment when the temple only allowed women. Juliette and her cousins had been gifted the honor of playing bodyguards. It was unlikely that there was any need for protection at a women-only temple, but such was life as a figurehead of a criminal empire. At the thought, Juliette walked back to her vanity and slotted an extra knife into her sleeve.

"Yes, I expect so, but that's not what I'm talking about," Kathleen said, waving the question away. "Were you aware she has some secret lover in the city?"

Juliette whirled around, her mouth parting. A hint of glee slipped out as she exclaimed, "You're joking."

Kathleen propped her hands on her hips. "Can you sound a little less excited about this?"

"I'm not!"

"Your eyes are *glowing*!"

Juliette tried her best to school her expression, feigning earnestness. She pushed her coat farther up her arm before it slipped from her elbow. "I didn't know about this, but it's not so bad. You were worried about Rosalind falling into trouble with merchants. Isn't a lover better in comparison? Now, I really have to go—"

Kathleen held her arm out, physically preventing Juliette from leaving. With the way that her cousin was eyeing the coat on her arm, she wouldn't be surprised if Kathleen stole it next, just so Juliette couldn't walk out.

"Allegedly, the lover *is* a merchant," Kathleen said. "You're not the least bit concerned why Rosalind hasn't *told* us?"

"Biǎojiě"—gently, Juliette eased Kathleen's arm away from the door—"we can ask her about it when we see her. I have to go. I'll meet you later?"

With a grumble, Kathleen stepped aside. Juliette thought she had finally gotten through, but as she stepped into the hallway, unfolding her coat, her cousin said, "Don't you get tired of all this?"

Juliette paused in her step, pulling her coat on. "Tired of what?"

Kathleen's lips curved up. She squinted into the doorknob, its golden gleam bouncing her reflection back at her in miniature.

"Chasing answers," her cousin replied, dabbing a finger at the corner of her mouth. The line of her lipstick was already a perfect bow. "Eternally running around trying to save a city that does not want to be saved, that is hardly *good enough* to be saved."

Juliette hadn't expected such a question; nor had she expected to reel from trying to answer it. Down the hallway, the voices were still communing in their meeting, leaving her out of whatever plan would soon beset the city. The men who governed this place did not want her help. But she was not doing it for them; she was doing it for everyone else.

"I'm not saving this city because it is good," she said carefully. "Nor am I saving this city because *I* am good. I want it safe because I wish to be safe. I want it safe because safety is always what is deserved, goodness or wickedness alike."

And if Juliette didn't do it, then who would? She sat up here on a throne encrusted in silver and dusted with opium powder. If she didn't use her birthright to offer protection where she could, what was the point?

Kathleen's frown only deepened, but there was too much to unpack, especially while Juliette was hovering on her toes, rushing to leave. All that her cousin managed was a soft sigh and then: "I beg you to be careful."

Juliette smiled. "Aren't I always?"

"You look a mess."

Juliette rolled her eyes, pushing past Marshall to get inside. She could smell the city on her skin: that mix between the windblown salt coming in from the sea and the unidentifiable jumble of fried food-stuffs permeating the streets. There was no avoiding it whenever she rode through on a rickshaw.

"I have a question," Juliette said immediately, pulling the locks on the safe house door.

Marshall wandered deeper into the room—not that there was any-where to go in such a small space—and collapsed on his mattress. "Is that why you have arrived without gifts to bear?"

Juliette palmed a knife into her hand and pretended to throw.

"Ah!" Marshall yelped immediately, throwing his arms over his face. "I jest!"

"You'd better be. You certainly pick up enough things to eat and drink whenever you go outside."

Juliette put her knife away. With a stride that could be described more as stomping than walking, she made her way over to the mat-tress too and dropped down beside him, her dress clinking with noise.

"You're my only White Flower source right now," she said. "What do you know about your communication with the Communists?"

"The Communists?" Marshall echoed. He had been lying back, elbows propped on the sheets, but now he sat up straight, brows knitting together. "Most of the Russians in this city are Bolshevik Revolution refugees. When have the White Flowers ever liked the Communists?"

"That's what I want to know," Juliette grumbled. She blew a piece of hair out of her eyes, and when that did nothing to get the lock away from her face, she huffed extra loudly and pushed it back, smooshing it with the rest of the tangle.

"Given, it is not as if I am very up to date with the latest White Flower goings-on." Marshall reached for something tucked near the wall, his whole arm straining to make contact without moving from position. When he finally retrieved it, he returned to Juliette with a flourish. "May I? It's hurting my eyes to look at you."

Juliette squinted at what he was holding, trying to pick out the label in the dim light of the safe house. She snorted when it registered. Hair pomade.

She inclined her head toward him. "Please. Make me pretty again."

In silence, Marshall scooped a clump of pomade and started to brush through her hair with his fingers. He made fast work of re-forming her curls, though his tongue was sticking out in concentration, as if he had never tried shaping longer hair but he would be damned before Juliette told him he was doing it wrong.

"You should ask Roma," Marshall said, finishing a curl near her ear. "It's his job, is it not?"

"That's a little difficult right now," Juliette replied. The blood feud pushed away her answers about the blackmailer. Politics pushed away her chances at protecting the city so they wouldn't *need* answers about the blackmailer. Why did everybody in this city insist on making life so *difficult* for themselves? "None of this would even be happening if General Shu would just let us distribute the vaccine."

Marshall froze. He tried to hide it, tried to resume with the curl as if nothing happened, but Juliette sensed the delay, and her head swiveled to him, interrupting his work.

"What?"

"No, nothing—let me—"

"Marshall."

"Can I just—"

"Marshall."

The edge in Juliette's voice got through. With the slightest shake of his head, Marshall continued to feign casual, but he said: "I had some ties to the Kuomintang before joining the White Flowers, that's all. General Shu is bad news. Once he latches on to something, he won't let go. If he doesn't want a Scarlet vaccine distributed across the city, it's never going to go out."

Juliette supposed she wasn't surprised at that, given what she already knew about the man. But:

"Weren't you a child when you joined the White Flowers?"

Marshall shook his head again, more firmly this time. "It was a youth group. Now . . ." He shifted one last curl in place. "You no longer look like a rickshaw runner dragged you through the mud. Happy?"

"Overjoyed," Juliette replied, getting to her feet. Something still sounded a little off, but she hardly had the time to prod at it. "I'll take my leave now, but—"

"Stay inside, I know." Marshall waved her off. "Don't you worry about me."

Juliette shot him a warning glare as she walked to the door, but Marshall only grinned.

"Goodbye, you menace."

Twenty-Two

As it turned out, when Lady Cai said that she needed accompaniment to the city temple in the afternoon, she meant the very minute noon passed, and now Juliette was late. When the car came to a stop, Juliette leaned into the rearview mirror and retouched her hair once more before tumbling out, searching for her mother and her cousins. She tried not to bristle when indeed she found Rosalind and Kathleen alongside her mother, as well as *Tyler* with a group of his men.

Since his stunt with the safe house, the Scarlets had praised him with vigor. She was having quite some trouble doing the same.

"We almost thought you wouldn't come," Rosalind said as Juliette joined her, eyes still fixed on Tyler. He was cleaning his pistol, twisting a cloth roughly along the barrel. If he wasn't careful around the trigger, it was going to go off and then one of his men would have a hole blown through the stomach.

"I didn't think everyone left so early." Her mother had sighted her now and was coming this way. "What is Tyler doing here?"

"He came with your mother," Kathleen supplied, standing to Rosalind's other side with her arms crossed. "Extra protection for the walk."

Juliette tried not to grit her teeth so hard. She was going to put a crack in her jaw at this rate.

"Ready?" Lady Cai asked, smoothing her qipao down and waving them along. Tyler stayed put where he was, his men spreading out along the entrance into the temple walls, but Juliette gave him one last look before turning and following after her mother.

"So, I heard an interesting rumor."

In synchrony, Juliette and Rosalind lifted a foot over the protruding threshold into the temple. Anytime Juliette needed to do this to enter a building, she could gauge its age—gauge that it had been built before the roads were entirely smooth and the people had needed to protect against the possibility of floods. The temple itself was a quaint building, but a vast courtyard circled its perimeter, protected by tall, sun-faded walls with two golden gateways to the north and south, each facing the sides of the dusty red temple.

Rosalind's eyes slid over. "Quoi?"

"Une rumeur," Juliette repeated, perhaps with an unnecessary bout of flourish as she switched to French too. "Floating around the city."

"You know better than to—" Rosalind stopped suddenly, looking beside her. When Juliette turned too, she realized it was because Kathleen had stalled behind, pausing just after the entranceway, looking around the courtyard. It appeared like she was waiting for something.

"Mèimei," Rosalind called. "You okay?"

A small smile played at Kathleen's lips. "I'm fine."

Juliette and Rosalind waited for her to catch up, walking again only when Kathleen had fallen back in step. They passed a silver xiānglú—one that was so enormous it looked like a giant bowl fitted with an awning. Three women stood around it to light their incense, delicately holding their sleeves so as not to get caught in the flames in the basin.

"We were just talking about Rosalind's lover," Juliette said to Kathleen.

"Shh!" Rosalind immediately hissed, her gaze snapping up to make sure Lady Cai hadn't heard.

"Then it *is* true," Kathleen exclaimed.

"Do the both of you want to yell any louder?"

"No one here understands us, c'est pas grave." Juliette bounced in her step. "Why haven't you told us? Where did you meet?"

Rosalind's expression tightened. "You really should not trust what the whispers say."

"Rosalind." Kathleen sounded stern now, as if she just wanted an answer. "Why are you being so secretive about this?"

"Because . . ." Rosalind swept another look around. By then they had almost reached the temple building, trailing far behind Lady Cai, who was climbing the steps up. There was no one around them, no one to overhear their conversation even if they happened to speak French.

"Because?" Kathleen prompted.

And all in one breath, Rosalind said, "Because he's associated with the White Flowers, okay?"

Juliette felt a sudden lump in her throat. The smell of incense permeated the entire courtyard, getting stronger with the closer they approached the temple. It clotted in her nostrils, almost choking her airways if she didn't just *exhale*—

"That, I didn't expect," Kathleen remarked evenly. "Here I was thinking it was politics, and you gave me blood feud instead." Meaningfully, Kathleen caught Juliette's eye. Rosalind didn't know about Juliette's past with Roma . . . but Kathleen had some idea, even if it was not the full picture.

"It's not ideal, Rosalind," Juliette finally choked out. *Speaking from personal experience. From very, very personal experience.* "If my parents find out—"

"Which is exactly why they won't." Rosalind lifted the edge of her qipao, starting up the steps. Kathleen made to follow, but Juliette's skirts swished around freely at the knees. "We were first introduced in a bar on neutral territory, and I only ever see him in places that switch between Scarlet and White Flower just about every second day. Give it some more time and I'll have convinced him away from the White Flowers. No one has to know."

Juliette tried to shake off her terror. She nudged her cousin, hoping that a faked brightness would inject real energy into her outlook. "No one has to know," she echoed. "We'll help you—right, Kathleen?"

Kathleen, on the other hand, was not afraid of grimacing. She didn't even try to look happy. "Ugh, I suppose. It's a dangerous game, Rosalind. But we're on your side."

It was a dangerous game, but nowhere near as dangerous as the one Juliette was playing. She had to remind herself that it wasn't the same. That Rosalind could be happy, that they didn't all have to end in bloodshed.

"The three of you walk so slowly," Lady Cai said when they finally caught up. Inside the temple, the daylight seemed muted, stopping outside the open doors like it didn't have an invitation. Instead, the red of the shrines took on its own glow, casting the temple in a warm sheen.

"Merely taking in the parameters, Māma," Juliette replied.

Lady Cai blew out a short breath like she didn't believe her. "I see the client. Don't go far, Juliette. Maybe—" Her mother waved her hand at the far wall, where a smattering of women knelt in front of symbolic deities. They would kētóu three times, foreheads briefly touching the floor mats, then plant their incense into the shrines. "Qù shāoxiāng ba?"

Juliette scoffed. "I think the ancestors might strike me down if I initiate any contact with them. I'll just wait here. Kathleen and Rosalind can go if they want."

Kathleen and Rosalind exchanged a glance. They both shrugged.

As Lady Cai left to approach the client, Juliette's two cousins found their own incense sticks and went back outside to light them, leaving Juliette to wander about the temple.

"Don't be offended, ancestors," Juliette murmured under her breath. "I'll bring you a few extra oranges next time." She cast a glance at her mother. The meeting seemed mundane: two women speaking to each other about matters designated as more delicate than their husbands could handle. The woman handed over a stack of papers. Lady Cai scanned through them. Juliette turned back to the shrines, chewing on her thoughts.

A Frenchman, a monster, a blackmailer. Communists, Nationalists, civil war.

A vaccine, ready to circulate.

She simply wasn't working with enough information. All she had was conjecture. No names, no sources. And while she was supposed to be thinking about fixing the state of the city, she was thinking about Rosalind's plight too, and how unfair it was that even after the black-mailer was gone, the city would always, always be divided.

Juliette scanned their surroundings again, patient as her mother's conversation went on. It was this time that she sighted the long pew in the corner of the temple and became fixated there, finding some-thing of note. As Juliette stepped closer, she saw one girl seated alone, reading a small book. Something about her blond hair was familiar.

Juliette stiffened. She spared another glance over at her mother to ensure Lady Cai was not looking her way, then, as quickly as she dared, hurried over to the pew.

"Alisa Montagova," Juliette hissed. "This is Scarlet territory. What are you *doing* here?"

Alisa's head jerked up, her eyes widening. She slapped her book closed, as if the illicit activity at present was her reading.

"I—" The girl winced. "I wasn't going to stay long. I just didn't think anyone would care about the blood feud in a women's temple."

"Okay, but"—Juliette looked around again—"*why?* Why are you here?"

Alisa blinked, seeming to realize that Juliette's panic was not over her presence alone. She had tried to seem tough, but now her expression was tightening in confusion. "We had a funeral in the cemetery a few streets over. I got tired of standing, so I snuck away."

The cemetery a few streets over . . . Juliette tried to envision the layout of the city in this region, knowing immediately which cemetery Alisa was referring to. In her head, she traced their route out, assuming attendees were to move from that section of White Flower territory and into the east of the city, where most of them lived. No matter what, they needed to pass the front of the temple, where Tyler was currently waiting with all his men.

Juliette spat a curse. "Who was present, Alisa? Your father? Inner circle?"

By now Alisa had gotten to her feet. Juliette's concern was scaring her. "No, not Papa. But Roma and Dimitri—"

A bullet went off in the distance, outside the temple walls. To anyone else, it could have sounded like a rickshaw crash or a food cart coming up hard against the sidewalk. But Juliette knew better. She shot off, tearing through the courtyard, already reaching for the weapons on her body. By the time she was approaching the gate of the temple walls, the scene was already unfolding before her: twenty, thirty gangsters, and civilians—so many civilians nearby, looking stunned.

Too many civilians for gunfire. Too many likely victims of stray bullets. The gangsters in the brawl had realized too, else there wouldn't be so many going at hand-to-hand combat now, else there wouldn't be a White Flower half strangling Tyler, almost pressing her cousin to the floor.

Without slowing in her run, Juliette jumped over the threshold of the temple entrance and pulled the knife sheathed at her thigh. When she threw, the blade pierced into the White Flower's neck smoothly, striking its target with nary a sound before the White Flower pitched sideways and fell.

"You're welcome," Juliette snapped, coming to a stop in front of Tyler and holding out a hand.

Tyler grinned. He gripped her fingers and stood. "Thank you, dearest cousin. Duck."

Juliette dove to the side without questioning it. A White Flower lunged forward, and Tyler engaged, but as Juliette spun around, still locked in her crouch, her gaze shot through the chaos and locked right with another figure who had paused in the fray.

"Tā mā de," she muttered. *Roma.*

A sudden prickle of an idea occurred to her. As Roma marched forward, locked on her for a target and probably intent on running a dagger through her heart, Juliette formed her plan. He wouldn't respond to her messages, wouldn't work with her any longer, but she needed him. Who better to know whether there was a White Flower sect collaborating with the Communists than Roma Montagov, heir of the White Flowers? If he would speak to her only to fight the blood feud, then Juliette would use the blood feud.

Juliette shot to her feet, trying to make a break for it. She could cut an easy path through the brawl. She could stay low and dart through that empty pocket of space. . . .

Someone grabbed her by the back of the neck. Juliette sensed a blade—or *something*—about to come down on her, and her hands launched up. She pulled, yanking the arm over her shoulder until she heard a socket pop. Her attacker shouted. Just as he tried to bring the knife in his other hand down, Juliette darted out of the way and spun around, pressing her forearm against her attacker's neck, both of her feet braced against the concrete road.

It wasn't Roma who had grabbed her; it was Dimitri Voronin. A quick snap of her eyes confirmed Roma was still trying to fight through the thick of the brawl, but he was on the move toward her.

"Juliette Cai," Dimitri greeted, acting like they were exchanging pleasantries. "I heard you grew up a socialite. Where did you learn to grapple like a street urchin?"

"I gather you don't know much about socialites."

Using his height against him, she hooked a foot behind his knee, grabbed a fistful of his hair, and slammed Dimitri's head into the ground. She kept moving, emerging from the fight and scanning the temple walls quickly. Alisa had followed her out, peeking from the archway of the temple entrance.

Juliette shot a look over her shoulder. Roma was still watching her. Good.

"Come with me."

Alisa blinked, taken aback by Juliette's sudden appearance before her. "What?"

Without waiting for an answer, Juliette hauled Alisa by the arm and took off.

Twenty-Three

Juliette pulled Alisa back into the courtyard. Briefly, she thought she caught Rosalind and Kathleen out of the corner of her eye, but her cousins needed to stay by her mother's side, and so they did not come after her, nor ask what she was doing.

"I promise I'm not going to hurt you." Juliette glanced over her shoulder again. Roma had made it out of the crowd, a splatter of blood on his collar. His eyes were ablaze, vivid in their violence. "I just need to bait your brother somewhere quiet. *Run!*"

They ran until Juliette found a thin alleyway. She shoved Alisa in fast, sparing no time before she kicked several trash bags, stacking them tall so they acted like a barricade. Then she pushed Alisa to hide, slotted behind the bags and out of view.

It wasn't that she was trying to scare Roma. She simply had a feeling that Alisa didn't need to see whatever was going to happen next.

Roma came into view, his chest rising up and down from exertion. With one glance at the tight grip he had on the pistol in his hand, Juliette knew she was right.

"Why are you doing this?" Roma spat. His expression was hateful—but his words were tortured. Like he wished she would just disappear instead, so that he didn't have to deal with her, so that he didn't have to be vengeful. "What the hell are you doing?"

Juliette held out her hands. As if showing that she was unarmed would make any difference.

"Listen to me for a second," she pleaded. "I have information. About the blackmailer. It might be coming from within the White Flowers. I'm here to *help*—"

Juliette flinched, narrowly sidestepping his first shot.

"I was going to make it quick," Roma intoned. "As a mercy. For what we once were."

"Will you listen to me?" Juliette snapped. She sprang forward, and the gun went off again, missing her, but so barely that she felt the heat skim her shoulder. His pistol was still smoking when she closed her hand around the middle of the barrel. Roma tried to shoot again, but by then Juliette had turned the pistol skyward, letting him empty out three bullets before she thumped a hand hard on the inside of Roma's elbow. His arm slackened, and she threw the gun out of his grip.

"This wasn't hard for you to understand a month ago," Juliette hissed. "The city is in danger. I can *help* you."

"And you know what I have realized since then?" His hand darted into his pocket for another gun, and Juliette tackled him fast, throwing him to the ground of the alley and using her two hands to pin his arm to the floor. The move was familiar, like that first time Roma ambushed her near Chenghuangmiao, but if the memory meant anything to him, Roma didn't show it.

"I have realized," he continued, keeping his arm still for that moment, "I do not care about this city, or the danger it brings onto itself. I cared for people, and now the people are gone."

He kicked out, and Juliette rolled away to avoid the hit, swallowing her wince of pain when she landed hard on her elbows and her forehead nearly smacked into the rough wall of the alley. Roma was up in the blink of an eye, looming over her with the gun, and she didn't think; she just lunged. This was a true fight now—vicious and unflinching. Each time Roma tried to shoot, Juliette tried to disarm, but he had not known her so long for nothing, and he predicted her moves well enough that Juliette's head was soon spinning from colliding against the concrete ground multiple times. Throwing herself out of harm's way too fast and too hard was painful, but it would sure as hell be more painful if she didn't avoid his quick hits and strikes.

"Roma!" Juliette spat. Her elbow slammed hard against a stack of bricks, having finally writhed out of their grapple with his blade in her hand. *Victory.* She threw the blade, hearing it clatter and spin out of the alley. "Listen to me!"

He stilled. She almost thought she had gotten through to him, but then his eyes narrowed, and he hissed, "The time for listening has long passed."

He dove for the blade.

From the very moment he raised his arm, Juliette knew he had aimed too high. Roma had always been a bad thrower, which never made any sense because he was so damn good with his bullets. But he loosed his grip from the end of the alley, and time slowed down; Juliette tracked the blade, predicting it to sail so far above her head that it was comical—

Then Alisa Montagova stood up from her hiding place, scrambling to her feet and calling out a plea to end the fight.

"Please, don't hurt each other—"

Before Juliette could think, could even take a moment to *gasp*, she shot up, diving in front of Alisa. She didn't realize what she had done—not really—until she came to a stop in front of the other girl and there was the hard *thunk!* by her ear.

Alisa's eyes grew wide, her words cutting off and her hand flying to her mouth.

The pain did not come at first. It never did: a blade entering always felt cold and then foreign. Only seconds later, as if her nerve endings had finally registered what happened, did intense, sharp agony reverberate outward from the wound.

"Mudak," Juliette managed, turning to look at the blade half-embedded in her shoulder, then at Roma. His jaw was slack, face drained of color. The wound, meanwhile, immediately started to bleed, a steady stream of red running its way down her dress. "You just had to throw the one with a jagged edge?"

That seemed to startle Roma into action. He walked forward, slowly at first, and then at a run, nearing Juliette and grabbing hold of her arm. She watched him examine the wound. Even if Juliette were uninjured, she didn't find a reason to be frightened. His anger—however momentarily—had dissipated.

"Alisa, run to the nearest safe house and get the emergency first-aid box."

Alisa's eyes grew to enormous proportions. "Are you planning to stitch her up yourself? She needs the hospital."

"Oh, that would go down well," Roma said tightly. "Shall we take her to a Scarlet or a White Flower facility? Who will shoot a little slower?"

Alisa balled up her fists. Juliette was still alert enough to pick up the clamor of the fight coming from a distance, but she couldn't quite feel her fingers anymore, nor squeeze her own fists.

"It's only down the road, Alisa." Roma pointed forward. "Hurry."

With a huff, Alisa spun on her heel and hurried off.

Juliette breathed out. She almost expected to see her breath, as she would on a cold winter's day. Instead, there was nothing: the coldness was coming from inside her. A numbness was flooding her limbs, little prickles like every cell in her body was trying to go to sleep.

"Put pressure on the wound, would you?" she asked casually.

"I know," Roma snapped. "Sit."

Juliette sat. Her head was spinning, doubles and triples appearing in her field of vision. She watched Roma tear his jacket off, balling it up and adjusting the fabric around the blade, pressing as hard as he dared to stop the blood from running. Juliette did not protest. She only bit down on her lip, bearing the pain.

"What is *wrong* with you?" Roma muttered after a while, breaking the silence. "Why would you do that?"

"Stop you from knifing your own sister?" Juliette closed her eyes. Her ears were humming with white noise. "You're welcome."

Roma's frustration was tangible. She knew exactly what he was thinking—why take a hit for Alisa when she had been the one threatening to shoot his sister at the hospital? None of this made any sense. Of course it did not make sense. Because Juliette couldn't make up her damn mind.

"Thank you," Roma said, sounding like he could hardly believe he was saying those words. "Now open your eyes, Juliette."

"I'm not going to sleep."

"Open. Them."

Juliette snapped her eyes open, if only to glare at the alley space in front of her. It was then that Alisa returned clutching a box to her chest, her cheeks red and her breath coming in gasps.

"Ran as fast as I could," she huffed. "I'll watch the alley while you . . ." Alisa trailed off, not knowing precisely *what* Roma was going to do.

She dropped the box by her brother, then ran for the other end of the alley. When Juliette strained her ears again, she realized that there was no shouting in the distance anymore. Alisa had likely noted the same thing: the fight was over. The gangsters would be fanning out soon, looking for them.

If Juliette was going to talk to Roma, she needed to do it now, before it was too late. He had already stopped trying to stanch the wound, flipping the box open and unscrewing a bottle of something pungent. He set it aside.

"I'm cutting your coat off," Roma said. Another blade appeared in his hand, slicing through the fabric at her neck before Juliette could protest. When he peeled the coat away from her thin dress, all Juliette could smell was the metallic tang of blood. If her shoulder hadn't been in overpowering pain, she would have thought some stray alley cat was giving birth nearby.

Muttering a curse, Roma put his fingers to the zipper at the back of Juliette's dress.

"You know," Juliette said, barely stopping her teeth from chattering, "you used to ask before you undressed me."

"Shut up." Roma tugged the zipper down. Just before he peeled aside the dress, he yanked the blade out.

"For crying out—"

"I do suggest keeping it down," Roma said tightly. "Would you like a handkerchief to bite?"

Juliette's head was too light to respond immediately. She was going to faint. She was definitely going to faint.

"I'll bite nothing unless it's your hand," Juliette muttered. "Raw. And detached."

In response, Roma merely passed her the blade he had stabbed her with.

"Hold this."

Juliette reached for it with the arm that did not have a weeping gouge in its attached shoulder, then clutched the blade to her chest, holding her dress up. She blinked hard to keep herself alert, then watched Roma as he shifted to a crouch beside her, making quick work of finding a clean rag in the box and dousing it with the foul-smelling bottle.

It took everything in her willpower to hold back her scream when Roma clamped the rag to her wound. The antiseptic stung like a thousand new cuts, and Juliette had half a mind to ask whether Roma was actually poisoning her instead. His eyes were not on his task; he was scrutinizing Juliette instead, searching for a reason, for the slightest fracture in her face that would give way to an explanation.

Juliette blew out a slow breath. Despite the agonizing pain, she could feel the bleeding crawl to a stop. She could feel her head clear up, the fuzz lessening.

She had a job here to do.

"You've been infiltrated by Communists." Juliette turned her head ever so slightly—not enough to disturb her shoulder but enough to lock eyes with Roma. "There's a sect in the White Flowers working with them, giving over your resources and weaponry. I suspect the monsters are emerging from this very collaboration."

Roma did not react. He only removed the rag and retrieved what looked to be a needle and a thread. "I'm going to suture the wound."

Juliette's first instinct was to snap that he couldn't. She had no doubt that he would do a fine job; running about in this city meant knowing how to snap an enemy's leg with two fingers and also how to piece an ally's body back together. But was she an ally? Would he piece her together with a steady hand?

Roma made an impatient noise, waving the needle. Though she imagined she could probably get up and get to the hospital with a gaping hole in her shoulder, Juliette winced and relented.

"Wait."

She dropped the blade she was holding and reached for the lighter in her pocket. Wordlessly, she flipped its lid and struck her thumb on the spark wheel. When the flame sprang to life, Roma brought the needle near to sterilize it without being asked, like he had already read Juliette's intention. It was easy sometimes to forget how well they had known each other before everything went awry. To forget that they were once as familiar as halves of the same soul, predicting each other's next words. Here, with Roma absently tapping the back of his hand against Juliette's, asking her to put the flame away when the needle glowed red, Juliette could not forget.

"Don't stitch too deep. I don't want a scar," she grumbled, snapping her lighter closed.

Roma frowned. "You're hardly in the position to negotiate the size of your scars."

"*You* threw the knife at me."

"And now *I'm* stitching you up. Do you have any more complaints to air?"

Juliette resisted the urge to strangle him. "Did you hear any of what I said before?" she asked instead. "About the Communists?"

"Yes," Roma replied evenly. He pulled the thread into the needle. "And it doesn't make sense at all. We don't want the Communists taking the city. Why would we help their revolution?"

Roma leaned in, and the first prick of the needle entered her skin. Juliette gritted her teeth hard but otherwise withstood the pain. She had suffered worse, she tried to remind herself. She had suffered worse simply by smashing wine bottles too hard in New York, which had ended with her needing stitches all along her arm.

At least those had been done in a hospital.

"I don't know why," Juliette said tightly. "But it's happening, and right under your nose."

Her shoulder twitched, and Roma's hand came around her arm immediately, holding her still. His fingers were hot, burning into her skin.

"And what," Roma asked, pulling the thread through again, "do you want me to do about it?"

"What you were supposed to," she replied. "Find the Frenchman. The monster on the train."

The needle went in too deep. Juliette gasped and Roma cursed, his grip tightening to stop her from leaping up.

"Stay still," he commanded.

"You're clearly trying to kill me."

"I'm obviously not very *good* at it because you remain alive, so stay still!"

Juliette exhaled sharply through her nose, letting Roma resume the last of the stitching. Though she tried not to move, she continued eyeing him until he shifted uncomfortably, his eyes flicking to her and narrowing.

"The monster," Juliette said again. "Everything will be clearer from him onward."

But Roma shook his head and held his hand out. Juliette passed him the blade beside her—the very same one he had stabbed her with—and he cut the thread at the end of his stitching.

"I can't," he said shortly. "My hands are full. As you can see"—his jaw tightened, and he inclined his head toward the other end of the alley where Alisa was keeping guard—"the blood feud is whittling us down alongside our mass casualties from the madness. I fear sending resources into finding the blackmailer will only incite more attacks, and while I hear you have your vaccine already, we—"

"I'll give it to you. Samples. Papers. Take it to your labs to re-create."

Roma's look of vexation faded for complete surprise. It didn't take him long, however, to shake himself from his stupor and get back on task with a frown, retrieving a bandage from the box and laying it over Juliette's shoulder.

"You have permission?"

Of course not, Juliette scoffed silently. In what world would the Scarlet Gang be willing to pass their vaccine on to the White Flowers? No one in that gang did anything out of the goodness of their hearts unless a good heart could bring in a fortune on the black market.

Aloud, Juliette only said, "No."

Roma narrowed his eyes again and pressed down too hard on the bandage, not entirely by accident. "I somehow doubt that you are willing to betray your people, Juliette."

"It is not betraying my people," Juliette said, taking the stinging sensation. "It is going against my father. My own people will not suffer if the White Flowers suffer less too. Your loss is not my gain."

Roma taped down the bandage. Seeing that he was done, Juliette used her uninjured arm to reach for the fabric of her dress and yank it over the wound, congratulating herself for not letting out a pained shriek.

"Isn't it?" Roma asked. He shifted behind her again and reached for her zipper, but he did not immediately pull it up. His fingers hovered there, a hairsbreadth away from her skin, yet she could still feel the proximity like a physical touch against her bare back.

"Not when it comes to the madness." Juliette's throat was dry. She could not see his face. She did not know how to read this. "I can help you orchestrate a break-in"—Roma suddenly pulled the zip up—"but in return, give me the monster in the White Flowers. I will get to the root of this."

She felt his warm breath curl around her neck, as heavy as everything unsaid between them. A sudden pressure came on her other arm then, and she realized Roma was helping her stand. Almost as one, they rose upright, following the path of the breeze as it blew into the alley and swept skyward.

Juliette turned around. The wind settled. By all means, it was cold in that alley, but she couldn't feel it. Her coat was in two pieces on the ground, and her dress was torn at the back. Roma's jacket was kicked aside, soaked with blood, and his sleeves were pushed up his arms, kept away from his stained hands. When they stood like this, close enough that their heartbeats were in conversation, Juliette did not know what coldness was.

"Agreed?" she asked, her voice almost a whisper.

Roma stepped back. Like that, the chill crept in, swirling the front of Juliette's dress, raising goose bumps all along her arms.

"For the vaccine," Roma said. "Agreed."

One more day of survival. One more day of Roma letting her off the hook without putting a gun to her head. How long could she keep this up? How long before she either caved or just let him shoot his goddamn bullet?

Juliette bobbed her head in a mock curtsy, turning to go. Only then Roma held his arm out, stopping her before she could take a single step.

"Why did you do it?" he asked. "Why did you jump in front of Alisa?"

Juliette's lips parted. *Because I cannot bear to see you hurt, even when I am the one hurting you the most.*

She wanted to say it aloud. It was on her tongue. It burned the whole length of her throat, begging to be let out. What was the harm in another secret between them? What could they not withstand if they had already fought a monster and the stars themselves?

Then Alisa, from the other end of the alley, called, "We've got people incoming. Juliette, perhaps you should go."

Juliette heard the voices too. They were still some distance away, but keenly audible, overlapping one another in Russian. Laughing, they spoke of dead Scarlets, of her people falling to the ground with their lifeless eyes staring up at the sky.

It was that which had Juliette remembering herself. It was that which jolted the truth back to the forefront of her mind, like a slap to her face.

This wasn't about fighting for love. This was about staying alive.

"You ask why?" Juliette said quietly. She swallowed hard—leaving nothing but lies studded in her mouth like extra teeth. "It stopped you from trying to kill me, did it not? I keep telling you, Roma—I need your cooperation."

In an instant, the tentative readiness for peace fled from Roma's expression. He was a fool if he thought the truth would make it easier. It would only tear them apart to think that this could end any other way: both of them consumed by the blood feud.

"Thursday," Juliette said. The White Flower voices were getting closer. "Chenghuangmiao at the ninth hour. Don't be late."

Juliette walked away before the other White Flowers could happen upon the alley, before Roma saw the tears rise to her eyes, utterly, utterly frustrated that this was what they had been reduced to.

Roma breathed out, kicking his bloody jacket. It was unsalvageable, but he hardly cared.

"Roma!" one of the White Flowers exclaimed, seeing him in the alley. They looked between him and Alisa, noting the blood on Roma's hands and his haggard appearance. There was definitely a bruise or two on his face after his fight with Juliette. "What are you doing here?"

"Leave us," he snapped.

The White Flowers hurried away without another word. Slowly Alisa walked back to him, cocking her head to the side. Instead of hurrying to ask what had just happened, she started packing up the first-aid box.

"Dammit!" Roma hissed aloud. He had had her. Right here. He could kill however many bodies he wanted on the streets, land perfect shots upon the Scarlets that ran at him with knives. But none of that mattered if he couldn't strike a killing blow on the heart of the Scarlet Gang. On Juliette. Revenge on disposable parts was not revenge at all, but cowardice. And maybe he was a coward. He was a coward who couldn't stop loving a wicked thing.

"What was that all about?" Alisa asked plainly.

Roma scrubbed at his hair. A dark lock fell into his eyes, covering his whole world in black. "I should be asking you if you're all right first." He sighed. "Are you hurt?"

Alisa shook her head. "Why would I be?" She sat down, leaning up against the wall. "Juliette jumped in front of that knife."

She had. And Roma could not comprehend a single reason why . . . or at least one that made sense, no matter what Juliette had said.

"So?" Alisa prompted. "Why were you trying to kill Juliette?"

Roma decided to sit too. He shuffled beside his sister like they were awaiting a bedtime story, not hiding out in an alley stained with blood.

"Well, two generations ago, her grandfather killed ours. . . ."

Alisa wasn't buying it. "Leave the blood feud out of this. You were collaborating with her, and then suddenly you're not. I've heard the rumors—the ones that seem logical and the ones that are so preposterous to be laughable. What is the truth?"

231

Roma pushed his hair out of his eyes. His pulse was still raging, his palms slightly damp. "It is . . . it's complicated."

"Nothing in this world is complicated, only misunderstood."

Roma peered at Alisa, his nose scrunching. Alisa scrunched the exact same button nose back, and the siblings suddenly seemed like mirror images of the other.

"You are entirely too wise for your young age."

"You are nineteen. It is not far by much." Alisa tapped her knee. "Does Papa know?"

"It was his idea," Roma muttered. Seeing that he could not keep his sister in the dark anymore, he started at the beginning, from the moment Lord Montagov called him into his office to discuss the plan and then the snide, knowing glance Roma had caught from Dimitri in the living room.

"The last of it was in Zhouzhuang," he finished. "Then the Scarlets blew up our safe house, and I figured the alliance was called off."

Alisa was staring at the wall of the alley, clearly mulling through the events. The gears in her head were turning, her frown deepening. She wouldn't be able to make sense of anything. It was a waste of energy to try.

"I almost wanted to stay."

Alisa's frown disappeared quickly, surprised by his sudden pivot. "In Zhouzhuang?" She snorted. "It's so quiet."

"We need a little quiet. This city is always so loud." Roma tipped his head up, staring at the flurrying clouds. The desire to run had been pulling at the edge of his mind for years: a constant whisper surrounding the idea of escape. He remembered one late night leaning on his windowsill, his cheek still smarting from Lord Montagov's discipline, wishing he could pick himself up and fade into a life somewhere outside these city boundaries. He wanted air that didn't smell like factory smoke. He wanted to sit under the cover of a large tree, lean upon the trunk and see nothing but green for miles. Mostly, that night in 1923, he wanted Juliette back, and he wanted to take her and run, far from the clutches of their families.

Only he also knew exactly what that meant: leaving the White Flowers without an heir, carving open a space that any hateful soul could fill.

"It is loud because you listen," Alisa said.

"It is loud because everybody's always talking at me." Roma sighed, pressing the heel of his bloody palm into his eyes. Constant demands from the White Flowers. Constant demands from his father. Constant demands from the city *itself*. "I entertain that it must be nicer to live simply instead. To catch fish and sell it on the fresh market every day for livable wages instead of trading mounds of opium for amounts of cash we'll never need."

Alisa thought on it. She pulled her legs up to her chest and leaned her arms on her knees. "I think," she said, "that is something you say because we have been rich all our lives."

Roma smiled tightly. Indeed. They had never been born for a simple life, and so they did not deserve it either. It had taken generations to climb to where they were now, and who was Roma to throw it away?

All the same, that part of him never seemed to go away. The part that wanted to run, the part that wanted a different life. If only he could erase every memory of his earlier years, maybe he could erase these thoughts too, but he would always remember lying in a park with Juliette—fifteen and carefree, his head in her lap and her lips pressing a soft kiss to his cheek, the grass under his fingers and the birds fluttering in song on the branches above him. He would always remember that little nook where nothing could disturb them, a world of their own, and thinking *this—this is the only complete happiness I have ever felt*.

It was *that* part of him he could never kill, and when Juliette was stitched into those memories like a finished hem, how could he ever kill *her*?

A sound came from the other end of the alley then—a pebble skittering across the pavement. Seconds later Benedikt came into view, frowning at the sight of his two cousins on the ground.

"What are you doing? We need to go."

Roma got to his feet without argument, nudging the first-aid box out of sight and reaching a hand out to Alisa. "Come on." He ruffled her blond hair as she stood, the two of them trailing after Benedikt as they made their way home.

It wasn't until they were trekking back into White Flower territory and Alisa started dragging her feet upon the gravel that Roma suddenly blinked, his eyes coming to the back of Benedikt's head. He hadn't thought much about how his cousin had found them. But now, as Benedikt chided Alisa to walk properly and stop ruining her shoes, he realized that he had heard no footsteps before Benedikt's approach.

So how long had Benedikt been lingering outside the alley, listening to their conversation?

Twenty-Four

In a factory in the east of the city, on a dreary Thursday afternoon, the machines go quiet at once. The foreman lifts his head from his desk, dazed and sleep-fogged, a thin trail of drool smeared across his chin. He wipes at his face and looks around, finding no workers before him, only their crowded tables and their materials laid out in a mess, strewn onto the floor.

"What is this?" he mutters under his breath. Their deadline is tight. Don't the workers know? If they cannot deliver their materials within the week, the big bosses at the top will be angry.

Oh, but the workers care not about such matters.

The foreman turns around, and with a start, finds them standing behind him, armed and at the ready. One slash, that's all it takes. A knife over his throat and he's twitching on the floor, hands clasped around the wound in a futile attempt at holding the blood in. The red seeps regardless. It does not stop until he is naught but a body lying in a scarlet pool. It soaks the shoes of his workers, his killers. It is carried from street to street, the faintest red print pressed upon crumbling pavement and into the roads of the Concessions, marring stains upon the clean white sidewalks. This is what revolution is, after all. The trailing of blood from door to door, loud and violent until the rich cannot look away.

But the revolution is not quite there—not yet. The people are trying again, but they are still scared after the last uprising was quashed, and no matter how loud they rage, their numbers are small. They cannot be heard in Chenghuangmiao, where two girls sit at a teahouse and plan a heist, sketching charcoal upon paper while the cold breeze blows through the window. There is a momentary shout, and the one in the glittery Western dress stiffens, leaning out the teahouse, body half dangling out the second floor in search of trouble.

"Relax," the other says, brushing a crumb off her qipao. "I heard the police stopped the riots before they got very far. Focus on finishing your outrageous plan for stealing our own vaccine."

A sigh. "*Have* they stopped the riots? It looks as if another is starting here."

The heir of the Scarlet Gang tips her chin toward the scene outside, where a small group is holding signs, calling for unions, for the ousting of gangsters and imperialists. They make their plea, speaking as though it is a matter of connection, of garnering enough sympathy until the tide turns the other way.

But the city does not know their names. The city does not care.

A group of White Flowers comes along then—an ordinary bunch, nothing more than muscle and eyes for the gang, keepers of the territory. The shoppers nearby hurry away, certain that they should not witness this, and they are correct. A thick cloud blows over the sun. The lapping pond water underneath the Jiuqu Bridge darkens by a shade. The White Flowers peruse the scene, whisper among themselves, and then—quick as only a practiced maneuver can achieve—they raise their weapons and shoot half the group dead.

Up in the teahouse, the girls flinch, but there is nothing to do. The remaining protesters scatter, only police officers are already waiting, ordered in by the White Flowers. The surviving rioters kick and hiss and spit, but what good will it do? For now, all their fury can do is burn holes in their chests.

"I used to think this city I am to inherit was descending into one ruled by hatred," the girl says into the cold wind. "I used to think that it was our doing, that the blood feud ruined all that was good." She looks at her cousin. "But it has been hateful for a long time."

Hatred has been lurking in the waters before the first bullet was fired from Scarlet to White Flower; it's been there since the British brought opium into the city and took what wasn't theirs; since the foreigners stomped in and the city split into factions, divided by rights and wrongs that foreign law put into being.

These things do not fade away with time. They can only grow and fester and ooze like a slow, slow cancer.

And any day now, the city will turn inside out, corrupted by the poison in its own seams.

It was concerning how many messengers Benedikt had paid in the last hour, but Marshall tried not to jump to any conclusions. He was already having a hard time finding a good hiding spot, staying far enough that Benedikt would not feel watched but close enough to pick out what was going on.

"Are you planning a takeover?" Marshall muttered. "What could you possibly need this many White Flowers for?"

As if hearing him, Benedikt looked up suddenly, and Marshall ducked fast, pressing along the roof wall. They were near headquarters, in the busier part of the city, where the street corners were loud and the alleys were crisscrossed with hundreds of bamboo poles hanging laundry to the wind. Even if Benedikt thought he caught movement from afar, Marshall was confident that his best friend would merely think it to be a trick of the eye, triggered by a large frock waving with the breeze.

Marshall had grown so pale from being indoors all the time that he probably *resembled* a white frock.

"That's all, then," he heard Benedikt say, waving the messenger off. If it weren't some task Benedikt was having the messenger do, then Marshall imagined the only other possibility was collecting information. When Marshall poked his head out farther, trying to get a better look, Benedikt turned just right, giving Marshall a glimpse of the red ribbon in his hands.

Marshall scratched his head. "Don't tell me you went and got a lover," he grumbled. "I've only been dead for five months and you're already buying women presents?"

Then Benedikt brought out a lighter and started to burn the ribbon. Marshall's eyes bugged.

"Oh. Oh, never mind."

His confusion only grew as Benedikt dropped the ribbon and let it burn, leaving the alley for the direction of home. Marshall didn't follow—that would be too risky—but he did sit there for a while longer, watching the last of the ribbon turn to ash, his brow furrowed. The answer for what was going on with Benedikt didn't seem to be emerging anytime soon, so he dusted himself off and climbed down the roof, making his way back to the safe house. He had plenty to help his disguise: a coat, a hat, even a covering over his face, feigning sickness.

Marshall had almost reached the building when a host of shouting echoed from the end of the street, and his head jerked up, searching for the sound. It was the very edges of a protest, and he would have thought little of it if it weren't for the group of Nationalist soldiers who were running in from the other road, coming upon the workers with their batons ready. Quickly Marshall turned away, but one of the soldiers had made eye contact with him, trying to gauge if he was part of the protest.

He can't recognize you, Marshall told himself, heart thudding. Nothing of his face was visible. There was no possibility.

All the same, when Marshall opened the door to the safe house and pulled the lock behind him, when the protest had been pushed away from the street and dispersed elsewhere so it wasn't so close to foreign territory, he still felt as though someone was watching.

Juliette had found her way back to Chenghuangmiao early. After splitting from the teahouse to run their separate errands, she and Kathleen had set to meet again at nine in the evening—once the sun had descended and the night was dark—but here she stood almost a quarter of an hour ahead of time. Her nose twitched, picking up the smell of blood that remained from the workers who had been gunned down in the daytime.

"I heard there was a riot here."

Juliette almost jumped. She turned to face Roma, who approached by the dim glow of the shops, half his face illuminated with sharp angles and the other half cast in shadows. He was wearing a hat, and when he came to a stop beside her and nocked it low, enough of his features were hidden that only Juliette, staring directly at him from two paces away, would be able to identify him.

"It was hardly a riot," she replied. "Your men worked fast."

"Yes, well . . ." Roma sniffed the air. Despite the cold that numbed their noses, despite the smells of roasted meat that wafted from the restaurants nearby, he sensed the blood too, could feel what had spilled on the ground here. "They can be a little heavy-handed some-times."

Juliette pursed her lips but otherwise did not respond. She waited for a group of elderly to pass by, then tilted her chin ever so slightly to the right, to the base of the building beside them.

"This is our lab," she said. "But we must wait for Kathleen to arrive. She will help you go in while I distract Tyler."

Roma arched a brow. "Tyler is here?"

"He's been *living* here." Juliette pointed up, to the windows that were aboveground. "We have apartments. He's paranoid that White Flowers will steal our research."

"And yet here you are, aiding a White Flower to steal your research."

"He is shortsighted," Juliette said simply. "Have a look, Roma."

"At the lab?"

Juliette nodded.

Roma seemed suspicious as he inched closer to the small windows, to the few inches of glass that jutted up from the concrete ground. Though the workers had gone home, the lights were bright inside, showing only Tyler at the foreman's desk, flipping through a book next to what looked like a very large blue mountain.

Roma shuffled back quickly lest he be spotted. "What *is* that?" he demanded.

"The vaccine," Juliette answered. "We created it in solid form instead. It's easily dissolvable for distribution through the water system but intensely flammable while solid."

At least that was what Juliette had understood from her father's quick briefing after the meeting that day. They would drop it into the water supply throughout all Scarlet territory, immunizing the civilians within range and protecting their own people.

Roma nodded once, indicating that he understood what she was implying. "It is clever," he said. "White Flowers do not live in your territories, and those who sneak into some household or another to drink the water will surely risk getting caught and having their lives forfeit. Communists are far from your territories too, likely in the poorer areas or the outer peripheries."

"And so it is only a Scarlet solution, through and through," Juliette finished. "Those who seek immunity must pledge allegiance to the Scarlets and physically come under our protection, pay rent under our roofs, add more numbers to those of Scarlet loyalty. I cannot take any credit for it, alas. It was all Tyler's doing."

"And was *this* Tyler's doing too?"

Juliette swiveled around, alarmed by the unfamiliar voice. For the briefest second, her heart seized, her hand twitching for a knife with half a mind to kill the potential threat. Then her eyes adjusted to the dark, and she recognized the speaker to be *Rosalind*, following beside Kathleen, who came to a stop with a huff.

"I did not invite her," Kathleen reported, adjusting her sleeve and giving Roma a polite nod. "She thought I was hiding something and came on her own insistence."

Roma nodded back.

"Juliette," Rosalind emphasized when she didn't get an answer. "Didn't your collaboration with the White Flower heir *end*?"

Juliette had neither the time nor the energy for this. She pressed at her hair, choking back a deep exhale. The chiming of bells sounded nearby, signaling nine o'clock.

"I'm working with him willingly."

"Willingly . . ." Rosalind's echo trailed off, the confusion and absolute disbelief in her expression deepening. Her eyes flicked from Juliette to Roma and then back again, and Juliette resisted the urge to flinch, knowing that her cousin could not possibly see what Juliette was afraid she might see. "You're openly colluding with the enemy. You have a straight shot, right now, through his head—"

Rosalind spoke as if Roma weren't standing right there, listening to her plot his death.

"Just trust me on this." Juliette tried to sound reasonable. "There is an incredible amount of difference between killing an enemy too soon and killing them when the time is right. This isn't a good time."

Rosalind took a step back. "It always comes to this," she said softly. "You decide when the blood feud does and does not matter. The Cais decide when they are enemies and when they are not, and the rest of us must fall in line."

"Rosalind," Kathleen said sharply.

Juliette blinked, surprised by the accusation. She wanted to guess that Rosalind was just being spiteful, that Rosalind thought it unfair Juliette could collaborate with Roma without consequence while she had to sneak around with her lover. Only that didn't quite align with the resentment in Rosalind's voice. It felt larger than that. It felt *older*—not a burst of anger from the heart but something that had been building up from the sludge of the gut.

Rosalind shook her head. "Whatever," she said softly. "I need to go to my shift at the burlesque club."

She turned and walked off, heels clicking quickly into the crowd of Chenghuangmiao, leaving a pocket of silence in her wake. Juliette's eyes flitted to Roma. He did not give any indication that this had shaken him in any way. All he appeared was bored, and it was too dark for Juliette to check for his other tells.

"We're wasting time," Juliette said, her voice raspy when she spoke up again. "I'm going to pull the electric panel at the back of the restaurant and then lure Tyler up to his apartment upstairs. On my cue, Kathleen, you can accompany Roma into the lab. Between the two of you, I'm sure you can figure out which papers are relevant. Are we ready?"

Kathleen nodded. Roma, too, offered an affirmative shrug.

Juliette sighed. "All right, then." She plunged into the restaurant.

"I suppose we should have clarified what exactly Juliette's cue will be," Kathleen remarked when the restaurant fell dark. A few of the patrons inside gave a shout of surprise. Otherwise, they merely continued eating.

"Yes, well," Roma Montagov said, "given that it is Juliette, I am sure it will be loud and obvious."

An unbidden sound of amusement escaped from Kathleen, and though she clamped down on it immediately, Roma's expression twitched too—not entirely enough to qualify as amused, but certainly not stoic, either. Kathleen's inappropriate levity turned to scrutiny. As they fell into a taut, waiting silence, she bit her lip, fighting the urge to speak further. This was far from the first time she had observed Roma Montagov and Juliette working together despite their multiple attempts to kill the other. And if Juliette would not say anything about why . . .

"I hope," Kathleen said, unable to resist the temptation, "you understand that Juliette is doing you a great favor."

Roma immediately scoffed. "There are no favors in this city. Only calculation. You heard what she said to your sister, did you not?"

Kathleen had. *There is an incredible amount of difference between killing an enemy too soon and killing them when the time is right.* And it seemed she was the only one who had heard the hitch in her cousin's voice that indicated she was lying. How strange it was. Both that Roma Montagov seemed angered by Juliette's intent to destroy him and that Kathleen could see Juliette didn't intend to at all.

"She is saying what she thinks Rosalind wants to hear."

Roma frowned. "I do doubt that."

Kathleen tilted her head. "Why?"

This time Roma really did laugh. It was a disbelieving sound, like Kathleen had asked him if it were possible to breathe without air.

"Miss Lang," he said, his voice still soaked with incredulity, "in case you forgot, Juliette and I are blood-sworn enemies. You and I, too, are blood-sworn enemies."

Kathleen looked at her shoes. They were getting dusty, picking up the weird bits and pieces always littered about the sidewalks.

"I do not forget," she said quietly. She bent down to wipe at the strap across her heel. "I used to think this feud could be stopped if both gangs would just understand each other. I used to draw so many plans to send to Juliette when she was in America. So many things we could say, we could propose, we could put into effect so the White Flowers would see that we were people who didn't deserve to die."

She straightened up. There was still no cue from Juliette. Only a dark, foreboding building, rumbling with confusion as some of the restaurant patrons wandered outside. Roma lowered his hat to avoid recognition, but he was listening.

"Only it's not that, is it? It was never the problem of alienation. It doesn't matter how deeply we tell the White Flowers of our pain. You know. You have always known, because you tell us of your pain too."

Roma cleared his throat. "Isn't that the whole point of a blood feud?" he finally asked in response. "We are equals. We do not try to colonize the other, as the foreigners have done. We do not try to control the other. It is only a game of power."

"And isn't that mightily tiring?" Kathleen demanded. "We destroy each other because we wish to be the only ones in this city, and we care little how much the other will hurt. How do we live like that?"

Silence. Roma's expression was tight, like he suddenly couldn't remember how he got pulled into this conversation. Above them, the clouds were blowing in, gathering with thickness to prepare for what would be a storm.

"I am sorry."

Now it was Kathleen's turn to blink. "Whatever for?"

"For not having a solution, I suppose."

Was he really, though? How could any of them truly be sorry when they did nothing to stop it?

"It is no good to be sorry," Kathleen said plainly. She knew clear as day that Juliette had realized this a long time ago. That was why her cousin had never put into effect any of her plans. Why her cousin had always brushed the topic away, had resisted from engaging directly, speaking of her parties and speakeasies instead in her letter replies. "So long as the Scarlet Gang and the White Flowers have hope for a future where they are the only mighty power, the blood feud lives on."

Roma Montagov shrugged. "Then there is a solution. Destroy the gangs."

Kathleen lurched, almost colliding with the wall that they stood alongside. "No," she said, horrified. "That might be worse than having a blood feud."

That would be unending grappling, rulers ousted at every turn or politicians who lied at every moment. No one would be as loyal to this city as gangsters were to it. *No one.*

It was then that the sound of smashing glass interrupted Kathleen's train of thought, and her gaze whipped up to find a book falling through one of the third-floor windows. There was a shout from inside the building, then a whole series of footsteps thundering up—a voice that sounded like Tyler calling for backup.

"There is our cue," Roma Montagov said, already striding for the entrance.

Heart pounding, Kathleen made to follow, goose bumps rising at the back of her neck. She was always on edge when she had to perform tasks that could get her in trouble, and breaking into their own Scarlet labs was certainly more troublesome than going undercover at Communist meetings.

"Best to hurry," Kathleen warned. "There's no telling how long Juliette can hold Tyler's attention away for."

They descended into the lab quickly. It was pitch-dark. Kathleen squinted in haste to avoid colliding with a worktable, her hands groping about to find her way. Roma did not seem to have the same problem, pulling a small burlap sack from his coat and using the thinnest stream of moonlight coming from the windows to light his way. He made fast work of taking samples from the mountain in the center of the lab. The texture was as malleable as clay, as light as dust.

"Miss Lang, where are the papers?"

Kathleen wrinkled her nose, still squinting without much success. "They made almost a dozen copies, so they're all around us. Just make sure you find a complete set, not duplicates of the same page."

Roma set down the burlap sack and dug into his pocket again, coming out with a small box in his hand. Kathleen didn't register what he was doing until there was a *whoosh!* sound and a flame burst to life between his fingers, eating up the matchstick.

"Are you mad?" Kathleen hissed. "Put that out! The vaccine is *flammable*."

With a grimace, Roma pinched the match out. "No fuss," he said. He reached for a stack of papers right beside him. "I think I've got it."

Kathleen huffed, wiping a thin sheen of sweat from her forehead. She had had one job—to watch him—and this place had almost gone up in flames.

Above them, there came the rumbling of more footsteps. The sound of glass shattering again echoed inside the building, and then, almost scaring the life out of Kathleen, a fast tapping came on the windows to the lab. When her gaze whipped to the moonlight, she found Juliette gesturing frantically for them to hurry.

"You have everything?" Kathleen asked Roma.

Roma gestured to the materials in his hand. "Thank you for aiding a White Flower break-in, Miss Lang."

Juliette waited outside impatiently, half thinking that it would be Tyler emerging before Kathleen and Roma did. The timing could ruin this whole scheme. All it would take was Tyler freeing himself from the bonds that she had secured over him, bonds that she had secured rather hastily after attacking him from behind with a bag over his head. Time had been of the essence: it was more important for her to get out than it was to keep him tied down all night.

At last Kathleen and Roma emerged from the restaurant, stepping back into the busyness of Chenghuangmiao. At the same moment, there was a shout from above, loud because of the broken window. A few late-night strollers glanced up but did not pause, paying no heed to the strange events that occurred in these places.

A *bang*. Tyler had freed himself.

"I'll try to keep him distracted," Kathleen said, already moving back in the direction of the restaurant. "Both of you, go!"

They didn't need more prompting. Side by side, Roma and Juliette kept a steady, nonsuspicious pace until Tyler burst out from the building, bellowing into the night and asking for the intruder to show himself. By then enough time had passed that they had faded into the crowd and could pick up speed. Though there weren't as many people here in the night as in the day, it was enough cover to blend in and step into an alleyway out of Tyler's sight utterly.

"Come on," Juliette whispered, forging ahead. The alley walls loomed alongside them, tall and foreboding. "Remember your bargain, Roma. Find me the Frenchman."

"I will work as fast as I can," Roma said from behind her. "I promise that—*oomph!*"

Juliette whirled around with a gasp, alarmed by Roma's muffled shout. For a startling moment, she did not even think to draw a weapon. She could only wonder how Tyler had found them when she thought she'd lost him. She *thought* that he wouldn't have been able to move through the crowds at such speed.

Then her vision focused, and she realized Roma was not being attacked; whoever had ahold of him was pressing a *cloth* to his face, and when Roma dropped to the ground, falling unconscious, the figure set him down without malice.

It was not Tyler who had found them.

It was Benedikt Montagov, who stood to his full height, pushing back the hood of his coat and walking toward her.

Tā mā de.

"I didn't gauge you to be the type to murder your own cousin," Juliette snarked, slowly inching back. If she bolted now, chances were that she could make a run for it. There was another alley across from this one, leading into a busier street that might give her shelter.

"He is only knocked out," Benedikt replied coldly. "Because he could not do what needs to be done."

The gun came out in an instant. He had not been holding it before, but then it was in his hand, the stark, sleek weapon glinting under the moonlight and only three paces away from being pressed directly to Juliette's forehead.

There was no way out of this. There was no way Juliette could run fast enough without a bullet entering one body part or the other, and then she would bleed out here, like another one of the workers rioting for life. Benedikt was not like Roma. He had no hesitation with her life.

"Listen to me," Juliette said very carefully, holding her hands up.

She imagined her brains blown upon the wall, pink and red smeared with the tiles. She would accept her death when it came someday, but not *now*, not under a false revenge that this Montagov cousin had taken upon himself.

Benedikt's finger tightened on the trigger. "Don't waste yourself on last words. I will not have it."

"Benedikt Montagov, it's not what you—"

"For Marshall," he whispered.

Juliette squeezed her eyes shut. *"He's alive. He's alive!"*

The bullet did not come. Slowly, Juliette eased her eyes open again and found Benedikt with his arm slackened, staring at her in aghast disbelief. "I beg your pardon?"

"You fool," Juliette said, the insult coming softly. "Do you not remember Lourens's serum? In all this time, I have half expected one of you to realize the truth. Marshall Seo is alive."

Twenty-Five

Benedikt didn't put away his weapon as he followed Juliette through the city. He didn't trust her. He couldn't guess how she might sidle out of this, couldn't pick out the clear sign of a lie when she had winced at Roma's unconscious form in that alleyway and waved for Benedikt to walk alongside her, but there was plenty of time between now and wherever they were going for Juliette to run—or God forbid, retrieve her own weapon and shoot.

She didn't pull out any weapon.

She only continued walking forward, her step certain, like she had walked this route a thousand times before. Benedikt was developing a tic in his cheek. He could hardly think long on what Juliette had said lest he lose his mind before he saw the truth for himself. He had the urge to smack his palm against something, to stamp his feet down until his shoes were in pieces. He did nothing. He only followed, obedient and blank-faced.

Juliette stopped outside a nondescript building, its exterior small and faded enough that it blended right into all the walls and windows nearby. There were three steps that went up into the building, and through the open entranceway, there was a single door pressed right by the entrance, two or three paces away from a staircase that continued winding up. Benedikt listened. Past the howl of the wind, there was very little to be heard. The upper levels of this building were likely vacant.

Benedikt jumped, the gun in his hand twitching, when Juliette plopped herself down upon a crate outside the apartment door.

"I'll wait out here," she said. "Door's unlocked around these times."

Benedikt blinked. "If this is a trick—"

"Oh, spare me! Just *go in*."

His hand came down on the handle. For whatever reason—or for every reason, he supposed—his heartbeat was raging like a war drum in his chest. The door eased open, and he stepped into the dim apartment, eyes adjusting while the door clicked behind him on its own. For a moment he did not know what to look for: a stovetop, papers scattered on a table, a shelf, and then . . .

There. Like a goddamn specter raised from the dead, Marshall Seo was lounging on a shabby mattress. Hearing the intrusion in the room, Marshall casually glanced up from the wood carving he was working on, then did a rapid double-take, bolting to his feet.

"Ben?" he exclaimed.

He was paler. His hair was shorter, but uneven, as if he had taken a pair of scissors with his own hands and hacked away, doing a piss-poor job at the back.

Benedikt could not move, could not say anything. He gaped like a fish, all wide eyes and loose hanging mouth, staring and staring, because this was *Marshall*, alive and walking and right in front of him.

"Benedikt," Marshall said again, nervously now. "Say something."

Benedikt finally jolted to action. He picked up the nearest object he could find—an apple—and threw it at Marshall with all his strength.

"Hey!" Marshall yelped, jumping out of the way. "What gives?"

"You didn't think to contact me?" Benedikt shouted. He picked up an orange next. It bounced off Marshall's shoulder. "I thought you were *dead*! I mourned you for months! I slaughtered Scarlets in your name!"

"I'm sorry! I'm sorry!" Marshall kept darting around, trying to avoid being target practice. "It had to be this way. It was too dangerous to tell you. Juliette's reputation is on the line if this gets out—"

"I don't care about Juliette! I care about you!"

Suddenly Benedikt and Marshall both froze—the former remembering that Juliette was still within hearing range and the latter realizing that she must be outside if Benedikt was here.

There came a shuffling sound on the other side of the door and then Juliette, clearing her throat.

"You know what?" she called. "I think I might go take a walk."

Her heels clicked off, fading into the distance. Benedikt felt like a hole had been punctured in his lungs as he leaned up against the table, all that fury and anger he had been carrying inside him finding nowhere to go and opting to deflate and deflate and deflate instead. He had expected to explode outward, to at last rid the darkness in his chest by seeking revenge and directing a very sharp object at Juliette. Instead, the darkness had turned to light, and now he was an overwrought light bulb, close to implosion when the vacuum space inside shattered.

"She didn't have to save me," Marshall said softly, when it looked like Benedikt was at a loss. Benedikt remained staring at the table, both his hands pressed to the flat surface. Slowly, Marshall crept nearer until he was right beside Benedikt. He opted to lean against the table, the two of them facing different directions. "She could have killed me and secured complete power, but she didn't."

"She has been hiding you?" Benedikt asked, his head lurching up. "Here? All this time?"

Marshall nodded. "If Tyler Cai finds out, it is not merely a fight that will result. It is Juliette's entire position. She will be ousted."

"She could have avoided pretending to kill you in the first place," Benedikt muttered.

"And have us all die at the Scarlets' hand in that hospital?" Marshall asked. "Come on, Ben. I already had a bullet in my stomach. If she hadn't sent them running in those few minutes, I would have bled out."

Benedikt scrubbed at his face. Try as he might to be resentful, he had no alternative to offer.

"Fine," he grumbled. "Perhaps Juliette Cai knew what she was doing."

Marshall reached out and punched Benedikt's shoulder. It was something he had done thousands of times before. Benedikt's pulse picked up regardless, like the weight of his newfound knowledge added to the weight of the hit.

"I owed it to her to lie low," Marshall said, not noticing the turmoil unraveling right beside him. "Well, when people on the streets weren't trying any funny business, at least. Otherwise I was lying low."

"Funny business?" Benedikt echoed.

Marshall picked up a cloth on the table and mimed tying it to his face. In a flash, Benedikt saw that dark figure on the rooftop again, the one who had shot all those Scarlets when he had been badly outnumbered.

"That was *you*."

"Of course it was," Marshall replied, his dimples deepening. "Who else would keep such a close eye on you?"

Benedikt's breath left him in a whoosh. The air in the room grew still, or maybe that was just him, his lungs reaching critical deflation. *I love you*, he thought. *Do you know? Have you always known? Have I always known?*

A notch in Marshall's brow formed, accompanying his hesitant smile. Marshall was confused. Benedikt was staring, and he could not stop, all the terror and devastation that had wrecked him these past few months lodged right in his throat like a physical block.

You could reach for him. Ask if he loves you back.

"Ben?" Marshall asked. "Are you okay?"

If he loved me too, wouldn't he have told me? Wouldn't he have come to me, come hell or high water?

Benedikt reached over suddenly, but only to hug his friend close, only to do as he had always done in all these years they had known each other. Marshall jolted but was quick to return the embrace, laughing as Benedikt pressed his chin hard into Marshall's shoulder, like the physical sensation was enough to confirm that this was real; this was all real.

"Don't ever do that to me again," he muttered. "Don't *ever* do something like that again."

Marshall's arms tightened. "Once is plenty, Ben."

He's alive, Benedikt thought, pulling back with a thin smile. *That's all that matters.*

Roma awoke with a deep cough, rolling onto his side and wheezing for breath. By the time he came to, the moon was directly above him, shining into his bleary eyes. His neck was in pain. His back was in pain. Even his *ankles* were in pain.

But the vaccine still lay beside him, the bag untouched. So too did the papers, tucked inside.

"What the *hell*?" Over his head, the birds perched on the electric lines flew off at once, startled by Roma's shout. He hadn't seen who had knocked him out. Juliette was gone too, but there was no sign of a struggle, no blood in the alley or even a sequin fallen from her dress.

Roma got to his feet. He could only assume that it had been a Scarlet, and Juliette had either dealt with the situation or was off elsewhere leading them away. There was nothing he could do now except take the vaccine to Lourens as he had planned.

Roma trudged off.

In that alley, the birds did not come back in his absence. They knew to flee as something else stirred in Chenghuangmiao, lumbering in on two upright feet. If the people in the market had paid attention, they might have known to go too. Instead, not a soul in Chenghuang-miao thought to move until the screaming started and they looked up, finding five monstrous creatures tearing a path into the clearing.

Juliette came in through the front door of her house, shrugging her coat off when one of the maids gestured to take it. There was still activity in the kitchen, some aunt making a late-night snack, the warm glow of light crossing into the otherwise dark living room.

"Go to bed," Juliette told the maid after she hung up the coat. "It's late."

"I'll fetch you some slippers first," the maid said. She was on the older side, likely a mother by the way she was frowning disapprovingly as Juliette rolled off her sharp and impractical heels.

Juliette sighed and collapsed sideways into the couch. "Xiè xiè!"

"Āiyā," the maid chided, already marching out of the living room. "Bù yào shǎ."

The maid disappeared into the hallway. If only the people of the vast and expansive Scarlet empire could see Juliette now. She looked like a paper doll more than she looked an heiress with blades for teeth.

Then the front door burst open, and Juliette jolted to her bare feet immediately, braced for war. A gust of cold came blowing in, then Tyler, dragging someone behind him. When Tyler came closer, he pulled his hostage forward too, and it was Kathleen who came into the light, stumbling to a stop in front of Juliette.

"What is the meaning of this?" Juliette demanded. She reached for Kathleen's shoulders, giving her a cursory pat. "Are you hurt?"

"No. I'm fine," Kathleen said, shooting Tyler a deathly glare. She rubbed her arm harshly. "Your cousin just has barnacles for brains."

"I know you did it, Juliette," Tyler spat. "I could smell your perfume everywhere. What was in it for you? Power? Money?"

Juliette exchanged a glance with Kathleen, who shrugged, seeming flabbergasted as well.

"What are you talking about?" Juliette asked.

Tyler's expression turned livid. "Why are you feigning ignorance?"

"I *am* ignorant—what are you accusing me of?"

"The monsters, Juliette! Monsters stormed the lab and took every bit of the vaccine."

Horrified, Juliette staggered a step back, her legs hitting the couch. She tried to school her expression, but she doubted it worked, not when a cold sweat had broken out from head to toe.

Monsters? Right after Juliette's heist? On the same night? How could this possibly be a coincidence?

The maid returned with Juliette's slippers then, but she took one look at the scene before her and set the slippers down by the kitchen, making a quick exit. A *click* echoed through the living room, the hall-way door closing. Above, the chandelier gave a single chime, picking up that faint whisper of the wind.

"Did you see anything?" Juliette asked. "Was it all of them?"

"All five of them," Kathleen answered. "We caught the last glimpse of the monsters disappearing, and yet Tyler still thinks I had a hand in it despite catching up to me from three streets away *before* the monsters attacked."

Kathleen must have done as she said, distracting Tyler so Roma and Juliette could get away without being caught. But who was to know that *monsters* would suddenly add themselves into the equation too?

Of course . . . it wasn't the monsters, was it? It was that damn blackmailer.

"Why else were you even there?" Tyler snapped at Kathleen.

"That's *my* business, Cai Tailei! Regardless, you chased me all the way out of Chenghuangmiao. You saw how far I was from the monsters!"

"That wouldn't have prevented you from summoning them. That wouldn't have prevented *you*"—at this, he pointed a finger at Juliette—"from summoning them."

Kathleen shook her head. "You're being ridiculous. I'm going to go fetch Lord Cai to handle this." She trekked up the steps before Tyler could say otherwise, disappearing from view. In her absence, the living room fell quiet: Tyler watching Juliette carefully for any tell of her guilt, and Juliette racking her brain for how it was possible that the blackmailer would strike at the same time as her. It couldn't have been the White Flowers. Roma had been lying unconscious in an alleyway. Benedikt Montagov had been with her. No one else knew of her plans, unless Roma had sent people after him, which she could not imagine, for otherwise he would have had to explain how he came across the information.

So *what* happened?

"Listen," Tyler said. His voice had lowered. "If you just come clean, I can help you. There's no shame in admitting that you're simply misguided."

Juliette shook her head. "How many times do you need to hear of my innocence, Tyler?"

"It is not your innocence I want to hear. I'm trying to steer you to do what's right. Why can't you see that?"

There was the shuffle of footsteps from upstairs. It could have been Kathleen popping in and out of the rooms. It could have been the household staff slinking near to witness the drama. Either way, Juliette was so irritated that she could only splutter for a moment, temporarily losing grasp of every language she spoke.

"Your idea of what's right is not gospel," she finally managed. All she could see in her mind's eye was the people of Shanghai dying, gouging at their own skin from a preventable madness, all because the people at the top—because people in this very household—couldn't find it in themselves to care. "Who do you think you are to tell me what's *right?*"

"I am your family," he snapped. "If I don't keep you in line, who will?"

"Hey!"

Kathleen's voice cut through the argument. She was leaning upon the second-floor banister, her head visible from where Juliette and Tyler stood.

"Your father's not here," she reported once she had Juliette's attention. "It's almost eleven o'clock."

Juliette blinked. "Lái rén!"

Almost immediately, the maid came back. She had been waiting in the hallway just outside the living room. "Would you like me to make a call to see where your father is, Miss Cai?"

And apparently there wasn't even any shame in pretending like she wasn't listening.

"Yes, please."

The maid disappeared, and Kathleen came back down the stairs. As they waited, hovering in the living room, Kathleen loosened her braid and smoothed her fingers along her scalp, as if the weight of her hair was giving her a headache. Quietly, Juliette pulled a thin, needlelike knife from her sleeve and offered it. Kathleen took it with a grateful look, then stuck it into her hair for a pin.

The maid returned.

She was pale.

"Scarlet reports say Lord Cai is at the burlesque club," she said. Juliette was already starting toward the door, ready to report to her father what nonsense was happening with the blackmailer, but then the maid went on: "The place has been locked down. He's not letting people in."

Juliette paused in her step, turning over her shoulder. On instinct, she looked at Kathleen, then Tyler, and they both appeared equally puzzled.

"For what reason?"

The only times she could remember her father shutting down a club or a restaurant was when someone had misbehaved, and he needed to . . .

A bolt of ice sank down Juliette's spine. Suddenly she thought she could smell metal under her nose: the phantom scent of blood, the scent that soaked the ground each time a deal had fallen through or a secret had slipped and the men of the Scarlet inner circle needed to pay for it.

"Punishment," the maid reported, turning even paler. "He's just arrived. For Miss Rosalind."

"Rosalind?" Tyler exclaimed. "The hell did she do?"

Oh *merde*. Juliette ran for the door, but even as she tore into the night, the maid's answer followed her out.

"She's the White Flower spy."

Twenty-Six

Juliette practically slammed into the two Scarlets guarding the door to the burlesque club, narrowly halting before a collision. Kathleen was close behind, her breath coming fast.

"Let me through."

"Miss Cai." The Scarlets exchanged a glance. "We can't—"

"Stand aside. Now."

One of them shifted out of her way, drawing a glare from the other, but that small gap was enough for Juliette. She squeezed past and pushed through the door, barging into the dark interior of the club, the smell of smoke bringing an immediate sting to her eyes.

And inside, all she could hear was screaming.

For a moment Juliette was frozen in shock, uncertain what she was witnessing. The club had been cleared out, the tables and bar emptied of patrons and workers. The only people present were her father's men, seated around him and at the ready while he lounged at one of the largest tables, arms splayed across the velvet of the half-moon couch.

He was facing forward.

Facing the stage, where Rosalind was being whipped.

The lash came down again on her back, and Rosalind cried out, her whole body shuddering. They didn't allow her to crumple to the floor: there were four Scarlets around her, two to hold her upright, one with the whip, and one standing just to the side.

"Oh my God," Kathleen whispered. "Oh my—"

Juliette charged for the stage. "Stop it!" she demanded. She was upon the platform in three fast steps. When the Scarlet standing guard tried to stop her from lunging in Rosalind's direction, Juliette was faster, pushing at the arms that tried to grab her. The guard tried again, and Juliette immediately struck her fist across his face. He stumbled away, finally letting Juliette throw herself before Rosalind, her own body a shield for the next lashing.

"Xiao Wang, stand down."

At Lord Cai's call, the Scarlet who held the whip frowned. Droplets of blood were splattered across the front of his shirt, but he seemed not to notice. He didn't stand down. His arm pulled back, half-prepared to strike again, as if he would release the whip.

"Go ahead," Juliette said, her words curling into a sneer. "Whip me, and see how many pieces I'll cut you into afterward."

"Xiao Wang." That was Lord Cai again, his voice rising over Rosalind's whimpers. "Stand down."

The Scarlet listened. He lowered the whip, and Juliette spun around, hands outstretched for Rosalind. As soon as the Scarlets released their hold on her, she collapsed, and Juliette scrambled to catch her cousin, softening her fall onto the stage. By then Kathleen had reached them too, cursing and cursing under her breath.

The burlesque club was silent. Waiting.

"Rosalind," Juliette said. "Rosalind, can you walk?"

Rosalind mumbled something beneath her breath. Juliette couldn't hear what Rosalind was saying, but by Kathleen's stricken expression, she had understood immediately.

"Deserve what?" Kathleen asked, her voice a mere rasp. "Why would you say that?"

It was only then that the mumble registered to Juliette. *I deserve it, I deserve it.*

"Because she does."

Juliette's head snapped up, seeking her father. He had spoken in such plain declaration, without room for dispute nor debate.

"Bàba," she whispered, horrified. "You know Rosalind. You know who she is."

"Indeed," Lord Cai replied. "And so she should have known better. She should have had more loyalty, but instead she has been feeding Scarlet information out."

Juliette felt her throat grow tight. When she shifted her hold on her cousin, her palm came back entirely slick with blood, the mangled gashes in Rosalind's qipao weeping bright and red from her wounds. Juliette was torn between the same indignation that had dragged her father out here to make an example out of Rosalind and utter outrage that this was *Rosalind*—no matter what she did, where was her chance to explain herself?

"Is this about her lover?" Kathleen asked quietly. Her voice shook. "He is a mere merchant. She said he would soon leave the White Flowers."

"He is no mere merchant," Lord Cai replied. With disconcerting speed, he leaned off the couch, grabbing a stack of papers upon the table. In his hand, he flipped through them, then selected one to pass to a Scarlet beside him, indicating in Juliette's direction. "He is no merchant at all. According to the letters we found, he is a White Flower through and through, and he has been siphoning our clientele lists through Lang Shalin for months."

What?

The Scarlet presented the single piece of paper. Juliette scanned the Russian script briefly, reading a report about the members of the inner circle. This was one among hundreds. One day logged out of months.

"Who?" Juliette demanded. "Who were these letters being sent to?"

"Well—" Lord Cai gestured toward Xiao Wang, toward the whip

that trailed blood across the stage. "That's what I wanted to know too."

By now it seemed that Rosalind was close to losing consciousness, her body growing still. Juliette tapped her face, but her cousin's eyes had fallen shut, thick lashes fluttering up and down each time Juliette urged for a response.

"Come on, Rosalind," Juliette hissed. "Stay awake."

Lord Cai arose from his seat suddenly, and panic surged through Juliette's every cell in response. She had never responded like this before when it came to her father, whom she had always seen as fair, even when he was the one holding the whip. Nothing had changed. Her father was and had always been the leader of a ruthless gang, the head of a criminal empire. He had never hesitated to give punishment where punishment was deserved, and Juliette had never blinked until now—now, when punishment was still fair, but fair brought the blood of one of her best friends.

"We are done here, I suppose," Lord Cai said. "If you want to interfere, Juliette, you can help by getting a name out of your cousin. She protects him even now, and it will not stand." He waved at the men around him. "Help her home. Call a doctor."

Kathleen made a noise of protest as they leaned over to grab Rosalind, but Juliette relinquished her hold. The time for punishment had passed, and the Scarlets weren't fond of unnecessary cruelty. They were careful, avoiding Rosalind's injuries.

This whole event wasn't about hurting her; it was about making a point.

"Juliette," Kathleen whispered when the Scarlets started to clear out from the club. "Did Rosalind lie to us?"

"Yes," Juliette replied, certain. She squeezed her hands, and blood crusted into the lines of her palms. Rosalind had lied, had betrayed the Scarlets for whatever reason, and Lord Cai had not hesitated to make her answer for it.

Juliette looked at the bloodred stains on the stage. The men were moving the tables into their original formation, glasses clinking together, voices yelling at one another to summon the car out front. She could feel her father's eyes on her, calm in inspection, digesting her every reaction. She needed to keep her expression composed—no particular horror at the violence, no undue sympathy for a traitor.

But all she could think was: if Rosalind was whipped like this for leaking Scarlet information and protecting an ordinary White Flower, then what was Juliette's fate if they were to ever find out about her past with Roma Montagov?

Benedikt wouldn't have run the message himself if it weren't such a late hour, but the clock was nearing midnight, and he doubted any of the White Flowers were sober enough in the main headquarters to be summoned to a task. This was urgent.

Though these few months, he supposed just about everything in this city was.

"I cannot concentrate with you hovering over me like this."

Benedikt heard Lourens's booming voice before he saw him, pushing through the lab doors and scanning across the few technicians working overtime. Eventually, he sighted Lourens and his cousin near the side tables, both of them squinting at something under a microscope. Or technically, Lourens was the one with his face pressed to the eyepiece. Roma was looming over him and invading the scientist's personal space.

"Is that the vaccine?" Benedikt asked.

"Stolen right from the Scarlets," Roma answered, having recognized Benedikt's voice without bothering to look up as he approached. "But Lourens is saying he doesn't think he can re-create it."

"I cannot *read* any of these papers," Lourens shot back. "Moreover, this sample is not pure. It has been manipulated for additional solubility . . . or flammability. One or the other, I'm sure."

"Well," Benedikt interrupted, "it just became a lot more valuable. The Scarlets had their entire supply stolen. By monsters."

Roma finally looked up, taking a step away from the microscope. "What? I was there only a mere hour ago."

"I know." Benedikt nudged a thumb toward the doors, indicating the rest of the city outside. "That's why there are rumors that you orchestrated it. White Flower credibility went up. Scarlet security went down. There will be blood feud fights on the streets tonight, I'm sure."

"Me?" Roma muttered under his breath. "That's rich. I *wish* I did."

Lourens, meanwhile, made a thoughtful noise, his eye still pressed to the microscope. "I really would recommend finding the source of this rather than counting on our re-creation of the vaccine, Roma."

Roma didn't say anything in response. He was good at internalizing; if Benedikt took a listening device to his cousin's head, he was sure he would hear an utter scramble of panic, but on the exterior, Roma simply folded his arms.

"Just try your best. Even if I can find the blackmailer, who's to say if I can find the rest of the damn monsters?"

Lourens pushed the microscope away wearily. "I am not paid enough for this." He reached for the drawers along the worktable, retrieving a scalpel. "Speaking of which, there was someone who came poking around in the evening, seeking you."

Benedikt pulled a face, though Roma was too busy with his own surprise to notice.

"To the lab?" Roma said. *"Here?"*

"I do not know how he found his way over either. He was called General Shu."

Why did that name sound familiar? Benedikt combed through his memory but came up empty. Roma, on the other hand, immediately reared back. "He's a top Nationalist official. What does he want with *me*?"

Lourens merely heaved a sigh, like the topic was wearing him out. "I suspect he circulated all the places you are known to frequent. He left as soon as I said you were not present."

"Are you in trouble?" Benedikt asked.

"With the Kuomintang?" Roma replied, scoffing. "No more than the usual level they want me dead." He stepped away from the work-table, leaving Lourens to his task. "Shall we go?"

Benedikt nodded. He was still mulling over Lourens's strange report when Roma opened the doors for him, the smack of cold wind forcing him alert.

"You look better today," Roma remarked, starting in the direction of headquarters. "Are you getting more sleep?"

"Yes," Benedikt replied plainly. *And mere hours ago, I found out that Marshall is still alive.*

He wanted to say it aloud. He wanted to scream it from the roof-tops and declare it to the whole world, so that the world could end its mourning with him. But now Benedikt had been roped into Marshall's promise to Juliette. Benedikt was another piece in a larger chess game, one with Juliette on one side and Roma on the other, and to keep Marshall from falling off the board, it seemed that he had to start playing for Juliette's strategy.

"Good," Roma replied. A slight crinkle appeared in his brow. Perhaps confusion, perhaps relief. His cousin heard the lift in his voice and couldn't quite pinpoint a cause, but he was not direct enough to ask outright.

A streetlamp flickered above them. Benedikt rubbed at his own arms, easing his chill. When they turned a corner, deep enough in White Flower territory that he felt assured they wouldn't be attacked anytime soon, he said:

"You did not seem concerned by the news I brought you. I expected some exclamation when told that monsters robbed the Scarlets of their vaccine."

"What's the point?" Roma replied tiredly. "The Scarlets never would have distributed to us."

"The concern isn't the Scarlet loss. It's the use of monsters for such a trivial task with no attack on the people."

Roma blew out a breath, fogging the air around him. "I'm almost convinced at this point they'll never go away," he muttered. "They will keep coming and coming, and Juliette will keep appearing before me, dropping to her knees to ask for help just one last time, right before she puts a blade in my back."

Benedikt remained silent, not knowing what to say. The lack of argument must have seemed suspicious to Roma, because he threw a quick glance over, mouth opening again. But Roma didn't begin his next sentence. Instead, so quickly that it scared the living daylights out of Benedikt, Roma pulled his gun and shot into the night over Benedikt's shoulder, his bullet already echoing before Benedikt had whirled around and caught sight of movement disappearing from the mouth of the alley.

"Who was that?" Benedikt demanded. He glanced around, taking inventory of their surroundings—the shop signs written in Cyrillic and the Russian bakeries all lined up in a row, though they had retired for the night. This was about as far into White Flower territory as one could go. "A Scarlet?"

Roma frowned, drawing closer to the alley. His target had long disappeared—possibly struck, possibly only grazed, given the distance at which Roma had shot from.

"No," he replied. "A Nationalist, uniformed. I thought I heard someone behind us, but I chalked it up to my imagination until they came closer. We were followed almost immediately upon leaving the lab."

Benedikt blinked. First an official appearing at the lab. Now they were picking up a tail on the streets, right in their own territory? It was bold—far too bold.

"What did you *do?*" he demanded.

Roma didn't answer. He had sighted something on the alley floor: a wad of loose-leaf paper. It looked like an old advertisement, but Roma picked it up anyway and unfolded it.

His eyebrows shot straight up. "Forget about what *I* did." Roma turned the slip of paper around, and a sketch of Benedikt's face stared right back at him. "What do the Kuomintang want by trailing after *you?*"

Benedikt took the paper. A cold sweat broke out along his spine. His neutral expression was colored in careful ink, the illustration better than his own self-portraits. The artist had been generous with his crop of curly hair. There was no doubt that this was him.

"I . . . haven't a clue," Benedikt muttered.

But his concern wasn't why the Kuomintang were following him. If they had been on his tail for some time now, the more important question was: How much had they seen from earlier in the day, when he was exiting the safe house and saying goodbye to Marshall, who was supposed to be dead?

Twenty-Seven

Rumor had it that there would be more protests today. The early morning had passed with a flurry in the Scarlet house, its hallways combating collision after collision of whispers. If it wasn't Tyler's relatives trying to clarify with one another what exactly Miss Rosalind had done to be hauled home covered in blood, it was their speculation about whether it was safe to enter the central city today when reports said that workers were attempting to strike yet again.

Tyler couldn't get out fast enough. A bunch of good-for-nothings, they all were, talking instead of doing. With the new hubbub, hardly anyone was paying heed to what had happened to their vaccine supply. The monsters had invaded a secure facility that only Scarlet inner circle knew about. Was no one suspicious? Was Lord Cai not the slightest bit concerned?

"—right?"

With delay, Tyler stubbed out his cigarette in the ashtray, then looked up at Andong and Cansun. They were across from him, pacing the length of the room, while Tyler remained seated upon a chaise lounge, granted a full view out the floor-to-ceiling window before him. Below, the intersection just outside the Bailemen dance hall was at high capacity of activity: the citizens and occupants of Shanghai bustling to and fro like there was hardly a minute to spare. Every so often, someone walking on the street would glance up, tracing their eyes across the block letters reading PARAMOUNT fixed outside the dance hall. They could likely see into the windows of the second floor, into the opulence and the vacant rooms open for Tyler to come and go as he pleased. The rest of Shanghai didn't have such leisure.

"Were you saying something?" he asked, frowning.

Andong paused for a beat, like he couldn't tell if Tyler genuinely had not heard him or if he was giving him another chance to reconsider what he had just said. When seconds passed and Tyler did not look angry, Andong cleared his throat and repeated, "I was only remarking on the uselessness of trying to disrupt the Communist forces. Our numbers are dwindling as it is, and theirs keep growing. We have a blood feud on the other side to take care of; they are single-minded in their objective."

Tyler nodded. He remained only half listening, and when he replied, it was also halfhearted.

"No one cares to follow what is good."

Tyler retrieved a new cigarette, but he didn't light it. *The blood feud*. The goddamn blood feud and the goddamn White Flowers, siphoning their resources and their members and their members' *loyalty* like some parasitic invasion of the mind. What was it about their maneuvers that had people turning against their family? Juliette, and her dalliance with Roma Montagov. Rosalind, and whatever nonsense she had gotten involved with.

Perhaps it was simply the women. Perhaps they were just weak.

Tyler struck a new match. Once his own cigarette was lit, he threw the pack into the air, and Andong's hand whipped out, hurrying to catch it before it could fall to the floor. Cautiously, Andong took one cigarette out. He worried it between his lips, and as if reading Tyler's thoughts, asked: "So what are you to do about Juliette?"

"What am I supposed to do?" Tyler replied immediately. He took a drag, then almost coughed. He had never liked these things. He smoked them for a lack of anything better to do. "If she won't admit to her wrongdoing, I can't force it out of her. She will merely keep rotting us from the inside out."

She didn't even know it. Tyler had no doubt that Juliette—his cousin who had grown up with everyone wrapped around her finger—would never for a second consider that she might be wrong. That her behavior was traitorous, even if she was not openly acting the traitor. Sympathy for the White Flowers was weakness. *Love* for the White Flowers was a direct strike against the Scarlets in the blood feud. Juliette may as well take a gun to her own head for all that she was doing to the future of the gang she was supposed to lead.

He still didn't know what to believe—whether she had something to do with the vaccine disappearing. Juliette was the one who had killed the last monster; was it so hard to believe that perhaps she had gotten her hands on five others? Juliette was the one who wanted the vaccine distributed to the whole city; was it so hard to believe that she would steal it for that purpose?

But why seek a vaccine at all if the monsters were under her control? It made no sense. Something didn't quite click.

Unless they weren't hers. Unless she was going along with it because they were under Roma Montagov's control, and she couldn't find it in herself to rebel against him.

Tyler jumped to his feet, drawing Cansun's curious attention. The window was flaring with light, a vendor's stall passing the street underneath with its reflective surfaces. They had initially come to a high vantage point to watch for the possibility of monsters in the city, but there had been no chaos of the supernatural persuasion, only human strikes and human protests.

If Roma Montagov was the perpetrator, then Juliette could still be saved. Tyler believed that. The Scarlets came first, and bitter as it was, that did include his cousin. Blood to blood—it was the same sort that ran in their veins. That had to count for something. If she were forced to choose sides, if she saw how this city was split, she would realize what was at stake. She would stop operating foolishly under a White Flower's thumb.

"What does Roma Montagov treasure most?"

Andong blinked, taken aback by the question. Meanwhile, Cansun folded his arms and brought his shoulders near his ears, considering the question. He was already slight and looked even more so when he stood like that, wasting into a stick figure.

"What do we care about Roma Montagov for?" Andong asked, but both Cansun and Tyler were looking out the window, tracing the crowds that gathered thicker and thicker.

Tyler dropped his cigarette in the tray. His fingers were dusted with ash, prickling at his skin. The human body was so fickle. He should have been born a beast instead. He could have used it well.

"Come on, gentlemen," he said, making for the door. "The protest starts soon."

The streets were full of people, blocking the entrance of the meeting hall that Kathleen needed to enter.

With a wince and an awkward sidestep, Kathleen tried to squeeze herself through, her elbows held out on either side of her. It did little to avoid the jostling, but it did streamline her path ever so slightly. The crowds could have been worse. They could have summoned a strike that incapacitated the whole city, but it seemed they remained localized in the central areas.

"Oh, Christ—"

Kathleen ducked, narrowly avoiding being smacked across the face by a worker's sign. The worker glanced at her momentarily before moving on, but Kathleen's gaze was drawn to the red rag tied around their arm.

Which color do you bleed? Juliette had asked so long ago, in that den not far from here. *Scarlet or the worker's red?*

When Kathleen brought her hand up to shield the sun off her face, the red thread at her wrist glimmered like jewelry. It was pristine and stark, dangling softly against her skin. This was Scarlet red. This was the clean edges of a color used merely for allegiance—for decoration. The worker's red was dirty, and spirited, and *desperate*. It had long exploded outward in all directions, spilling like a crowd growing frenzied.

Kathleen finally pushed her way in, sidling into the meeting hall. This was not the very worst it could get—far from it if the enthusiasm among the Communists here was any indication. The Communists and their unions would keep trying and trying, each time inciting revolt in one part of the city and hoping it would set off a chain reaction in the others. The better they prepared, the more likely they would succeed.

And when they did, that was no longer the protests of unruly workers on the streets.

That was revolution.

"Attention! Attention!"

The meeting had already started, switching from one speaker to another, so Kathleen slid into a seat, hoping she hadn't missed anything critical. It hardly seemed important now to keep an eye on their further plans—the Scarlets already knew: the Communists had almost reached the end of their planning, the final revolt waiting in the wings, ready to take to the stage.

"What are we rising for?" the speaker onstage asked. "What do we incite change for? Our own gain? Our own peace?"

Kathleen pulled at her braid. Her mind wandered to Rosalind, to her sister's silence last night when she had stirred back into consciousness.

"The state will continue to suppress us. The law will continue to cheat us. Anyone who deems themselves a savior of this city is a fraud.

272

All kings are tyrants; all rulers are thieves. It is not peace nor gain that revolution shall aim for. It is only *freedom*."

All through the meeting hall, Party members rose to their feet. Their chairs scraped back, the noise grating to the ear. Kathleen didn't move, only taking it all in. She wasn't worried about sticking out. No one was paying attention to the last row, too focused on the speaker at the front.

"The gangsters of this city sacrifice us for their pride, for their meaningless blood feud. The foreigners of this city sacrifice us for riches, for unending gold stockpiled on their ships. We will free ourselves from these chains! Who are they to tell us what to do? Who are they to punish us when they see fit?"

His words washed over her like a tidal wave. Kathleen suddenly wanted to clutch her stomach, unable to bear the truth knotting up inside her. Indeed, who was the Scarlet Gang to whip Rosalind bloody merely because they had decided she was not loyal enough? Why did they deserve the *power* to hurt another person? Why was this the way they lived, falling to their knees under Lord Cai just because it was the way it had always been? If he wanted them dead next, then Kathleen and Rosalind had no choice save to place their heads down for the sword's blow. Protection was nothing when it hinged on one family's whims and desires. This wasn't what Kathleen had sworn loyalty to. She wanted order—she wanted order under *Juliette's* control.

But if order needed to tremble under fear first, maybe it wasn't worth it.

"Rise!" the speaker onstage said. "Too long have we suffered and languished. We shall rise!"

At last Kathleen stood too, putting her hands together to clap.

Alisa chewed on her fork, her foot dangling off the roof edge.

At present, she was sitting at the very top of headquarters, face turned to the cold wind as her fingers flipped through a file swiped from her father's office. Her bedroom was directly below, warm and cozy, but her brother or other White Flowers could walk in at any moment, and she couldn't have that while she was snooping. In search of privacy, she had climbed up to the roof tiles instead, a plate of cake in one hand and the folder of papers tucked under her arm.

She stabbed her fork in for another bite, chewing thoughtfully. Just as she started flipping to the next page, there was a burst of noise from afar—the usual rowdy shouting of a fight starting. Alisa stiffened, knowing she would need to go inside if there was a blood feud conflict coming nearer, but she couldn't see anything other than the usual empty alleyways, even as the voices got louder. For several long moments, Alisa continued searching, but nothing moved in her periphery short of her blond hair waving with the wind.

"Strange," she muttered, content to stay put for the meanwhile.

Alisa flipped to the next page. The folder had been selected at random after she poked her head into her father's office for the briefest second and saw it lying on his desk. She had heard rumors of Communist spies infiltrating the White Flowers and was curious; Roma had been busy lately, though Alisa wasn't sure if he was looking into the same Communist spies or something else. No one ever told Alisa anything. No one ever paid her attention at all unless it was to barge in on her and tell her that her tutors were here.

Unfortunately, Alisa didn't think she had stolen anything very relevant. The folder contained profiles on the Kuomintang, but nothing past basic information. Some news clippings on Chiang Kai-shek. Some maps from spies who were tracking the Northern Expedition. The only thing that seemed briefly interesting was an investigation into General Shu, who had little information made public about his life. By the time Alisa scanned to the end, however, all she had gathered was that General Shu had a bastard son. Which was entertaining but hardly helpful.

"Hey!"

Alisa set the file aside and peered down from the roof. With that shout catching her attention, *now* she could see the fighting, though it seemed not to be a fight at all. She squinted, trying to pick out exactly what was coming in her direction, and only when she saw the signs did she realize that perhaps it was not a blood feud conflict moving down the main road but a workers' protest.

"Ooooh," Alisa said under her breath. "That makes more sense."

She tucked the folder under her arm, then gathered up the plate and the fork. In a hurry, she skittered across the roof, carefully lowering herself over the edge with the one hand she had free and sliding the whole way down upon one of the exterior poles. She landed in the thin alley around the back of the apartment complex, her shoes squelching hard in the mud, her elbow thwacking against a pot of flowers growing upon one of the first-floor windowsills. It wouldn't do to be spotted waving this folder around at the front of the house, and so she would merely use a back entrance, or else—

Alisa stopped when a figure stepped in her path. Before she even had time to run, the bag came down over her head.

In White Flower territory, the protests reached all-time heights, spilling over the footpaths and wreaking havoc in the buildings. When Roma exited the safe house he had been visiting—another stop on his search for the identity of the White Flower Frenchman—he was almost impaled by a shovel.

"By God," Roma spat, hurrying to the side.

The worker only eyed him, not seeming very sorry. Why would he be? There were no other gangsters in sight to put a stop to this.

With another muttered curse, Roma hurried back home, staying close to the buildings. His father should have sent men out for crowd control. Their numbers should have gathered by now, fighting back against the rioters with weaponry. So where were they?

Roma ducked into the alleyway that took him to headquarters, a hand above his head to protect himself from dirty laundry water. A heavy drop landed on his palm right as another colossal shout echoed down the road, driving unease into his bones. It seemed nonsensical that he was spending time searching for the Frenchman when there had not been an attack since the train cart. When instead all that had been wreaking havoc across Shanghai was the blood feud or the rioters, and as far as he knew, not a soul in the White Flowers had a plan of action to combat that sort of discord instead.

"You're full of *nonsense*."

Roma frowned, closing the front door after himself. The loud bang did not interrupt the voices shouting from the living room. A wave of heat from the radiators immediately warmed his stiff skin, but he did not shrug his coat off. He wandered into the living room, following the shouting, and found Benedikt and Dimitri in the heat of an argument, a plate smashed to pieces by Dimitri's feet, as if someone had thrown it.

"What is going on?" Roma asked, for what felt like the umpteenth time that day.

"That's what I want to know too," Benedikt replied. He stepped back, crossing his arms. "Alisa is missing."

An ice-cold sensation swept down Roma's spine. "I beg your pardon?"

"I heard her yell," Benedikt seethed. "From somewhere outside the house. And when I went to investigate, guess who the only person present was?"

"Oh, don't be tiring," Dimitri sneered. "I heard no children screaming. Nor any ruckus past the chaos on the streets. Perhaps you are imagining things, Benedikt Ivanovich. Men who do not assert themselves tend to—"

Roma did not hear the rest of whatever foolish thing Dimitri was surely to say. He was already charging up the stairs with a roar in his ears, taking two at a time until he was on the fourth floor, charging into Alisa's bedroom. Indeed, as Benedikt had said, it was empty. But that didn't mean anything. Alisa was always disappearing for large blocks of time. For all he knew, she was hidden in some air duct across the city, biting into an egg roll and having the time of her life.

"She's not in her room. I already checked." Benedikt's voice traveled up the staircase before he did, emerging with his hands buried in his hair.

"It's hardly unusual," Roma said.

"Yes." Benedikt bit down on his cheeks, turning his face gaunt. "Yet I heard her yell."

"Dimitri is right on one thing at least—there *is* plentiful yelling outside. The streets are rioting. I can hear yelling right now."

But Benedikt only gave Roma an even look. "I know what Alisa's voice sounds like."

The certainty was what had Roma on edge. Acting on a sudden instinct, he made a sharp pivot for his room. He didn't know why that was the first place he thought to check, but he did, easing his door open gently. Benedikt was close on his heels, peering in curiously too.

Three things became immediately apparent, one after the other. First: Roma's room was freezing. Second: it was because his window had been pulled open. Third: there was a letter fluttering on the window ledge, pinned down by a thin blade.

A wave of goose bumps broke out all down Roma's arms. Benedikt hissed in a breath, and when Roma didn't make a move to go fetch it, he did the honors instead, tearing the blade out and unfolding the letter.

When he looked up, his face was void of blood.

"Moy dyadya samykh chestnykh pravil," Benedikt read. "Kogda ne v shutku zanemog—"

He didn't have to finish it. Roma knew the next two lines that were coming.

"On uvazhat' sebya zastavil," he intoned. "I luchshe vydumat' ne mog."

The opening verse to *Eugene Onegin*. Roma marched forward and took the letter, immediately crinkling the edges with his grip. Past the famous lines of poetry, the letter proceeded.

> I hear dueling is the most noble way to kill someone.
> It's about time this blood feud earned some nobility,
> don't you think?
>
> Meet me in a week's time. And I'll give her back.

And beneath the text, there was a flourish of a signature, leaving no doubt who had devised this masterful scheme.

"They have taken Alisa," Roma rasped aloud to Benedikt, though Benedikt already knew. "Tyler Cai has taken Alisa."

Twenty-Eight

Rosalind was awake, but she was unresponsive. At this point, Juliette was almost getting worried, wondering if the injuries had extended to her mind, too.

"Could you give us a moment?" Juliette called to the Scarlet standing by Rosalind's bedroom door. He had his hands folded in front of him, rigid and on guard.

"I'm afraid not, Miss Cai," he said. "Your father said to keep watch."

"*I'm* already here keeping watch, so can't we have some privacy?"

The Scarlet only shook his head. "Whatever information you extract has to go straight to Lord Cai."

Juliette swallowed her huff of annoyance. "And does my own father suspect I would keep it from him?"

"Your father never suspected his niece, either, and yet here we are."

Juliette stood up from her chair, her fists clenched. The Scarlet paused, eyeing her stance. It wasn't as if Juliette's trigger-happy fingers were unknown to the gang. They had all heard the stories, and they had all seen the results—what mattered now was whether he feared Juliette's immediate threat more, or the eventual consequences of not following Lord Cai's exact instructions.

"I will stand outside, with the door open a crack," the Scarlet relented. He stepped out, and tugged at the door, the hinges squeaking.

Juliette flopped back into the plush chair. Rosalind had hardly blinked through the whole exchange. On any other day, she would have made some comment about Juliette being more bark than bite. Now she only stared, a glaze over her eyes.

Her cousin was in pain, Juliette knew. The wounds on Rosalind's back were severe, and Kathleen had almost swooned at the sight when the doctor was dressing them last night. Juliette was torn between sympathy and frustration. Torn between absolute horror that this had happened and a complete lack of understanding over *how* this had happened. Perhaps it made her a bad person. A bad friend, a bad cousin. Even while Rosalind was like this, so pained and dazed that she was reduced to absolute silence, Juliette couldn't help but feel betrayed that Rosalind had lied to her. And she didn't know if it was because this city had hardened her or if her heart had always been like this—cold, brittle, turning away with the first sign of disloyalty. Juliette was a liar too. When it came to telling the truth, Juliette was perhaps the most corrupt of them all, but that didn't stop her from flinching instinctively when she was dealt lies in response.

"I promised to protect you," Juliette said quietly. "But not like this, Rosalind."

No answer. She hadn't expected one.

"It was copies of your correspondences that they dug up at the post office. That's how you were found out. Not sightings, not rumors. Simple pen to paper and your handwriting." Juliette blew out a frustrated breath. "Was the merchant business all false, then? Is there even a lover, or did you play spy for no reason?"

Suddenly, Rosalind's eyes swiveled to Juliette, her gaze sharpening for the first time.

"You would have done the same," Rosalind rasped.

Juliette sat up straighter. She looked to the door, to the slight gap left ajar. "What?"

"I love him," Rosalind mumbled. A bead of sweat had broken out along her hairline. She was delirious, probably running a fever. "I love him, that is all."

"Who?" Juliette demanded. "Rosalind, you must—"

"It doesn't matter," she interrupted, almost slurring her words. "What does any of it matter? It is done. It is done."

None of this was making any sense. Even if this lover was a White Flower, what was the point of protecting a regular member? What consequence would there be, short of having him on a Scarlet hit list? He couldn't be high up. It certainly wasn't Roma, and it wasn't Benedikt. If not a Montagov, then why the torment? Why did Rosalind squeeze her eyes shut as if the world were bearing upon her?

A sudden knock on the door. Juliette jolted, her heart hammering in her chest as if she had gotten caught doing something bad. The Scarlet poked his head back in, scanning the scene. She expected him to remark on Rosalind's mumblings, but instead:

"Telephone call for you, Miss Cai."

Juliette nodded, then got to her feet, reaching out to pull Rosalind's blankets a little higher. Rosalind hardly stirred. She only closed her eyes, shivering and shivering, even once Juliette left the room, shutting the door after herself.

"Don't bother her," she warned the Scarlet. "Let her sleep."

"You're going too easy on traitors," he called after her.

Juliette thinned her lips, proceeding down the hallway. He was right. They were going too easy on her—*Juliette* was going too easy on her. And because Juliette had been the one to interrupt the whipping, her father would give the task to her just to teach her a lesson: if Rosalind gave no information soon, then it would be on Juliette to uncover why her cousin had betrayed them, by whatever means necessary.

Juliette swallowed hard, approaching the telephone. She had no doubt she could do it. She had never hesitated to garrote and cut her way through the other Scarlets that her father had sent her after, whether for rent money or a quick answer on a trade receipt. The question now was whether she wanted to, whether she believed that this was a stain on her conscience too large to bear.

Juliette picked up the receiver and pressed it to her ear. "Wéi?"

"Miss Cai?"

The voice was speaking English. And it sounded like—

"*Roma?*"

An uncomfortable cough. "Close, but no. It's Benedikt."

Juliette released a tight breath, pushing back her disappointment. She told herself it was because she had been expecting Roma to have found the Frenchman, not because she wanted to hear Roma's voice.

"Did something happen?" she asked, lowering her volume. A quick glance over her shoulder showed her there was no one else in the hallway, but that didn't mean no one was listening in on her conversation.

"Define what *something* is," Benedikt replied, his voice pitching low too. "I've been meaning to contact you for days, but this is the first time I managed to shake Roma off. Your cousin took his sister."

For a long moment, Juliette did not comprehend what Benedikt Montagov was talking about. Then, as the words registered, she spluttered, "*What?* Rosalind took Alisa?"

"No, no," Benedikt rushed to correct. English was far too simple a language for familial relations, and he sounded confused that she had leaped to that conclusion. "Your tángdì. Cai Tailei. Now Roma has torn through the whole city looking for Alisa, but she's nowhere to be found. I figured that when his back was turned I may as well ask if you knew anything."

Juliette pressed a hand to her eyes, biting back the burning urge to scream. Of course Tyler would pull a stunt like this now. As if one wayward cousin wasn't enough. Now *another* had to go poke at the blood feud.

"I do not," Juliette replied bitterly. "I did not even know that he had taken her. Is she safe?"

"He cannot harm her—won't harm her. She will have to remain safe and alive if he is to get his chance at killing Roma."

Juliette almost dropped the receiver. "I beg your *pardon?*" She looked around again. Two messengers were on the landing of the stairs, giving her a suspicious look. Juliette forced herself to refrain from shouting. "How do you mean?"

Benedikt was unspeaking for a long moment. It almost seemed he was regretful to have to deliver this news.

"A duel, Miss Cai. If Roma can't find Alisa in three days' time, then he's going to fight a duel with Tyler to get her back."

Juliette found Tyler hours later, among the dimly illuminated tables at Bailemen. It seemed like decades had passed since she was last here with Roma, like the city had shifted and grown so much wider underneath her feet. The dance hall, however, was as full as ever. A place like Bailemen would probably never fully clear out, even if there was war outside.

"Scatter," she spat at the men surrounding him, seating herself opposite her cousin.

They all looked to Tyler for instruction. Juliette's hand was already inching for the garrote wire around her wrist in case she needed it, but then Tyler nodded, and the four around him walked away, eyeing Juliette with a hint of disdain.

"What can I do for you?" Tyler asked. He leaned back into his seat, hands splayed on the armrests. In front of him, he had three empty drink glasses, but he did not look in the least bit inebriated. He hadn't been here for long; the moment a messenger reported the sighting to Juliette, she had rushed over immediately.

"Don't do it," Juliette said plainly. "It was never worth it, and it's not worth it now."

Tyler picked up one of the empty glasses in front of him. He waved it in slow circles, like there was some invisible liquor inside that Juliette could not see.

"I was wondering how long the news would take to reach you," he replied, watching the glass refract light. "Longer than I thought, I must admit."

"Not all of us have as many ears on the city as you do."

"Ah, but instead, you have a direct line to the Montagovs."

Juliette's blood turned cold. So this was what it was. Tyler had finally decided to call her bluff.

With a quick tug, she snatched the glass out of her cousin's hold. He was not to look at the dance floor, at the shimmering walls, at the phantom drinks. She forced him to look at *her*.

"I assume you have been reading your Pushkin," she said. "Russian duels allow for seconds, and seconds are allowed to ask the aggressor whether they would like to apologize instead. So I ask, Tyler—return Alisa and let this go. It is not worth your life."

Tyler let out one short laugh. It did not have the delirious ring that echoed around the rest of the dance hall, heightened by the dark night and erratic music. It was laughter hedged in ice, a sound that came from predators watching their traps snap into place.

"What are you *thinking*?" As quick as his humor came, it was gone. Tyler leaned into the table. "Who asked you to speak on Roma Montagov's behalf? Who asked for *you* to be his second?"

Juliette's fists tightened. One of her fingers crept around her wire again—not to use it but just to ground herself, just to twist the thread hard around her finger until the pain neutralized the hot ire burning in her throat.

"It was merely a turn of phrase."

Tyler stood up. "Don't lie to me." There was no glee in his voice, not this time. He was taking it seriously, anointing himself as some overseer of Juliette's loyalties. "You can act as *my* second, and you can either let this play out or forfeit the Scarlet Gang to me now."

Juliette lunged across the table in a fury, but Tyler met her just as fast. Her fist halted in midair, Tyler's sudden grip on her wrist stopping the blow from landing on his nose.

"You are out of your mind," Juliette hissed. "He is just as likely to kill you. You are not invulnerable."

"I am not," Tyler agreed. "But I *am* a Scarlet. And right now that is more than can be said about you." He pushed her fist away harshly, then tugged at his coat in preparation to leave. Juliette, meanwhile, grabbed hold of the table, steadying not only her physical body but her rapidly spinning mind.

"Monday morning, tángjiě," Tyler said. "Right outside the border of the Settlement, by the Suzhou Creek, shall we say? Don't be late."

Twenty-Nine

I can't talk him out of it," Benedikt Montagov said.

Juliette glanced at him. They were standing alongside the Huangpu River, looking out into the water. Two days until the duel, and the weather was starting to turn warm—or perhaps it was the glint of the sun over the choppy waves that made the day seem overly golden.

How strange it was that Benedikt would agree to meet her like this, hands stuck in his pockets, unflinching when she arrived. He maintained his berth, certainly. Even in making nice, there might always be a part of him that thought Juliette could shoot at any moment. But still, he had arrived. He had arrived and was sharing information like they were old friends, united on a cause.

"You're sure that we cannot break Alisa out?"

"I don't know where she is," Juliette replied. "This city is too big. Just as I can hide Marshall Seo, Tyler can hide Alisa Montagova for as long as he wishes."

"Then there is no way around it," Benedikt said plainly. "Tyler will get the duel he wants."

Juliette took a deep, deep inhale, holding it in her throat.

"He has dictated that it will be a Russian duel, so they both only get one shot," she said, her words coming out as a croak. "But this is Roma and Tyler. Someone is going to die."

In the duels of stories, that one shot often went awry—striking the ground instead, piercing through a cap instead. But neither Roma nor Tyler was capable of such ineptitude.

"It's worse," Benedikt said. "If we're really going by the old rules, the person who challenged the duel receives first shot. What are the chances that Tyler will miss?"

Juliette squeezed her eyes shut, bracing against the intense prickling that had started up in her head. The wind was not helping. The wind was luring out what terror she was trying to clamp in, asking for a dance.

"None," she whispered. "Absolutely none."

She didn't want to see this unfold. Scarlet against White Flower. Family against her whole heart, beating red and bloody.

"You can talk him out of it, Juliette."

Juliette startled, opening her eyes again and turning to look at Benedikt Montagov. He had switched to using her first name. Perhaps he didn't mistrust her as much as it seemed.

"I have tried. Tyler won't listen to me."

"Not Tyler."

Her stomach dived, wondering if Benedikt was implying what she thought he was. When the wind blew across her face this time, it was as frigid as ice. A tear had tracked down her cheek, running sharply and quickly, dropping to the concrete before it could be seen. They were silent for a few moments while the Bund rumbled around them, with Benedikt looking out into the river and Juliette looking at him, wondering exactly how much he knew.

She got her answer when Benedikt caught her gaze and asked, "Why don't you tell him?"

"Tell him what?" she replied. She knew, of course. *The truth. Tell him the truth.* Benedikt had been at the hospital that day. He had seen Roma's unwillingness to walk away from Juliette. It was not hard to put together what they were to each other.

-Lovers. Liars.

"It is not like Roma cannot keep a secret," Benedikt said. "He cares little for his own life because he cares so much about everyone else's. He would throw himself in harm's way for Alisa because she's all he has left. But if he knows he still has you, he might be less eager to rush into death. Tell him you lied. Tell him Marshall is alive. He'll have to find a different plan."

Juliette shook her head. Pretty as it might be to think it all came back to this—to her, to love—that was one mere fracture on a whole web of shattered glass.

"It won't do anything," she replied quietly. "Besides, I am not afraid of him revealing to the world that Marshall is alive. I am afraid of him forgiving me."

Benedikt swerved to face her. He looked aghast at her words. "Whatever is there to be afraid of?"

"You don't understand." Juliette hugged her arms to herself. "So long as he hates me, we are safe. If we love again . . . this city may just kill us both for daring to hope."

She would be saving him from one strike of death just to push him right into another.

Indeed, Benedikt's long silence seemed to say. *I don't understand.* Juliette had watched Benedikt walk into the safe house in search of Marshall Seo. She had almost taken a bullet to the face in Benedikt's vengeance for Marshall Seo. She knew that Benedikt understood fear. Fear of love and all the ways that it might not come back, all the ways that it could hurt. But he didn't fear a blood feud, and Juliette was glad he had been spared from at least one terrible thing.

"Spit it out, Benedikt Montagov," she whispered when the silence drew on.

Benedikt turned his back to the river.

"I think," he said eventually, so faintly that it seemed like his mind was elsewhere, "you do yourself a disservice by refusing to hope."

Before Juliette could think to respond, Benedikt had already given her a friendly pat on the shoulder and was walking away, leaving her standing at the Bund, one lone girl with her coat billowing in the wind.

Kathleen had leafed through the correspondences, read the information that had been passed on. There was no doubting it anymore, no matter which direction one looked at it from. All the times Lord Cai had made threats to the Scarlet Gang, warning of a spy in the inner circle. All the times he had gone around the house, making note of which relatives resided within earshot of his meetings, cutting down their numbers one by one in hopes that he had managed to purge the spy out. It had been Rosalind. It had always been Rosalind.

And Kathleen wanted answers.

She trekked up the stairs, single-minded in her task. Her sister had promised. Even oceans apart, it had been her, Rosalind, and Juliette—promising to protect one another, promising that they were untouchable so long as they stuck together. What was possibly more important than that?

Kathleen stopped outside Rosalind's door, ignoring the Scarlet standing guard. She knocked, her knuckles coming down harshly enough to hurt.

"Rosalind, open the door."

"She's hardly in a position to be walking around," the Scarlet said. "Just go in."

"No," Kathleen managed. "No, I want her to get up and look me in the eye."

Never had Kathleen felt such treachery stab her through the gut. She understood if Rosalind had lost her loyalty to the Scarlet Gang. She understood if Rosalind had finally snapped, determined to ruin the Cai name after years and years of being kept out from the core of the family. That alone was something Kathleen could forgive, even if it was a slap to Juliette's face.

What Kathleen couldn't comprehend was why *she* hadn't been told.

"Rosalind," she snapped once more.

She was answered with silence. Too much silence. When she finally tried to open the door, it was locked.

"How long has it been since you checked in on her?" Kathleen demanded.

The Scarlet blinked, staring at the handle that wouldn't turn. "Merely an hour."

"*Merely* an hour?"

Something was wrong. That much was immediately clear. The Scarlet quickly waved for Kathleen to take a step back. She shifted out of the way, and the Scarlet kicked the door hard, blowing it off its hinges with a thud. The door whipped back against the wall and the room came into view: an empty bed, a chair pushed over, and the window wide open, the gossamer curtains blowing in the breeze.

Kathleen rushed to the window. There was a rope hanging over the ledge, made entirely of bedsheets, secured to one of the legs of the four-poster bed. It trailed down, down, down to the flower beds below, where the roses were trampled into the soil.

Kathleen heaved a long, bitter sigh. "She made a run for it."

If Roma hadn't been polishing his pistol in the storage room on the ground floor, he wouldn't have heard the rustle in the alley outside.

The window was pulled open, the afternoon sunlight pouring into the dusty corners, reflecting off the brass lamps. When he set the cloth down, he heard a splash and then a quiet curse. It sounded like a girl whimpering in pain, footsteps coming nearer and nearer.

Roma's immediate thought was that it was Alisa—that she had managed to escape and had found her way back home. Without even thinking, Roma pushed the window as wide as it would go and climbed through, his shoes clunking down on the wet clay ground outside. Nothing on the northern side. He spun around.

And saw Rosalind Lang, dressed in what looked like a nightgown, a heavy coat thrown over her shoulders.

Roma resisted the urge to rub his eyes, wondering if he was hallucinating. His lack of sleep in the last few days might finally be getting to him, because if Rosalind's presence here wasn't strange enough, her bedraggled state certainly was.

Then a beat passed, and Rosalind pulled a pistol from her coat. She raised it fast, seeming to expect a fight.

Roma didn't return the gesture. He only raised his hands slowly and said, "Hello. What are you doing here?"

There was humor in this—it wasn't lost on him, despite the utterly unhumorous situation. Once upon a time, before Roma met Juliette, before Roma rolled a marble at her feet and fell in love with her, he had been sent into Scarlet territory with another mission.

He had been sent in for Rosalind.

That was why his father had started to suspect him in the end. Rosalind Lang had become the talk of the town as the best dancer the Scarlet burlesque club had ever seen, and there had been plans for Roma to mingle into the Scarlet crowds, to get closer to Rosalind and obtain Scarlet information under the guise of a great, star-crossed love affair. Instead, Roma had heard rumors of Juliette Cai's return to Shanghai and had switched gears while crossing onto Scarlet territory, wanting to see this terrible Scarlet heir for himself.

He hadn't stood a chance. The moment he saw Juliette Cai for the first time, saw that smile playing on her lips, standing there at the Bund, it was a done matter. That false star-crossed love affair pivoted and turned real. Roma would claim, in reporting back, he hadn't had any luck with their plan, yet he kept slinking into Scarlet territory regardless. Of course his father caught on.

How strange it was to find Rosalind Lang here, mere paces away from his father's domain, five years later.

"One shout," he said when Rosalind kept the pistol pointed in his direction. "That's all it takes before White Flowers rush out of the house and you are riddled with bullets. Think carefully, Miss Lang."

"About what?" Rosalind managed. Her hand was trembling. "I may think carefully and shoot you, or I may forget to think entirely and shoot you."

Roma frowned. When he took a step closer, he saw the redness in her eyes, like she had been freshly crying. "Teach me how one should forget to think," he remarked. "That sounds like a feat most valuable."

He did not know what he was quite stalling for. It didn't seem right, somehow, to draw forth a crowd of White Flowers and kill Rosalind Lang. Perhaps it was because he did not dislike her sister, and Roma had no inclination to bring hurt onto Kathleen Lang.

Perhaps it was because she reminded him of Juliette.

"Don't think I won't shoot," Rosalind spat. "Shout for help. Do it!"

Roma did nothing. He only stood there, frowning. *What could she possibly be doing here?*

Finally, Rosalind gave up, a fresh tear tracking down her face as she lowered the gun.

"How much easier it would have been," she whispered, "if it had been you instead. How good you are. How noble."

Rosalind quickly pressed the back of her hand to her lips, like she was stopping herself from saying more. With a hard blink to clear her eyes of tears, she charged forward and hurried by, her shoulder brushing Roma's as she passed. Roma stared on even after she disappeared, fixated on the mouth of the alleyway as if mere concentration could dissolve his bewilderment.

Maybe he should have shot her. It would have been what Juliette deserved. An eye for an eye. A life for a life.

Roma shook his head. But that wasn't who he was. It wasn't who he wanted to be. The Scarlet Gang had taken Alisa, and he would get her back honorably. The Scarlet Gang wanted to stoop low, and he would steer in an entirely new direction. He had washed his hands with enough blood. He was tired of it. Tired of the smell that permeated into his sleep, tired of hating so deeply that it burned him from the inside out.

Quietly, Roma climbed back in through the window.

Thirty

The sky was overcast, dark enough that the morning almost seemed to be nearing night. That would have been too much to ask for. If the whole day could simply skip past itself, then no duel could be fought.

But here they were, standing by the Suzhou Creek under clouds as plump and heavy as waterlogged laundry. Juliette couldn't make sense of how quiet it was, how there hardly seemed to be anyone present today on the roads. In the distance, the large gasworks factories sat utterly idle, not a single worker to be seen. Was there something happening that she did not know about? Some rally gathering all the numbers elsewhere in the city that she was not aware of?

"Look alert, Juliette."

Juliette cast a wary eye to Tyler as he hovered at the end of the alley, ready for the very moment that the Montagovs appeared. Directly ahead, the creek flowed on, filled with fishing boats and houseboats that seemed to sit unoccupied.

"I don't suppose we're following the actual dueling code, are we?" she asked. "Because there are quite literally five hundred rules, and my Russian vocabulary only goes so far."

In answer, Tyler pulled something from his pocket and tossed it Juliette's way. She caught it swiftly, the pages crumpling underneath her fingers. The cover was faded, but its text was still legible, surrounded by a border decoration: *Yevgeniy Onegin*.

"Thirty-two paces," Tyler replied evenly. "We can make that trash bag a barrier."

Juliette glanced over her shoulder, checking on Alisa again. The girl stood under the grip of two of Tyler's men. Another two Scarlets were posted at the other end of the alley. They were standing guard in case the White Flowers decided to rush in from the back roads and summon a turf war, but Roma would never be so thoughtless. There was no possible victory picking a fight within such a small space, surrounded by high walls and tiled rooftops that jutted into either side. All that could possibly suit a place like this was a duel.

Thirty-two paces. A barrier in the middle, which the dueler on each side could approach but could not retreat from once they had stepped forward. Tyler had one shot. If he missed, Roma could compel him right to the barrier, and when Roma took his returning shot, there was only one outcome possible. At such proximity, Roma could only strike true.

But that required Tyler missing first. And even at thirty-two paces, Juliette wasn't sure if it was possible. She could only hope that they wouldn't advance to the barrier. That they would both stay far, far from each other, and both would miss, and this duel would end with honor restored and without death, with Alisa returned to the White Flowers and Tyler mollified.

An utter joke, Juliette thought. Her heart was thudding a storm in her chest. Never could that happen. So how was this going to end?

"Hey," Juliette said, stepping closer to Alisa. "You need anything? Thirsty?"

Alisa shook her head. She tried to tug her arm out of her captors' hold, but it was a weak effort; she had long given up trying to escape.

"I just want to go home," she said frostily.

Juliette swallowed hard. "You will." She placed the copy of Tyler's novel at Alisa's feet. "Look after this for me, would you?"

Tyler had promised to give Alisa back at the duel's end, regardless of the result. So far, he certainly seemed to have kept his word. Alisa was unharmed—at most, she only looked annoyed to be here.

Perhaps, it occurred to Juliette suddenly, Alisa didn't even know that her brother was being summoned for a duel.

Footsteps sounded from the road outside the alleyway. Juliette inhaled sharply and straightened, her fists clenching hard. If Alisa didn't know why she was here, she would soon.

Roma and Benedikt appeared. They were visibly tense, coats pulled up to their necks to brace against the cold. For a moment, Juliette wondered if Roma might be wearing something protective underneath, but then he unbuttoned his coat, showing merely a pristine white shirt. There would be no tricks here. Tyler would see through any attempt.

"Tyler," Juliette snapped. Her voice drew Roma's attention, summoning his eyes to the back, where Alisa was being held. He lurched forward, but Benedikt grabbed his arm, warning him against any sudden movements. Another cold gale blew into the alley. The Montagovs were twin reflections of the same picture—one ablaze as a study of contrasts and shadows, the other a faded, blond replicant.

"No need to chide me," Tyler replied, striding toward her. "I'm getting into position."

Just as he started to walk, there was a loud *bang!* from nearby, and everybody in the alley flinched. No matter how blasé Tyler acted, he was just as tense as Juliette was. Where Juliette stood taut in fear, he stood white-knuckled to prepare for blood.

"Only a rickshaw runner, I'm sure," Juliette said. She offered Alisa another glance, trying to communicate with her eyes that everything would be all right, before walking to meet Benedikt in the middle of the alley. As seconds, this was supposed to be their last chance to communicate on behalf of the duelers, to resolve the matter and walk away.

"Any success?" Benedikt murmured.

Juliette shook her head. "No luck. What about with Roma?"

"He won't back down."

Knowing that they were speaking about him, Roma kept his gaze trained on Juliette. His expression was blank, revealing nothing.

"Roma," Juliette whispered. She knew that he could hear her. Even if she mouthed every word, Roma could probably read it. "Don't do it."

"I must," he said. There was no other argument. It was as simple as that. The blood feud was fated to run deep. Even Roma, who had hated the idea of it, couldn't resist its draw. It would pull him in, force him to kill.

Remember what you used to say, Juliette wanted to scream. *Astra inclinant, sed non obligant.*

She remained still, her breath caught in her throat. Her heart was pounding, so loud that it had to be audible, so loud that it was all she could hear. But Roma—Roma only idly turned and took his position at the end of the alley, sparing no second glance at Juliette or Benedikt.

The moment Juliette turned on her heel and started to walk, Benedikt snapped to attention too. He hurried to Roma and grabbed him by the elbow, hissing something that Juliette could no longer catch. With every three steps, she glanced over her shoulder, trying to make sense of what was happening, but each time, Roma did not look responsive. He only shook his head and brushed his cousin off.

"Tyler," Juliette called.

"Step behind me," Tyler replied. He did not look in Juliette's direction. "Unless you want to be within firing range?"

One breath in. One breath out.

"Tyler—"

This time Tyler did give her his attention, his pistol dangling at his side. "Yes?"

And Juliette's tongue stalled. What was she to say? Was she to beg for Roma's life? Was she to plead, drop to her knees, do all that Tyler expected her to do as that weak-hearted girl he had never thought could lead?

Juliette swallowed hard. She could not. She *would* not. She was the heir to the Scarlet Gang. Heir of mobsters and merchants and *monsters*, each and every one of them, blood frothing at the mouth. She kneeled to no one.

Tyler smiled. "Take your place, then."

But *God*, she wished she weren't. She wished she could just be a girl.

Juliette walked to the back of the alley, stopping beside Alisa. By now Alisa was starting to frown. She was putting together the pieces, watching Roma and Tyler face each other at opposite ends of an alley, pistols in their hands, as Benedikt said, "Tyler Cai. You may approach the barrier at your own pace."

"What's happening?" Alisa demanded suddenly. "Is this a *duel*?"

A crack dashed across Juliette's heart. She felt the gouge form like it was a physical sensation.

"Don't look," Juliette said to Alisa.

Tyler was walking far too fast. The fear of a Russian duel was that the first shooter would miss, that the closer they had approached the barrier for their own shot, and closer they were when it became their opponent's turn. But Tyler did not seem to have that worry at all. Tyler kept going, and going, and going, until he had closed in on the barrier entirely, his shoes stopping by the trash bag.

"What do you mean *don't look*?" Alisa shrieked. She was struggling, squirming like her life depended on it, doing everything in her effort to loosen the grip the Scarlets had on her arms. "He will kill him, Juliette! Tyler will *kill* him!"

"Alisa Montagova," Juliette snapped. "I said look away—"

Tyler raised his pistol. Aimed.

And just as Alisa started to scream, a shot rang into the early morning, as loud as the world ending.

The scream ended abruptly.

Tyler touched his chest, where a bloom of red was starting, flowing faster and faster. Roma took a step back, his eyes widening, searching the scene before him.

Because he had not made the illegal shot.

Juliette had.

Both her hands came around her smoking pistol. There was no room for regret now. She had done it. She had done it, and she could not stop there. She turned, and with a sob choked on her tongue, she shot each and every one of Tyler's men before they had even comprehended what was happening, bullets studding their temples, their necks, their chests.

The moment they were all down, Juliette threw her pistol to the ground too.

"*Dammit*, Tyler!" she screamed. Tyler turned around and looked at her—really looked at her. He dropped to his knees. Fell to his side. Rolled to face the dark, dark sky.

Juliette rushed forward. She had made the shot, all his men were dead, and yet still she reached out and tried to stanch his wound as if she would be more despicable if she didn't try, as if there could possibly be any coming back from this.

"Why did you have to keep pushing?" she cried. "Why couldn't you have just *left it*?"

Tyler blinked slowly. It would have been easier if he had answered Juliette in hatred. It would have been easier if he had spat at her and called her a traitor, used any of the names that he never had any trouble labeling her with. Instead, he looked confused. Instead, he touched his weeping wound over Juliette's hands and pressed down, and when his fingers came back covered in bright scarlet, it was absolute incomprehension that marred his face, like he never thought Juliette would hurt him this way.

"Why?" he rasped. He might have been echoing her. But Juliette knew he wasn't—he was asking a question of itself.

Juliette's hands came down harder, certain that if she just pressed enough, by sheer will she could close the wound, could stop the blood, could reverse the last minute of the world.

But even if she did, the city's feud would still go on.

"Because—" Juliette said. Her voice was no louder than a bare whisper. Yet in the quiet of the alley, with only Tyler's gasps, she was all that could be heard. "I love him. I love him, Tyler, and you tried to take him from me."

Tyler exhaled. Something like a dry laugh shuddered from his lungs. "All you . . . had to do," he said, "was . . . choose your people."

Juliette's jaw trembled. Nothing was ever as simple as "my people" and "your people," but to Tyler, it was. He thought himself capable of rising to the top, thought himself worthy of being the next heir, but all he had ever done in his eighteen years was act off orders from the top, tainted by the hate that ran like poison through their lives. How could she fault him for that?

In that fleeting moment, Juliette closed her eyes and tried to remember a time before it all. A time when Tyler tossed her his apple before breakfast because she was hungry and her little fingers couldn't reach the fruit bowl. When Tyler climbed onto the roof of the house to fix the electrical wiring and was hailed a hero by the household staff. When Juliette walked into his bedroom shortly after she'd returned from New York and found him curled into himself, crying over a picture of his father. He had slammed his door in her face, but she understood.

She had always understood.

By the time Juliette opened her eyes and whispered, "I'm sorry," Tyler was already dead.

Thirty-One

Numbly, Juliette removed her hands from Tyler's body. They were coated in red up to her wrists. Her fingers were wet, slick with the viscosity of blood.

For a long moment, the alley was quiet and still, frozen like a film that had become stuck on its reel. Then Alisa darted forward and flung herself at Roma, who opened his arms for her, his face shell-shocked. He stared at Juliette, Juliette stared at her hands, and the only one who seemed to have some sense remaining was Benedikt, who called, "Juliette, you should probably tell him now."

A harsh, salt-soaked gust of wind blew at Juliette's hair, obscuring her vision when she looked up. Some faint argument had broken out afar in tandem with dimly chiming bells—striking twelve times to signal noon, each echo adding to the white noise in her ears.

"Just my two cents," Benedikt added softly.

Roma's grip tightened on Alisa. He looked between Juliette and his cousin, his brow furrowing, still unable to erase the shock in his expression.

"What?" he managed faintly. His eyes shot to the corpses on the ground. "Tell me what?"

Juliette rose to her feet. It was a shaky effort. It was that feeling in dreams when she couldn't push up from the ground, her bones as heavy as metal.

Only before Juliette could respond, she was interrupted by another voice—one that came from above, from the roof of the building pressing in on the alleyway.

"That she beat me to the shot."

A blur of motion landed before her with a *thump*. Marshall Seo turned smoothly, as if he had not leaped down two stories, tugging off the cloth around his face and offering Roma a small smile.

Roma stared. And stared, and stared, and stared.

Then he ran at Marshall and hugged him so tightly that he had to thump his friend's back to work off his excess energy. Marshall hugged Roma just as enthusiastically in return, not at all minding the attack.

"You died," Roma gasped. "I saw you die."

"Yes," Marshall replied simply, "Juliette tried very hard to make sure of that."

Suddenly, Roma released Marshall, his eyes snapping to Juliette. She could feel her distress emanating off her skin like a visible aura. She didn't know how to stand or where to place her hands, didn't know whether it was appropriate to try to rub the blood off or if she was to pretend she wasn't occupying an alley with three White Flowers while all her Scarlets lay dead around her.

Roma's mouth opened. Before he could demand an explanation, Juliette was already speaking, her eyes turned back to her hands. She couldn't—*couldn't* look at him.

"I had to." Her voice cracked. "Tyler had to see your hatred. He would have destroyed us if he knew I—" Juliette broke off, her red fingers scrunching into fists. She hardly needed to elaborate. They had heard her. They all heard what she'd said to Tyler.

"Juliette."

Juliette looked up. She lifted her chin and faked bravery, faked it like she faked every damn thing in her life—all to survive, and for what? To piece together some pathetic excuse of living surrounded by material goods and not a single shred of happiness. Her heart had never felt so heavy.

"It doesn't matter," Juliette said. "He can't hurt us now, can he?"

Juliette turned away and started to walk. She could feel it—the shaking was already starting in her hands, and soon the tremors would shudder her chest, consume her whole body. She needed to leave before she could *break*, before her mind started to circle exactly what she had done here and how she would explain this away.

Tyler was dead. Tyler's men were dead. The only person left to spin the tale was Juliette. She could say whatever she wanted, and the thought felt too big for her to comprehend.

"Juliette."

Footsteps thundered after her. She picked up her pace a moment too late, a touch coming upon her wrist. Only as soon as Roma grabbed her arm, a horrific sound came from outside the alley, from North Suzhou Road, near the wide creek. They both ducked at once, heads turning toward the source.

"What was that?" Benedikt demanded. "Was that gunfire?"

The sound came again: a spray of bullets moving even closer. Like phantoms materializing from the mists, three men suddenly ran across the mouth of the alley—quickly enough that they did not sight Roma and Juliette standing there, but not so quick that Juliette couldn't sight the red rags tied around their arms. It all seemed to happen in seconds. Where it had been quiet, the roads suspiciously empty like its business occupants were taking the day off, the city suddenly roared to life: shouting at every corner, and gunfire. Constant gunfire.

"It's happening," Juliette said in disbelief. Today was the twenty-first of March, by the Western calendar. "Revolution."

"Where are they? Where are Juliette and Tyler?"

Kathleen peered down the second-floor banister, frowning at the sudden commotion. The front door slammed and the volume in the foyer increased, voices shouting atop one another. Lady Cai seemed to be giving instructions, but with so many other people speaking too, she had grown inaudible.

Kathleen hurried down the stairs. "What's going on?" she asked.

Nobody paid her any attention. Lady Cai continued giving orders, her posture stick straight, her arms gesticulating—grouping men together and sending them out the door as if she were merely conducting some orchestral show.

"Niāngniang." Kathleen slid herself right in front of Lady Cai. At any other time, she would never have dared. Right now, the house was in so much chaos that her aunt couldn't tell her off. "Please. Tell me what is happening."

Lady Cai tried to brush Kathleen aside.

"Communists are acting against Kuomintang instructions for patience," she said distractedly. "Separate uprisings are happening across the city in an attempt to take Shanghai for the Northern Expedition." It was then that Lady Cai cocked her head, looking at Kathleen properly. "Aren't you our inside source on this business?"

"I—yes," Kathleen replied, tripping over her words. She hoped she wasn't about to get the blame for this. "I am your source. And I've told everyone again and again that the strikes will get larger, that their numbers will rise—"

"Nothing to worry about," Lady Cai interrupted, her no-nonsense mode returning. "No matter what the Communists take, the Nationalists will take it back, and then it will again be in our hands. Our only problem now"—she waved her hands at the nearest group of men—"is finding where my daughter has gotten herself to before she gets herself killed."

Kathleen watched their gangsters hurry out the door. Heard them mumble Tyler's name, Juliette's name.

Rosalind was missing too. And yet there was hardly a single gangster worried. They pushed and shoved to get out, piling onto the streets while the workers caused chaos, but only because they had been given the instruction to find the younger Cais, somewhere out in the city. If Lady Cai had not commanded it, would they still care?

Kathleen breathed out, stepping away from Lady Cai. Even here, at the mansion, which sat along the city's outer boundaries, there came the sound of gunfire in the distance. There came the deep, deep rumble of the ground shifting, like something colossal had just blown up.

Juliette would be fine. She would not be so easily taken down.

Shanghai, on the other hand, was a different question.

And Rosalind, too, was another matter entirely.

Kathleen pulled her coat off the rack. She merged with a group of messengers heading out of the house, piling into a car heading for the heart of the city. She needed to find Rosalind. She needed to get her sister back before this city burned down around them.

Lady Cai walked upon the driveway, her arms folded, and locked eyes with Kathleen through the window of the car.

When the car drove off, Lady Cai did not protest.

Juliette watched a brothel owner wander out onto her balcony, her silk billowing in the wind. In seconds, she was shot from below, and with a spray of red, tumbled over the railing onto the hard cement ground.

The worker who had fired the bullet did not pause. He was already moving on, joining a crusade of others in their hunt for another target.

Juliette slammed back inside the alley, her hand flying to her mouth, the metallic tang of the drying blood hitting her tongue. She knew violence. She was used to it, used to bloodshed and hatred . . . but *this*? This was on a scale wholly unknown. This was not a feud between gangs in a contained face-off. This was the whole city rising up from the gutters, and it seemed riots and protests were no longer enough.

Once the workers were finished, the Nationalists would come in to claim an allied victory. And depending on when the blackmailer decided to show their face, it would soon turn into a civil war fought with monsters and madness. Juliette supposed she should be grateful this revolution was merely an exercise in bullets right now. The monsters were being conserved. Squirreled away until the real claim for power.

"We have to go," Benedikt declared. "I'm sorry, Juliette, but you'll have to leave the bodies here."

"No matter," Juliette replied quietly, wiping at her face. Perhaps when they were found later, the workers would be blamed for the deaths. Perhaps she wouldn't need to be more terrible. She could just be a murderer instead of a murderer *and* a liar.

Another round of heavy gunfire. They had to take the back roads out. There was no way they could venture along the main creek and not be shot immediately.

"Where are we going to go?" Alisa whispered. There was something in her hands. She had retrieved Tyler's book, hugging it to her chest. "What sort of—"

Marshall shushed her, then gestured for them to press against the wall, remaining very still while a group gathered close to the alley, yelling instructions at one another to fan out. This was not just an opportunity to incite chaos. With the machine guns coming out, the workers were trying to take Shanghai from the hands of imperialists and gangsters.

It was exactly what both the Scarlets and the White Flowers had feared.

"We have a safe house two streets away," Benedikt reported quietly when the gunshots seemed to move in the other direction. "Let's go."

Marshall touched Juliette's elbow. "Come with us."

Juliette startled. She could still feel Roma's eyes on her.

"No," she said. "No, I have my own."

The ground shook under their feet. Somewhere, somehow, something was blowing up. On the other side of the creek, the nearest factory's windows all shattered into dust.

There was no time to lose. They needed to disperse.

Juliette bent and picked up the pistol she had tossed, trying hard not to look at her cousin's body. "Stay inside until this blows over. When it ends, Shanghai will not be the same city." She made to leave, and for the second time, Roma lunged out quickly and grabbed her wrist. This time Juliette finally whirled to face him, her teeth gritted.

"Roma, let go."

"I'm coming with you."

"The hell you are."

"Quit running from me," Roma snapped. "We need to talk."

"Really?" Juliette exclaimed. A bullet struck the mouth of the alley, and Juliette knew that they had been spotted. "You want to talk *now*? While the city undergoes revolution?"

Behind them, Benedikt and Marshall were wide-eyed, uncertain if they needed to step in and facilitate this. They could either demand that Juliette accept it, or persuade Roma to back off, and neither option seemed very likely to have success. Only Alisa offered a little thumbs-up as Roma turned over his shoulder, waiting to see if another bullet was coming.

"Benedikt, Marshall," he said. There was a note of awe in his voice that he could at last say those two names together again, the way that things were supposed to be—the return to a normal he knew even if the world around him was splitting apart. "Please take Alisa to the safe house."

"Roma—"

"I'm standing here until Juliette agrees to talk," he warned. "If the workers storm this alley, then they themselves can move me."

Juliette stared at him, flabbergasted. "You have lost your mind."

True to his word, he was unmoving as Benedikt and Marshall

exchanged a quick nod, nudging Alisa to hurry and go. Alisa reached over to squeeze Roma's arm as they passed by, whispering a quick, "Stay safe," before the three of them disappeared. Then it was only Roma and Juliette and an alley soaked in red.

"It is not a difficult choice, Juliette," he said. Voices now, coming right by the main road, seconds away from turning into the alley. "We can leave, or we can die here."

Juliette felt the press of his fingers on her wrist. She wondered if he noticed her pulse beating a cacophony under his touch.

"For crying out loud," she said darkly, shaking his grip loose so that his fingers entwined with hers instead, blood mixing on skin, pulling him away from the mouth of the alley. "You are so dramatic."

Just as the workers rounded into the alley and loosed their ammunition, Juliette and Roma disappeared through the narrow back passages and merged into the city.

Thirty-Two

Blockades were already forming on the streets, an attempt to close the Concessions before the havoc traveled here, too. Roma and Juliette reached their intended destination in the nick of time, turning onto a thin street before British soldiers could rope it off. Every window they hurried past had its curtains drawn tight. The sounds of gunfire followed on their heels. Fighting would soon arrive in the vicinity.

"Quick," Juliette whispered, opening the door to the safe house. After accepting that he was going to keep playing vigilante, she had warned Marshall to keep his temporary residence unlocked when he was not there—to ensure that it seemed unoccupied if any Scarlets were to come looking—and she was relieved to find that he had listened. This was the closest Scarlet location. She figured there was no harm in taking shelter here, especially when it was outside proper International Settlement territory, hovering at the edges of Zhabei.

Just as Roma hurried in and Juliette bolted the door, there came shouting from the British soldiers at their makeshift barricade. Their voices coursed down the street, bringing a hush upon the apartments as every resident inside waited for chaos to erupt.

"Are the windows boarded?" Roma demanded.

Juliette didn't answer; she only waited for Roma to beeline for the windows and pull at the curtains, breathing out in relief when he found them to be nailed shut with wooden panels.

"The darkness didn't give it away?" she muttered, bringing her lighter to a candle on the table.

The first echoes of shooting began outside. Perhaps Juliette should have tried to get home instead, tried to organize the Scarlets to fight back. Somehow, she had a feeling it would not make a difference. For the first time, the gangsters were not only outnumbered but vastly overpowered.

Roma pulled the curtains shut tightly. He waited there for a moment, then turned around, folding his arms and leaning up against the boards. There was nowhere really to sit: Marshall had made the place cozy, but it was still as small as a crawl space. One chair, propped near the stove, and a mattress on the floor, the blankets resembling a nest atop it.

Juliette opted to lean up against the door. They remained like that, on opposite ends of the room, unspeaking.

Until Roma said: "I'm sorry."

Juliette's eyes widened a fraction. For whatever reason, there was anger roiling in her belly. Not anger at Roma. Just anger—at the world.

"Why are *you* sorry?" she asked quietly.

Slowly Roma inched away from the window. She watched as he trailed his fingers across the surface of the table and found no dust, a hint of fascination flashing in his eyes before his gaze flickered to the coat hanging on the wall. It seemed Roma had come to the realization that this was where Marshall had been living.

Roma took another step across the room. In answer to her question, he gestured at the blood on her hands.

"He was still your cousin, Juliette. I'm sorry."

Juliette closed her fists, then tucked them under her arms, folding her posture. Her head was a storm. She had fired on her cousin. Fired on his men—her own men—Scarlets, all of them. Still, she couldn't quite regret it. She would live with this forever, live with her cousin's blood on her hands, and in the dark of night when no one could hear her, she would cry her tears and mourn the boy he could have been. She would mourn the other Scarlets just as she mourned the White Flowers she had destroyed in the blood feud, and even more so, because their loyalty should have been their protection, and yet Juliette had turned on them.

She didn't regret it. She hated it, and she hated herself. But standing there, in front of her, was the reason for everything she had done, and to look upon him alive and well was enough to push back the loathing she had for the blood on her hands, for the city that had made her into this monster of a person.

"This kindness is disconcerting," she managed. "Whatever turmoil exists in my heart, I deserve it."

Roma sighed. It was a vast sigh, one that might have formed smoke had he huffed just a tad harder.

"You are a liar, Juliette Cai," he said. "You lied to me until I wanted you dead."

Juliette couldn't bear how soft his voice had grown. "Because I could not risk the consequences. I could not risk my own cousin taking your life because I was too weak to let you go." She loosened her fists, feeling the dried blood itch in the lines of her palms. "And yet he pursued your death nonetheless."

Roma inched forward once more. He was careful, careful even to look at her, afraid that she might bolt. "You think so intently of protecting me that you did not consider whether I wanted to be protected. I would have rather died knowing you are as you are than lived a long life thinking you cruel."

"I *am* cruel."

"You are not."

Juliette swallowed hard. How quickly he forgot. How quickly he tried to convince himself otherwise. "Your mother, Roma."

"Oh, please," he said, "I already know."

He . . . what? A tremor hastened through the room: Juliette staring at Roma and Roma staring right back. "What do you mean?"

"I know how these things *work*, Juliette." Roma tore a hand through his hair, exasperated. His dark locks became so mussed that the longer strands fell loose over his forehead, and all Juliette could think was that this stone-cold, perfect image of a boy was at last giving way for the real one underneath. "I know we were a risk to each other from the very beginning. And I know you far better than you think I do."

"Do you?" Juliette challenged.

But Roma wasn't buying her pity party. He folded his arms. "In what world would you have sent men after my mother, no matter how upset you were? You didn't know her. She had no personal gain to you, and if I never knew that you did it, then it wasn't to spite me, either. No, you told someone. In a fit of recklessness, you gave her address, however you found it, and then the blood feud did the rest of the work." Roma strode two, three steps more, stopping at arm's length in front of her. "Tell me I'm wrong."

Juliette looked away, her eyes prickling with tears. Somehow, he had found the heart of the matter and told it so generously that it seemed undeserved.

"You're not wrong," she managed.

Roma nodded, his shoulders straight and assured. By flickering candlelight, he appeared all the more sturdy, like nothing could phase through his bravado. Only as Juliette tried to blink away the emotion threatening at her eyes, she peered at Roma and found that he was struggling to do exactly the same.

"We live," he said, "with the consequences of our choices. I know that better than anyone, Juliette. I am the only one in this entire damn city who feels exactly as you do. You should have known that I would *understand*."

He didn't have to say it aloud. They both knew. Nurse. He was talking about Nurse, and the explosion at the Scarlet house.

"You're right," Juliette said tightly. "You do know. You know that all we do is take from each other, break each other's hearts in turn and hope the next time won't shatter us completely. When does it end, Roma? When will we realize that whatever sordid affair we have between us isn't worth the death and the sacrifice and—"

"Do you remember what you said?" Roma interrupted. "That day in the alley, when I told you my father made me set the explosion."

Of course she remembered. She was incapable of ever forgetting a single moment between them. Depending on how she looked at it, it was either a great talent or a mighty curse.

Juliette's voice shrank to a whisper. *"We could have fought him."*

Roma nodded. He swiped hard at his eye, getting rid of the moisture there. "Where has that attitude gone, Juliette? We keep bending to what the blood feud demands of us, letting go of what we want in fear that it will be taken first. Why must we *wonder* when this mutual destruction will end? Why don't we fight it? Why don't we just *end it?*"

A bitter laugh crept up from her lungs, echoing faintly into the room. "You pose questions that you know the answer to," she said. "I am *afraid*."

She was so damn afraid of being punished for her choices, and if it were easier to shut down, then why would she not? If there were an easier way to live, to choose ease over pain, how could she not?

But Juliette knew she was lying to herself. Once, she used to be braver than this.

Roma closed that final breath of space between them. His fingers grasped her chin, and he turned her gaze upon his. Juliette did not frighten, did not jolt out of the way. She knew his touch. Knew it to be gentle, even when it had tried being violent some few days or weeks or months ago.

"What are you afraid of?" Roma Montagov asked.

Juliette's lips parted. She exhaled a short, abrupt breath. "The consequences," she whispered, "of love in a city ruled by hate."

Roma drew his hand away. He remained quiet. A terrified part of Juliette wondered if this was it; if they had reached the end of the line. Try as she might to tell herself they were better off if she and Roma were finished, that future flashed suddenly before her eyes—one without this love, one without this fight—and the sorrow almost cleaved her in two.

"Answer me something," Roma said suddenly. His words sounded eerily familiar, and with delay, Juliette realized why. He was echoing her. He was echoing her that day behind the newspaper building, that day she had collapsed in the grass with hands just as bloody as the ones she held in front of her now. "*Do* you love me?"

Juliette felt her heart wrench. "Why are you asking?" she croaked. "Less than an hour ago, you wanted me dead."

"I said I wanted you dead," Roma confirmed. "I never said I didn't love you."

Juliette gave a weak splutter. "There's a difference?"

"Yes." His fingers twitched, like he was going to reach for her again. "Juliette—"

"I love you," she whispered. And in echo of *his* words so many months ago, "I have always loved you. I'm sorry I lied."

Roma was unmoving for one slow thud of a heartbeat. Their eyes locked, baring the truth their words left behind. And when Juliette's lip started to tremble, Roma finally pulled her into a tight embrace— so tightly that Juliette squeaked, but she clutched him back just as fiercely. In the end, this was all that they were. Two hearts pressed as close as they dared, shadows melding into one by the flickering candlelight.

"I missed you, dorogaya," he whispered against her ear. "I missed you so much."

The city was in chaos, and yet Kathleen wandered the streets in some dreamlike trance, left alone by the workers with rifles, left alone by the gangsters with broadswords. It was as if they did not see her, but they did: she made eye contact with each and every one of them, and they merely looked onward, finding no reason to bother one lone girl walking like she had nowhere to be, hard shoes coming down on the rough pavement.

She didn't know where to begin looking for Rosalind. She had tried the usual places, but the burlesque club was locked down and the restaurants were all barred. Their favorite shops were ransacked, windows smashed and doors torn straight off the hinges. Where else could Rosalind even go? What else could Kathleen do except walk the city and hope that some invisible string was pulling her to her sister?

Kathleen put one foot in front of the other. She had always had the skill to look like she belonged somewhere. Act like she had been invited in, because if she did not, then she would be waiting forever for an invitation that was not coming.

Who could have known that it would work during a revolution too?

"Ow!"

Kathleen turned around, thinking she heard a voice nearby. It sounded like a child, but why would a child be out during this time?

She turned the corner and identified the source of the cry—indeed, there was a little girl, sprawled along the sidewalk. The girl dusted herself off, awkwardly brushing her palms together, then shaking the folds of her skirt. Something about her tugged at Kathleen's memory, but Kathleen couldn't immediately recall why.

"Are you okay?" Kathleen hurried over and crouched down, the edges of her qipao brushing the dirty ground. It didn't matter; at least then she would match with the stains on the girl.

"Is okay," the girl said shyly. She showed Kathleen the gauze in her hands. "I was sent to fetch supplies. Wanna come?"

"Supplies?" Kathleen echoed. Who was sending a little girl for supplies in the middle of revolution? When she took too long to answer, the girl took her silence for a yes and looped their hands together, dragging Kathleen along.

A round of gunfire sounded from afar. Kathleen grimaced, then hurried the girl along, hoping they weren't far from wherever they were going. The little girl didn't protest their hastening speed; she trotted along gallantly, and when Kathleen ducked down suddenly, moving them into an alley to avoid a group of Nationalists, the girl said, "I like your hair."

It was then that Kathleen finally recognized the kid, because she had said the very same thing in one of the Communist meetings. Suddenly it made much more sense. She was the child of workers. She was out here because there was nowhere else to be.

"I like yours too," she replied. "Are we almost there?"

"Right here."

They turned into the next alley. Where the others remained empty, this one hosted a whole group of workers—judging by their state of dress—and *active* workers in the uprising too, if their injuries were any indication. This was some rest area, some makeshift space of recuperation—workers leaning on the walls and clutching large gashes in their torso, some sitting and cupping a palm around a bloody eye. It was hard to see: the sun was starting to set, and the city was awash in a hazy orange. Colors blended together like a rain-stained paint palette, broken bodies and fading shadows looking exactly alike.

The little girl ran off, tasked with getting the gauze to wherever it was needed. Left now to her own devices, Kathleen kneeled beside a man some few years older than her, examining his bleeding forehead without being asked. That was the trick. Pretend that she had been assigned everywhere she went; avoid letting a single second of hesitation slip through.

"Who did this?" she asked. "Police or Scarlet?"

"What's the difference?" the man retorted. "But neither. White Flower." He pulled his knees closer to his chest and spat on the concrete beside him. "We're close to taking almost all territories except Zhabei. The Russian bastards are putting up a hell of a fight there."

Kathleen prodded his cheek. It was bruised too, but he would survive. Head wounds bled more seriously than they actually were.

"Are we really?" she remarked casually.

The man grew more wary then. He looked her up and down, a slower appraisal than the initial quick scan when Kathleen crouched beside him.

"You don't look like you're a part of the cause."

Kathleen stood, brushing her hands on her skirt. She gave a thin smile. "And what do people of the cause look like?"

The man shrugged. "We don't have clothes that nice, that's for sure."

When the sun went down on the city, the alley felt it immediately, felt the chill sweep in and set into the bones of those already hungry and tired. This was a place of final destinations. A place people were tossed when they could go on no longer, the fire dampened in their heart.

"And what *do* you have?" Kathleen asked. "Impatience? Exhaustion?"

The man jerked back, his head almost colliding with the rough brick of the wall. "How dare you—"

"Stand up," Kathleen snapped. The night stirred around her, prickling to life by the bite of her voice. "You are sitting ducks here, waiting for slaughter."

"But—"

"Stand *up*."

Without her noticing, the rest of the alley had fallen quiet. The injured and tired were listening, watching Kathleen, watching this girl who had come out of nowhere but sounded just like one of them. She swiveled a slow turn on her heels, and though the moon was yet to grace the skies, her eyes could pick out each and every one of their expressions.

The man stood.

"Good," Kathleen said. Her ears perked, hearing the sound of striking batons. Police—no matter under which jurisdiction, no matter under whose control. They were coming, and coming fast.

"Now." She looked at the alley full of workers. "Are we going to lie down and die, or are we fighting to live?"

The gunfire continued into the night. Juliette had figured it would surely come to an end by twilight, but the sounds did not stop even when the candle burned out and the room fell into darkness, matching the dusk outside.

"It's likely your White Flowers who are holding the fort here," Juliette whispered, blowing at her hands. Her fingers were ice cold, but at least they were clean now, the blood scrubbed away.

"It's a lost cause," Roma said quietly. The thick of the fighting echoed from the north, which was White Flower territory. "The workers are armed. They outnumber the gangsters, and judging by the sounds outside . . . there could be hundreds of thousands throughout the whole city."

Juliette leaned her head against the wall behind her. She and Roma were seated on the mattress, huddling among the blankets to brace against the cold. Through the boarded-up window, there was only a sliver of glass uncovered, letting in a beam of light that cut a line between the two of them.

She hoped her father and mother were safe. She hoped that the house was far enough in the outskirts of the city that it went unharmed, that the workers wouldn't think to target the Scarlet Gang there and cut down the head of the dragon. It seemed unlikely, even if the workers hated gangsters. The Scarlet Gang had their alliance with the Nationalists, and the Nationalists and Communists were still allied on paper. If the Communists had a say in it, they would instruct the workers to stay far, far away from harming the Cais.

At least that was what Juliette was telling herself so she didn't lose her mind from worrying.

Juliette blew another hot breath onto her hands. Noting her discomfort, Roma shifted onto her side of the light beam and grasped her fingers. Juliette's first instinct was to hold on to him. When Roma gave her a wry look, biting back his amusement, she loosened her grip, letting him rub her hands to get some warmth into them.

"Roma," she said. "The chaos outside . . . It won't just end tonight as it always does. It won't go back to the way it was."

Roma smoothed his thumb across her wrist. "I know," he replied. "While we weren't watching, we have lost power."

While the Scarlet Gang and White Flowers were busy chasing a blackmailer, busy maintaining their business to stay atop each other, a third threat had risen quietly among the noise.

The gangsters still had weapons. People. Connections. But they would not have land to operate on. If the revolt outside was victorious, come morning, Shanghai would be a workers' city. No longer under a false government, lawless for the gangsters to run amok. No longer a self-contained paradise for trade and violence.

"It seems so fruitless," Juliette grumbled. "The Communists are armed, the workers are taking the city. There has been no monster attack, no madness. Perhaps it will come once the Communists clash with the Nationalists, but for all we know, this blackmailer was never even a threat upon our people. We kept chasing after monsters, and politics was what swept the rug from right under our feet."

Roma's hands stilled. By now Juliette's fingers were plenty warm. Still, Roma didn't let go. He held on.

"It's not our fault," he said. "We are heirs of a criminal under-world, not politicians. We can fight monsters, not the turning tide of a revolution."

Juliette huffed, but she hardly had anything worthy of argument. She leaned toward Roma, and he let her settle against his chest.

"What are we to do, Roma?" she asked, her voice careful. "What are we to do when we get out of here?"

Roma made an inquisitive noise. She felt the vibration against her ear. "We survive. What else is there?"

"No, that's not what I meant." Juliette lifted her head, blinking into the hazy darkness. Roma smiled the moment he peered down and met her gaze, like it was an instinct. "What are *we* to do? On two sides of a feud, in a city that might crumble before our families stop killing each other."

Roma was silent for a moment. Then he wrapped his arms around her and collapsed the both of them backward—him with a firm plop and Juliette with an ungainly noise, taken by surprise.

"This is warmer," Roma explained, yanking the blankets over them.

Juliette lifted a brow. "Trying to get me into bed already?"

When Roma let out a soft laugh, it almost felt like the world would be okay. Juliette could fool herself into thinking the rounds of gunfire outside were fireworks, the same sort of celebration that had hurtled through the city during the New Year. They could pre-tend it was January again, revert back to a time when the city was still.

But even when it was still, it had been teetering toward something, on the brink of metamorphosis. Nothing was going to remain idle and unchanging when there was so much anger lurking just beneath the floating surface. The gangsters would no longer be the power in charge when the city outside fell quiet again, but the Scarlet Gang and the White Flowers would still be at war.

Juliette felt her heart sink right down to her stomach. She retrieved her hand from inside the blankets and brought it to Roma's cheek.

"I wish we had been born as other people," she whispered. "Born into ordinary lives, untouched by a blood feud."

Roma's hand came up too, curled loosely around hers to keep her touch remaining upon him. For a long while, he looked at her, taking in her eyes, her mouth, gaze roaming like he had once been starving and this now was a feast.

"No," Roma finally said. "Then we would not have met. Then I would have lived an ordinary life, pining for some great love I would never find, because ordinary things happen to ordinary people, and ordinary people settle for something that satisfies them, never knowing if there would have been greater happiness in another life." His voice was rough, but it was certain. "I will fight this war to love you, Juliette Cai. I will fight this feud to have you, because it was this feud that gave you to me, twisted as it is, and now I will take you away from it."

Juliette searched his face, searched for any hint of hesitance. Roma didn't waver.

"What pretty words," she whispered. She tried to play it cool, but she knew Roma could hear her breathlessness.

"I mean them all," Roma replied. "I would engrave them onto stone if that would have you believe me more."

"I believe you." Juliette finally let herself smile. "But you shall not engrave it onto stone, because I don't need you to take me away from the feud. I'll be running by your side."

Roma rose onto his elbows. In a blink, he was hovering above her, their noses already brushing, lips so close that the proximity was itself a tangible sensation. "Don't be afraid," he whispered. "Not of us. Not ever."

His hand brushed her neck; his thumb smoothed across her jaw. Time seemed to crawl to a stop, creating a little pocket for just the two of them.

"I will stare fear in the face," Juliette promised quietly. "I will dare to love you, Roma Montagov, and if the city cuts me down for it, then so be it."

A beat passed. Another. Then Roma pressed his lips to hers with such ferocity that Juliette gasped, the sound immediately muffled when she pushed herself up and drew closer. Despite his burning energy, Juliette felt Roma's mouth move with sincerity, felt his adoration while he trailed kisses all down her neck.

"Juliette," he whispered. Both of their coats came off. Roma had the zip of her dress pulled in seconds too, and Juliette lifted her arms to accommodate. "My darling, darling Juliette."

The dress fell to the floor. With some disbelief, Roma suddenly blinked, his eyes clearing for the briefest moment while she worked at his shirt buttons.

"Are you trying to impale me?" he asked, pulling the knife from the sheath around her thigh and setting it aside.

His shirt joined her dress on the floor. Juliette ripped the sheath off too, tossing it onto the pile.

"What's a little light stabbing between lovers?"

Juliette had intended it as a joke, but Roma turned serious, gazing at her with his dark eyes. His hand had been curled around her elbow, but now he trailed his touch up her arm, drawing goose bumps in his wake. Juliette didn't quite understand the hesitation until his fingers settled gingerly at her shoulder, tracing the newly healed wound there. The one he had made.

"Is it going to scar?" he whispered.

"Let it," Juliette replied. "It'll remind you that you can't get rid of me that easily."

A smile quirked at his lips, but still he didn't let Juliette brush the matter away. What Juliette tried to shake off, to tamp down and forget, Roma hauled out into the light and forced them both to face. What Roma refused to combat, Juliette fought head-on, dragging them both into the scuffle. That was why they worked so well together. They balanced the other depending on what the other needed.

Roma leaned down. He brushed his face against hers, then pressed a kiss to her shoulder.

"I'm sorry, dorogaya."

"Qīn'ài de," Juliette whispered back, tucking an errant piece of his hair behind his ear. "I'm sorry too."

She pulled Roma close once more, meeting his lips. It was hard to voice the extent of their penance, hard to put into words exactly how much they needed to apologize for the bloodshed between them. Instead, they begged for a lifetime of pardon from each other through touch, through tender caresses and pounding hearts raging in tandem.

With effort, Juliette finally managed to get Roma's belt off. It hit the floor beside the mattress and clanked against her knife, striking a discordant sound that made Roma jump. Juliette let out a small laugh, cupping his face. "Well, don't be nervous."

In the dim moonlight, Roma arched a brow. "Nervous? Me?" He kissed her again, intent on proving it. And again, and again.

"Juliette," he whispered eventually.

"Mhmm?"

"Is this okay?"

"It's perfect."

Outside, the night raged on, awash with warfare and terror. There was no telling when it would stop, when the shelling would cease and the picket lines would fall back. There was no telling if this city would ever be whole again. With each passing moment, the world could fall to pieces; with each passing moment, a total collapse approached, some inevitable finality that had been looming since the first lines of division were drawn in this city.

Juliette breathed out, sinking her hands into the sheets.

But that was not here yet. That was not the present; that was not this moment, this heartbeat of time locked in by heady breaths and gentle worship. It was distant to Juliette, and she would let it remain at a distance, so long as she could have *this*—here, now, perfect: her soul as boundless as the sea, her love as deep.

Thirty-Three

The grass under Juliette's feet was damp, leaving dew on her polished shoes as she shifted under the shade of the tree. She scratched at her ankle, then winced when her finger caught the metal of her shoe buckle. She inspected her hand. No blood. No scratch. Instead, she felt covered in grit, an unwashable taint upon her skin. Shanghai was now under the rule of the Nationalist Army—under Chiang Kai-shek, their commander in chief. Juliette shouldn't have been surprised that it had come to this. He had already seized much of the country, after all; the Northern Expedition had been building for *months,* after all. But it was the workers who had ravaged the city until it was awash in red. It was the Communists who had led the effort. Then the Communists had asked their workers to give way when General Shu marched his men into the city and set up Nationalist bases before the dust had even settled.

Something was afoot. The tension was a pungent smell in the air, waiting to see whether it would be the Nationalists or the Communists who struck at the other first. And Juliette knew—she just knew—that the Scarlet Gang was involved, but no one would tell her how.

Juliette cast a glance to her side, reaching out and putting a hand to Kathleen's wrist. Kathleen jolted, then realized what Juliette was indicating. Her cousin stopped tapping the side of her qipao, resolved to clutch her hands in front of her instead, her feet planted firmly in the short cemetery grass.

Last week, most of the Scarlets had escaped the chaos on the streets relatively unharmed. There were casualties, certainly, but few enough that this was the last of their funerals. Instead of mass lives, what they had lost was control.

Nanshi, and all the industrial roads south of the French Concession—taken.

Hongkou, the narrow strip of land surrounded on three sides by the International Settlement—taken.

Wusong, jammed amid ports leading into the Huangpu and Yang-tze Rivers—taken.

East Shanghai—taken.

West Shanghai—taken.

Zhabei, where the workers were most densely populated of all—taken, though their fight with the White Flowers had lasted through the night. When morning broke, whispers flew through the city to report that the White Flowers had at last relinquished, slinking into their homes with broken bones and letting the streets take a different ruler. By six o'clock, Shanghai was quiet, occupied by the workers.

Officers had been ousted out of police stations, call centers raided and trashed, rail stations bombed to render them ineffective. The web of connections that powered Shanghai had been snipped at every juncture point save for inside the French Concession and International Settlement, which the foreigners now guarded with chain-link fences and barbed wire to keep the Nationalists out. In the Chinese parts of the city, there was no such thing as Scarlet-controlled or White Flower–controlled territory anymore. For a fleeting moment, it had seemed that Shanghai was some malleable place, humming with the possibility to grow anew. Then the Nationalist armies marched in and the workers gave way, letting the soldiers take over. Now everywhere they looked, there were Nationalist soldiers stationed along the streets, the city under occupation.

The most outrageous thing was, these few days had still passed as normal. Though the clubs were closed, though the restaurants were closed, though the city was ghostlike in its stillness as it waited for the next political move, her parents acted like nothing was wrong. Private dinners hosted at the mansion went on, albeit with more Nationalists present. Private parties went on, albeit with more Nationalists present.

And funerals went on, albeit with more Nationalists present.

". . . may he go on to the next life peacefully."

It didn't make sense. The blackmailer was still out there. Unless Juliette had been utterly mistaken this whole time, the blackmailer *had* to be aligned with the Communists in some way. Yet in this crucial moment, why hadn't the monsters come out? Why not fight the Nationalist Army off with madness?

"Juliette," Kathleen whispered. "Now you're the one twitching."

Juliette shot her cousin a quick glance, conveying her annoyance. In the same motion, she caught sight of three Nationalist soldiers to their left, eyeing her.

The Communists' fight was a long one, Lord Cai had said after the takeover. Their fight encompassed not just this city but the whole country. Why would they upset their alliance with the Kuomintang so soon? Why *wouldn't* they pretend that all this rebellion and bloodshed had been a joint matter of sticking it to the imperialists, of taking Shanghai back under the control of a true unified government, and bide their time for class revolution? Would it not be sensible to revolt against the Kuomintang only when they actually had a true army alike to the Nationalists? Red rags and anger could not stand up against soldiers and academy training.

Lord Cai had sounded convincing. He had not sounded one bit worried. Their whole city had just been overturned by a force so mighty, and he cared not? Their entire way of life was at a standstill, waiting to see how the Nationalists would organize their rule, how the Nationalists would come to an agreement with the foreigners, and Lord Cai was content to stand by and let it happen?

It was unlikely. Juliette wondered what she was missing.

"If all who wish to speak have spoken, then let us bid Cai Tailei a safe passage away."

The priest stepped aside, gesturing for the relatives nearest to him to begin saying their goodbyes. Each person in the cemetery today clutched a flower in their hands: a faded pink, for though it was customary to use white for mourning, the Scarlet Gang would never use white flowers under any occasion.

Lady Cai stepped up and tossed her flower into the grave. The casket already lay inside, closed, as shiny as the headstone. Once the procession finished, the grave would be closed with dirt and laid softly with new grass.

Juliette clenched her fists tight, nodding as her mother motioned for her to go on. How fortunate it was that she was a modern girl who did not believe in the afterlife. Otherwise, she would certainly burn in hell for this.

"Oh, Juliette." Lady Cai brushed her daughter's face as she passed. "Don't look so somber. Death is not the end. Your dear cousin performed tremendous feats in his time alive."

"Did he?" Juliette said softly. There was no challenge in her voice. It would be foolish to voice resentment now, when she was standing and Tyler was dead.

"Of course," Lady Cai reassured her, taking her daughter's monotony for grief. She clutched Juliette's hands, holding them steady. "He made the Scarlets proud. He stopped at nothing to protect us."

He should never have had the power to do so. We should not have the power to do this. And yet it was all a lost cause, wasn't it? If it were not the Scarlets stopping at nothing to consume the city, it was someone else.

"I will go pay my respects," Juliette rasped, swallowing every bitter word that she wanted to throw in her mother's face.

Lady Cai smiled, and with a squeeze on their enjoined fingers, stepped back to let Juliette proceed. For the briefest moment, Juliette imagined what her mother would say if she knew—knew what blood had once tarnished her palms, knew what blood was running traitorous inside Juliette's veins.

Perhaps there was a possibility that she might be forgiven.

But mercy and blood feuds had never mixed well together.

Juliette approached the grave, peering down at the casket. There was already an abundance of flowers scattered upon the smooth wooden lid.

"Maybe you *would* have made a better heir, Tyler," Juliette whispered, crouching to throw her flower in. When it landed, its petals appeared far paler than the others. "But I have a feeling the title is soon going to be rendered null."

Once, Juliette could never have considered a future without the Scarlet Gang—a future where they were not in power. That was before a monster tore through their numbers, before a madness incited revolution. That was before politicians marched their armies in and filled the streets with their artillery.

Once, she had wanted power. But beneath it all, maybe it was never power she wanted.

Maybe it was safety.

Maybe there was another way to get it, away from being heir to a crumbling empire.

Juliette rose to her feet. Her hands felt clawlike, still folded over an invisible flower. Someone was coming up behind her and it was time to take her leave, but for a second longer, she hovered around Tyler's headstone, committing its features to memory.

"I'm sorry," she said, her voice so quiet she could be heard only by herself . . . and Tyler, wherever he was. "If there is a life after this, one that is free of the blood feud, I hope we can be friends."

❧

Juliette slipped away from the funeral after-activities without notice, tipping her hat low and falling out of step with her relatives once they exited the cemetery. Kathleen quirked a brow in her direction, but Juliette shook her head, and Kathleen merely looked to the front of the footpath again, pretending not to see. The Scarlets walked onward in the direction of their parked cars, and Juliette pivoted onto a smaller street, melding deeper into what was once Scarlet territory.

Soldiers. Soldiers everywhere. Juliette pulled at the sleeves of her dress and tried to walk without letting her posture slump. The French Concession and International Settlement were closed: no one in, and no one out. That could not last for long—the foreign concessions were never built to operate as their own self-contained territories, and once they came to an agreement with the Nationalists, the barbed wire and makeshift fences would go down. For now, people steered clear in fear of the armed soldiers along Boundary Road, and so that was where Juliette went, to the rooftop of a building at the outer bounds of the Chinese part of the city, just out of view of the foreign soldiers peering through their rifle scopes. There was no telling what this building once was. Perhaps a small noodle shop, or a tailor's parlor. When Juliette trekked up, she saw shattered glass and ripped ledgers left behind on the emptied shelves.

Juliette eased open the rooftop door, her shoes coming onto the cement carefully. She kept her breath in her lungs, scanning the space . . .

Her exhale came out with relief. Silently she bounded over to the figure standing in the corner and wrapped her arms around his shoulders before he could turn around, setting her chin at the crook of his neck.

"Hello, stranger."

Roma relaxed under her grip, tipping his head back so that his hair brushed her cheek. "Is this an attack?"

"Perhaps," Juliette replied. She shook the knife from her sleeve and pressed the blunt side to his throat. "One lone White Flower, out in the middle of nowhere?"

Juliette felt a sudden pressure on her ankle. She hardly had a moment to gasp before she realized Roma had hooked his foot over her leg and *pulled* her off-balance. For the briefest second, she was falling backward, before Roma turned around fast and caught her waist, swiping the knife out of her hand and pressing the flat side to her throat instead.

"You were saying?" Roma asked, grinning.

Juliette shoved his shoulder. She was scowling, vexed to be caught off guard, but then Roma dropped the knife and pulled her closer. Their lips met, and she forgot what exactly she was going to rebuke him for.

"I missed you," Roma said when he pulled away.

Juliette quirked a brow, placing her hands upon his face. "You saw me yesterday."

"To talk business."

"We're here today to talk business too."

"Semantics—" Roma stopped with a frown, noticing the headdress twined around her hair. It was pale pink, just as the flowers at the cemetery were, a far lighter color than a Scarlet would usually dare to wear. "Another funeral?"

"Tyler's," Juliette answered quietly.

Roma touched the fixture in her hair, adjusting it carefully so it would hold back the strands from her eyes. When he had it in place, he smoothed his hand along her neck.

"Are you okay?"

Juliette leaned into the touch, exhaling. "What other choice is there?"

"That's not an answer, dorogaya."

Juliette pulled away gently with a shake of her head. The warmth and kindness were too distracting—it fooled her into thinking that all would be well, that the city was not crumbling under their feet. Instead, she twined her arm around his to drag them to the edge of the rooftop. There, they looked out upon the streets, upon the casual sprawl bleeding outward to the horizon.

"I'm okay," she said. "Surviving. That's the best one could hope for now."

Roma cast her a sidelong look like he was going to argue, but Juliette shook her head, directing the topic back to true business. They were meeting today because Roma had sent a note about new information on the blackmailer, and to tell the truth, Juliette had been surprised. Much as she wanted to eradicate the threat once and for all, it hardly seemed important in the grander scheme of things. The monsters had not attacked in so long. Now Roma and Juliette's search for the blackmailer was not so much in fear of the madness or in desperation to protect their people—it was simply for something to do, something to keep themselves from sitting idle while their city fractured to pieces on a level the teenage gangsters could not touch.

"What did you find?" Juliette asked.

A hint of pride flickered upon Roma's expression. "I got a name for the Frenchman," he said. "The one who turned into a monster on the train. Pierre Moreau."

Juliette blinked, the name striking a nerve of familiarity. Roma was still speaking, but Juliette had stopped listening, desperately searching her memory for where she had heard the name before. Had it been an introduction in the French Concession? No, she would have remembered if she had *met* the Frenchman before. Could she have seen his name in their records? Their guest lists? But then why would she have seen a White Flower on Scarlet lists?

". . . sailed into the city some few years ago to start trading."

332

Finally, Juliette remembered.

She almost dropped to her knees.

"Roma," she said breathlessly. "Roma, I've seen that name before. A slip of paper on Rosalind's desk. She said he was a patron at the Scarlet burlesque club."

Roma furrowed his brows. She had told him about Rosalind's disappearance, about her affair with a White Flower whom she wouldn't name. Roma had reported back a brief sighting of Rosalind near the White Flower headquarters the day she went missing. Because the Scarlet grapevine wasn't working as well as it used to, that was the last time anyone had heard from or seen Rosalind.

"Impossible," Roma insisted. "I may not have known the man by name, but he is prominent enough to be recognized in your clubs. He would have been identified immediately as a White Flower."

"Then . . . ?" Juliette physically felt her gut twist, her fingers pressing to her stomach. "Then he was never a patron at the club. Rosalind just happened to have a list of names, the first of which happened to be a monster."

Juliette needed to find the list again. There were four other names on it.

Four other names, four other monsters.

"Could it be?" she whispered.

She met Roma's eyes, a reflection of her own horror, having reached the same conclusion. Rosalind was raised in Paris, as passably French as anyone in the Concession could be.

"Is *Rosalind* the blackmailer?"

Thirty-Four

Dammit, dammit, dammit!"

Juliette slammed the drawers of Rosalind's desk shut, striking her hands so hard against the surface of the table that her palms stung. Rosalind playing spy was one matter. People were lured into betrayal across blood feud lines all the time—it was why their numbers were always shifting; it was why there were always eyes trying to penetrate the inner circle. But setting a monster on the city was another matter altogether. Using monsters to aid politics was something so absurd coming from Rosalind that Juliette couldn't even *comprehend* a reason for it. Unless the only motive was destruction. Unless the only motive was to burn the whole city down.

"Is that why?" Juliette asked aloud. She lifted her head, peering into the mirror opposite her, acting as if her reflection was a sullen Rosalind staring from some faraway place.

Sooner or later, Juliette would have to reckon with her own guilt. She could keep thinking of herself as mighty because she knew her way around a blade. But it was not the blade nor her ruthless tendencies that pushed her to the top. Perhaps they kept her there.

What had gotten her there was her birth.

"It hardly makes sense," Juliette whispered. She reached out with her fingers. The cold press of the mirror sank into her skin. "Be angry at me for how we were born. Be angry that you were born a Lang. But you never wanted Scarlet heirdom. You never wanted the city. You wanted to be important. You wanted adoration."

So why would she be the blackmailer? How did gathering guns and money help? How did lurking in the shadows with monsters and madness bring her *anything* that she might desire?

"Lái rén!" Juliette called.

A maid popped her head in immediately at the summons. She must have been waiting nearby, hearing the ruckus Juliette was making. "How may I help, Miss Cai?"

"Can you make a call to Kathleen?" Juliette waved her arm, trying to think. The Communist strongholds kept moving. The gangsters were still trying to dissolve them at the Nationalists' command, but otherwise it had been relatively quiet. The Communists, too, were waiting to see how this would turn out. "She should be at the . . . Mai Teahouse? Or maybe—"

"Can't, xiǎojiě," the maid interrupted politely before Juliette could waste more time guessing Kathleen's location. "Since the takeover, the telephone control centers have not been restaffed yet. Some lines near the railway station are down too as they fix the tracks."

Juliette cursed under her breath. So communication across the city was piss-poor. Without workers at the control centers, there was no one to direct and connect calls.

"Fine," Juliette grumbled. "I will send a messenger the old-fashioned way, then."

Rosalind's room had been cold, but Juliette didn't realize she was shivering until she returned to the warm hallway again, hurrying down the steps and into the living room. As soon as she started to scribble a note by the tables, the front door opened, and Kathleen stepped in.

"Kathleen!"

Kathleen didn't hear her. She continued walking, her eyes glazed. She looked deep in thought.

Juliette set the pen down, hurrying into the first-floor hallway in pursuit. "Kathleen!"

Still no response. Juliette finally got close enough to set her hand on her cousin's shoulder.

"Biǎojiě!"

At last Kathleen turned around, registering Juliette's presence with a start. She put a hand to her heart, her black gloves fading into her deep blue qipao.

"You scared me," Kathleen said breathlessly.

"I called your name at least three times!"

Kathleen blinked. "Did you?"

"Well—" Juliette looked around. There was no one else in the hallway, so she joked, "Technically not?"

Kathleen quirked her brow. Juliette waved a hand, seeing that she was getting sidetracked, and hooked her arm through her cousin's, dragging her back out into the living room and up the stairs. As they walked, she talked as fast as she could, covering what Roma had told her and what conclusion she had come to, ending with how she had run home immediately and started searching through Rosalind's things, only to find nothing upon her desk.

"Wait, wait, wait," Kathleen said, coming to a firm stop at the top of the staircase, the two of them on the second floor, right outside Lord Cai's office. It was presently empty. He was out somewhere: maybe in the Concessions, gauging the temperament of the foreigners; maybe meeting with Chiang Kai-shek himself, drawing up the final collaboration plans between Scarlets and Kuomintang.

"You were looking for a slip of paper on her desk?"

Juliette nodded. "It may have been moved since I last saw it, but she had so *much* paper there, and now there's nothing—"

"They're all in my room!" Kathleen exclaimed. "Juliette, I've been sifting through them for days, trying to find clues for where she went."

Juliette stared at her cousin for a long moment. Then she made fists and pretended to thud them down on Kathleen, raining light blows on her shoulder. "Why didn't you *tell* me? I spent so long digging through her room!"

"Tell you?" Kathleen echoed, slapping her hands at Juliette's fists. "How was I to know you would need something among those papers?"

"Oh, hush—" Juliette windmilled her arms, gesturing for Kathleen to lead on. They hurried, almost ramming into a servant, before piling into Kathleen's room, where the curtains stirred with the open window. Juliette could hardly remember the last time she had come in here; she couldn't remember the last time she had sat down among Kathleen's magazines and shoe racks, upon the thick quilt piled on her bed. It was always in and out, poking a head through to call her cousin to attention, or it was Juliette's room where they congregated.

"Voilà," Kathleen said, pulling Juliette from her brief reverie. With a quiet "oof!" Kathleen dug forth an arm's cradle of papers from her shelf and tossed it all atop her bed. Ink and prints glimmered under the late-afternoon sun streaking through the window, and Juliette got to work, sifting through the papers. She only wanted the list. Then she would know if Pierre was a mere coincidence. Maybe they could even find Rosalind by finding one of the names on the list.

Just as Juliette's eye snagged on a smaller piece of paper at the corner of Kathleen's bedspread, there was a loud knock on the door downstairs. The sound reverberated through the house. Curious, Kathleen walked to her doorway and peered out, listening while Juliette lunged for the paper and shook it from the pile.

"It's this!" Juliette cried. "Kathleen, it's the list!"

"Wait, wait. Hush for a second," Kathleen chided, pressing her finger to her lips.

Juliette tilted her head right as the voice wafted up:
"An attack! There's a monster attack in the city!"

Deep in the French Concession, where the city remained yet quiet, Rosalind was making a racket trying to get into an apartment on Avenue Joffre. She could see people passing on the street below her, but the duplex walls were thick, and the glass of its windows muffled the sound. Even the gardens below were rustling quietly with the wind, green shrubbery and yellow flowers entwining together. So peaceful with its own business, like every person she had passed on her way here. She hated it. She wanted them all to burn, to suffer as she was suffering.

"Open this *door*," she demanded. Her voice bounced in the corridor. No amount of polished tiles and chandeliers could soften her pitch or her near hysterics. "Is this how it's going to be? Has it all been a *lie* to you?"

Rosalind knew the answer. Yes. It was. Like some pitiful creature, she had ensnarled herself in a trap, let herself be sheared and skinned and slaughtered, and now the hunter was walking away with the job well done. She had been waiting in one of their other Concession safe houses for the past week, sending word along that she wanted to run. He had said he would come for her; she just needed to be patient as he finished up his business.

"Goddammit." Rosalind gave up on the door, her arms trembling with exertion. It wasn't love that she had chased—at least not in the physical sense. If all she had wanted was a warm body, she had her pick at the burlesque club: an unending list of men who would throw themselves at her for consideration. She didn't care about that. She never had.

A honk came from afar. Cars, rumbling down the residential driveways.

She merely thought she had found a companion. An equal. Someone to see her—*her*, just as she was, not a Scarlet, not a dancer, but *Rosalind*.

It was her fault for thinking that she was enough to change someone. Monsters and money and the city on strings—up against Rosalind, who hadn't even wanted to go along with it in the first place, who had only done so out of hope that he would be happy once he had the city, that they could be happy and no one could touch them. The world in one palm and her in another.

But someone who wanted the world would never stop before they had it, everything else be damned. It was hardly a competition.

She was foolish to think that her friends could be kept safe, that she could be the hand guiding him away from chaos. She had never possessed any power here. She had never *mattered*. Days had passed in that safe house with no change. In the end, this was the harsh truth: Rosalind had left everyone she cared about for someone who was not coming. Rosalind had hurt everyone she cared about, risked their very lives, all for someone who was long gone.

Rosalind tore her pistol from her pocket and shot at the door handle. The sound grated on her ears as the bullet struck once, twice, three times. The walls seemed to shrink from her, smooth silver and gold wallpaper inching back from the violence rarely brought into places like these.

The handle fell. The door inched open. And when Rosalind nudged into the apartment, she found it entirely vacated.

She couldn't help it. She laughed. She laughed and she laughed, tracing her eyes along every missing thing. The apartment had never been well decorated to begin with, but now the papers on the table had disappeared; the maps atop the grand piano were gone. When she peered into the bedroom, even the sheets were stripped.

"We can live here forever, can't we?"

She had twirled with those sheer curtains, splaying the lace across her head like some bridal veil. Had thrown her arms up, delirious in her happiness.

"Don't get too excited, love. We're only here until we rise higher."

"Must we? Can we not live a quaint existence? Can you not be a good man?"

"A good man? Oh, Roza—" Rosalind trailed her hands along the bookshelf, finding only dust, even though it could not have been more than a few days since the worn paperbacks were cleared away. *"Ya chelovek bol'nói. Ya zloi chelovek. Neprivlekatel'nyi ya chelovek."*

When the monsters were sent in for the Scarlet vaccine, she had said she didn't think she could do this anymore. Had that prompted the decision to abandon her? Or was it because she had gotten caught, because she could no longer supply Scarlet information?

"I would have abandoned them for you," she admitted to the empty room. She had always known who he was. She had always known him as a White Flower. The truth was that she hadn't cared. The blood feud did not stoke a fury in her heart like it did to others in Shanghai. She had not grown up here, had no ties to the people. The fighting on the streets seemed like a show she might catch in the theaters; the gangsters running their errands were interchangeable faces she could never keep track of. Kathleen had a kind heart, Juliette had blood ties, but Rosalind? What had this family ever given Rosalind to deserve her loyalty? Incompetence from her father and irreverence from the Cais. Year after year, the bitterness festered so deeply that it had developed into a physical hurt—one that stung as much as the current injuries on her back.

Had they just accepted her, had they seen her for what she could do, she could have offered the Scarlet Gang her life. Instead, they gave her scars and wounds—she was marked if she bit her tongue and stayed; she was marked if she tried to make something of herself and strayed. Scars upon scars upon scars. She was a girl with nothing else now.

Rosalind walked to the desk and was startled to find a slip of paper pinned to the wood of the table. For a second, as her heart leaped to her throat, she thought it might be an explanation, instructions on where she could go now, something to say that she had not been left behind.

Instead, as she drew closer, she read:

Goodbye, dear Rosalind. Better to part now than
when the havoc really begins.

He had known she would come looking. He had long planned to clear out the apartment and leave her with nothing but a pitiful note. Rosalind tore the paper out, bringing it closer to her eyes as if she might be misreading the messy scrawl. *When the havoc really begins?* What more was coming? What more would descend on the city?

Rosalind turned around, facing the apartment windows. She watched the trees wave, watched the sun beat on.

And in that very moment, a loud scream tore through the streets, warning about a monster on the loose.

"See anything yet?" Roma asked, putting aside the eighth folder he had finished going through.

"Rest assured," Marshall replied, "if we find something, we're not going to remain silent and wait patiently for you to ask."

Without looking, Benedikt reached over with a wad of paper and thudded Marshall over the head. Marshall nudged out with his foot to kick Benedikt, and Roma grinned, so pleased to have the three of them together again he hardly cared that they were cramped in the tiny Scarlet safe house where Marshall was living, papers spread out on every inch of flooring. No matter how small, he would always be fond of this apartment now. It had kept Marshall safe.

It had brought Juliette back to him.

"Don't be a clown," Benedikt said. Though he was also flipping through a folder with one hand, he held a pencil in the other, scribbling miniature sketches on the discarded pieces of paper. "Focus, or we're not going to finish going through the profiles."

There was a sect within the White Flowers working with the Communists; to find a lead, they would have to sift through all the information they had on their own gang. Receipts, import logs, export logs—gangsters who ran anything on behalf of the White Flowers had to keep an account of their ongoings. Technically, at least. In truth, it was not as if gangsters were very good at bureaucratic records; that was why they were gangsters and not politicians. When Roma carried over the boxes, he had managed most of the haul on his own, with Benedikt holding only one so that Roma's vision was not obscured.

"I cannot help it." Marshall threw the file in his hands aside, picking up another with a sigh. "I've been bottling up my wisecracks for months, and now they must come out all at once."

Benedikt scoffed. He thwacked Marshall again, this time with his pencil, but Marshall grabbed his whole hand instead, grinning. Roma blinked, the paper in front of him suddenly the least interesting thing in the room.

He met his cousin's eyes. *Does he know?* Roma mouthed.

As Marshall let go and turned to fetch the last file in his pile, Benedikt mimed a slash across his throat. *You shut your mouth.*

Benedikt!

I mean it, Benedikt mouthed furiously. *Stay out of this.*

But—

There was almost an audible clack from Roma's jaw when he snapped his mouth shut, his teeth biting together the moment Marshall turned around again. Marshall looked up, sensing something in the air.

"Did something happen?" he asked, bewildered.

Roma cleared his throat. "Yeah," he lied. "I—uh—heard something." He pointed in the direction of the door. "Maybe off Boundary—"

Benedikt jolted forward. "Wait a minute. There really is something."

Roma arched a brow. His cousin really knew how to act. He had even drained his face of blood, his cheeks as white as the paper sheets on the floor.

Then he heard the screaming too, and he realized that Benedikt wasn't playing along. "You don't think—"

"Guài wù!"

The White Flowers bolted to their feet. Roma was the first one out, scanning the street in disbelief, his hand going to his gun. Benedikt and Marshall followed closely. Perhaps it was not a good idea to be out in the open, especially for Marshall, in what would be Scarlet territory. Mere weeks ago it would have been a declaration of war; now they were already in the midst of one, and no one had the energy to fight another.

"There hasn't been a monster attack in months," Roma said. "Why strike now?"

"We don't even know yet if it *is* an actual attack," Benedikt replied. Streams and streams of civilians ran past them, their shopping bundled to their chests, hurrying children and elderly along by the elbows.

Marshall started in the direction where the civilians were running from. Roma and Benedikt followed, moving fast but warily, eyes searching for the source of the chaos. They sighted no madness quite yet. Nor were there any insects skittering on the streets.

"This is pandemonium," Marshall remarked, spinning around quickly to take inventory of their surroundings. His eyes widened. "Why?"

Roma knew exactly what Marshall was asking. It was only then that he started to run. "Where the hell are the soldiers?"

He had his answer as soon as he turned the corner, coming upon the railway station. There had previously been an abundance of Nationalists stationed here, standing sentry to make sure their political opponents weren't trying to escape from the city. Only now they were not guarding the station but fighting *monsters*, rifles and guns pointed, shooting at the creatures that lunged at them.

"Oh God," Benedikt muttered.

One of the monsters lunged, swiping a claw against a Nationalist soldier's face. When the soldier staggered up against the railway station, his cheek was hanging off.

Roma would have blanched if he were not stunned beyond belief. He had glimpsed Paul Dexter's monster, and he had seen the one on the train. These monsters before him were no different in appearance, but it was broad daylight, the weather warm and almost pleasant, and to watch them with their blue-green muscles rippling in the sun almost frightened him enough to run.

"Marshall, stop," Roma snapped, holding his arm out. He could read Marshall's intent in the tension of his shoulders; while Roma considered scrambling backward, Marshall had planned to surge *forward*. "This doesn't involve us."

"They'll all die—"

"That's their fight." Roma's voice trembled, but his instruction didn't waver. More than anything, he was *confused* by the scene in front of him. There were still a few civilians nearby, huddled by the sidewalk and frozen in fear. Five monsters, all of them tall enough to bowl over an ordinary human, and yet they had eyes only for the Nationalists. Five monsters, all of them with the ability to release thousands upon thousands of insects and induce a madness that could sweep the city and have it on its knees . . . and yet they did not.

"Roma," Benedikt said quietly. He pointed, near the feet of one of the monsters. "Look."

A dead man. No—a dead White Flower, identifiable by the white handkerchief hanging from his work pants.

"And over there," Marshall whispered, tilting his chin at the bench in front of the railway station. Another corpse was collapsed there, the red cloth around their wrist looking like a gash of blood. "A Scarlet."

With a deep shudder, Roma took a few steps away from the scene, leaning against the emptied restaurant behind them. The Nationalist soldiers continued shooting, yelling at one another to report on where reinforcements would be. Their numbers were dwindling. Even without madness, they could not win against indestructible creatures.

"Nationalists, White Flowers, Scarlets," Roma said aloud, his brow furrowed as he worked through the puzzle pieces. "What game are they playing at here?"

"Stop!"

The shout came from the perpendicular road, coming nearer and nearer the railway station. Roma poked his head out, suddenly gripping Benedikt's arm in alarm.

"Who is that?" he demanded. "Where is it coming from?"

It sounded familiar. Too familiar.

"*Not* Juliette—don't get hasty," Benedikt immediately replied. "It's . . ."

The figure came into view, throwing herself in front of one of the monsters, arms waving wildly. Her hair resembled a tangle of black wire trailing down her back. Though she was significantly more disheveled since the last time he had sighted her, it was undoubtedly Rosalind Lang.

"What the hell is she doing?" Marshall exclaimed. "She'll get herself killed."

Bewildered, the three White Flowers watched Rosalind Lang dart in front of a soldier, screaming incoherent commands at the monster. The monster, however, loomed ever the closer, not deterred by gun nor girl.

"She could be the very blackmailer," Roma said.

"Then why does she look so frantic?" Benedikt asked. "Would she not have control of them?"

"Maybe she lost control," Marshall suggested.

Roma made a frustrated noise. "So *why* aren't they releasing their insects?"

The million-dollar question. Suddenly the monster reared back and charged right toward Rosalind. At the last minute, she spat a curse and dove out of the way; the monster hardly seemed interested in her anyway. It attacked and pounced on the Nationalist so viciously that the blood came up in an arc, splashing down on Rosalind until her face was sprayed with red. She lifted her head from the ground, elbows propped on either side of her, visibly trembling even from this distance.

"Do we . . . ?" Benedikt started hesitantly. "Do we help her?"

Another round of gunfire from a rifle that made no dent. Another cry, another soldier down.

With a sigh, Roma put his gun away and tore his jacket off. "*Help* isn't quite the right word," he said. "Shed your colors. I think they're only attacking gangsters and Nationalists."

Marshall peered down at himself. "I don't think I'm wearing any to begin with."

"Do any of us ever carry around a white handkerchief like some errand runner?" Benedikt added.

With his eyes pinned on the scene before him, Roma pushed his sleeves up, then grabbed a plank of wood from nearby.

"Shed anything identifiable," he clarified. "Then hurry up and help me pull Rosalind Lang out of there so we can knock her out."

"Wait, what?" Marshall yelled. "Knock her out?"

Roma was already marching forward, lifting the plank of wood. "How else are we supposed to take her to Juliette?"

Thirty-Five

Bàba!" Juliette exclaimed. "Please, tell me what's going on!"

The house was in disarray, overtaken by activity. At first Juliette had thought they were assembling their forces to fight against the attack. Messengers had been sent out the door at rapid speed, but as soon as she listened in on exactly what her father's men were saying, it seemed that it was not a defense they were putting up. They were summoning Nationalists to the door, gathering forces inward. They were bringing together the Scarlet inner circle, the business tycoons who held properties in the city.

Now they were here in abundance, greeting Lord Cai briefly and hurriedly, eyes darting back and forth like there was something urgently pressing on their heels. The moment her father came up the stairs, Juliette lunged for his sleeve, holding on tightly.

"What's going on?" she tried again when he continued walking forward. "Why would the blackmailer strike *now*—"

"It was never one blackmailer," Lord Cai replied evenly. Pausing before his office, already humming with noise inside, he eased her grip off his sleeve, then smoothed the fabric of his shirt down until it was free of wrinkles. "It was the Communists. It has always been the Communists."

Juliette felt her face furrow, all her muscles pinching together. "No, I told you, they're working with the Communists, but those were *Paul's* insects. One of the monsters is a *Frenchman*."

Lord Cai opened his office door, then gestured for Juliette to stay put. He wasn't allowing her to follow him in.

"Not now, Juliette," he said. "Not now."

The door closed in Juliette's face. For a minute Juliette could only stand there, blinking in disbelief. It had been laughable of her to think that she would be accepted into this gang once Tyler was gone, that Tyler was the only thing standing between her and complete recognition. They let her feel powerful, running about the city like she could solve all its problems, but as soon as true trouble came . . .

They closed the damn door in her face.

Juliette took a step back, practically seething through her teeth.

"Miss Cai?"

A pitter-patter of footsteps came up behind her. Juliette turned and found a young messenger holding a note out for her.

"For you," he said.

Juliette scrubbed a hand over her face, then took the note. "How come you weren't sent out into the city with everyone else?"

The messenger grimaced. "I—er—if you don't need me, I'll be off now!"

He fled before Juliette could get another word in. She almost called out again to summon the messenger back, but then she unfolded her note and stopped short. It was written in Russian. The messenger had not been a Scarlet at all, but a White Flower.

> Come quickly. The safe house. We have Rosalind.
> —♥

"Kathleen!" Juliette bellowed. She was already sprinting down the hallway, coming to a sharp stop outside her cousin's bedroom, her heels practically making skid marks in the flooring.

Kathleen scrambled up from her bed. "Do we know what's happening?"

"We have something better," Juliette said. "Get your coat. Roma found Rosalind."

When Roma opened the door to the safe house, it was so dark inside that Juliette could hardly see anything past his shoulder. As soon as she and Kathleen stepped in, Roma closed the door again and the apartment fell into utter black.

"What is this, an ambush?" Juliette remarked, flipping her lighter on. The first sight that flickered to life was Benedikt and Marshall, both standing by the stove and grimacing like they were bracing for something.

The second was Rosalind, gagged and tied to a chair.

"Oh my God," Kathleen cried, starting forward immediately. "What—"

"Make her promise not to yell before you take that out," Roma cut in quickly. He finally flicked on the overhead light, then sighed when Kathleen didn't listen, yanking at Rosalind's gag. It was only a small wad of fabric that once bundled vegetables; if Rosalind had really tried, she might have been able to spit it out.

"No yelling," Marshall emphasized. "One shout and the Nationalists will come knocking."

"Don't you tell me not to yell," Rosalind grumbled. "I'll—"

"Rosalind," Juliette cut in.

Her cousin fell quiet. There was no running this time. There was nowhere to go. The streets outside were crawling with soldiers, their numbers gathered thickly after the panic that had erupted near the railway station. The attack had happened too close to the International Settlement. One wrong move, and the British would start firing along the borders.

Juliette walked to the window, unwilling to face Rosalind quite yet. She pulled at the boards, peering through the slivers.

"How did they stop the attacks?" she asked.

"They didn't," Benedikt answered. "The monsters retreated of their own volition."

Juliette sucked in a tight breath. Thinned her lips. Crossed her arms—maybe crossed them a bit too tightly and looked as if she was reaching for a weapon, gauging by the way Benedikt made a noise of alarm.

Roma rolled his eyes at his cousin, gesturing for him to step back and get out of the way as Juliette wound around the table, coming to a stop beside Kathleen, in front of Rosalind.

"Was it because of you?" Juliette asked quietly. "Did they retreat because of you?"

"No," Rosalind replied.

Across the room, Benedikt and Marshall exchanged a nervous glance. Roma leaned into the table, his body inclining in Juliette's direction. Kathleen bit her lip and shifted to her left until she was against the wall.

"Rosalind," Juliette said. Her voice cracked. "I can't help you unless you tell me what you did."

"Who said I needed help?" Rosalind replied. There was no malice in her tone. Only a faint, faint sense of dread. "I am a lost cause, Junli."

If the table hadn't been behind her, Juliette would have staggered back, guts twisting at the sound of her name. The last time Rosalind might have used it was when they were children. When they were barely taller than the rosebushes in the gardens, jumping over each other in a game of leapfrog, diving into the piles of leaves the household staff were trying to sweep and giggling when they messed it all up.

"Oh, don't *try* that with me."

"Juliette!" Kathleen hissed.

Juliette didn't relent. She plunged her hand into her pocket and dug out the list they had retrieved, unfolding the paper with a brisk snap. "This was on your desk, Rosalind," she said. "*Pierre Moreau, Alfred Delaunay, Edmond Lefeuvre, Gervais Carrell, Simon Clair—* five names, and if my guess is correct, five *monsters*. It is a simple question: Are you the blackmailer?"

Rosalind looked down in lieu of answering. Juliette threw the paper to the floor with a loud curse, her foot stamping on the list.

"Wait, Juliette." Roma bent over to pick up the piece of paper. Under normal circumstances, she wouldn't have made much of the curiosity in his voice. Only then Benedikt and Marshall surged forward too, the three of them pale under the hazy bulb light, leaning in to read the list like it was something incomprehensible.

"What is it?" Juliette demanded.

"Simon Clair?" Benedikt muttered.

"Alfred Delaunay," Marshall added, rocking back on his heels. "Those are . . ."

"Dimitri's men," Roma finished. He passed the list back to Juliette, but Kathleen reached over and intercepted it. "Those are all Dimitri Voronin's men."

For all Juliette knew, the ground underneath her feet had crumbled to pieces. She was in free fall, her stomach suspended in motion. Rosalind did not deny it, did not offer another explanation. Nor did she do anything to resist when Juliette reached forward and pulled out the chain around her neck. It glimmered under the light, but Juliette paid no attention to hidden jewels. Instead, she flipped over the flat strip of metal at the necklace's end, running her finger across the engraving on the other side.

Воронин

Juliette choked out a laugh. Half gasping, half guffawing, she was almost struggling to catch her breath when Roma pulled her back gently, easing her grip off Rosalind's necklace before she could rip the chain off and strangle her cousin with it.

"Don't judge me," Rosalind said. Her eyes flickered between Juliette and Roma. "Not when you clearly did the same."

"The *same*?" Juliette echoed. She couldn't stand here anymore. She pushed off the table and marched to the other side of the room, gulping in air.

If Juliette had thought hard enough, perhaps she could have worked it out sooner, could have stopped this. She had always known: Rosalind was angry—angry at the world, at the place she had been given. But what she wanted was not to change her place; it was to find something that made her place worth it.

Juliette turned to Rosalind, her eyes stinging. "*I* decided to love a White Flower," she managed, each word slicing at her tongue. "*You* helped a White Flower set destruction onto this city. It is not the same!"

"I loved him," Rosalind said. She denied none of it. She was too prideful to deny it once she had been caught. "Tell me, if Roma Montagov had asked, wouldn't you have done it too?"

"Don't speak about me as if I'm not right here in the room," Roma interrupted before Juliette could answer. His tone was stern, if only to disguise how shaken he was. "Juliette, sit down. You look as though you are near fainting."

Juliette folded herself upon the floor and dropped her head into her hands. Wasn't Rosalind right, in a way? However it had happened, she had loved Dimitri enough to betray her family, feed him information to whatever ends he wanted. Juliette had loved Roma enough to kill her own cousin in cold blood. Rosalind was a traitor, but so was she.

Marshall cleared his throat. "Just to be sure that I am following," he said. "Dimitri Voronin . . . is the blackmailer? And you are his lover—"

"Not anymore," Rosalind cut in.

Marshall took the correction in stride. "You *were* his lover, both his source for Scarlet information and his"—he trailed off, thinking briefly—"what? Monster keeper?"

Rosalind turned her head away. "Untie me, and I will give you answers."

"Don't."

The command came from Kathleen, who had remained quiet until now. The ceiling light flickered, and underneath it, Kathleen's eyes looked utterly black.

"You owe us that much, Rosalind," Kathleen said. She tossed the paper onto the table; by now, Kathleen had scrunched up the list so much that it was nothing but a tiny ball, bouncing off the surface and flying to the floor. "I won't tell you how deeply you have betrayed us. I think you know. So speak."

Slowly, Juliette put a hand on the floor and started to get back onto her feet. "Kathleen—"

Kathleen spun. "Don't defend her. Don't even think about it."

"I wasn't going to." Juliette straightened to her full height, dusting off her hands. "I was going to ask you to take a step back: Rosalind is about to stand."

Just as Rosalind shifted, Benedikt lunged forward and yanked Kathleen toward him, stopping Rosalind from bowling her sister over with the chair's leg and making a run for the door. Heavens knew how she expected to escape her bindings even if she got to the door.

"Yes, fine!" Rosalind snapped, finally reaching a breaking point as her chair came back down with a defeated *thump!* "Dimitri wanted to take over the White Flowers, and when one of his associates came in contact with Paul Dexter's remaining monsters, I went along with his plan to destroy this city. Is that what you want to hear? That I am weak?"

"No one ever said you were weak," Marshall replied. "Merely

foolish—as the best of us have been known to fall prey to."

Roma waved for Marshall to stop speaking.

"Backtrack," Roma said. He looked over his shoulder briefly and exchanged a glance with Juliette. "What do you mean, *take over* the White Flowers? Paul Dexter's last note went to someone in the French Concession—how did Dimitri even get ahold of it?"

If Rosalind had her hands free, this would have been the time she placed a delicate palm to her forehead, smoothing down the long wisps of hair around her face. But she was bound, subject to interrogation by family and enemy, and so she only stared ahead, her jaw tight.

"Your search through the French Concession would never have led anywhere," Rosalind whispered. "*In the event of my death, release them all.* It was an instruction to the servants at a different property Paul owned in the Concession, on White Flower territory. When they didn't pay rent, Dimitri stormed the place and found the insects before they could be released." Her eyes closed, like she was remembering the scene. No doubt she would have been called upon to examine their findings; no doubt she must have seen to the fates of the servants, perhaps a simple bullet to shut them up, perhaps thrown into the Huangpu River so no one could follow Paul Dexter's last trail.

"Lord Cai will kill you for this," Kathleen said quietly.

Rosalind blew a harsh breath through her nose, feigning an amusement that didn't land. "Lord Cai hardly has the time. Don't you wonder why Dimitri thinks he can stage a coup? Don't you wonder where he got the nerve?" Her gaze shot up, landing right on Juliette. "The Scarlets and the Nationalists are working together to purge the city of Communists. As soon as the Kuomintang armies are ready, they will open fire on the city. Dimitri is waiting. He waits for that moment, and in the struggle, it will be him who comes in like a savior with his guns and money and allied Communists, driving the Nationalist effort back. It will be Dimitri who rises just as the workers are at their lowest, and he will give them hope, and when he is the prize force of the revolution, he will have the power he wants."

The safe house fell quiet. All that could be heard was faint shouting outside, as if soldiers were nearing. Quickly, Marshall walked to the window and peered through the cracks again. The others in the room remained where they stood, ignoring everything beyond their four walls.

For whatever absurd reason, Juliette's mind went to the assassin who had come after the merchant at the Grand Theatre. There was no greater scheme; there never had been. It was merely Dimitri trying to stir trouble with Roma's tasks. It was merely Dimitri, intent on taking the White Flowers for himself.

"Where did you hear this from?" Benedikt asked in horror. "Why would *you* have information about secret Scarlet plans when even Juliette does not?"

Another laugh. Another dry, bitter sound that held no humor.

"Because Juliette is not a spy," she replied. "I am. Juliette did not lurk in the corners listening to her father. I did."

Juliette's pulse was beating so hard that the skin of her wrists trembled with movement. Roma reached over and squeezed her elbow gently.

"How long might we have?" Juliette asked, the question directed at Kathleen. "If the Nationalists decide to purge everyone with Communist alignment out of the Kuomintang?"

Kathleen shook her head. "It's hard to say. They haven't come to an agreement with the foreign concessions yet. They might wait until jurisdiction settlements are made. They might not."

A purge itself was bad enough. But monsters and madness loosed on the gangsters that went in with guns blazing? It would be slaughter on both sides.

"We have to stop Dimitri before the Scarlets do anything," Juliette said, almost speaking to herself. It was impossible to put a stop to politics. But monsters could be found, and the men who controlled them could be killed.

"Should we?"

Juliette looked at Kathleen sharply. "What?"

"It might help," Kathleen said quietly. "If the Scarlet Gang is organizing massacre, setting chaos onto our side might help save the workers."

"Don't get brainwashed." That was Marshall—cutting in. "You can't control an infectious madness. Besides, your Scarlets have practically been overtaken by the Nationalists. You haven't had true power for months. You cut down a few of your numbers, and the armies only bring more in."

The room grew quiet again. There was no easy answer to any of this.

"Benedikt," Roma said after a long moment. "Do we know where Dimitri is?"

Benedikt shook his head. "I haven't seen him since the takeover. I don't think *anyone* has seen him since the takeover. He hasn't been around the house. All his men are scattered. Lord Montagov even suspected he might have been killed during the battle in Zhabei."

"But he is alive," Juliette said, her eyes pinned on Rosalind. "Isn't he, biǎojiě?"

"Alive," Rosalind confirmed. "Only I don't know where."

"Then I'll ask again . . ."

A click echoed through their tight space. Juliette knew it was disbelief that had every gaze in the room reacting so slowly, that caused the stunned, gaping alarm when Juliette pointed her pistol at her cousin, the safety off.

"I want his location," Juliette said. "Don't think I won't do it, Rosalind."

Kathleen started forward, panic setting into her eyes. "Juliette—"

"Wait." Roma stepped in front of Kathleen quickly, keeping her out of Juliette's way. "Just wait."

"I am telling the truth," Rosalind snapped. She pulled against her ropes to little avail. After all these years, she knew that Juliette did not wave around her pistol to make an empty threat. Juliette might not aim for the heart, but a body had many expendable parts. "You wouldn't even have caught me if I hadn't heard screaming about a monster attack and followed the sounds in an attempt to stop it. That was out of my own *goodness*. I have been *trying* to find Dimitri too! The men inside the monsters don't listen to me anymore!"

Juliette's grip tightened. The pistol in her hand trembled.

"I don't know where he is!" Rosalind spat, increasingly agitated. "He used to base his operations from an apartment on Avenue Joffre— the one he took over from Paul's people—but he moved. He wouldn't risk it with the French Concession so carefully watched after the take-over. He is out of my reach!"

"Forgive me," Juliette said, "if I don't believe you."

Her hand stilled. In her head, she counted to three, just to afford her cousin one last chance.

But when she reached three, it was not her gun that deafened the safe house with sound. It was the door, shuddering with explosive effort—once, twice, and then before Juliette and Roma could dart for it and hold it closed, it had blown open, halting the two in their tracks.

Juliette's pistol was still raised when General Shu came in, followed by so many soldiers that half of them were forced to remain outside, lest the apartment overspill.

"Not one step farther," Juliette demanded. Her eyes darted to the side. In that brief second of eye contact, she and Roma were silently asking each other how the Nationalists had found them and what the Nationalists wanted—but neither had an answer. All that was for sure was they had been found: Juliette Cai and Roma Montagov, colluding together.

But General Shu, as he ignored Juliette and took a step in, was not even looking at them. Nor did he take note of Rosalind in the corner, bound to a chair. With an expression akin to amusement, he merely examined the room, like he was a new tenant searching for a place to rent.

"Put your weapon down, Miss Cai," General Shu said, finishing his perusal and resting his hands at his belt. There, a vast selection of handguns sat at the ready, dangling from the leather. "I'm not here for you."

Juliette narrowed her eyes. Her finger twitched on the trigger. "Then why bring so many soldiers?"

"Because"—he signaled for the men behind him—"I heard that my son was alive and well, and I have come to fetch him back."

At once, the soldiers raised their firearms, pointed at one person in the room.

"Hello, Bàba," Marshall spat. "You have terrible timing."

Thirty-Six

Havoc erupted within the safe house.

Roma was shouting, Benedikt was shouting, Kathleen had pressed herself up against the wall, Rosalind was trying to free herself, and Juliette barely managed to get out of the way before the soldiers were surging out the door, Marshall clasped between them in captivity.

"Stop!" Roma bellowed. "You can't just *take* him!"

He was fast to follow, almost colliding with the building wall before barreling out from the front archway. A beat later, Juliette made to follow him, only Benedikt grabbed her wrist, stopping her midmotion.

"Don't let Mars get caught in the crossfire," Benedikt said in one breath. "You protected him once, Juliette. I know you have it in you to look out for him again."

"No use telling *me* this," Juliette hissed, grabbing Benedikt's arm and yanking him out with her. "Help me fix it. Kathleen, watch Rosalind!"

Kathleen's mouth opened as if to protest, only Juliette was already running out. She surveyed the scene—guns, soldiers, *Roma*. Marshall had long ceased struggling, but Roma had rooted himself in their path, stubborn until the very end.

The street around them was quiet. Give it some minutes more, however, and this would grow into a scene, gawkers at every corner. It was almost bizarre that Juliette's first thought was *I can't be seen with White Flowers*. The city had been taken, territory lines had turned as fluid as flowing river water, and yet still the blood feud raged on—as if it had any meaning, as if it *ever* had any meaning.

"Does my father know that you are hassling Scarlets?"

General Shu stopped. He turned around. When all his men were forced to halt too, Marshall made a valiant effort to tug himself free, but their hold upon him was iron. No matter how he lunged, there were too many in a small circle holding him in and too many in a larger circle that kept Roma at a distance by the threat of their rifles.

"Does your father know you lie about White Flowers being Scarlets?"

Juliette lifted her chin. At the far side of the soldier cluster, Roma's head snapped up, trying to catch Juliette's eye. He made a motion at her, urging her not to stick her neck in, to let him handle it. Fool. If he was sticking his neck in, she was already there too.

"How are you to prove that Marshall Seo is a White Flower?" Juliette asked.

General Shu pulled a revolver from his holster. He did not point it at her, at anyone. He merely examined it, opening and closing the cylinder to check his bullets.

"What would you prefer, Miss Cai?" he said. "The letter he wrote when he ran from me, declaring his intent to survive on his own in Shanghai by joining the White Flowers? News clippings I've kept over the years that report him to be the Montagov heir's right-hand man? I have them all—just give the word."

Juliette bit down on the inside of her cheeks, throwing Benedikt a glance, hoping he had some idea of their next move.

But Benedikt looked startled beyond description. When General Shu put his revolver back into its holster, the street was quiet enough that Benedikt's low murmur could be heard very clearly.

"*Ran* from you?"

Marshall grimaced, looking away. He had stopped struggling.

"He never told you?" General Shu asked. "I assume he said that we were all dead, didn't he?" He looked at Marshall. Now, out in the light, the resemblance appeared. The same face shape, the same lines crinkling at the eyes.

"You are," Marshall seethed, his voice a sudden crack in the air. He had never before seemed so furious: careless, cheery Marshall, who had never angered once in Juliette's presence, was now red in the face and shaking, the tendons in his neck standing at attention. "When Umma died and you weren't home, for all that it mattered, *you* were dead to me too."

General Shu didn't flinch. If anything, he looked a little bored. He didn't even seem to be listening.

"I will not discuss your mother with you in the middle of the street. We may have a nice sit-down later if you wish to talk. Mr. Montagov, would you please get out of the way?"

Roma remained firm. His brows were drawn. Juliette knew that look: he was trying to buy time, but the problem was that more time was not going to help the present situation.

"This is not your jurisdiction," Roma said quietly. "When Miss Cai says you can go, only then may you go."

General Shu put his hands behind his back, behind all the weapons at his belt. When he spoke again, he really did address Juliette, like Juliette had any control over what was to happen here.

"I have no interest in whatever strange arrangement between gangsters this is. All I want is to take my son home with me. I stay quiet about your business; you leave my business to me."

A wad of spit narrowly missed his face. General Shu stepped back, but Marshall looked like he was gearing up to do it again.

"You think you can just march in here," Marshall exclaimed. "You march into this city even though you did none of the work to take it.

You march in and grab me like I'm your damn property. Where were you all these years? You *knew* I was here. You could have fetched me at any point. But you didn't! The Revolution was more important! The Kuomintang was more important! Everything but *me* was more important!"

General Shu said nothing. Juliette's grip tightened on her gun, tightened on the trigger. She wondered what would happen if she shot him. She wondered if she could get away with it. A year ago it would have been nothing. Today it would be a declaration of war against the Nationalists, and the Scarlets—tough as they were—could not fight such a war. It would be annihilation.

"But now," Marshall went on, "now that you're in Shanghai anyway, you may as well tie up your loose ends, right? Everything is falling into place: your country and your happy little family." He spat again, but it wasn't aimed at his father this time. Merely an expulsion of the anger within his body, like popping a bullet out from its exit wound.

"Well, Miss Cai?"

Juliette started. Despite Marshall's speech, his father was still speaking to her. "It sounds like he doesn't want to go," she said tightly.

At once, by some signal that Juliette had not caught, the soldiers all stood to attention, saluting. Then they aimed their rifles at Roma, ready to shoot.

"Don't make things difficult," General Shu said. "Staying with the White Flowers is a death sentence. You know what is coming. I'm keeping him safe."

"Don't," Benedikt muttered from beside Juliette. "Don't believe it."

But this wasn't a matter of believing or not. This was . . . truth. This was knowing that the gangsters were near collapse. No more territories. No more thriving black market. How long could they hold on for? How long could the White Flowers survive, given they didn't have Nationalist support like the Scarlets did?

"Roma," Juliette called shakily. "Step aside."

"No!" Benedikt snapped. "Juliette, stop."

Juliette swiveled around, her fists clenched. "You heard what Rosalind said," she hissed. Though she attempted a volume only for Benedikt, there was no doubt that everyone present could hear her. "You know what *violence* is to come. How many Communist meetings has Lord Montagov sent Marshall to? How many times has his face been sighted there? Who is to say if his name is on a kill list when this city erupts? This is a way to keep him *safe*."

Benedikt reached for his gun. Juliette smacked it out of his hands immediately, her wrist crossing with his, her eyes ablaze. Benedikt did not try it a second time. He knew he would not win. In his expression, there was only hard disappointment.

"Is it for his safety?" he asked, hoarse. "Or is it for Roma's?"

Juliette swallowed hard. She released her hold on Benedikt Montagov's wrist. "Roma," she called again, unable to look over. "Please."

A long moment of silence passed. Then: the sound of rifles clacking against shoulder straps, heavy boots starting to walk. Roma had stepped aside.

Benedikt kept his eyes pinned on Juliette, like he didn't dare to look away, didn't dare watch Marshall be hauled off. The least that Juliette owed him was to hold his gaze, own up to the decision she had made.

"He will be safe," she said. The marching footfalls grew farther and farther away.

"Safe inside a cage," Benedikt replied, his jaw tight. "You sent him off to a prison sentence."

Juliette would not be chided like this. As if there had been any other choice. "Would you rather your cousin be shot?"

At last Benedikt turned away. Miraculously, no onlookers had come to see the commotion. Miraculously, even after the soldiers marched off with Marshall, the street remained empty, and now it was only the three of them out in the open, Roma standing by the sidewalk with his arms to either side of him like he didn't know what to do with himself.

"No," Benedikt said dully. He started to walk, toward the city center. Merely three paces away, he paused again and spoke over his shoulder. "I would rather the two of you not burn the world down each time you choose each other."

Thirty-Seven

J uliette wasn't one who liked relying on eavesdropping, but she was out of options. With her heels and dresses, she wasn't the sort of person who was very *good* at being sneaky, either, which meant her current predicament was truly a last resort. At any moment, she almost expected someone to wander out into the gardens and ask what she was doing, hanging from a guest bedroom balcony, leaning as closely as she could to the open window of her father's office.

"... *forces?*"

Juliette shifted forward, trying to hear more than a few snippets of each sentence. Fortunately, it was past dusk, and the purpling hour of the night obscured her strange position against the walls of the house. There weren't many Scarlets around the house to catch her like this anyway. She had been sitting on the couch all afternoon, observing the quiet around her. For however many hours Juliette wasted away in the living room, dragging a sharp nail down the armrest, the front door had not opened once—no one coming in, no one going out.

In the twenty-four hours that had passed since learning Dimitri Voronin was the blackmailer, Juliette had assigned messengers to watch every corner of the city. Until Rosalind gave up a location, there was no way to seek Dimitri. Until the Nationalists actually acted, until the *Scarlets* acted, there was no way to know how the coming fight would unfold if Dimitri were truly going to unleash madness on behalf of the Communists. Lord and Lady Cai feigned ignorance. When Juliette gave them Rosalind's accusation about the coming massacre, passed off as a rumor on the streets, her father had waved her off with assurances that this was nothing she needed to concern herself with. Which made no sense. Since when was the heir of the Scarlet Gang supposed to remain unconcerned? This was her *job*.

"*. . . numbers . . . unknown.*"

Juliette cursed under her breath, hooking her leg over the balcony when it sounded as though the meeting in Lord Cai's office was ending. The thing was, she had been waiting to hear something—*anything*—from the eyes she had placed across the city. Scarlet messengers were commonly prone to false reports. Even when nothing was awry, the more dramatic ones who wanted to prove themselves always came in with a whisper or two picked up from unreliable sources.

Juliette was playing eavesdropper in her own house because she had received absolute silence. And silence didn't mean the city had settled into peace and harmony. It meant the messengers weren't reporting to her anymore. Someone—multiple someones—had clammed them up, and after all, there were only two people in this gang higher-ranked than her. Her parents.

"*Have you seen Juliette?*"

Juliette froze right in the middle of the guest bedroom. Slowly, when it seemed the conversation was only passing in the hallway, she crept forward to press her ear to the door.

"*She was in the living room earlier, Lady Cai.*"

For a second Juliette wondered if she was finally being summoned. If her parents were going to sit her down and explain what the Scarlet Gang was planning, assuring her that they would never collaborate with Nationalists if collaboration meant bathing their city in a wave of red.

"*Ah, well. Her father asks to keep her away from the third-floor sitting room if you see her. We have a meeting.*"

The voices faded. Juliette's fists clenched tight before she even realized what she was doing, carving her nails deep into the skin of her palms. She could not fathom the meaning of this. Her mother was the one who told her time and time again that Juliette deserved to be heir. Her father was the one training her to take over, who summoned her into his meetings with politicians and merchants alike. What was different *now*?

"Is it me?" she whispered into the bedroom, her breath disturbing a fine layer of dust gathered on the wall. Juliette was a traitor. Juliette was a child. When push came to shove, maybe her parents had decided she wasn't competent enough.

Or maybe it was them. Maybe whatever plans were being dreamed up behind closed doors were so horrid that they were too ashamed to pass them on.

Juliette pulled the door open, popping her head out. At the other end of the hallway, a group of gossiping relatives bade one another a good night and dispersed, parting ways like they were taking separate exits in a stage play. Only when the coast was clear did Juliette slink out, trekking down the stairs and poking her head into the kitchen, where Kathleen was skinning an apple.

"Hey," Juliette said, leaning her elbows onto the counter. She switched to French, in case any maids were listening. "We need to do something."

"And by something," her cousin replied, thumb still working at the apple peels, "what are you referencing?"

Juliette's gaze roamed around. The kitchen was empty, the hallways otherwise quiet. It was eerie for there to be so little noise, for the household to be absent of messengers dropping in and out. It made the mansion feel unwell, like some dark shroud had crept into the walls, muting sound and blocking sensation.

"I think we need to scare Rosalind," Juliette said. "Juste un peu."

The knife in Kathleen's hands came to a stop. Her eyes flickered up. *"Juliette,"* she said sharply.

"I can't sit around like this!" The days were counting down. The clock kept ticking forward. "I cannot claim to stop the Nationalists. I do not claim to have the power to stop a whole political movement. But we *can* stop Dimitri from making it worse. Rosalind is sitting on his location. I *know* it!"

When Juliette fell quiet, she was breathing so hard that her chest heaved up and down. Kathleen was unspeaking for a moment, letting Juliette put herself together again, before shaking her head.

"What does it matter, Juliette?" Kathleen asked quietly. "Don't rush to answer me. Really ask yourself it first. What does it matter? Whatever is about to break out, what is one more element of chaos? It will be bullets against madness. Gangsters with knives against monsters with claws. It will be a fair fight."

Juliette bit down on the inside of her cheeks. Of course it mattered. One life was one life. One life did not become forgettable merely because it was lost in the masses. She wouldn't regret the lives she had taken, but she would remember them.

Before Juliette could say so, however, she was interrupted by the quiet groan of the front door opening. Its hinges squealed despite the messenger's effort, and when Juliette rushed into the living room, his wince was immediate.

It was dusk. The house was dim with shadows. Nevertheless, Juliette immediately zeroed in on the letter the messenger held, marching his way.

"Give me that."

"I'm sorry," the messenger said. He attempted a firm tone, but his voice shook. "This isn't for you, Miss Cai."

"Since when has *anything*," Juliette exclaimed, "in this house been *not for me*?"

The messenger resolved not to answer. His lips thinning, he simply tried to push by, heading for the staircase.

When Juliette was twelve, she had felt a sudden flare of pain inside her abdomen while watering the flowers over her Manhattan window. The feeling had spread like an internal invasion, had felt so hot and severe that she'd dropped the watering can with a spasm— watched it fall and smash to pieces on the pavement four stories below when she crumpled to the floor. Later, they would tell her that her appendix had ruptured, had refused to keep on functioning and had torn a hole in its own wall, pushing infection into the rest of her body.

That was what her anger felt like now. Like something had died, and now its vicious pus and poison had *burst* inside of her.

Juliette unwound the garrote wire from her wrist. In one lunge, she had it around the messenger's throat, silencing his cry before it could escape.

"The letter, Kathleen."

Kathleen snatched it quickly, and Juliette held on to the stranglehold for just a second longer until the messenger slumped. The moment he did, Juliette loosened the wire and let the messenger collapse in unconsciousness. By then Kathleen was already reading the letter. By then her hand was pressed over her mouth, so much horror in her eyes that she could have been a painting rendered by tragedy.

"What?" Juliette demanded. "What is it?"

"It's for your father, from the highest command within the Nationalists," Kathleen answered shakily. *"The Central Control Commission of the Kuomintang have made their decision. The Communist Party of China is anti-revolutionary and has undermined our national interest. We have voted unanimously for them to be purged from the Kuomintang—and from Shanghai."*

"We knew it was coming," Juliette said quietly. "We knew."

Kathleen thinned her lips. The letter was not finished yet. Having paled tremendously, she didn't speak the rest aloud, she merely flipped the letter around so Juliette could read it for herself.

Powers of execution should be reserved for the
elite, imprisonment for the masses. All members of
the Scarlet Gang are to report for duty at the turn
of midnight on April 12. The White Flowers may be
treated as Communists when the purge begins. When
the city wakes again, we shall have no adversaries. We
shall be one combined beast to fight the true enemy
of imperialism. Put the Montagovs' heads on pikes
and be rid of them once and for all.

In their very living room, the clock tolled for ten o'clock.

Juliette staggered back. "At the turn of midnight on April twelfth?" A faint buzzing started up in her ears. "Today . . . today is April eleventh."

Put the Montagovs' heads on pikes. Was that what this blood feud had come to? Total and utter annihilation?

Kathleen broke for the front door, the letter fluttering beside the unconscious messenger. She had already burst outside, progressing several steps down the main path before Juliette caught up to her, grabbing her cousin by the wrist and halting her in her tracks.

"What are you doing?" Juliette demanded. The night was cold and dark around them. Half the lamps in the gardens were turned off, perhaps to save on electricity, perhaps to hide the fact that there was not a single guard standing sentry by the front gate.

"I'm going to warn them," Kathleen replied, her words a tight hiss. "I'm going to help the workers fight back! They're allowing execution powers! It will be a bloodbath!"

The truth was, the bloodbath had long been building. The truth was, execution powers were already being used; it was only now coming right into the open.

"You don't have to." Juliette looked up at the windows across this side of the house, all illuminated. The night seemed so dark in comparison, its shadows almost liquid. When she lowered her voice, she almost thought she would choke on her next breath, like the darkness was pressing against her chest. "We can run. It's over. Shanghai has been taken over by Nationalists. Our way of life is dead in the ground."

Everything—either dead or dying. Juliette almost keeled over with the thought. All that she had worked for, all that she thought was her future: none of it mattered. Territories disappeared in minutes, loyalties switched in seconds, and revolution bowled over anything that was in its path.

"Mere moments ago," Kathleen said tightly, "you were resolute to stop Dimitri."

"Mere moments ago," Juliette echoed, her voice breaking, "I didn't know that there was an execution order for Roma's head. We have two hours, biǎojiě. Two hours to leave. To run far, far away. Gangsters never belonged in politics anyway."

Slowly, Kathleen shook her head. "*You* have to leave. I'm not going anywhere. They're going to kill them, Juliette. Civilians. Shop owners. Workers. That letter was a pretense—there will be no imprisonment. With the force of gangsters alongside the soldiers, anyone who takes to the streets in support of the Communists will be shot on sight."

It would be terror. Juliette did not deny that. If she went to her parents right now and demanded answers, they would not deny it either. She knew them too well to think otherwise. Maybe that was why she was afraid of confronting them. Maybe that was why she was choosing to run instead.

"Do you realize?" Her tears refused to fall, but they hovered in a thick sheen over her eyes. "We have passed violence, passed mere revolution. Nationalist against Communist—this is civil war. You're enlisting yourself as a soldier."

"Maybe I am."

"But you don't have to!" Juliette did not mean to yell. But here she was. "You're not actually one of them!"

Kathleen pulled away vehemently. "Aren't I?" she asked. "I am at their meetings. I draw their posters. I know their protest calls." She tore her jade pendant off. Held it up, in the moonlight. "Short of these riches, short of my last name, what is stopping me from being one of them? I could just as easily be another face in the factories. I could just as easily have been another abandoned child thrown onto the streets, begging for scraps!"

Juliette breathed in. And in. And in. "I am selfish," she whispered. "I want you to come with me."

Around them, the lamps flickered, then turned off completely. With only moonlight illuminating the gardens, Juliette wondered briefly if this was some indication that trouble was coming to the Scarlet house. It was not; at times like these, trouble no longer needed to act under the guise of darkness. Trouble was a roaring, raging fire.

Kathleen offered a small, shaky smile, then tied her pendant back on. "We have been allowed selfishness," she said. "But so many others in this city have not. I cannot find my own peace unless I help them, Juliette. I cannot find my peace with this city unless I stay."

Juliette knew what a losing argument looked like. A long second passed, and Juliette waited to see if her cousin would falter, but she did not. Kathleen's expression remained determined, and some part of Juliette knew that this was a goodbye. Her face crumpling, she reached for Kathleen, pulling the two of them close in a tight hug.

"Do not die out there," she snapped. "Do you understand me?"

Kathleen choked out a laugh. "I'll try my best." Her embrace was equally fierce, as was her expression when they released each other. "But you . . . We're under martial law. How are you to—"

"They can block off our trains and dirt roads, but we're the city above the sea. They cannot monitor every swath of the Huangpu River."

Kathleen shook her head. She knew how stubborn Juliette was

when she needed something done. "Find Da Nao. He's a Communist sympathizer."

"Da Nao the fisherman?"

"The one and the same. I'll get a note to him telling him to wait for you."

Juliette felt a hot stone of gratitude roil in her stomach. Even at a time like this, Kathleen was running tasks for her. "Thank you," she whispered. "I don't care if this makes me too much of a Westerner. I need you to hear my indebtedness."

"You only have two hours, Juliette," Kathleen said, waving her off. "If you're going to run . . ."

"I won't make it, I know. I'll buy everyone more time. I can hold off the purge until morning at least."

Kathleen's eyes widened. "You're not going to approach your parents, are you?"

"No." Juliette didn't know how they would react. It was too risky. "But I have a plan. Go. Don't waste time."

Afar, a bird had started cawing. The sound was high-pitched, a warning from the city itself. With a firm nod, Kathleen stepped back, then gave Juliette's hand one last squeeze.

"Keep fighting for love," she whispered. "It is worth it."

Her cousin disappeared off into the night. Juliette allowed herself one ragged breath. She let the quavery sound rush outward and tear a rip into her composure before she inhaled deeply and clutched her hands over the silk of her dress.

When Juliette stepped back inside her house, the living room remained silent, the messenger still lying on his side. She picked up the fallen letter and lifted her head, staring up the staircase. The light in her father's office was off. Now she knew: in the third-floor sitting room, her parents and whoever else they had deemed worthy to invite in were discussing senseless massacre for the sake of the Scarlet survival.

Juliette squeezed her eyes shut. The tears fell then, finding an easy path down her cheeks.

Keep fighting for love. But she didn't want to. She wanted to hold love to her chest and run, run like hell so the rest of the world couldn't touch it. It was exhausting to care about everyone in the city. She thought she had the power to save them, protect them, but she was still one girl, shut out of everything important. If she was going to be treated like a mere girl, then she would act like one.

The wind blew into the living room, the front door still cast ajar. Juliette shivered once, then suddenly couldn't stop shivering, the tremors rocking from head to toe.

I will fight this war to love you, Roma had said, *and now I will take you away from it.*

Enough was enough. In this moment, Juliette decided she did not care. This was a war they had never asked to be a part of; this was a war that had dragged them in before they had the chance to leave. Roma and Juliette had been born into feuding families, into a feuding city, into a country already fractured beyond belief. She was washing her hands of it.

She was not fighting for love. She was protecting her own, everyone else's be *damned*.

Thirty-Eight

The uniform was less itchy than Marshall had expected.

He had grumbled like high hell when his father had tossed it at him upon his arrival, opting to fold his arms and demand that they throw him in a cell instead. General Shu had stared at him blandly, as had all his men, as if Marshall were a child throwing a tantrum in a candy store. It had seemed rather silly then. To stand around and waste time, achieving nothing meaningful save for being a big headache. It was only that if he remained petulant, he could fool himself into believing that someone was coming for him. That the city might stop fighting, that the gangs would go back to normal, that the White Flowers would storm the place, waving for him to hurry and come home.

But Marshall had been hiding out for months. The White Flowers thought he was dead. The city had given up on him. There was no use digging his heels in and being difficult.

Marshall inspected the cuff of his sleeve, his attention drifting from the Nationalist currently speaking. This was General Shu's residence, and his father and twenty-odd men were presently convening around the heavy wooden table in the council room, letting Marshall listen too, as if he were here to learn. There were no more seats available at the table, so Marshall stood by the door instead, leaning on the fraying wallpaper and eyeing the ceiling, wondering if the creaking he heard late at night from his bedroom one floor above was the footsteps of his father, pacing the council room at odd hours.

"Érzi."

Marshall jumped. He had zoned out. When his eyes focused on the table again, the men were clearing out, and his father was staring at him, his hands behind his back.

"Come sit a minute."

At the very least, Marshall hadn't missed anything. He had heard all he needed in the other meetings. The Communists needed to go. Shanghai was theirs. The Northern Expedition would succeed. *Blah, blah, blah—*

"No campaigns to rush off to?" Marshall remarked, dropping into a seat.

General Shu didn't seem amused. The door closed after the final Nationalist, and Marshall's father returned to the table, selecting the seat two away from Marshall.

"You are not being forced to remain here."

Marshall snorted. "Given the soldiers stationed around this house, you and I have very different definitions of what being forced means."

"Mere precautions." General Shu rapped his knuckles on the table surface. Marshall's eyes shot to the sound immediately, stiffening at the move. It was how his father used to get his attention at the dinner table on the rare occasions he came to visit. *Visit*, as if it weren't his own family. "You are young. You don't know what is best yet. What I must do is keep you within the most ideal conditions, even if I must compel it, and only then can you—"

"Stop," Marshall pleaded. They had had enough low-toned, mean-spirited back-and-forth yesterday. He was hardly in the mood to start hashing out again how exactly a childhood kept out in the countryside qualified as an "ideal condition." "Get to the point. What am I doing here? Why do you *care*?"

For several long moments, General Shu said nothing. Then: "This country is going to war. I was content to let you run yourself wild as a gangster when there seemed no harm, but it is different now. The city is dangerous. Your place is here."

Marshall resisted the urge to laugh out loud. Not in humor—in belly-deep, stinking resentment.

"I survived as a gangster in Shanghai for years. I can manage, thanks."

"No." General Shu turned to his side, looking across the top of the chair between them. "You didn't, did you? At the merest provocation, the Scarlet heir asked you to play dead, and you did."

Marshall was so tired of this being some crime. What was *wrong* with hiding? What was *wrong* with retreating and lying low, if only to survive and recoup, if only to fight another day?

"I bear no ill will to the Scarlet heir."

"Maybe you should. She is reckless and volatile. She is everything wrong with this city."

"I ask again," Marshall repeated through gritted teeth. "Is there a point to this?"

His father could say that it was for his own good. He could pull up the city's every obituary, could show Marshall the sheer numbers that had been lost in these recent few years to the blood feud, a bullet through the chest for no reason other than wandering too close to the wrong territory. It didn't matter. It was all an excuse.

The Nationalists shunned the imperial monarchy, but when they marched into this city and took it, they acted just as conquering kings and empires did. Different titles, the same idea. Power was only long-lasting if it were a reign, and reigns needed heirs. Marshall's father never cared to find him when he was a child surviving off scraps. It was only now, when appearances became key, that he remembered Marshall existed.

General Shu sighed, dropping the brewing argument. Instead, he reached into his jacket, his hands brushing past the flashing medals pinned to his lapel, and retrieved a small, square card.

"I divulge this information because I care." The card landed upon the table, faceup. "There is an execution order from the Kuomintang on the Montagovs."

In a flash, Marshall shot to his feet, lunging for the small card and scanning the telegram. *The stroke of midnight. No prisoners left alive.*

"Call it off," Marshall demanded. His voice turned to steel. He hated when he sounded like this. It wasn't him. "Call it off *now*."

"I can delay it," General Shu said evenly. "I can continue delaying it. But I cannot call it off. No one has that power alone."

Marshall's fists tightened. He imagined marching out right now, through the line of soldiers, past the tall, tall walls bordering the mansion. . . .

"So you tell me as if I should be grateful?" he asked. "You tell me as if I should bless the Kuomintang that they are only *soon to be* dead?"

General Shu was not bothered by Marshall's outburst. He never was. "I tell you so you realize what is left out there. Your former gangsters whose lives hang on a thread. Your Scarlet heir under her father's thumb, your White Flower heir with nothing left under his command. What remains for you? The only place where you are needed is here. As the Kuomintang leadership flock into the city, as the number of meetings rise, as they look to see where the next generation of capable leaders may stem from—you are needed."

The telegram crinkled under Marshall's fingers. He was biting the inside of his cheeks so hard that he could taste the metallic tang of blood. The White Flowers were crumbling. The White Flowers hardly qualified as a gang any longer, never mind an empire that could exert power against the city.

"You cannot help your friends by running out," General Shu continued. "But you can help by staying with me. I am willing to train you in your studies, your potential for leadership. I am willing to bring you up the chain of command, to be my son in proper public view."

A Nationalist prodigy. An obedient son, one who had stayed in the house that day he found his mother dead, who hadn't fled the very second he envisioned living only with his stranger of a father. He wondered how much of his past he needed to erase, whether it was his history as a gangster or his history flirting with boys that would be more of a scandal.

"Do you promise?" Marshall asked hoarsely. "We can save my friends? You will help me?"

You will not abandon me? You will not leave me to fend for myself?

General Shu nodded firmly, rising to his feet too. "We can be a family again, Marshall, so long as you do not fight me. We could do grand things, make grand change."

Marshall released the telegram, let it flutter back upon the table.

"I will keep your friends safe," General Shu finally said. "I will protect them to the very best of my ability, but I will need your help. Don't you want a purpose? Don't you want to stop running?"

"Yes," Marshall replied quietly. "Yes, I would like that."

"Good," General Shu said. He dropped both his hands on Marshall's shoulders, giving a squeeze. It almost felt fatherly. It almost felt gentle. "Very good."

If Roma looked at one more map, he feared he would fry his brain.

With a huff, he pushed all the papers out of the way, dragging a hand through his hair and mussing his careful combing beyond repair.

A mess. Everything was a goddamned mess, and he couldn't begin to imagine how the White Flowers could survive this. His father kept himself locked in his office. The other powerful men in the White Flowers were either mysteriously missing or had outright signaled their intent to disappear. It hadn't been like this immediately after the takeover, but it seemed the more time passed, the clearer it was that there was no reverse button. Their contacts in the foreign concessions were lost; their agreements with militia forces across all territory had collapsed.

Lord Montagov had very few options. Either gather his numbers together and wage outright battle on two groups of politicians— Communist and Nationalist alike—or tuck tail and disintegrate. The first was not even in the realm of possibility, so the second it needed to be. If only his father would actually open his door when Roma knocked. So many years of Roma trying to prove himself, and for what? They would have ended up here anyway, a city in flames, whether Roma behaved or not.

"Roma!"

Roma sat upright, stretching his body so he could peer through his half-open door. It was late at night, the light at his desk flickering at random. Something was wrong with the wires in the house, and he suspected it was because the electric factories and power lines across the city were still sitting in ruins.

"Benedikt?" Roma called back. "Is that you?"

His lamp made a sound. With a suddenness that almost gave Roma a fright, the bulb went out completely. At the same time, footsteps were thudding up the stairs and down the hall, and when Benedikt burst through Roma's door in a complete rush, Roma's immediate instinct was to assume his cousin had had an epiphany for Marshall's rescue.

Then Benedikt slumped to rest his hands on his knees, his face so pale as to look sickly, and Roma bolted to his feet. *Not an epiphany.*

"Are you okay?" he demanded.

"Have you heard?" Benedikt gasped. He staggered forward, looking as if he would fall.

"Heard what?" In half-darkness, his sight guided only by the light of the hallway, Roma smacked his hands along his cousin's arms. He found no wounds. "Are you injured?"

"So you haven't heard," Benedikt said. Something about his tone brought Roma's eyes up, snapping to attention. "There are confirmed reports. Nationalists, Communists, Scarlets—they're all talking about it. I wager it was not supposed to leak past the Scarlet circles, but it did."

"About what?" Roma resisted the urge to shake his cousin, if only because color still had not returned to Benedikt's pale cheeks. "Benedikt, what are you talking about?"

Benedikt did stumble to the floor then, landing hard into a sitting position. "Juliette is dead," he whispered. "Dead by her own hand."

Juliette was not dead.

She was, however, at risk of collapsing from overexertion, given how hard she had run across the city. In an effort to hurry as fast as possible, she had possibly twisted her ankle and blown out her lungs. Perhaps lungs did not blow out so easily, but the tightness in her chest said otherwise. Affording herself a mere minute of rest, Juliette pulled her hat low over her face and leaned against the exterior wall of White Flower headquarters, heaving for breath behind the building.

She had managed to push the purge to four in the morning. Any later than that and her ruse could fall through if the Nationalists demanded further explanation.

The plan had unfolded so smoothly that Juliette just *knew* something was going to go wrong. She had succeeded in sneaking into her father's empty office, succeeded in forging a letter with his handwriting, and stamped it in his name. To the Chinese, a man's personal stamp was as good as an unforgeable signature, never mind how insensible that was given Lord Cai locked his in a drawer Juliette knew how to open. She had succeeded in pressing down the ink, in folding up the letter with its contents brief and succinct: *My daughter is dead, a dagger to her own heart. While I understand the importance of revolution, please allow all Scarlets to mourn until daybreak before any action is taken.* She had even succeeded in prodding the unconscious messenger awake and threatening him at knifepoint to take the letter and deliver it to the same Nationalist who had sent Lord Cai the last correspondence, promising that she would peel his skin like a sliced pear if he tattled about Juliette being alive.

The moment the messenger ran out the door, Juliette charged for the nearest phone. She needed to warn Roma: warn him that there was an order for his execution, and warn him that she was very much alive, no matter what the streets were about to say.

That was when Juliette remembered the lines were down.

"Tā mā de!" She tried, of course. Tried calling and calling in case the operator centers had one or two workers mingling around. The line refused to connect. There was not a single messenger around the house to run a warning to the Montagovs; they were all out, dispersed across the city, lying in wait like live snakes in tall grass.

Now it was already past midnight. She had spared precious time in packing first: jewelry and weapons and cash shoved into a burlap sack slung around her shoulders. If she was going to run, she was going to run with all the means possible to survive. Who was to say how long it would be before she could come back? Who was to say if Shanghai would ever heal enough for her to come back at all?

Juliette slunk around the side of the building, then took a sharp turn in her route, hurrying into another thin alley. She was not walking toward the front door of headquarters; instead, she needed to get to the building *behind* their central block. From above, the darkness of the clouds beat down as if it were oppressive heat, so heavy that the lone streetlamp some paces away seemed like the only salvation for miles.

Juliette came to a stop outside the other building. Listening for sound and hearing nothing, she knocked.

The shuffle of footsteps came immediately, like the occupant inside had been waiting for someone. When the door opened and a flood of light bled into the heavy night, a woman was blinking at Juliette—young, Chinese, wearing an apron dusted with flour.

This used to be how Juliette snuck into the Montagov house in the few times she had dared it. It had been years since her last attempt; by now the people living behind the central block had long moved, bringing in strangers for replacements.

"Which apartment are you in?" Juliette asked, not bothering with pleasantries.

"I—what?"

"Which apartment?" Juliette repeated. "You don't occupy the whole building, do you?"

The woman blinked again, then with delay, shook her head. "I am only this floor," she said, gesturing behind her. "Some renters in between, and at the top is my elderly father—"

Juliette withdrew a clump of money and pressed it into the woman's hands. "Let me through, would you? I just need to use his window."

"I—"

After a long second of staring at the sum of money in her hands, the woman made a stammering noise and let Juliette into the building.

"Thank you," Juliette breathed. She spared a glance over her shoulder before stepping through the threshold. "If you're waiting for someone to come home tonight, I urge you to stay in. Don't leave, understand me?"

The woman nodded, her eyebrows knitting together. Juliette didn't wait for further invitation—she surged forward, trekking up the nearest set of stairs that appeared. All the buildings in these parts of the city were built in a labyrinthine manner, windowpanes shooting out from staircase banisters and rooms leading into rooms leading into other rooms, which held the next set of stairs up.

Juliette finally found the floor she wanted, her memory withstanding the years. When she eased open the door into the dark bedroom, she found an elderly man sleeping in his bed, the curtains to his window undrawn, a flood of silver illuminating his frail form. Careful not to let her shoes click on the hardwood floor, Juliette crept to the window and lifted it, shivering with the gust of wind.

The back of this building was directly facing the back of White Flower headquarters. And they were so close to one another that when Juliette reached out, she easily slid open Roma's window and climbed over. For one exhale, her body was dangling four floors aboveground, one wrong twitch away from falling and shattering into pieces. Then she had ducked through the window, softly touching down in Roma Montagov's bedroom.

Juliette looked around. The room was empty.

Where the hell is he?

"Roma," Juliette called softly, like he might possibly be hiding. When there was no response, she cursed viciously. *Think, think.* Where could he have gone?

Juliette hurried to the door and pulled it open quietly, eyeing the empty hallway. There was considerable noise coming from downstairs, like White Flowers were still entertaining themselves despite the late hour. For a moment Juliette simply did not know what to do, short of slipping into the hallway and closing Roma's bedroom door behind her, her heart pounding a crescendo in her chest. Then she turned to her side and found a small face watching her from the crack of a shoe cupboard.

"Oh my God," Juliette whispered in Russian. "Alisa Nikolaevna, are you trying to give me a heart attack?"

Alisa climbed out of the small cupboard, straightening to her full height. "You're supposed to be dead."

Juliette reared back. "How did you know?"

"How did I know . . . that you were *dead*?" Alisa asked. "I heard

Benedikt bring the news in. Roma ran out as soon as he heard."

Oh. Oh, no, no, no—

"Where did he go?" Juliette breathed. "Alisa, where did he go?"

Alisa shook her head. "I don't know. I've just been thinking in the cupboard since then. I was about to mourn you too, you know. It was only ten minutes ago."

Juliette pressed her fist to her mouth, thinking fast. Within the house, there came a chiming sound, and she was willing to bet that it was signaling the hour: one o'clock, the new morning.

"Listen to me." Juliette kneeled suddenly, so that she wasn't looming over Alisa. She clamped her hands on the girl's shoulders, her grip tight. "Alisa, there's a purge coming. I need you to go downstairs and warn everyone, warn as many people as you can. Then I need you to pack whatever you cannot bear to live without and come with me."

Alisa stared forward. Her eyes were as big as a doe's, amber brown and filled with concern. "Come with you?" she echoed. "To where?"

"To find your brother," Juliette answered. "Because we're leaving the city."

Thirty-Nine

Where could he *be*?"

Juliette kicked a shopfront wall, scuffing her shoes with dust and mud. Patiently, Alisa waited for Juliette to kick three more times, chewing on her nails. There was a loud noise in the distance, and at once, Juliette and Alisa peered down the dark, silent road. No result came of the noise. All around them, the city simply sat waiting.

"Perhaps the Bund," Alisa suggested. "Along the Huangpu."

"At two in the morning?"

Before vacating the house, Alisa had warned as many White Flowers as possible to run and hide within the city while there was still the shield of night; word had likely gotten out to the wider circles that something was soon to come. There was something in the air already. A high note, ringing beyond the human ear. An inaudible hum, operating on some different frequency.

"He thinks you're dead—who knows where he might go?"

"No. He hates vast spaces. He wouldn't go near the water to mourn."

Juliette paced along the street, smacking lightly at her own face as if physical sensation could draw forth some ideas. Alisa kept chewing on her nails.

"It didn't just seem like he was running out to get away from the news," Alisa said slowly. "It seemed like he had something he needed to do."

Juliette threw her hands in the air. "We had little else to do except—"

Find Dimitri. Stop the madness.

"Did he say anything about going after Dimitri Voronin?"

Alisa shook his head. "I thought you didn't know where Dimitri was."

"We don't." Juliette gave Alisa a sidelong glance. "How did you know that?"

With a roll of her eyes, Alisa tapped her ear. It was hard to believe this was the same girl who had fallen comatose so many months ago, waking thin and frail on her hospital bed. She seemed to have grown a spine that was twice as thick in the time since then.

"I know everything."

"All right, Miss I-Know-Everything, where is your brother?"

Alisa only sagged in reply, and Juliette immediately felt terrible for her attitude. How old was Alisa Montagova now? Twelve? Thirteen? Pain at that age was an eternal thing, a feeling that might never fade. It would, of course. Pain always faded, even if it refused to fully disappear. But that was a lesson that could only come with time too.

"I'm sorry," Juliette said. She slumped against the wall. "I'm scared for him. If we can't find Roma before the Nationalists release their men onto the streets, they will get to him first." They would not hesitate. The Kuomintang had held back for so long. Had looked upon this city for years and years as it lived its glory age of jazz clubs and silent films, had broiled in anger to see Shanghai singing while the rest of the country starved. Perhaps their true target of anger were the imperialists hiding behind their chain-link fences in the Concessions. But when one held guns and batons in their hands, did a true target of anger even matter? What else mattered except, at last, an excuse for *release*?

Alisa suddenly perked up again, her head tilting to the side. "Even if Roma doesn't know where Dimitri is, what if he is still trying to stop him?"

Juliette pushed off the wall. She started to frown. "In what manner?"

"This." Alisa grabbed Juliette's arm, then tapped her inner elbow, indicating to the blue veins running translucent under her skin. "The vaccine."

The answers struck. With a gasp, Juliette started to push at Alisa, steering them down the street.

"Lourens," Juliette said. "He's with Lourens."

It was the man who believed her first. The same one from that alley, whose head had been bleeding something fierce. He certainly looked healed now, if a little rough, standing behind the faces of the General Labor Union's leadership—faces that Kathleen was sure she should recognize, though she couldn't quite put a name to any of them.

The most important Communist powers were scattered about the city, doing whatever it was that revolution depended on. Those who were supposed to keep house below them—the ones who were camped out now at the stronghold that Kathleen rushed into—had only frowned when she tried to explain what was coming, when she insisted that those workers flocking onto the streets with labor union bands on their arms were not workers at all but Scarlets intent on slaughter.

The man had to have been someone's son, someone's something-important. It took a whisper from him—a whisper to another whisper to a throat being cleared, and then the man at the center of the room, taking his glasses off, said, "If there is massacre coming and you have arrived to warn us, how can we possibly stop it? The Nationalists hold an army. We are only the poor. We are the ordinary."

Kathleen folded her arms. She considered the group seated before her, thinking how typical it was that they would say such things. These people here, seated around the table, were not the poor and the ordinary. They were the ones privileged enough to lead a movement. If she could, she would blast her voice up into the heavens and warn the people—the true poor and ordinary people—directly, because *that* was who she wanted to protect. Not the few thinkers, not the men who thought themselves revolutionaries. At the end of the day, movements survived, but the individual could be replaced.

That was all she was. One girl, doing all she could for peace.

"They thought they had the element of surprise," Kathleen said evenly. "So tell your leaders to flee before they can be imprisoned—regroup, wait for another day. Tell your people to rise up, become so mighty that the gangsters will struggle to bring their swords down upon innocents on the street."

When she looked up, the whole room was watching.

"It is very simple," she finished. "When they come, be ready."

They started to move. They started to pass messages, write notes, prepare telegrams for different cities in case the attack spread farther. Kathleen merely watched, sitting primly on one of the tables. There was some bubble of emotion stirring in her chest. Some strange feeling in realizing that she was not here because she had to be, because the Scarlets had sent her. In this space, at this time, she was not a Scarlet at all.

Perhaps she would never be a Scarlet again. She had spent all these years watching, mimicking, adapting. Making herself into the loyal inner-circle member, someone willing to die for the family. But she wasn't willing—had never been willing. It had always been about maintaining whatever approach necessary to ensure order, but now order was gone.

Kathleen peeled her gloves off, scrunching up the rich silk fabric until it was balled in her hands. The Scarlet way of life was dead. The safety net was gone, but so too were the constraints. No more family members watching for the faintest sign of disloyalty. No more hierarchy and Lord Cai dictating their every move. All these years, Kathleen Lang breathed when the Scarlet Gang breathed. Kathleen Lang walked when the Scarlet Gang told her to walk. Kathleen Lang didn't *exist* except to be someone in line with the Scarlet Gang, except to be the perfect image of someone who was worthy of protection and safety.

And when the Scarlet Gang faded away, so too would Kathleen. When the Scarlet Gang removed itself, Kathleen Lang halted like a music box ballerina—a dead girl's name who spun for their eyes.

The gloves fluttered to the floor.

The Scarlet way of life was dead. Kathleen Lang was dead, had always been dead. But Celia Lang was not. Celia had always been here, biding her time, waiting for the moment she could feel *safe*.

"So how did you come across this information?"

The man suddenly came to sit down, his shoes stepping over the fallen gloves without noticing, eyes too focused on the frantic scene before them.

"Doesn't really matter, does it?" she replied. "You can see it is true. You only have to send people out to poke around the corners of the city, and you will see the gangsters dressed pretending to be workers."

"Hmmm." The man's gaze flickered to her now. "Your face looks familiar. Aren't you Scarlet-affiliated?"

Celia stood up, fetching her dirty gloves and dropping them into the trash can.

"No," she said. "I am not."

Benedikt slammed up against the doors of the lab, blocking the exit with his body. Some paces away, a tired Lourens who had been awoken from his sleep was blinking in trepidation, not knowing why Roma was acting this way.

"Listen to me," Benedikt said lowly. "You'll be shot on sight."

"Move aside."

Roma's voice was lifeless. So too were his eyes, a mass of darkness swallowing up his stare. The strangest thing was that Benedikt recognized himself in that expression, recognized that same twisted sense of rage that showed itself in recklessness.

Is that what I looked like?

"You said we were coming here to check on the vaccine!" Benedikt hissed. He made another grab for the jar in Roma's hands. "Now, instead, you're running off with some concoction to blow up the Scarlet house a second time. That's not what Juliette would have wanted!"

"Don't tell me what Juliette would have wanted!" Roma snapped. "Don't tell—"

Benedikt took his chance to dive for the jar. Roma saw it coming and darted back two steps, but Benedikt outright lunged, pushing his cousin to the linoleum floor and pinning his arm down. Lourens made another concerned noise but otherwise remained motionless by the tables, his eyes swiveling about the scene.

"At least wait," Benedikt said, his knees on Roma's stomach. "Wait to see why. Since when did Juliette have any reason to take a dagger to her own heart—"

"So they killed her," Roma seethed. "They killed her, and they're going to get away with it—"

Benedikt pushed on Roma's attempt to sit up. "This isn't some murder on the streets, this is the Scarlet Gang! You've always known the danger of gangsters. You live it every day!"

Roma stilled. He breathed in, then again, then again, and suddenly Benedikt realized it was because his cousin was struggling to fill his lungs.

"She would never," he managed. "Never."

Benedikt swallowed hard. He couldn't allow this. It was for Roma's own good.

"There are Scarlets everywhere in the city right now," he said slowly. "They're plotting something. You cannot go make it worse."

His words had the opposite effect. Benedikt had intended to pacify, and instead a vein started to throb at Roma's neck. Roma shoved Benedikt off, fast, and got to his feet, but Benedikt wouldn't give up so easily. He lunged for the jar again. When he only managed to catch Roma's wrist, he switched from trying to wrest away the explosive and simply grabbed ahold of his cousin with both hands, keeping him from opening the lab's doors, keeping him from running through the building and out into the night.

Roma came to a halt. Slowly, he turned around. The deadness in his eyes had acquired a murderous glint.

"Tell me," he said. "Were you not the one who sought revenge when you thought Marshall was dead?"

Benedikt scoffed. That was a mistake. The fire in Roma's eyes only grew stronger.

"I never stormed into the Scarlet house. I never did anything rash!"

"Maybe you should have."

"No," Benedikt spat. He hardly wanted to think about Marshall right now, when he was trying to talk Roma out of a death wish. "What good could it have done?"

"What good?" Roma hissed in echo. "It doesn't matter, does it? He came back to life!"

Roma tried to pull away; Benedikt would not relinquish. In a flash, Roma had his pistol in his free hand, but it was not to point at Benedikt.

He brought it to his own temple.

"Hey." Benedikt froze, afraid that any sudden movement would nudge at the trigger. All he could hear through his ears was the sound of rushing blood. "Roma, don't."

"Roma, do not be a fool," Lourens urged from where he stood.

"So let go of me," Roma said. "Let go of me, Benedikt."

Benedikt let out a low breath. "I will not."

It was a standstill, then. It was a matter of Benedikt believing that his cousin could not be this lost, and yet he was not certain. He could not know if in the next few seconds Roma would call him on his bluff and splatter his brains across the lab.

Benedikt let go.

And at that very moment, the lab door flew open, illuminating the figures who stood at the threshold.

"Roma! What are you *doing*?"

Roma whirled around, releasing an audible gasp at the sound of the voice. Benedikt, already facing the doors, could only blink. Once. Twice. It wasn't a hallucination. Juliette Cai was really standing there, wearing a ridiculous hat, with Alisa behind her, both of them panting for breath as if they had been on a long run.

"Look," Benedikt said faintly, hardly hearing his own words as they slipped out. "You got your resurrection too."

Roma didn't seem to hear him. He was already dropping his pistol like it had burned him, dropping the jar in his other hand. Benedikt dove to catch it, not daring to find out how explosive materials would react when thrown against the hard floor. By the time he had caught the jar, saving it from smashing upon the linoleum at their feet, Roma had already reached Juliette, kissing her hard on the mouth. The embrace was so fierce that Juliette immediately stretched one of her hands back, trying to cover Alisa's eyes.

Alisa darted under Juliette's hand and mimed a gag to Benedikt. Benedikt was still in such shock that he couldn't laugh along.

"Are you okay?" Roma and Juliette asked in unison the moment they broke apart.

Benedikt got to his feet. The jar remained intact. He passed it to Lourens, and Lourens took it quickly, shelving the explosive away. They were hurrying to put it out of Roma's sight, but with Juliette here now, Benedikt doubted Roma even remembered why he wanted that jar.

"I thought you were *dead*," Roma was saying to Juliette. "Don't *ever* do that to me."

"The better question is," Benedikt cut in, "why are you *so* fond of faking deaths?"

Juliette shook her head, her arm twining around Roma's as she hurried him back into the lab. She gestured for Alisa to come along too, letting the doors fall closed.

"Faking my death would have required actually producing a false corpse, as I did for Marshall," Juliette said evenly. "All I did here was lie. I never meant for it to reach you. It shouldn't have leaked past the Scarlet circles." She sighted Lourens, still warily hovering by the worktables. "Hello."

"May I return to bed now?" Lourens asked wearily.

"No," Juliette answered before any of the Montagovs could. "You need to hear this too. There's a purge coming. That's why I lied. To push it off."

"A what?" Roma was still in a daze, blinking rapidly to clear the mist over his eyes.

Juliette placed her hands on one of the tables. It looked like she was physically bracing herself, and when she lifted her head to speak . . . it was not Roma she was looking at but Benedikt.

"There's an execution order for your heads. White Flowers are to be treated as Communists, and just before dawn breaks, Scarlets and Kuomintang soldiers alike are going to start shooting and arresting. The command has been given. Anyone opposing the Nationalists is to be eliminated. We have to go."

"Wait—*what?*"

Roma's voice rose another octave, prompting Alisa to reach out and hug his arm. Benedikt, meanwhile, simply exhaled a breath, letting the information sink in. A full-city purge. At last the Nationalists had pushed themselves into full throttle, intent on taking Shanghai.

"We can't," Roma continued. "Dimitri is still out there with his monsters. I will accept stepping out of politics. I will accept high-tailing it out of the way if it's the Nationalists and Communists colliding against each other. But while we can stop Dimitri, we must."

Was it even possible at this point? How could they stop him? How could they kill men who turned to monsters when the monsters seemed so indestructible?

Juliette grimaced, her eyes flickering again to Benedikt as if to ask for help. Before she could speak, it was Lourens who cleared his throat, interrupting her.

"You may not need to." Lourens gestured to the back of the lab. One of the machines had been humming away, lit from the inside. "The vaccine stops the madness, no? It won't solve the physical monster problem, but it will take away a large portion of their power."

Roma's eyes grew wide. "The vaccine is ready?"

"Not at this precise moment. But give it a few days, perhaps. I have the formula. I have the supplies. I can dump it in the whole city's water supply. No one even has to know that they're being inoculated."

"Which means," Juliette said quietly, "we have done all that we can here, Roma. For the sake of your life, we have to leave. All of us. Right now, before dawn breaks."

Benedikt finally understood why Juliette's gaze kept drifting back to him.

"Okay," Roma said, defeated, in collision with Benedikt's sudden *"No."*

The room fell quiet, nothing but the sound of machines humming. Then, when Benedikt was sure he had summoned everyone's attention: "Not without Marshall."

Juliette clicked her tongue. "I was afraid you would say that." She finally glanced away. "If Marshall is with his father, he is safer than he would be anywhere else."

"He may be safe, but he will be trapped there for however long. If we're getting out of the city, out of the *country*, we get out for good. We're not leaving him behind."

Roma made a thoughtful noise. He wiped a smear of dust off Alisa's cheek, who, to her credit, had remained quiet through all this.

"Benedikt's right," he said. "If there is indeed a purge coming, it doesn't stop with one event. Let's say Lourens distributes the vaccine. Let's say the madness disappears and the city returns to relative normalcy. But with this violence on the Communists and the White Flowers . . ."

"The city will never return to normal," Juliette finished heavily, like she didn't want to say it aloud.

One purge was never one purge. The Nationalists were not only forcing out all opposition. They also had to maintain their control. No Communist could show their face on these streets again. No White Flower could continue living within the city's borders, at least not without hiding their identity. The purge would never end.

"So," Benedikt finished, "we need to get Marshall."

Juliette tossed her hat off, throwing it to the table. Her hair was a tangled mess. "As much as I agree, *how* do you propose we do that?"

"I go alone."

All heads in the room snapped to Benedikt. Even Lourens looked flabbergasted.

"Are you trying to get yourself killed?" Juliette asked. "I *just* said that all White Flowers seen on the streets upon daybreak will be slaughtered."

"I am not as recognizable as Roma is," Benedikt replied easily. "Especially not if I dress as your Scarlets will be. I have already seen them. They are in workers' overalls, with a band over their arm." He gestured to his biceps. "They seek White Flowers to execute by *looking* for White Flowers. Who is to say what I am if I look just like them?"

"It's a good plan," Roma said.

"It's a horrible plan," Juliette said.

Roma picked up Juliette's hat. "But all the Nationalists will be on the streets. Marshall will probably be unguarded."

Juliette snatched the hat back. "Why do you think they have allied with the Scarlets? They always send the smaller men to go do their dirty work, their bloody work. You cannot guarantee that General Shu himself won't have his eye on Marshall."

"At the very least, he will not have backup." Benedikt pushed up his sleeves, heaving an exhale. "We waste time by arguing. It is this or nothing. The two of you cannot even consider following me. *Especially* into a Nationalist stronghold. You will be hauled off in a blink, no matter how many ugly hats you wear."

Juliette threw the hat at Benedikt. He dodged easily, though even with Juliette's deathly aim, the soft article would have bounced off him anyway. The lab fell silent again. Alisa's eyes darted back and forth, trying to follow the situation.

"Under one condition," Roma finally said. "If you cannot get to him, you must give up. Marshall's own father will not put a call out for his head. But if caught, they will execute *you*."

Benedikt's mouth opened to argue, but then, just subtly enough that Roma didn't notice, Juliette raised her hand to her lips and pressed a finger there, shaking her head.

"I have a contact at the Bund who can smuggle us out," she said, closing her fist and appearing normal the moment Roma turned to look at her. "Martial law cannot restrict him from sailing to catch fish, but the latest we can depart is noon. Any longer, and I suspect I will be found." Juliette's stare was harsh upon Benedikt, communicating alongside her words. "You must meet us at the Bund then. No matter what."

Benedikt knew what Juliette was trying to say even if she didn't say it aloud. If he was not there, they still needed to leave. She would knock Roma and Alisa out and drag them if she needed, but she would not risk their lives and let them remain behind for him.

Benedikt nodded, a smile—a true smile—coming to his lips. For perhaps the first time, he trusted Juliette wholeheartedly.

"At noon," he promised.

Forty

They had boarded up the lab, going as far as to smash one of the windows in advance, so Scarlets passing by would think it already scouted and searched. Any moment now, the bugle call would sound across the city, summoning all those under Nationalist command.

Juliette wondered if any Scarlets mourned. If, in hearing of her death, they had felt a genuine drop of sadness, or if she was merely a figurehead they had been forced to respect. By now her parents had surely poked through her scheme, had received condolences back from the Nationalists about their dead daughter and searched through the house to find her missing. It would not take long to put two and two together and figure that Juliette was the one who had announced her own death.

"Miss Cai."

Juliette lifted her head off Lourens's kitchen table. His apartment was at the back of the labs, and after throwing a pile of shelves onto the floor to make the hallways look ransacked, they had deemed it unlikely any of the gangsters or soldiers would find their way here. Still, Juliette had shoved a knife across the door latch, and if anyone was to try barging through, they would have to snap the steel first.

"Yes?"

Lourens passed her a thin blanket. Juliette had trouble reaching for it, only because she could not see where she was reaching. She had been awake for long enough that her vision was starting to blur, and there was only one candle for light, flickering in the adjoined living room. The sun would be up any second, but they had just finished taping the windows of Lourens's apartment with layers upon layers of newspapers, blacking out the outside and preventing the outside from looking in.

"If all is settled, I am going back to sleep," Lourens announced.

Roma looked up suddenly, frowning from across the apartment. He was on the sofa with Alisa, a needle and thread in his hand as he fixed a rip in Alisa's sleeve, leaning the both of them so closely into the candlelight that there was a risk Alisa's blond hair would catch aflame.

"Lourens," Roma said, almost chidingly as he finished his stitching. "How can you sleep? There's about to be mass slaughter outside."

"I highly suggest you children do the same," Lourens chided back. He plucked an orange from his fruit bowl and set it down in front of Juliette. "Take it from someone who ran once too: when you leave all that you know, you want to be well rested."

Juliette picked up the orange. "Thank you?"

Lourens was already shuffling away, moving from the kitchen into the living room. "Miss Montagova, you will take the spare room, yes? Miss Cai, you should find that the sofa will suffice, and, Roma, I will find a floor sheet for you."

Juliette watched Roma frown, watched him look at the sofa and mentally measure its width, finding it would probably fit two.

"You don't have to—"

"Thank you!" Juliette repeated, cutting in. Lourens disappeared down the hallway.

"Juliette, what—"

"He's old, Roma." She pushed herself up from the kitchen table and took the orange with her, peeling the skin into neat strips. "Are you trying to horrify him with your social impropriety?"

"Social impropriety while there is mass slaughter outside," Roma grumbled.

Juliette pulled an orange segment free and plopped it in her mouth. She started to walk around the living room, inspecting the various vases that Lourens owned. As she poked her nose here and there, she heard Alisa begin to mutter to Roma, only Alisa's version of muttering was loud enough that each word was quite clearly enunciated.

"Roma."

"What is it?" He prodded her sleeve. "Another rip?"

"No," Alisa whispered, frowning and drawing her arm away. "So did you . . . ? Did you *marry* Juliette Cai?"

Juliette choked, the orange immediately lodging in her throat.

"I—" Even by the dim light, Roma looked faintly red. "We are well acquainted."

Half spluttering, half holding back the most inappropriately timed laugh, Juliette managed to cough the orange out of her windpipe. Roma, meanwhile, cleared his throat, getting to his feet and nudging his sister up too.

"Come on, Alisa. Go get some rest."

He quickly pushed Alisa down the hallway, exchanging some words with Lourens before Lourens retired into his room. Juliette thought she heard *vaccine* and *are you certain?* There was some more murmuring from the guest room before Roma emerged again, fumbling around in the dark with something that looked like a mat.

"Lourens insisted I take this," Roma explained, setting it onto the floor.

By now Juliette had finished her orange and calmed down, seated upon the sofa. The humor was an instinctive reaction; the city was collapsing outside, and blood was going to run so thickly that the roads would turn to an ocean of red. Laughing was the only way she wouldn't cry.

"And will you?" Juliette asked.

Roma's head jerked up. His eyes narrowed, trying to gauge if Juliette was asking a genuine question or teasing.

She smiled. Roma exhaled in relief, kicking aside the mat.

"No one holds a straight face like you do," he said, joining her on the sofa. "I'm still mad at you, dorogaya."

Juliette reeled back, placing a hand to her heart. "Mad at *me*? I thought we already got past that."

"I already forgave you for everything else," Roma said. "I'm mad at you for having me think you were *dead*. Do you know how horrible that was?"

Juliette shifted her knee. It pressed up against Roma's leg. He didn't move away. She would take that as a forgiving sign. "Benedikt lived with the same feeling for *months*."

"Which is why I didn't think you would pull it twice," Roma said. "Which is why I thought it to be true."

Juliette reached out with her hand. Gently, she pressed her palm to his cheek, fingers skimming softly on skin, and Roma reached up to clasp his hand on hers.

"I should be mad at you too," she said quietly. "How dare you take a gun to your head as if your life is something that can be thrown away."

Roma leaned into her touch with a sigh, his eyes fluttering closed. He looked young. Vulnerable. This was the boy she had fallen in love with, underneath all the harsher layers he needed to wear to survive. But in her mind's eye, she was remembering the sight before her when she had pushed open the doors to the lab. Roma, his pistol pressed to his temple. Roma, looking ready to shoot.

"I panicked," he said. "I wouldn't have pulled the trigger. I only needed Benedikt to believe I would so he could let me go."

But the threat had to have come from somewhere. The very fact that Benedikt had believed it meant Roma was capable of doing it. Of threatening his own life just to get to her. Juliette couldn't shake off her own ill ease. She didn't want to be a girl who incited harm. She didn't want it, but perhaps by mere virtue of being Juliette Cai, she was the embodiment of this city's violence.

"You can't ever do that." Juliette tightened her fingers. "You can't choose me above everything else. I will not accept it."

A beat passed. The candle was dancing vigorously atop the table, casting them both in moving shadows.

"I won't," Roma whispered. When he opened his eyes again, slowly to adjust to the dim light, he added, "Don't leave me, Juliette."

It sounded like a plea. A plea to the heavens, to the stars, to the forces that drew their fates.

"I would never," Juliette replied solemnly. Too many times had she done it already. "I will never leave you."

Roma loosed a soft breath. "I know." He pressed a kiss to the inside of her wrist. "I think I was more afraid that they took you from me."

Oh. His admission stirred a tightness in her throat. This was their lives. Constantly operating in fear, even when they were supposed to have power. Wasn't power supposed to provide control? Wasn't power supposed to solve everything?

Juliette pulled her hand away, only so she could extend her pinkie finger instead. "With my whole heart," she promised, "if I have any say in the matter, you will never lose me."

The candlelight flickered. Roma's eyes, too, flickered up and down, from her face to her hand.

"Is this . . . ," he said, "a strange American custom?"

Juliette huffed a short laugh, grabbing Roma's hand and hooking her pinkie with his. "Yes," she answered. "It means I cannot break my promise or you may chop my finger off."

"That's the Japanese interpretation. Yubikiri."

Her eyes snapped up. "So you *do* know what it means!"

Roma didn't give her the satisfaction of being caught out. His expression forcibly serious, he only lifted her hand and smoothed out her fist, so that all her fingers were separated, her palm held facing him.

"What if I don't want this one?" he asked, tapping her pinkie. He moved his touch to the one beside—her ring finger—and grazed the length of it. "What if I want this one?"

Juliette's heart started to thud in her chest. "So morbid," she remarked.

"Hmmm." Roma continued to draw a circle about her finger, leaving no question for what he was implying. "I'm not sure if morbidity was what I was going for."

"Then what?" Juliette wanted to hear it. "What were you going for?"

Roma breathed a laugh. "I'm asking you to marry me."

All the blood in Juliette's body rushed to her head. She could feel her cheeks blazing red, not out of embarrassment, but rather because there was such an uproar swirling inside her that the hot surge of emotion had nowhere else to go.

"My pinkie promise isn't good enough for you?" Juliette teased. "Did Alisa put you up to this?"

This time it was Roma's turn to press both his palms on Juliette's cheeks. She had thought it would be too dark to notice her blush, yet Roma noticed, a smile twitching on his lips.

"She doesn't have the power to put me up to this," he said. "Marry me, Juliette. Marry me so we can erase the blood feud between us and start utterly anew."

Juliette inched forward. Roma's hands dropped to her neck, smoothing back the loose hair curling around her shoulders. He seemed to think that she was leaning in for a kiss, but she was in fact reaching behind him, and with a start, Roma blinked, sighting one of Lourens's many copies of the Bible in her hands.

"I wasn't aware that you were religious."

"I am not," Juliette replied. "I thought you needed a Bible to get married in this city."

Roma blinked. "So you're saying yes?"

"Shǎ guā." She raised the Bible, pretending to beat him with it. "Do you think I'm holding it for a weapon? Of course I'm saying yes."

Quick as a flash, Roma had his arms around her, pushing her upon the sofa. The Bible fell to the floor with a *thump*. A burst of laughter rose to Juliette's lips, muffled only by Roma's kiss. For a moment that was all that mattered—Roma, Roma, *Roma*.

Then there was the faintest sound of gunfire, and both of them gasped, breaking apart to listen. The windows were blacked out. They were safe. Only that didn't change the reality, didn't mean the world outside was not brightening with light and running with red.

It had started. Although faint, a bugle call could be heard reverberating through the whole city, trickling even into this apartment. The purging had started.

Juliette sat up, reaching for the fallen Bible. She doubted Lourens would be happy if they scuffed it up.

"I should have tried sending more help," she whispered. "I should have sent more warning."

Roma shook his head. "It's your own people. What were you to do?"

Indeed, that was always the problem. Scarlet or White Flower. Communist or Nationalist. In the end, the only ones who seemed to benefit from so much infighting were the foreigners sitting pretty behind their Concession borders.

"I despise it," she whispered. "If my people can fire on the masses merely because they have Communist sympathies, I despise them."

Roma did not say anything. He only brushed her hair behind her ear, letting her tremble in her anger.

"I will be free of my name." Juliette looked up. "I will take yours."

There was a moment of stillness, a moment where Roma gazed

upon her like he was trying to commit her features to memory. Then:

"Juliette," he breathed. "It is not as though my name is any better. It is not as though there is less blood on mine. You can call a rose something else, but it remains yet a rose."

Juliette flinched, hearing a shout outside. "So we are never to change?" she asked. "We are forever blood-soaked roses?"

Roma took her hand. Pressed a kiss to her knuckles. "A rose is a rose, even by another name," he whispered. "But we choose whether we will offer beauty to the world, or if we will use our thorns to sting."

They could choose. Love or blood. Hope or hate.

"I love you," Juliette whispered fiercely. "I need you to know. I love you so much it feels like it could consume me."

Before Roma could even respond, Juliette lunged for a ball of yarn on the table. Roma watched her in confusion, his brow furrowed as she measured a length of string and pulled a knife from her pocket to slice.

He grew less confused when Juliette took the string and started to wind it around his finger—his right hand, as was customary for Russians. She had remembered. Remembered from their whispered conversations five years ago about a future where they could run away and be together.

"I take you, Roma Montagov," she said, her voice soft, "to be my lawfully wedded husband, to have and to hold, until death do us part." She tied a small, secure knot. "I think I'm missing some vows in between."

"As well as an officiant and some witnesses"—Roma reached for her knife, cutting his own bit of string—"but at least we have a Bible."

He took her left hand. Carefully, he wound the string around her fourth finger, making such a delicate effort that Juliette didn't want to breathe for fear it would distract his task.

"I take you, Juliette Cai," Roma whispered in concentration, "to be my lawfully wedded wife, to have and to hold, until . . ." He looked up as he finished the knot. Paused. When he spoke again, he did not look away. "No, scratch that. To have and to hold, where even death cannot part us. In this life and the next, for however long our souls remain, mine will always find yours. Those are my vows to you."

Juliette closed her fist. The string really did feel like a ring: as heavy on her finger as any band of metal. These vows were as substantial as any made in front of a priest or audience. They didn't need any of those things. They had always been two mirrored souls, the only ones who understood the other in a city that wanted to consume them whole, and now they were joined, mightier when together.

"Even death cannot part us," she echoed fiercely.

It was a promise that felt colossal. In this life they had been born enemies. In this life they had blood for miles between them, wide enough to run a river, deep enough to forge a valley. In the next, maybe there would be peace.

Outside, metal clashed against metal, an echo ringing all across the city—again, then again. Here, within these four walls, all they could do was hold each other, waiting for noon to come, waiting for the moment they could be free.

Forty-One

Celia seemed to have ended up a soldier, perusing the battleground from above. All she had ever wanted was a quietly revolving world. And she had slapped her hands over her ears, hoping that silence in her head meant silence outside too.

That would work no longer. The world had grown too loud. The city had come to a crescendo.

"Three Scarlets from the north, likely bringing more," Celia reported. Immediately, the girl who had been idling by the balcony, in wait for her observations, ran off to report. The message would travel from house to house, building to building.

"Your note has been handled," an incoming girl reported now, nodding to Celia. "We reached Da Nao."

Celia nodded back, then turned her focus to the streets again. She never thought she would end up a soldier, and . . . she supposed she wasn't. She was not among those gathering below, holding bricks and batons and weapons in wait for the gangsters and Nationalists. When the first of the fight broke out, the people only needed to resist until the city could awaken, until their numbers could pour outward and do what they had always done best: incite chaos, take to the streets, overwhelm all the higher hands trying to control them.

"Get ready," Celia called down.

On cue, the Scarlets approached, startling upon sighting the workers already waiting outside their apartment blocks. They exchanged a glance, as if asking if they should still proceed. When their eyes lifted, sighting Celia from above, a flash of recognition seemed to register.

Celia stepped inside from the balcony.

Not a soldier, but the watching eyes.

Not a soldier, but the beating heart of resistance.

Benedikt pulled at the band on his arm, shedding it as soon as he was off the main roads. The strip of white fabric soaked into a dirty rain puddle, and he shuddered, a brief chill skating down his back.

They were all wearing it, the Scarlets with their knives and guns. Faces smeared with a bit of dirt as if that disguised them as the masses, their armbands printed with the Chinese character for "labor," as if this was the workers' cause firing back upon its leaders. He had wagered that he could blend among them unnoticed, and he had been right. It had only taken a quick change of clothes, and hardly any of the Scarlets on the roads stopped to consider him, even if he was running in the opposite direction.

Benedikt paused now, crouching behind a telephone post when he heard a rumble of commotion in the distance. The Concessions were open. He didn't know when that had happened, when all the foreign soldiers had been commanded to depart their posts. For whatever reason, Route Ghisi was unguarded, and the roads—formerly blocked with sandbags and makeshift chain fences—were now cleared.

The commotion came nearer. Benedikt ducked just in time to hide from the group of Scarlets as they hurried out of the French Concession.

He shouldn't have been surprised. The Scarlets and Nationalists had come into an agreement with the foreigners, then. The foreigners had allowed this, had known about the purge and warned their people to stay indoors. No matter how much the Nationalists proclaimed their need to retake the country, too much of this city was under the foreigners. Too many Nationalist offices and Nationalist headquarters sat on French land to risk upsetting them.

"Hurry up. Jessfield is low on reinforcements."

Another group ran past the telephone post, and Benedikt sank lower, though the post would surely cover him from view. Only when the voices faded again did he stand, poking his head around to watch the Kuomintang men disappear from sight.

The French Concession was empty. Benedikt had never seen its early mornings so vacant, not a single vendor in sight even while the sky slowly brightened into a hazy gray. But that didn't mean it was quiet. Sirens were shrieking all across the city, most of them coming from the south. If Benedikt took a guess, he would say they were coming from the gunboats, those floating upon the parts of the Huangpu in Nanshi.

He started to run. No use being subtle now. Each second wasted was a second closer to noon. Benedikt knew where General Shu's house was located. His only concern was whether Marshall would be there or if the house would be inhabited at all. For all he knew, they were no longer in Shanghai. For all he knew, they were in any location across the city, outside of foreign land and far from the fighting.

"Hey!"

With a start, Benedikt turned over his shoulder, finding a group of Scarlets emerging from a narrow side street. They were dressed as he was, rifles in hand. Benedikt's first instinct was to run, but the Concession was too wide and vast; there would be no way to lose his pursuers, not unless he could disappear into thin air.

"What?" Benedikt shouted back, as if their call was nothing more than an annoyance.

"Where are you going?" one Scarlet within the group bellowed. "Command said to congregate in Zhabei. We've got protesters trying to march on Second Division headquarters."

"Oh?" Benedikt feigned ignorance. He tried to think if he even knew where the hell the Nationalists' Second Division headquarters were. Baoshan Road? "I was not made aware. I'm running a message."

"For?"

They were getting suspicious. Benedikt steeled his expression.

"Lord Cai is having a direct note brought to Chiang Kai-shek. He's already mad enough about Juliette's stunt. Do you want to be the ones to go back and explain why his note is so late?"

The Scarlets all grimaced, some more severely than others. "Go on, then," another in the group said. Before Benedikt even moved, they were already off in a different direction, muttering among themselves about Lord Cai.

Benedikt exhaled, continuing onward with his pulse beating a racket in his chest. That had been a risk. For all he knew, Lord Cai might not have publicly announced what Juliette had done. Fate was on his side this time.

His target finally came into view. A tall wrought-iron gate, painted black. It didn't seem like there was anyone standing guard. It didn't seem like there was anyone keeping watch within the compound either. All Benedikt could hear were distant sirens—distant sirens and the whistling wind, whipping through his hair and obscuring his vision.

Benedikt palmed a gun and slunk around the gate. His boots came down hard on the shrubbery that surrounded the residence, rustling with every step. The ground inclined slightly uphill here, rising as the trees grew thicker, branches drooping low. In this part of the French Concession, the houses were built far apart enough that each had a garden and a long, winding driveway. Some chose enclosures to block people from looking in, while others let their flowers and shrubs be gawped at freely. When Benedikt finally found a lump of dirt tall enough to step on, he used the boost to launch himself up on the walled gate, peering over to discover not only one outer enclosure but a second fence erected just inside.

"Is this a house or a military compound?" he muttered. There seemed to be no movement between the fences. With a grunt, Benedikt swung his legs over the first wall, almost rolling right off and narrowly landing on his two feet. A twinge of pain shot up his ankle.

Please don't be sprained. Please don't be sprained.

He took a step forward. The pain worsened.

Oh, for crying out loud.

Half hobbling, Benedikt grabbed ahold of the second fence, shoving his left foot through one of the notches. This one was chain-linked rather than a smooth wall, but as soon as he had hauled himself halfway up, he heard voices coming near. Cursing furiously under his breath, Benedikt stuck his right foot into the fence, biting right past his screaming ankle, and scrambled over the sharp wire at the top. It was possible that he had torn a rip through the cuff of his trousers. It was possible he had scratched his arm and was leaving a trail of blood through the grass. None of it mattered enough to slow him down, afraid that he would be spotted at any moment now that he was in, hurrying along the edges of the garden.

The house loomed into view: one prominent front door, then two wings to either side of it, the second-floor balconies hanging atop its first-floor garages. Gauging by the number of shiny black cars parked outside the house, there were plenty of visitors inside.

Benedikt paused, trying to figure out his best course of action. If he listened hard, he thought he heard the steady hum of conversation from inside, which meant they were possibly hosting an early-morning function. He could hardly comprehend how. The Nationalists had just set the command for slaughter on the city. How did any of these men find the stomach to congregate together and continue with their day when their soldiers were laying waste to the people outside?

"Marshall, where the hell are you?" Benedikt whispered to the empty gardens. Carefully, hunching close to the ground, he started to make his way around the gravel paths, sticking close to the cover of the trees. Too close to the house and he feared being spotted through the large windows; too close to the fence and he feared being sighted by the patrolling soldiers. It wasn't until he came around the back of the house that he dared straighten a little, hobbling close to the painted white walls. Somehow, he needed to find a way in. Perhaps if he stripped out of the overalls, he could pretend to be a Nationalist's assistant and claim that—

Benedikt halted. He had passed a window, only now he doubled back, peering in more closely. There was a flag hanging over the desk inside: deep blue with a white sun. This was an office. This was *General Shu's* office.

The two windowpanes were latched, but that was no problem. Benedikt retrieved his pocketknife and triggered the thin blade, sliding it right between the two panes. All he had to do was push up, and then the latch was nudged out of the way, the window hinges creaking softly when Benedikt nudged at the glass.

He almost couldn't believe it. With care not to bring the dirt of the gardens in with him, he climbed through, wincing when he landed on the carpet. The office stayed silent—no alarm going off, no secret guard waiting in the corner. Only the flag fluttering with the slightest disturbance, dust settling over the papers on the desk and the early sunlight casting a slash across the wall. One door opposite the desk likely led out into the hallway. Another door near the flag was smaller—a storage unit.

Benedikt's gaze caught on the desk. He hardly had the time to dawdle, yet he paused all the same, trying not to put more pressure on his ankle as he walked over and picked up the two pieces of paper left at the center.

The first was messily scribbled, its characters almost bleeding off the page in a hurry.

Intercepted this.
We've sent word ahead to Lord Cai.

Benedikt blinked, a bad feeling sinking into his stomach. The second piece of paper was far thinner, ink visible through the sunlight even before he unfolded it. This message was written in a much more careful hand, addressed to . . .

"Oh, *no*," he muttered.

Da Nao—

Cai Junli and Roma Montagov seek safe passage with you to leave the city. You must take them onboard. Both of them. For the good of the country, for the good of the people. Please do this favor.

—Lang Selin

The Nationalists knew. The Scarlets knew. They would be assembling their forces right this moment, intent on stopping Juliette from leaving. And if they caught them, then Roma would be hauled away for execution.

Benedikt set the papers down. He had to find Marshall. They had to get out, get to the Bund, deliver the warning.

But then came the sound of footsteps down the hall. Then came the boom of voices, coming closer and closer.

They were heading for the office.

Panic set his pulse into breakneck speed. Benedikt eyed the window, calculating the time he needed to climb back out. With no time to spare, he pivoted instead for the other door in the office and opened it to find a storage room for filing cabinets—barely wide enough to let one person walk through, but long enough to leave darkness on the other end. He squeezed right in, his back pressed against the cabinets lining the walls, shoulders almost colliding with the sharp metal edges.

Click. Benedikt pulled the door after himself just as the burst of

414

voices entered the office. They settled into the room, chairs scraping back, heavy bodies sitting down—discussing the Communists, discussing the massacre.

And then: "We have complaints from the Scarlet Gang about the Montagov kill order. Said it was dishonorable."

Benedikt wasn't sure if he had heard correctly. He turned rigid with surprise, listening closer. So the Scarlet Gang hadn't been entirely on board. He didn't know whether to respect them for voicing their concern or hate them for going through with it anyway.

With fear coating his skin like sweat, Benedikt pushed at the door as carefully as he could, allowing it to open just the barest sliver. He didn't have a perfect idea what each high-ranking official in the Kuomintang looked like, but he recognized General Shu, if not by his resemblance to Marshall, then by the image permanently seared into his head when General Shu was taking Marshall away from him.

"Forget it," General Shu said. "My command stands. We will never again have a chance like this for eradicating our enemies; we must take it."

Benedikt's fists curled by his sides, twisting at his sleeves for something to do, for some way to exert energy so he didn't move and make noise. Since when were the White Flowers enemies to the Nationalists anyway? Dimitri had allied with the Communists, but was that enough to condemn every White Flower? If it were the Scarlets demanding the White Flowers be pulled into the purge, that was one matter, but General Shu insisting on it instead . . .

There were only four Montagovs left in the city. Unless the kill order wasn't a strike against the White Flowers at all, but an effort to take everyone Marshall loved away from him.

Benedikt exhaled slowly. The Nationalists continued with their discussion, the smell of cigarette smoke wafting into the closet space. All the while, trying not to move a single muscle, Benedikt was trapped.

Forty-Two

Rain had been falling in a light drizzle over the city, washing at the stains marring the sidewalks, turning the lines of blood into one long stream that ran through the city like a second river.

When Juliette picked her way out of the lab building, emerging cautiously into the late morning, the street was empty. It had been quiet for some time now. The gunshots and shouting and clanging metal had not gone on for long; the Nationalists and the Scarlets had stormed the city with military-grade weapons, after all. Those at the other end of their violence had submitted quickly.

"Something's not right, dorogaya."

Juliette turned around, watching Roma emerge into the open, clutching Alisa's hand. His eyes shifted nervously.

"It's too quiet."

"No," Juliette said. "I think it is only that all reinforcements have been called elsewhere. Listen."

She held up a finger, tilting her head into the wind. The rain started to fall harder, turning the drizzle into a proper downpour, but beneath the din, there came the sound of voices, like a screaming crowd.

Roma's expression turned stricken. "Let's move."

The first cluster of people they came upon was a surprise. Roma panicked, Alisa froze, but Juliette pushed at both of their shoulders, forcing them to keep moving. These were protesters—university students, gauging by their simple fashion and plaited hair—but they were too caught up in their slogan-shouting to even notice the three gangsters passing them.

"Keep moving," Juliette warned. "Head down."

"What's happening?" Alisa asked, raising her voice to be heard over the rain. "I thought there was a purge. Why aren't they afraid?"

Her blond hair was plastered to her neck and shoulders. Juliette was not faring much better; at least she hadn't bothered with finger waves, so it was only black locks stuck to her face, not pomade running in a sticky mess.

"Because you cannot kill everyone in one day," Juliette replied bitterly. "They went for their most prominent targets using the element of surprise. After that, the workers still hold the numbers. As long as people at the top are putting out the call, there will be people at the bottom ready to answer."

And answer they did. The farther Roma, Juliette, and Alisa walked—delving deeper into the city and closer to the Bund—the more the crowds thickened. It became startlingly clear that those on the streets were all congregating in one direction: north, away from the waterfront and in the direction of Zhabei. It wasn't only students anymore. Textile workers were on strike; tram conductors had abandoned their posts. No matter how powerful the Nationalists had grown, they could not hide the news of a purge. No matter how much fear the Scarlet Gang once incited, they had since lost their grip on the city. They could not threaten its people back into submission. The people would not stand for murder and intimidation. They would be heard.

"No one is going in our direction," Alisa noted as they turned onto a main road. Here, the numbers were almost paralyzing. If the back gave one rough push, the crowd would gridlock. "Won't we get caught leaving by sea?"

Roma hesitated, seeming to agree. That slight moment of pause had him almost colliding with a worker, though the worker hardly blinked—he merely resumed with his call: *"Down with the imperialists! Down with the gangsters!"* and continued onward.

"We have to take our chances," Roma said, his eyes still tracking the worker. When he turned away, he caught Juliette's gaze, and Juliette tried for a small smile. "There is no alternative."

"What about the countryside?" Alisa kept asking. Her pace faltered. "It is chaos here!"

They were coming upon the Bund. The usual picturesque buildings rose into view—the Art Deco pillars and tall, glowing domes—but everything looked muted in today's light. The world was covered in a sheen of gray, a cinema picture that had been filmed with a lens not wiped clean.

"Alisa, darling," Juliette said, her voice soft. "We're already under martial law. The Communist leadership is scrambling to run, and the Nationalist leadership is scrambling to eliminate. By the time we skirt into the countryside and reach another treaty port for escape, the Nationalists will have taken over there, too, and we will be stopped. At least here, we can take advantage of the chaos."

"So where are they?" Alisa asked. As they arrived at the Bund, coming within sight of the Huangpu River's rocking waves, Alisa looked around, searching beyond the protesters, beyond their shouting and sign-waving. "Where are the Nationalists?"

"Look at where everyone is going," Juliette said, inclining her head. *North.* With so much freshly spilled Communist blood on the ground, the Kuomintang were focusing their attention on newly vacated police stations and military headquarters, ensuring they had their people behind the desks. "The Nationalists are off straightening all their bases of power. The workers will go there too—will flock to those bases in hopes of making some difference."

"Don't get too relaxed," Roma added. He turned his sister's face, nudging her chin until she looked upon a particular tense spot in the crowd. "Though there are no Nationalists, they have placed Scarlets."

Juliette gave a small intake of breath, mostly lost when a clap of thunder came over the city. She brushed Roma's elbow, and his hand came to grasp hers. The both of them were soaked to the bone, as was the string around their ring fingers, but Roma held on gently, like they were merely reaching for each other on a morning stroll.

"Come on," Juliette said. "With all these people, let's find a good place to wait."

In Zhabei, the surviving leadership of the General Labor Union were shouting over one another and banging their fists against the tables. People in suits mingled with people in aprons. Celia sat back and looked on, her face utterly impassive. They were occupying a restaurant refashioned into a stronghold, tables and chairs pushed into clusters, with one large cluster in the middle leading the work. She couldn't comprehend how anybody was being heard over the uproar, but they were—they were communicating and acting as fast as they could.

A petition was being drawn up. *Return of seized arms, cessation of the punishment of union workers, protection for the General Labor Union*—these were collated into demands and then rolled up, prepared to be brought to the Nationalists' Second Division headquarters. Even if it killed them, the Communists did not accept defeat.

"Up and at it, girl!" someone bellowed into her ear. They were bounding through the crowd and screaming at others before Celia could even turn and see who it was. The workers pumped their fists into the air and yelled at one another, chants ringing from their mouths before the demonstration through the city could even begin.

"No military government!" they roared, laughing as they tackled one another, bursting onto the streets and into the pouring rain. "No gangster rule!" They joined the crowds already present in west Shanghai, merging into one, unearthly procession larger than life itself.

Hands pushed at Celia to rise, and then she was up, her head still ringing.

"No military government!" the old woman beside Celia yelled.

"No gangster rule!" the child in front of Celia yelled.

Celia stumbled out from the restaurant, onto the pavement, and into the rain. The streets had come alive. This wasn't the glittering, glimmering old money of Shanghai: bright lights and jazz music shining from the bars. This wasn't red lanterns and golden lace trim on the dresses of dancers in the burlesque clubs, one swish of fabric that pulled the crowds into exuberance.

This was animation from the gutters of the city, rising amid the ash of low-ceilinged factories.

Celia raised her fist.

It was the new set of footsteps entering the office that finally forced Benedikt to perk up, shaking himself out of the near trance he had put himself in to remain quiet. It was the way the sound came in: shoes dragging, deliberate.

Benedikt didn't have to see Marshall to know that it was him. Nor did he have to see him to guess that Marshall had his hands stuck in his pockets.

"The cars that Lord Cai sent are here," Marshall said. He was feigning casual, but his voice was tight. "They're ready for everyone."

Benedikt listened hard, trying to gauge how many Nationalists were pulling their coats off the backs of their chairs and filtering out of the room. The office hadn't been that full to begin with, yet he didn't hear enough footfalls exiting. Indeed he was right when another conversation started up between General Shu and someone else, debating their next move for the Communists who had escaped.

"Érzi," General Shu said suddenly, summoning Marshall to attention. "Where are the letters for central command?"

"You mean the nasty envelopes I personally licked to close?" Marshall asked. "I put them in there. Do we need them now?"

There had been a pause in his speech. With delay, Benedikt realized the missed beat had been because Marshall was pointing. And the only place to point at . . . was this filing closet.

"Fetch them, would you? We need to be off in a few minutes."

"Yessir."

Footsteps, dragging his way now. Benedikt looked around frantically. At the end of the closet space, there was a small cardboard box, which he had to assume was what Marshall was coming in for. He walked toward the box, then faltered, freezing three steps away from it when Marshall opened the door, stepped in, and closed the door after himself.

Marshall hit the light switch. He looked up. Widened his eyes.

"Ben—"

Benedikt clamped a hand over Marshall's mouth, the effort so aggressive that they slammed into one of the filing cabinets, bodies locked. Benedikt could smell the smoke clinging to Marshall's skin, count the lines crinkling his brow while he tried not to struggle.

What the hell are you doing here? Marshall's eyes seemed to scream.

What do you think? Benedikt silently responded.

"What happened?" General Shu called from outside. He had heard the loud thud.

Carefully, Benedikt eased his hand away from Marshall's mouth. The rest of him didn't move.

"Nothing. I stubbed my toe," Marshall called back evenly. In the same breath, he lowered his voice to the quietest whisper and hissed, "How did you get in here? The Kuomintang have an execution order for Montagovs, and you deliver yourself right to the door?"

"No thanks to your father," Benedikt shot back, his volume just as low. "When were you going to tell me—"

"Bad time, bad time," Marshall interrupted. He heaved an inhale; their chests rose and fell in tandem. Marshall was dressed in uniform, each polished gold button on his jacket digging between them. It seemed the walls were closing in with how close they were, the space shrinking smaller and smaller.

Then Marshall swerved away suddenly, squeezing through the narrow passage and retrieving the box. Benedikt leaned back against the cabinets, his breath coming short.

"Stay here," Marshall whispered when he walked by again, holding the box. "I'll come back."

He turned off the lights and closed the door firmly.

Benedikt resisted the urge to kick one of the cabinets. He wanted to hear the thud of its metal echo, have it ring so loud and forcefully that the whole house was brought here to him. Of course, that would be incredibly, incredibly ill advised. So he stayed unmoving. All that he allowed was his rapidly tapping fingers. How much time did Roma and Juliette have at the Bund? How close was it now to noon?

After what seemed like eons, the door opened again. Benedikt tensed, prepared to pull his weapon, but it was Marshall, his expression stricken.

"You can come out," he said. "They've all departed for the Scarlet house."

"And left you behind?"

"I feigned a headache."

Benedikt walked out, almost suspicious. His ankle stung, slowing his movements, but the hesitation was intentional too. He didn't know what had gotten into him; he had come here resolute to rescue Marshall and leave as quickly as they could, yet now he looked at Marshall and felt utter bewilderment. There was a hot stone in his stomach. He had imagined Marshall getting tortured, abused, or otherwise at the mercy of people he could not stand up against. Instead,

Benedikt had found him moving around this house as if he belonged here, as if this were his home.

And maybe it was.

"I thought I was coming to break you out," Benedikt said. "But it looks like you could have broken yourself out at any point."

Marshall shook his head. He stuck his hands back into his pockets, though the posture was incongruous with the ironed smoothness of his trousers. "You *clown*," he said. "I was trying to help you from the inside. My father was going to delay the execution order."

A coldness blew into the room. At some point, while Benedikt was hiding, a steady rain had started up outside, turning the sky a terrible, dark gray. The droplets came down on the windows, sliding along the edges and collecting in a miniature puddle on the carpet. Benedikt blinked. Had he latched the windows after climbing in? He could have sworn he did.

Did he?

"You would have been too late," Benedikt reported. "Executions started at dawn. It was Juliette who came to warn us." Or rather, warn Roma, and Benedikt was roped in by virtue of proximity.

Marshall jerked back. "What? No. No, my father said—"

"Your father lied." As Marshall had. As Marshall seemed to be doing with increasing frequency.

"I—" Marshall broke off. His attention turned to the window too, looking irritated by the water dripping in. He walked toward it. "Then why would you come here, Ben? Why venture right into enemy territory?"

"To save *you*." Benedikt couldn't believe what he was hearing. With Marshall's whole past crumbling as a lie, perhaps his entire persona, too, was an untruth. *Is Marshall Seo even his real name?*

"Of course it is."

Benedikt had muttered that last part aloud.

"Seo was my mother's family name," Marshall went on, pushing the window closed. "I figured everyone would ask fewer questions if they thought I ran from Korea after Japanese annexation, an orphan with no ties. Less complicated than running from the Chinese countryside because I couldn't bear to live with my Nationalist father."

"You should have told me," Benedikt said quietly. "You should have trusted me."

Marshall turned around, arms crossed, leaning up against the glass. "I do trust you," he muttered, uncharacteristically quiet. "I merely would have preferred to maintain a different past, one of my choosing. Is that so wrong?"

"Yes!" Benedikt snapped. "It is if we had no idea that you were going to be in danger when *Nationalists* marched into this city."

"Look around. Do I appear in danger?"

Benedikt could not respond immediately; he feared that his words would come out too sharp, too far from what he really meant. This never used to be a worry, not with Marshall, not with his best friend. Of all the people in the world that he trusted would understand him no matter how unfiltered his thoughts ran, it was Marshall.

But something was different now. It was fear that had settled into his bones.

"We have to go. Roma and Juliette await at the Bund with a route out, but the Nationalists have already sent people after them. If we wait any longer, either martial law will shut the city down with no means of escape or Juliette is going to get hauled away."

"I *can't*." Marshall tugged at his sleeves, trying to straighten out the imaginary crinkles. "I have their trust, Ben. I am more help to you as a docile Nationalist prodigy than anything else."

Somewhere in the house, a grandfather clock started to chime.

"Whether or not my father lied about the timing of the purge is irrelevant," he went on. "What is relevant is that droves of White Flowers will be hauled into imprisonment to await execution alongside the Communists, regardless of whether we were truly working with them. I can stop it. We won't have to run. *Roma* won't have to run, so long as I stay. If I can steer my father into protecting us, the White Flowers *survive*."

When Marshall paused for breath, his chest was rising and falling, appearing exhilarated by the weight of his role. And without hesitation, Benedikt said: "In all my years knowing you, I've never imagined you could make such a daft decision."

Marshall's expression fell. "I beg your pardon?"

"They're lying!" Benedikt exclaimed, the sound harsh. "Why would they ever allow the White Flowers to continue onward when the Nationalists have an alliance with the Scarlet Gang? We're *finished*, Marshall. The gang is in shambles. There's no going back."

"No," Marshall insisted. He stood firm. "No. Do you know how much violence I witnessed as a phantom in this city, Ben? The view from the rooftops is utterly, utterly different from the view on the street, and I saw everything. No matter the bloodshed, I saw how damn much every White Flower cared for us, for *you*, for the Montagovs. I can save them."

"Is that what this is?" Benedikt resisted the urge to march over and *shake* his friend. He knew; he knew that physical force was not the right method of persuasion here, that if anything, it would merely rile Marshall into further stubbornness. "Some display of loyalty for the gang that took you in? It was never about the White Flowers, Mars. It was about what we believed in—*who* we believed in. It's Roma, it's a city where we belong, a future. And when that topples, then it is up to us to flee too."

Marshall swallowed hard. "I have power here by mere virtue of my birth. You would ask me to abandon it, abandon the possibility of helping people?"

"What real help can you be?" This wasn't what he meant. This was what was coming out anyway. "Will you march upon the front lines and massacre the workers to win your father's trust? Rough up a few Communists for the freedom of White Flowers?"

"Why are you being *like this*—"

"Because it's not worth it! Power is never worth it! You keep making trades upon trades, and you get nothing in return. Roma is running from it. Juliette is running from it. What makes you think *you* can handle it?"

A flicker of hurt—real hurt—flashed across Marshall's face. "Is that what it is?" he asked. "You think I am too weak?"

Benedikt bit back a curse, swallowed his anger until it slid down his throat. How had this happened? He knew he shouldn't have spoken so fast. He knew he shouldn't have run loose with his words. There was never any good to come from it. And yet he could barely think. It was the oppressive air of this room and the steady trickle of rain from outside and that *clock* still chiming from someplace in the house.

"I never said you were weak."

"Yet you would have me walk away. I'm trying to *help* us. I'm trying to have us survive—"

"What use is the gang's survival if *you* do not survive?" Benedikt cut in. "Listen to me, Mars. No matter how much they trust you, this is civil war. This city will overflow with casualties—"

Marshall threw his hands up. "You and Roma may run. You are Montagovs. I understand. Why should I follow?"

"Marshall—"

"No!" Marshall exclaimed, his eyes ablaze, not finished with his rebuke. "I mean it. Why should I? With all that I am promised here, with all the protection I have, why would *I* run unless I was a coward? Why would I abandon such prime opportunities—"

"Because *I love you*!" Benedikt shouted. At once, it was like a dam in his heart had broken, smashing past every barricade he had built up. "I love you, Mars. And if you are gunned down because you want to fight a war that doesn't belong to you, I will never forgive this city. I will tear it to pieces, and you will be to blame!"

Absolute silence descended upon the room. If Benedikt had thought it oppressive before, it was nothing in comparison to the weight of Marshall's wide-eyed stare upon him. There was no taking it back. His words were out in the world. Perhaps those were the only words he had ever said that he didn't *want* to take back.

"Good grief," Marshall finally managed, his voice hoarse. "You had ten years to say something, and you choose now?"

And for whatever absurd reason, Benedikt managed a weak laugh. "Bad timing?"

"Horrific timing." Marshall closed in with three strides, coming to a halt right in front of him. "Not only that, but you choose to *blame me* in a declaration of love. Didn't anyone teach you manners? God—"

Marshall clasped his hands around Benedikt's neck and kissed him.

The moment their lips pressed together, Benedikt was hit with the same rush of a gunfight, of a high-octane chase, of the thrill that came with hiding in an alleyway when the pursuit came to an end. He hadn't ever thought much about the act of kissing, hadn't much cared no matter who was on the other end of it. He had never craved it, had only thought about it like an abstract concept, but then Marshall leaned into him and his veins lit on fire, and he realized it wasn't that he did not care. It was only that it had to be Marshall. It had always been Marshall. When Benedikt reached up and sank his fingers into Marshall's hair and Marshall made a noise at the base of his throat, all that Benedikt could think was this was what it meant to be holy.

"Please," Benedikt whispered. He pulled back for the briefest of moments. "Come with me. Leave with me."

A breath jumped between them, an exhale into an inhale. Marshall's hands trailed over Benedikt's shoulders, down his chest, to his waist, gripping the loose fabric of his shirt.

"Okay." His answer came shakily, the single word heavy like a sacrifice. It was a choosing—it was turning away from the commitment of family and following Benedikt wherever he was to go. "On one condition."

Benedikt's gaze snapped up. Marshall was looking at him with his eyes wholly black, pupils blown large, his expression pensive and serious.

"Anything."

A grin slipped out. "Say it again. I didn't pine all these years to only hear it once."

Benedikt gave Marshall a shove—a force of habit, really, and Marshall stumbled back laughing.

"Idiot," Benedikt chided. "In all these years, why didn't *you* say anything?"

"Because," Marshall said simply, "you weren't ready."

Idiot, Benedikt thought again, but it was with such fondness that his chest burned with it, a red-hot iron of affection that branded every inch of his skin.

"I'll say it however many times you want. I'll romance you until you get sick of me. I am horrendously, horrendously in love with your dreadful face, and we need to go, *now.*"

The smile that Marshall made was something glorious, so big that it felt uncontainable by the room, uncontainable within the house.

"I love you just as horrendously," he replied simply. "We can go, but I have an idea. How certain are you that my father is lying?"

Benedikt wasn't sure if this was a trick question. He hardly had the time to reel from the quick switch in topic. "Entirely certain. I heard him say the execution order was his command."

Marshall pulled at the cuffs of his sleeves, rolling them up to his elbows as he wandered about his father's desk, eyes searching through its contents.

"If the order is still in effect, we're dead if we get caught," Marshall said. He withdrew a piece of blank paper, then a pen, and started to write. "But not if we overturn the order on an emergency command."

"With what?" Benedikt asked, flabbergasted. He squinted at what Marshall was writing. "A permission slip for any officer who catches us?"

"A permission slip"—Marshall finished writing with a flourish—"approved by *General Shu*. His stamp should be in his meeting room. Let's go."

Marshall was out of the room before Benedikt could even register the plan, digesting what they were trying to do. Benedikt's ankle protested as he picked up speed too, catching up to Marshall in the long hall, winding around the house to come to the foyer.

Benedikt came to a dead stop. "Mars."

"It's just up there," Marshall said. He pointed to the stairs, not noticing Benedikt's terrified expression. "We—"

"*Mars.*"

Marshall jumped, then turned around and followed Benedikt's gaze. Through the delicate archway of the foyer, the living room unfolded in front of them: the unlit fireplace, the floral vases, and General Shu, reading a newspaper on the leather couch.

"Oh," Marshall said quietly.

General Shu laid his newspaper down. In one hand, he was holding a pistol, pointed in their direction. The other hand was gloved, matching the thick fabric of his outer coat, like he had come back inside the house without bothering to get comfortable.

"Did you think," he said slowly, "that I wouldn't notice my window wide open?"

"Well, you caught us." Marshall might have been taken aback upon first sighting his father, but he recovered fast, his voice injected with grace. He walked right up to him, not faltering when his father rose, not faltering even as he walked right up to the pistol. "*You* promised that you would help me, help the Montagovs. So here we are."

General Shu was watching Benedikt. Studying him.

"Your place for helping them is through official channels," General Shu said evenly.

"This right here is an official channel. Unless, of course"—Marshall's voice turned cold—"you lied to me."

Silence. The ticking of the grandfather clock, its pendulum swinging left and right inside the glass casing. Slowly, General Shu set his pistol down on the table beside them.

"There is an order to the way things must work," he said. His eyes darted to Benedikt again, some flare of irritation in the momentary glance. "We cannot make things happen just because we want it. That is tyranny."

How fast could Benedikt reach for a weapon if he needed to? The pistol on the table mocked him—close enough for General Shu's immediate retrieval but just far enough to give hope that it was not a threat.

"Bàba, it is just one question," Marshall said. "If I asked for help to save my friends, are you with me or against me?"

General Shu made a dismissive noise. "There exactly is your problem. You think everything can only be good or bad, heroic or evil. I have taken you in to teach you to be a leader, and you cannot stay true to your word."

"My word—"

General Shu pushed on. "We follow the rules that come down from command. We eradicate those who want to threaten a peaceful way of life. You are my son. You will do the same. There is no other respectable option."

Rain clattered down around the house, the droplets seeming far away because of the hollow sound. Benedikt was almost afraid that Marshall was listening, that this pull of family and legacy was too strong to resist.

Then Marshall said, "You forget. I was not raised respectably. I was raised as a gangster."

And before General Shu could stop him, Marshall picked up the pistol his father had set down and hit him hard across the temple.

Benedikt hurried forward, his eyes wide as Marshall caught his father and eased him back onto the couch. General Shu's eyes were closed. His chest looked still. "Please tell me you didn't just commit patricide."

Marshall rolled his eyes. He put his finger under his father's nose, confirming that General Shu was still breathing. "You don't think I've perfected how to knock someone out by now?"

"I'm just saying the pistol looks a little sharp—"

"Oh my *God*, you are impossible." Marshall mimed a zip across his lips, forbidding Benedikt from arguing further. "Time is ticking. Let's find that stamp."

Forty-Three

D o you see them?"

"No," Roma answered, his jaw tightening. "It is our misfortune that the waterfront is so damn crowded."

"If we had known, I would have decided on a less vague meeting point," Juliette muttered. With a sigh, she shifted, trying to hold her arms over more of Alisa's head, blocking off the rain. She might as well be a helpful umbrella while Roma trekked up and down the boardwalk, running reconnaissance.

This wouldn't do. The rain was messing with their visibility; Juliette could see the protesters and strikers moving, but she couldn't make out faces past a few feet in front of her. Roma and Juliette were in plain clothes, which let them blend in with the rest of the city, but it would be impossible for Benedikt and Marshall to sight them even if the two were already present at the waterfront. They were used to searching for Roma's clean pressed white shirts and Juliette's beaded dresses. Neither of those items was present today.

"Roma, it's almost noon."

"They'll come," Roma insisted. "I know they will."

Juliette looked out onto the river, biting her lip. Along every ramp, there were boats jammed in tight capacity, making space for foreign warship after foreign warship, flags of red, white, and blue marking the sides. The foreigners had summoned them here as a threat. A reminder that they had won a war on this land once before, so they could do it again. A reminder that Shanghai could jostle up in civil unrest however much it liked, but it better settle down in due time before the foreigners got too annoyed and started using these war vessels.

"How about this?" Juliette said. She tried to wipe the rain off her brow. It was pointless when the downpour fell so fast. "I'm going to find my contact. I'll have him at the ready and try to stall beyond noon. Soon as your cousin shows, we run."

"Soon as he shows with Marshall," Roma corrected. Then, seeing Juliette's frown, he leaned in and pressed a kiss to her cheek. "Go on. We'll be here."

Juliette was still worrying her teeth against her lower lip when she turned and started to pick her way along the boardwalk. The wharf she wanted was within sight—to the left of the one that Roma and Alisa were standing nearest. So long as the Montagovs didn't move, she had them in the corner of her eye as she walked, careful not to slip on the wet surfaces.

These wharves were usually bustling with activity. Today, Juliette couldn't tell if it was merely the ruckus on the streets that overshadowed everything or if the fishermen were too afraid to venture out.

"Da Nao." Juliette had spotted her contact, a big-bellied man chewing on his toothpick. He stood under the awning of his tiny boat, a vessel that looked pocket-sized in comparison with the warship docked on its right. Hearing Juliette's call, Da Nao looked up, his whole body freezing before he could finish untying his boat from the wharf.

"Cai Junli," he said. "I thought your cousin's note was a prank."

"This is no prank. Are you willing to take us away?"

Slowly, he stood to his height, his eyes darting left and right. "Where are you hoping to go?"

"Whichever coast you reach first," Juliette answered easily. "I . . . I cannot stay any longer. Not with the Scarlets turning like this."

For the longest moment, Da Nao said nothing. He bent down again and continued gathering the rope at his feet. Then:

"Yes. I can take you away. I can sail south."

Juliette breathed out in relief. "Thank you," she said quickly. "I'll pay you however much you need—"

"Who else are you bringing?"

His question came abruptly, choked out like he couldn't speak the words fast enough. A pinprick of suspicion registered in Juliette's mind, but she brushed it aside, hoping it was only the stress of the situation currently unfolding in the city.

"Roma Montagov," Juliette answered, praying that her voice would not shake. Da Nao was a Communist sympathizer, Kathleen had said. Even with his double life as a Scarlet fisherman, he cared little for the blood feud. "Along with his sister and two of his men."

Da Nao had finished gathering the excess rope. There remained only one thin line keeping his boat docked. "You're traveling with Montagovs now? The seas are still being watched, Miss Cai. We may have trouble leaving the territory."

"I'll pay you however much to hide us. Just get us out."

Though Da Nao had finished tidying everything in his vicinity, he continued scanning the floor of his boat. "Are they forcing you to help them, Miss Cai? You can tell me if they are."

Juliette blinked. The rain was stinging her eyes badly. She had not even considered that the fisherman might think she was acting against her will. Why was that his first thought, and not the easier conclusion that Juliette had simply betrayed the Scarlets?

"No one is forcing me to do anything," she said. Her fists curled. "Roma Montagov is my husband. Now, can I come aboard and get out of this rain?"

The toothpick in Da Nao's mouth bobbed up and down. If he was surprised to hear her admission, he did not show it.

"Certainly." Only then did he finally look at her, taking the tooth-pick out of his mouth. "You will have to shed your weapons before you come on board. I mean no offense, Miss Cai, but I know you gangster types. All in the water first."

Juliette stiffened, her gaze darting back along the boardwalk. Even at a distance, she could sense that Roma was watching her and had noted her unease. She raised a hand, signaling that she was fine, and with a sigh, pulled out the blades tucked against her thighs. Short of the cash in the bag hanging from her shoulders, she had thought the weapons on her skin could be traded as valuables.

"Okay," Juliette said, her blades hitting the water with a slap. They floated for a second, then sank into the dark waves.

Da Nao threw his toothpick to the floor. "All weapons, Miss Cai."

With a sigh, Juliette snapped off the garrote wire around her wrist and hurled it into the water. "Happy?"

"No, not really."

There was a sudden motion from behind Da Nao. A man stepped out, a pistol held to Da Nao's head, his expression tight. Juliette rec-ognized him. He was a Scarlet—he had once run a message for her.

"Please understand," Da Nao said, his voice barely audible as the river rolled beneath him, "that as much as I want to help you, Miss Cai, your Scarlets have always been watching."

The Scarlet fired, and Da Nao fell with a spray of red, the bullet in his head killing him instantly. With a horrified gasp, Juliette lunged forward, preparing for a fight, but the Scarlet did not turn his pistol to her next. He turned it upward and fired once, twice, three times, each bullet piercing through the awning of the fishing boat and studding into the sky, its *bang! bang! bang!* loud enough to be heard over the storm.

It was a signal.

No.

Juliette turned fast on her heel. She sighted Roma and Alisa's blurry forms immediately, but by then there was countermovement in the crowd, and the Scarlets who had been playing guard were on their way to the waterfront, merging into a task force.

"ROMA! ALISA! RUN, RUN NOW!"

Someone tackled Juliette from the side.

"Stop!" she shrieked. "Get off of me!"

Sheer instinct kicked in. She threw her head back as hard as she could, colliding with her attacker. There was a sickening crunch that sounded like a nose breaking, and when her attacker momentarily loosened his grip around her arms, she pulled free and ran.

They had intercepted her cousin's note. They had been one step ahead of her this whole time, waiting with Da Nao. Juliette should have known there would be eyes everywhere in the city after her little scheme. She should have known that her father and mother would pull out every stop to figure out what game she was playing at after disrupting Scarlet business and disappearing into the night.

Juliette skidded off the wharf, frantically wiping at the rain on her face to clear her vision. *There*—she spotted Roma and Alisa again, circled in by a group of Scarlets with firearms. Roma still had his weapons; with a pistol in hand, he managed to take down two Scarlets.

But he was outnumbered. Before Juliette could reach them, the Scarlets had him disarmed.

"Don't touch him!"

The moment Juliette ran close, the nearest Scarlets dove at her. She tried her best to dispatch them, ducking fast and sliding under outstretched arms, but she was one girl without weapons and they were loyal to her no longer. Just as Juliette stood again, one of the Scarlets pressed the barrel of his gun to Roma's head.

And Juliette came to a complete stop.

Two of the Scarlets grabbed her by the shoulders. All the faces here were familiar, all of them names that she was sure she could recall if she thought a little harder. Under the pour of vicious rainfall, they could only look upon her in hatred.

"Don't," Juliette managed. "Don't you dare hurt him."

"It is your own fault for delivering him right to us." The Scarlet who had spoken looked even more familiar than the rest, undoubtedly a leader among them, undoubtedly one of Tyler's former men. He had a hint of glee in his eyes, that same old bloodlust Juliette was so tired of seeing. "Thankfully for you, you don't have to watch. Take her to Lord Cai."

"No!" It didn't matter how much she kicked. With a Scarlet on either side of her, the men lifted her easily by her arms and started to lead her away. "How dare you—"

Of course they dared. She was no longer Juliette Cai, the heir of the Scarlet Gang, to be feared and revered. She was a girl who had run away with the enemy.

"Don't touch them!" Juliette screamed, throwing her head over her shoulder.

The Scarlets didn't listen. They started to lead Roma and Alisa in the other direction, pulling at Alisa so roughly that she cried out. Even as the distance between them grew and grew, Roma had his eyes latched on Juliette, his face so pale under the shadow of the sky it was as if he were dead and executed already. Perhaps Juliette had an ill-divining soul. Perhaps she was seeing his future, perhaps by the day's end he would be lying at the bottom of a tomb as the last of the Montagov line.

"Roma, hold on! Hold on!"

Roma shook his head. He was shouting something, again and again, the sound lost to the rain, and he did not stop until Juliette was out of sight, dragged away from the Bund and onto another main road.

It was only then that Juliette realized what he had been saying, his eyes stricken like he had already lost hope of seeing her again.

I love you.

The rain came down like a tidal wave, but it did not discourage the crowds moving through the city.

Even if Celia had suddenly decided to abandon the procession, she had no route out. She was boxed in on all sides, surrounded by workers and students and ordinary people who looked no more like revolutionaries than she did. Yet nonetheless, they were here and screaming—screaming at the top of their lungs, long banners in their best penmanship unfurled into the air.

"Protect the union!"

They were coming into Baoshan Road, approaching their destination. Celia did not shout with them, but she took it all in. Among so much chaos, she became bigger than herself, bigger than any physical body, any physical form.

"No surrender!"

Not a soul in the procession carried firearms, only signs running with ink. They were here to make a point clear. They could achieve their goals with nothing except might. They were the *people*. A city was nothing without its people; a city could not thrive without its people.

The government should fear *them*.

"Down with the military government!"

They turned around a bend in the street, and Celia was flooded with immediate horror, sighting lines and lines of Nationalist troops in their way. On sheer instinct, her steps ground to a halt, but the procession did not appear to be stopping, and so she could not stop either, jostled back into movement.

"No," Celia murmured.

The soldiers stood to attention. Those on the ground were armed with bayonets; those on higher platforms had their eye glued to the telescopic sights of their machine guns. A barricade of wooden stakes cut the street off abruptly, and a hundred paces behind it, all the soldiers' barrels were pointed at the crowd, ready to fire. They looked somber. They crouched at attention behind stacks and stacks of sandbags, using them for shields against retaliation. But there wouldn't *be* retaliation. The protest was *unarmed*.

They won't shoot, Celia thought. The crowd was getting nearer and nearer. *Surely they won't.*

The procession collided with the barricade. Workers pushed from their side, gangsters and troops pushed from the other. Celia couldn't breathe—she felt out of body, only soul, floating above the crowd and overseeing it all. She was already a ghoul floating above the mayhem, swirling in the rain.

"Down with gangster rule!"

The workers finally pushed over the barricade, making for the troops. Chaos on both sides—bodies and sound and noise, clashing at once.

It was then that a flash of light registered in Celia's peripheral vision, prickling up some sixth sense that told her something was awry. She twisted, her eyes making a sweep of the scene, breath coming fast. She saw two things at once: first, movement in an alley near the fallen barricade, something glistening and then slinking back into the shadows; second, the glint of metal held in the hands of a man some few paces away.

"Stop!" Celia yelled, diving forward, but it was already too late. Mr. Ping—the same Mr. Ping of the Scarlet inner circle—had his pistol pointed to the skies, and when she collided with him, his bullet had already burst into the air, its sound resonating tenfold into the crowd. All around him, the workers stared, unable to comprehend the sound.

"This is a peaceful demonstration!"

"Who is that? Why would he do that?"

"Get down. Get down!"

Celia staggered back, pressing her rain-soaked hands to her mouth. Mr. Ping stood there now, unmoving against the crowd that demanded an explanation. He had no need to explain himself. He had been planted here to do exactly this, forfeiting his life for the sake of the Scarlets. If the Scarlets asked for blood, the inner circle would offer their own.

Within the armed line of Nationalists, a voice screamed, "Return fire!"

"Let me *go*," Juliette hissed. "Let *go*!"

They had been walking for so long in the rain that Juliette was thoroughly soaked. Each time she attempted to shake herself free, her drenched hair flung left and right to disperse water. On any other occasion, the distance between the Bund and the Cai house would have required a car. Today, it was impossible to get any vehicle through the city. Better to walk it on foot, lest they were stalled behind a crowd and a rescue attempt came for Juliette. At least, that was what she had gathered from the two Scarlets holding her hostage, who found no problem with discussing such matters over her head. The one on her left was named Bai Tasa, she recalled. The one on her right remained stubbornly nameless.

"They have blocked off Baoshan Road," Bai Tasa was saying, making an effort to ignore Juliette's writhing. The streets here were emptied. They had entered Nationalist-guarded defense lines, needing only a single nod from Bai Tasa before the soldiers were ushering them through, pushing the other protesters back. Of course, even before they came into the guarded parts of the city, no one had offered Juliette a second glance no matter how loudly she yelled. Everyone else was yelling just as loudly.

"Do we care?" the Scarlet on the right snapped. "We are cutting behind the barricade anyway."

"It is only an extra ten minutes if we go around."

"Ten minutes that I do not have. These people are driving me up the wall."

Juliette tried to dig her heels into the pavement. All it did was grate at her shoes, rubbing at the soles.

"Hold on a minute," she interrupted. "What are we cutting behind? Are we passing the end of the protest?"

Though the Scarlets did not respond to her, it was a valid guess, what with the noise that was coming from the rapidly approaching intersection. The houses around her seemed to shake, their empty terraces and imposing exteriors slick with the gray day. She hadn't paid attention before, but now she saw Nationalist military vehicles parked all along the road. Only . . . they were empty, as if the men inside had been moved elsewhere.

"What's happening?" Juliette demanded again, though she knew the Scarlets wouldn't answer her.

They passed the intersection, and when Juliette turned to look down the other road, she saw the backs of hundreds of Nationalists. The sheer number struck panic into her bones, and that was *before* she realized they were braced behind sandbags and makeshift barriers with whole machine guns pointed down the street as the noise grew and grew.

Juliette summoned the last of her energy to throw herself to the ground. The Scarlets hadn't expected it; Bai Tasa stumbled, almost tripping over his own feet when Juliette sprawled before him. The other Scarlet grumbled, pulling at her arms while she struggled to stay down. Her focus was locked on the scene before her, on the strikers coming into view, surging against the wooden barricade. There were so many of them. Far, far more than the Nationalists hiding behind their makeshift shields, but the Nationalists had them surrounded at so many angles, firearms pointed forward. How was this supposed to end? How could this possibly end well?

Juliette scrambled up suddenly, deciding she had seen enough.

Before Bai Tasa could grab ahold of her again, *she* affixed her fingers on to *his* wrist like an iron vise.

"Call the order to stop! Find someone to draw them back!"

Bai Tasa, to his credit, did not wince. The other Scarlet pulled Juliette off of him quickly, snapping, "I told you we shouldn't have gone this way."

"My apologies, Miss Cai," Bai Tasa said, ignoring his companion. He turned to the scene before them, to the Nationalists in uniform and the workers pushing ever closer. It might have been Juliette's imagination, but he truly looked sorrowful. He put a hand on her lower back as if to offer comfort, as if any of that *mattered* here. "You're not in charge anymore."

A gunshot sounded from within the workers—

I don't think I was ever in charge, Juliette thought numbly.

—and the Nationalists, too, let loose their gunfire.

"*No!*"

The Scarlets lunged for her again before she could scarcely take two steps. Juliette had no energy to fight. She merely sagged in their hold, her voice growing softer and softer with each repetition—no, no, *no*.

A legion of lead fired onto the workers, the students, the ordinary people. One after the other, they collapsed atop each other as if someone were snipping at the strings that held them up, struck in the chest, in the stomach, in the legs.

Massacre. That was what this was.

The Nationalists kept firing, empty shells stacking up behind their safe line of defense. It was clear that the protesters would not—*could* not—fight back, and yet the bullets continued anyway. The rear half of the crowd had reversed in a panic and was trying to run, but still, the bullets followed, burying in their backs until their knees gave way, until they lay unmoving upon wet cement and tram tracks.

Even from here, the smell of blood was pungent.

"We have to move," Bai Tasa said suddenly, as if snapping out of a daze. The gunfire had lessened, but it had not stopped.

"Kathleen," Juliette muttered to herself. Had her cousin been in that crowd? Would she sense it like she sensed the city's death heaving beneath her feet—some wild animal on its last lap of freedom before the cage came down?

"What did you say?" the Scarlet to her right asked. This was the first time he had spoken directly to Juliette. Perhaps it was the shock of what they had just witnessed. Perhaps he had forgotten why he was hauling her off in the first place, forgotten exactly who he had placed his loyalty with. Much of those workers lying dead in the streets had likely been Scarlet-aligned not some weeks ago. Allegiance was supposed to keep them safe. Blood feuds and civil wars built themselves on the idea of allegiance.

What good was it? Things died and changed in the blink of an eye.

"Nothing," Juliette rasped, her eyes stinging. "Nothing."

She sighted movement in the alley by the Nationalists' line of defense. As the Scarlets pushed for Juliette to start walking, she could only stare aghast at the scene, at the insects that were slowly crawling across the ground, rushing for the Nationalists. Juliette could not have called a warning even if she tried; her voice had gone hoarse. As the last of the bullets stopped, the insects rushed upon the soldiers' shoes, crawling into their pant legs. The men behind the sandbags jumped to their feet and exclaimed in horror, but it was too late: they were infected. It would not set in immediately, not when the insect numbers were so low. The infection would build, and build, and build.

Lourens's vaccine would not be ready so soon. These soldiers were dead men. The Nationalists—each and every one of them still stained with the blood of the workers—knew what was coming. Bai Tasa blinked in bewilderment, hurrying to push Juliette away before the

443

insects could crawl over, and Juliette obliged, at last walking without resistance.

She wondered if the infected men would wait for madness to come, or if they would take their rifles to their own heads first.

Forty-Four

"Keep up. Keep up."

Benedikt winced, almost slipping right off the roof tiles. The rain was pelting down. On the plus side, it meant that the Scarlets they were tracking were unlikely to look up and see Marshall and Benedikt following from the rooftops—drawing near when they were bypassing the narrower commercial streets and keeping at a distance when the roads got wider with fewer buildings to use for cover. On the downside . . . Benedikt was very close to taking a tumble and landing with a splat on the sidewalks below.

"How the hell did you do this so often?" Benedikt asked, brushing his sopping-wet hair off his forehead. In seconds, the rain had pushed it back.

"I am simply more lithe than you are," Marshall replied. He turned back for a second, sparing a glance as the Scarlets below moved forward, at no risk of disappearing anytime soon. "Come *on*."

Marshall extended a hand. Benedikt hurried forward and took it, their fingers laced together, half to be near each other and half because he truly did need to be dragged to prevent his ankle from giving out entirely. Soon, the Scarlets seemed to be slowing, and Marshall halted, his lips pinched in thought as he watched them.

Benedikt peered over Marshall's shoulder. As he squinted through the rain, he couldn't stop the hiss that escaped when he tried to set even weight on both his feet. Marshall's attention pivoted to him immediately, looking him up and down.

"What's wrong?"

"Nothing," Benedikt said. "How are we to approach them?"

The Scarlets had stopped outside a building—what looked like police headquarters, though it was hard to read the faded French along the front. Marshall and Benedikt had arrived at the Bund too late. With horror, they had halted to a stop by the roadside just in time to witness Roma being dragged away, separated from Juliette and torn in the other direction. Marshall had almost hurried forward, intent on stopping them in their tracks with "General Shu's" new order, but it was risky—almost too suspicious for such timing. There was a better chance of success if they waited until the Scarlets reached their destination, instead of mysteriously appearing en route.

So Benedikt and Marshall decided to trail after Roma. He had not tried to escape through the entire walk: he remained wooden between the Scarlets who had ahold of him, saying nothing save for the occasional assurance to Alisa. Alisa, on the other hand, had bucked and kicked as hard as she could, going as far as to try biting one of the Scarlets. None of it worked. They did their best to ignore her, and the march onward only continued.

Now, at their destination, one of the Scarlets was arguing with a Nationalist standing guard by the doors. Roma and Alisa stood in the rain with their Scarlet captors, every single one of them looking out of place on these empty streets. There would have been more civilians walking about if the Nationalists hadn't cleared the roads with their military vehicles. There would be more civilians witnessing this bizarre scene—Montagovs under Scarlet control—if the Nationalists had not laid waste to everyone outside with bullets and gunfire.

"I think we may have to do it now," Marshall said, hesitating. "I don't know if they have a jail cell waiting inside or a firing squad."

"Then let's go." Benedikt made to shuffle off the roof tiles. He had barely gotten a step forward when Marshall's arm shot out.

"With your ankle like that? Stay here, Ben. It makes more sense when it is only me who arrives with the command anyway. You're still dressed like a worker."

Before Benedikt could protest, Marshall was already sliding off the roof, hanging along the gutters by his fingertips, then jumping down and landing cleanly.

"Keep an eye out," Marshall hissed from below. He disappeared quickly, ducking through the nearest alley and then emerging between two of the buildings, coming onto the main road. Benedikt didn't like getting left behind, but he had to admit it would have looked strange for him to accompany Marshall. From his vantage point, he watched Marshall approach the group, his posture stick straight, acting the Nationalist soldier. He started to speak with one of the Scarlets, pulling the forged note out of his jacket. All the while, the other Scarlet who had stepped out of the rain and under the awning of the police station was *still* arguing with the soldier standing guard. The Scarlet—as Benedikt eyed him—lashed out, whacking the soldier's hat and flipping it right off his head.

Benedikt wondered what could possibly be a point of contention at this precarious time. Was it not the Nationalists' mission to capture the Montagovs? Why would they keep Roma lurking outside for so long? Did they not worry about a rescue attempt?

"Hey!"

Roma's voice rang loud. The Scarlets, the two soldiers outside the station, Marshall—they all turned to look at him, taken aback, but Roma's attention was fixed on the soldier picking his hat back up.

"Why is your hat so big? It doesn't fit you in the slightest."

The rain suddenly eased into a light drizzle. Its raucous noise grew faint, and it was like Benedikt's ears had come unplugged, like he could think clearly again. He realized what Roma was implying. The man outside was not a Nationalist soldier. He had been planted there to stall.

The doors of the station burst open. And out poured a cascade of workers, armed with rifles.

"Ohhh—no, no, no—"

From the street side, Marshall's gaze snapped to Benedikt, his arm miming a slash across his throat. *Don't! Stay there,* Marshall was warning, just as Dimitri appeared behind the workers, coming to a stop at the top step of the station. The workers fanned out.

"I'll take it from here," Dimitri said. "Shoot the Scarlets."

The Scarlets didn't have a chance to fight back. Some managed to retrieve weapons, some managed one shot. But the workers had them surrounded, rifles already aimed, and with a *pop-pop-pop!* reverberating along the whole street, the Scarlets all dropped, eyes blank and glazed, fleshy wounds studded into their chests. The blood splashed generously. When Marshall raised his arms high, signaling his surrender, the left side of his neck was entirely splattered.

This is bad. This is so, so bad.

The last of the Scarlet groans faded into silence.

"May as well shoot us too while you're at it," Roma said into the deathly quiet. Loudest now were the clinking of bullet casings, dropping from the rifles and littering the ground. "Or do we receive the honor of being torn apart by your monsters?"

Dimitri smiled. "You get the honor of a public execution at nightfall for your crimes against the workers of this city," he said evenly. "Lead them there."

Marshall didn't resist, letting himself be nudged by the sharp end of a rifle. He fell into step beside Roma, arms still held up, and didn't glance up, though he had to know Benedikt was watching. It was to avoid Benedikt being caught too, he knew, but still he cursed Marshall for it, because if this was Marshall's death, if this was an inescapable fate, then he needed one last *look.* . . .

Benedikt scrambled up, his teeth gritted hard. He knew how to save them. He *would* save them.

Before any of Dimitri's men could see him, Benedikt hurried off the roof and started to run in the other direction.

Forty-Five

Do you care to explain yourself?"

Juliette touched the quilt over her shoulders, pulling at its loose threads. Her gaze remained unfocused, turned in the direction of her balcony, gazing out at the gray afternoon. The rain had stopped. As the ground grew quiet, so too did the skies.

"Cai Junli."

Juliette closed her eyes. The use of her birth name had the opposite effect that her mother had likely intended. Lady Cai wanted her to realize the severity of the situation; instead, Juliette felt as if her mother were addressing someone else, some false manifestation of the girl she was supposed to be. All this time, her parents had let her be Juliette—let her be wild, impulsive. Now they wanted the unknown daughter again, but Juliette only knew how to be Juliette.

"Do you even know what happened out there?" she whispered in answer to her mother's question. This was the first time she had ever seen both her parents in her bedroom at once. The first time that they had closed the door on a party going on in the house, their attention fixated on her instead. "Your precious Nationalists mingling downstairs with champagne—they opened fire on a peaceful protest. *Hundreds* of people, dead in an instant."

450

Never mind the infections. Never mind that the madness would soon break out among the soldiers. The Nationalists would put them in quarantine to prevent the spread of the insects, but Juliette doubted it mattered. The monsters would be working this very moment, quietly infecting as many as they could. Violence on both sides—that was how a city shrouded in blood would always be.

"You are hardly in a place to be lecturing right now," Lady Cai said evenly.

Juliette tightened her hold on the quilt. The Scarlets had deposited her in her bedroom when they hauled her back to the Cai house, had sat her upon her bed and demanded she wait while her parents came to her. She was to remain idle, some prisoner under confinement in her own home. This *was* her place. This was the *only* place she had.

"It was *massacre*, Māma," Juliette snapped, rocketing to her feet. "It goes against everything we stand for! What happened to loyalty? What happened to order?"

Her parents remained unbothered. The two of them could have been replaced by marble statues for all that it mattered to Juliette.

"We value order, family, loyalty," Lady Cai confirmed, "but at the end of the day, we choose to value whatever ensures our survival."

An image of Rosalind flashed in Juliette's head. Then Kathleen.

"And what about the survival of those on the streets?" Juliette asked. Each time she blinked, she saw them fall. She saw the bullets pierce their chests and cut through the crowds.

"Communists who threaten the fabric of society," her mother replied, her tone grave. "White Flowers who have been trying to snuff us out for generations. You wish for their lives to be saved?"

When Juliette turned away, unable to speak past the sour twist in her throat, her mother's gaze followed. There was little Lady Cai ever missed. Little that went past her appraisal and emerged untouched. Juliette knew this, and yet still she was surprised as her mother snagged

451

her wrist. Juliette's fingers splayed out against the overhead light. The yarn on her finger glowed white.

"They say you were found with Roma Montagov." Her mother's grip tightened. "Again, I ask, do you care to explain yourself?"

Juliette's eyes went to her father, who had yet to say anything. His composure was placid; Juliette felt turned inside out. While he stood there, occupying a space in her room, Juliette could sense *everything*: her own inhale-exhale of breath, the electricity droning overhead, the static murmur of conversation outside the door.

Her heart, thrumming just beneath her rib cage.

"I have loved him so long that I do not remember him as a stranger," Juliette answered. "I loved him long before we were told to work together in spite of the hate between our families. I will love him long after you tear us apart merely because you pick and choose when it is convenient to partake in the blood feud."

Her mother released her wrist. Lady Cai thinned her lips, but there was otherwise no surprise. Why would there be? It was not difficult to guess why else Juliette would be running away with him.

"We listened to the modern age and never thought to control what you do," Lord Cai said then, finally choosing to speak. His words were a low rumble that gave everything in the room a telltale tremor. "I see that it was our mistake."

Juliette choked out a laugh. "Do you think any of this could have turned out better if you had kept me trapped in the house? Do you think I would have never learned defiance if you had kept me in Shanghai all these years, educated only by Chinese scholars and their ancient teachings?" Juliette slammed her hand against her vanity table, swiping all her brushes and her powders to the floor, but it wasn't enough—nothing was enough. Her words were so bitter in her mouth that she could taste them. "I would have ended up the *same*. We are all held up on the city's strings, and perhaps you should first ask why we have a blood feud before asking why I defied it!"

"Enough," Lord Cai boomed.

"No!" Juliette screamed back. Her heart was pounding. If she had been in hyperawareness of the room before, now she could hear nothing except her raging, violent pulse. "Do you hear what the people are saying? This execution of Communists and White Flowers—they are calling it the White Terror, a *terror*, as if it is merely another madness that cannot be helped! It *can* be helped! We could stop it!"

Juliette took a deep breath, forcing herself to lower her volume. The more she yelled, the more her parents narrowed their eyes, and she feared that one more outburst from her would have them choose to stop listening. This wasn't over. She still had a chance to convince them otherwise.

"Both of you have always said that power lies with the people," Juliette tried, keeping her tone steady. "That the Scarlet Gang would have fallen apart if Bàba had not made membership a badge of pride with ordinary civilians. Now we let them die? Now we let the Nationalists slaughter whoever is suspected of unionizing? The blood feud was about fairness. About power and loyalty splitting the city. We were *equals*—"

"You wish to say," Lord Cai interrupted coldly, "that you would rather we return to a time when the White Flowers blew up our household?"

Juliette staggered back. Her chest squeezed and squeezed until she was sure there was no oxygen left in her lungs.

"That is not what I mean." She hardly knew what she meant. All she knew was that none of this was *right*. "But we are above massacre. We are above a *kill order*."

Her father had turned away, but her mother's gaze remained. "What have I tried to teach you?" Lady Cai whispered. "Do you remember not? Power lies with the people, but loyalty is a fickle, ever-changing thing."

Juliette swallowed hard. So this was the Scarlet Gang. They had said yes when the foreigners demanded an alliance, choosing capital over pride. They had said yes when the politicians demanded an alliance, choosing survival over all else. Who cared about values when the history books were being written? What did it matter if the history books rewrote everything in the end?

"I beg you." Juliette dropped to her knees. "Call an end to the White Terror, demand the Nationalists cease, demand the White Flowers be held separate from the Communists. We have no right to eradicate a populace. It is not fair—"

"What do you know about *fair*?"

Juliette lost her balance, folding sideways and sprawling upon her carpet. She could count on one hand the number of times her father had raised his voice at her. He had shouted so loudly just then that it hardly seemed real. She was half convinced the sound had come from elsewhere. Even Lady Cai was blinking rapidly, her hand pressed to the neck of her qipao.

Juliette recovered faster than her mother did. "Everything you taught me," she said. She pulled herself upright, the loose fabric of her dress gathering around her knees. "Everything about our unity, about our pride—"

"I will not hear it."

Juliette straightened to her full height. "If you won't do anything, I will."

Lord Cai looked to her again. It was either the electricity flickering at that very moment or a light in her father's eyes dimming. His expression turned blank, as it did when he encountered an enemy, as it did when he was readying to torture for information.

Her father, however, did not resort to violence. He only put his hands behind his back and let his volume sink into a steady quiet once more.

"You will *not*," he said. "Give up this malarkey and remain heir to the Scarlet Gang—remain heir to an empire that will soon be backing the country's rulers—or leave us now and live in exile."

Lady Cai swiveled toward him. Juliette's fists grew tighter and tighter, letting out all her dread so that it did not show in her face.

"Are you mad?" Lady Cai hissed to her husband. "Do not give such a choice—"

"Ask her. Ask Juliette what she did to Tyler."

Utter silence descended on the room. For a second, Juliette was experiencing that weightlessness right before free fall, her breath cold in her throat and her stomach upended. Then the significance of her father's words registered like a shock of ice water, and she was rooted once more in the thick threads of her carpeting. Suddenly his refusal to bring her in on Scarlet planning made sense. Shutting her out of the Nationalist meetings made *sense*. How long had her father known? How long had he known she was a traitor and kept her here anyway, let her pretend that everything was normal?

"I killed him."

Lady Cai reared back, her lips parting in shock.

"I shot him and his men," Juliette went on. "I live with his blood on my hands. I made the choice to put Roma's life over his."

Juliette watched her mother, the line of her brow furrowed and carved from stone. Juliette watched her father, his gaze as blank as ever.

"I suspected, when they said he was found with only one bullet wound," Lord Cai said. "I suspected, when all of his men went down with no struggle, which seemed odd given the workers of the uprising were ruthless in their artillery spray. It was only after I received reports about Tyler challenging Roma Montagov to a duel that my suspicions seemed to have motive."

Juliette slumped against the frame of her bed, her whole body collapsing against the footboard slat. She had nothing to say. No defense to give, because she was guilty to the very core.

"Oh, Juliette," Lady Cai said softly.

It was hard to tell whether her mother was admonishing her or pitying her. Pity that came not out of sympathy, but out of abhorrence that she could be so thoughtless.

"I had no intention of punishing her. No intention of asking for an explanation when this was the daughter I raised." Lord Cai brushed at his long sleeves, smoothing out the wrinkles in the fabric. "I wished to observe her. To see whether I could right her course, wherever she had strayed. Juliette is my heir, my blood. I wished to protect her above all else, even against Tyler, even against the Scarlets below us."

Her father walked close then, and when Juliette continued staring at her feet, he grasped her jaw, bringing her gaze up firmly.

"But we punish traitors," he finished. His fingers were like steel. "And if Juliette wishes to defect to the White Flowers' cause, then she may leave and die along with them."

Lord Cai let go. His hands dropped to his sides, and without another word, he swept out of her bedroom. The door closed behind him with a subdued click that seemed incongruous with the promise he had made. He would not break it. Her father had never broken a promise in his life.

"*Māma.*"

Those two words came out as a sob. Like that ragged screech for help in childhood when she had scraped her knee playing outside, summoning her mother to come comfort her.

"Why?" Juliette demanded. "Why do we hate them so much?"

Lady Cai turned away, shifting her attention to the mess on the floor. With her back to Juliette, picking up the brushes and powders, she remained quiet, as if she did not know what—or who—Juliette was talking about.

"There must have been a *reason*," Juliette continued, angrily swiping at the prickle in her eyes. "The blood feud has raged on since the last century. What are we fighting for? Why do we kill one another in a never-ending cycle if we do not know what the original slight was? Why must we remain enemies with the Montagovs when *nobody remembers why?*"

And yet wasn't that the root of all hatred? Wasn't that what made it so vicious?

There was never a reason. Never a good one. Never a fair one.

"Sometimes," Lady Cai said, setting the brushes back onto the vanity, "hatred has no memory to feed off. It has grown strong enough to feed itself, and so long as we do not fight it, it will not bother us. It will not weaken us. Do you understand me?"

Of course Juliette understood. To fight hatred was to upset their way of living. To fight hatred was to deny their name and deny their legacy.

Lady Cai dusted her hands, looking at Juliette's sullied carpet with little more than vague unsettlement in her eyes. When her gaze flickered over to Juliette herself, the expression turned to a deep, deep sadness.

"You know what you did, Cai Junli," her mother said. "Do not try to convince me, for I am finished here until you remember yourself."

Then Lady Cai exited the room too, each click of her heels reverberating tenfold in Juliette's ears. Juliette stood there in her lonesome, listening as the door was locked from the outside, unable to stop the sob that rose again to her throat.

"I regret nothing!" Juliette screamed, making no move to follow the receding footsteps. She did not bother banging on her door, did not attempt to tire herself out. The only thing that followed her mother out was her voice. "I refuse to remember a falsehood! *I defy you!*"

The footsteps faded entirely. Only then did Juliette crumple into a ball, squeezing herself as small as she could upon the carpet, and let herself cry, let herself rage and scream into her hands. For the city, for the dead, for the blood that ran in rivers on the streets. For this cursed family, for her cousins.

For *Roma*.

Juliette choked on her next sob. She thought she had killed the monster of Shanghai. She thought she was hunting new monsters, born of deviant science and greed. She was wrong. There was another monstrous entity in this city, worse than all the others, *feeding* all the others, rotting this whole place from the inside out, and it would never die until it was starved. Would no one starve hatred? Would no one take it upon themselves to cut off its every source of nourishment?

Enough.

Juliette took in a deep, shaky breath, forcing her tears to come to a staggering stop. When she wiped her eyes clear again, she looked around her room carefully, taking inventory of every item that had not been removed.

"Enough," she whispered aloud. "That's enough."

No matter how thoroughly her heart lay shattered, she would reassemble the parts, even only temporarily, even only to get through the next hour.

Before she was the heir of the Scarlet Gang, she was Juliette Cai.

And Juliette Cai was not going to accept this. She was not going to lie down and let other people tell her what to do.

"Get up. Get up. Okay—*get up.*" She rose to her feet, her fists tight. Upon her finger, the piece of string sat heavy, soaked with rain and dirt and who knew what else, yet still it clung to her skin with admirable strength.

They had cleared her bedroom—taken the pistol from under her pillow, the revolvers hiding with her clothes, the knives slotted in her bookshelves. The door was indeed locked, but she was not locked in. After all, there was still a balcony adjoined to her room. She could slide the glass aside and jump. She couldn't circle the house and disrupt the party downstairs—not without weapons—but she could run. Her father had meant it. Exile was an option.

But what was the point? What was the point of running if she had no one to run with? If she had no one to go to? Roma was either already dead or soon to be placed in front of a Scarlet bullet. Juliette was *one* girl—no power, no army, no means of enacting rescue.

Juliette reached into her wardrobe, retrieving the shoebox sitting under her dresses. Her arms brushed the beads dangling from the fabric, and as the room chimed with a light, musical tinkling, Juliette rocked back and sat down hard on the floor, her fingers braced on either side of the box.

She pulled the lid open. It was as she had remembered. The items remained the same.

A poster, an old train ticket, and a grenade.

The box had sat untouched for so long, a keepsake of knickknacks Juliette had once pulled from the attic because the items looked too glamorous to rot among the broken lampshades and discarded bullet casings. She wondered if the Scarlets had not removed this from her room because they had not thought to open the box, or if it was so absurd to think that she would use a grenade to do damage that they did not bother.

Juliette closed her palm around it. To her left, the reflection in the vanity mimicked her movements, the glass capturing her fretful expression when she glanced up.

"How would the war proceed if I killed them right now?" Juliette asked, speaking to herself, to the mirror, to the city itself as it ground to a halt in this cold, hollow room. "They mingle beneath me, prominent Nationalists and war generals. Maybe Chiang Kai-shek himself has stepped in. I would be a hero. I would save lives."

A burst of laughter echoed up from the floorboards. Glasses clinked together, toasts given to celebrate mass slaughter. The blood feud had been bad enough, but it was something Juliette believed she could change. Now it had grown to unrecognizable proportions, split bigger than it ever needed to be. Scarlet against White Flower,

Nationalist against Communist. Dissolving a blood feud was one thing, but a civil war? She was too small—far too small—to meddle with a war that spanned across the country, that spanned across their whole forsaken history as a nation.

Another burst of laughter, louder this time. Let her drop an explosive to her bedroom floor, and it would send down a direct blast, strike all the people in the living room. Juliette felt the rush of loathing take root in her. She condemned the city for its hate. She condemned her parents, her gang. . . . But she was equally terrible. One final act of violence to end it all. She was angry enough to do it. No more Scarlet legacy. No more Scarlet Gang. If she was dead too, she didn't need to live with the pain of her terrible act—herself and her parents, in exchange for bringing down everyone else in the house.

"Let the city weep," she hissed. "We are past hope, past cure, past help."

She pulled the pin.

"Juliette!"

Juliette whirled around, her hand tight around the grenade. For a fleeting second, she thought it was Roma on her balcony, perching on the railing once again. Then her vision sharpened, and she realized her ears were playing tricks on her, for it was not Roma sliding open her glass doors but Benedikt.

"What are you doing?" Benedikt hissed, striding in.

Juliette, on instinct, took a step back. "What are *you* doing here?" she demanded. "You have to go—"

"Why? So you can blow yourself up?" Benedikt asked. "Roma is still alive. I need your help."

The rush of relief almost caused Juliette to drop the grenade, but she tightened her hold just in time, keeping the lever pressed down. When she closed her eyes—overwhelmed by the sheer knowledge of this one little thing that the universe had granted her—she was so grateful that tears sprang up immediately.

"I'm glad you evaded capture," Juliette said, her voice quiet. "Of all people, you will be able to get him out."

"Oh, *please*."

Juliette's eyes snapped open, so shocked by Benedikt's tone that her tears receded. He pointed at the grenade in her hand. "Do you think that's worth it? What will it do to blow up a few Nationalists? They will build their ranks again! They will pick a new leader from Beijing, from Wuhan, from wherever else there are people. The war will still be fought. The conflict will go on."

"I have a duty here," Juliette managed shakily. "If I can do one thing—"

"You want to do one thing?" Benedikt asked. "Let's go blow up the monsters. Let's stop Dimitri. But this?" He jammed a thumb in the direction of her door. The sounds of the party outside continued to filter through. "This is inevitable, Juliette. This is civil war, and you cannot disrupt it."

Juliette did not know what to say. She closed both hands around the grenade and stared at it. Benedikt let her stand like that for a long moment, let her roil in her conflicting emotions, before turning on his heel and cursing under his breath, muttering, "First Marshall, then you. Everyone is just dying to self-sacrifice themselves."

"Marshall?"

Benedikt grimaced. As if remembering that he had broken onto enemy ground, he wandered out to the balcony again and peered around, watching for movement. "Dimitri intercepted the Scarlets and took Roma and Alisa. Marshall got looped in too when he was trying to rescue them. Now it's just me and you. We really do not have long, Juliette."

"Has Dimitri recruited the workers?" Juliette asked, her heart pounding in her ears.

"Yes," Benedikt confirmed. "At this point I don't even know if Dimitri is still intent on taking the White Flowers. With just about every gangster either dead or imprisoned or having fled the city, he's far more concerned with building a base of power among the Communists."

"Then why did he take Roma? If not to end the Montagov line—"

"It's symbolic, I suspect. Kill the gangsters. Kill the imperialists. Kill foreign influence in the city. A public execution as a last-ditch war cry for the workers in the city before Nationalists stomp them out. And then Dimitri and his monsters will flee south with the rest of the Communists, and the war will rage on."

Juliette sucked in a ragged inhale. Was that how this would end? Lourens could sneak a vaccine into the city's water supply, but the whole country? The whole world? If Dimitri fled with the Communists, high off the power that his acquired arms and money and *monsters* gave him, what was the limit? Where would it stop?

"Look," Benedikt said, cutting into Juliette's panic, his voice floating in from the balcony. "Either way, I think we can rescue them. Roma, Marshall, and Alisa—we can get them away from Dimitri and leave the city for good. But you need to help me."

The immediate agreement was on her tongue. And yet Juliette was having such trouble making the move to go.

We punish traitors. And if Juliette wishes to defect to the White Flowers' cause, then she may die along with them.

It wasn't a new development. She had turned traitor five years ago, that windy day on the Bund when she befriended Roma Montagov. She had turned traitor all those times refusing to push her knife into him. She had turned traitor long before she put her bullet in her own cousin, because if loyalty meant being cruel to a fault, then she could not do it.

Her parents would mourn. They would be mourning a version of her that did not exist.

"I love you both so much," she murmured, "but you are *killing* me."

Benedikt's head popped back into the room. "What was that?"

"Nothing," Juliette said, snapping into action. "I'll come."

"Oh." Benedikt almost seemed surprised by Juliette's turn in attitude. He eyed her as she eyed her room, allowing herself one last look around. "You're still holding . . . um—"

Juliette reached for the pin and slid it back into the grenade. Gently, she returned the weapon to her shoebox and tucked it into her wardrobe once more. Before she closed the doors again, she pulled out one of her flapper dresses.

"Let me change first. I'll be fast."

Benedikt frowned as if to advise against such a flashy choice, but then Juliette pulled out a coat too, her brow raised in challenge, and Benedikt nodded. "I'll wait on the balcony."

Enough time had passed for Juliette's hair to dry, but it had been a downpour outside, and her clothes were still sticking to her. In her effort to yank off her dress, it seemed she might have yanked a bit too hard, because as she shed it, there came a *plink!* of something hitting the carpet. Had she broken off a button? A sequin?

She squinted at the floor. No—it was something blue. It was . . . a small *pill*, its color as shiny as a gem. Beside it lay a slip of paper, slightly damp as it fluttered to a stop.

"Oh my God," Juliette muttered, unfolding the note. Bai Tasa's hand on her back. The quick swipe against her when he removed it. He had put these items into her dress pocket.

Use wisely. —Lourens

Bai Tasa was an undercover White Flower.

A disbelieving laugh burst through her throat, but Juliette choked it down fast, not wanting to concern Benedikt, who already seemed to think she was a moment away from leaping off the deep end. Juliette picked up the pill, examining it carefully. When she slipped on her new dress, she put it snugly into her new pocket, dry and clean, then transferred over the rest of what had not fallen out—her little lighter, a single hairpin. That was all. She had no weapons, no valuables, nothing save the clothes on her back and a warm coat, tightened around her waist with a sash.

She hurried to the balcony. When Benedikt turned around, his hair was ruffling in the wind, expression earnest and in such resemblance to Roma that it hurt her chest to look at him.

"Let's go."

Forty-Six

Dimitri announced the execution to be at night-fall, so I gather we do not have much time left."

Juliette looked up at the gray clouds, clutching her fists tight. "Yes, but for your plan to work, we must know exactly how the monsters transform. We cannot just pin our chances of success on sheer hope. *Now!*"

Juliette darted fast across the road, moving from the mouth of one alley to another before the soldiers at the tram light could sight her. Benedikt was fast behind her, though he winced when he slowed to a walk, the two of them picking their way through the narrow passageway.

"Are you injured?"

"Twisted my ankle, but it's fine. I thought we already knew the monsters transformed with water."

Juliette crouched when they came to the end of the alley, listening for sound. Soldiers patrolling along the left, but the right turned into a narrower walkway. It would take them farther from the safe house, but it was a better option than getting caught. She waved for Benedikt to hurry.

"Do we?" she questioned. "I saw one man splash something into his face on the train. We know that these monsters are different from the first, and even at the end, Paul managed to make alterations with how much water was necessary for Qi Ren's transformation. The new ones are transforming at will. We can't bet on it."

Which was why they were going to the safe house to free Rosalind and demand the information she held. They hadn't asked the right questions the first time, and then they had been interrupted by General Shu's appearance. Now Juliette knew better; now Juliette was setting aside her own feelings of betrayal, single-minded in getting one answer.

"If it is not water," Benedikt said, "then what?"

Juliette sighed. "I haven't a clue. But there's more to it—I can feel it."

Benedikt's plan was so strange that it seemed like it might just work. If Roma, Alisa, and Marshall were being hauled to public execution, it had to be outdoors to allow a crowd to gather. But now, after full-scale revolution, there were so few parts of the city where any gathering could be made that the only likely place was Zhabei, with armed workers standing guard.

The Communist effort—and their workers—were following Dimitri because he was supplying monetary funds and ammunition.

But they did not know how he had acquired them. They did not know he had used monsters to blackmail the gangs in Shanghai, and they did not know that he controlled such monsters. The people of Shanghai, though they had bravely fought a revolution, were still *afraid* of his monsters.

"So we incite chaos," Benedikt had explained. "The monsters must be standing guard as men. Dimitri wouldn't miss an opportunity to bring them. He needs the extra protection if Nationalists catch wind of what is happening, but they must blend in too. Force them all to transform, and the civilians on scene will panic. They run, they collide with the armed workers, and they distract everyone long enough that no one can stop us as we swoop in, grab the prisoners, and leave."

But what if it doesn't work?

"We're here."

Juliette paused. When there didn't seem to be activity on the street, she stepped out and approached the safe house building. It was strange—it looked so different since the last time she had seen it, but nothing had changed. It was only the city that kept changing.

"Go on," Benedikt said.

Juliette shook herself out of her daze. There was no use standing here, staring at the door. She reached for the knob and pushed through.

Inside, as light flooded into the apartment, Rosalind straightened up immediately, blinking hard. She looked weary, having been deprived of food and water for two days. Juliette couldn't stand the sight of this, and yet she thought she had it in her to force something out of her cousin?

She approached Rosalind's chair. Without a word, she started to untie the bindings.

"What has happened?" Rosalind croaked. "I heard gunfire. So much gunfire."

Juliette couldn't get her fingers around one of the knots. Her hands were shaking, and when Benedikt touched her shoulder, she stepped away, letting him take on the task instead.

The safe house was too dark. Juliette tugged hard on one of the panels nailed over the window, and when it chipped off, a triangular stream of fading gray light poured into the space. The sun would be setting soon. Nightfall was coming.

"The purge started," Juliette said, her voice hoarse. "The workers managed to gather their forces and march in protest. Nationalists fired on them. The bodies still haven't been cleared."

Rosalind didn't speak. When Juliette turned around, her cousin's expression was gaunt.

"And Celia?"

Juliette started, not expecting the switch in names. She supposed it was apt. Kathleen would never have joined the workers' efforts. That was all Celia, through and through.

"I don't know. I don't know where she is."

The first knot came undone. Rosalind could move her left shoulder.

"Juliette," Benedikt prompted. *Get to the task at hand,* he seemed to be saying.

Juliette paced the length of the room, digging her hands into her hair. She pulled at the strands, so unused to the straight cut that brushed her neck as she moved.

"We're letting you go," she said. "But we want to know everything you know about the monsters."

Rosalind pulled her right arm out as the bindings there came loose too. She had lost all her energy—finding no need to rush or agitate while the rope fell from her body.

"If I had information to give, do you not think I would have offered it by now?" Rosalind asked. "I have nothing more to gain by holding on to anything. Dimitri was only using me as a source into the Scarlets. He was using me long before he decided to blackmail us."

"You must have picked some things up, no matter how little attention you paid his business," Benedikt said, refusing to take her answer. He pulled hard on her ankle rope. Rosalind winced. "How did this begin? Were the monsters already active before he obtained control?"

"No," Rosalind replied. "He found the host insects in that apartment. Five of them, gargantuan and floating in liquid. *I* recruited the Frenchmen for him to infect." She squeezed her eyes shut. "He said it was a war effort. No mass killings, no chaos. Only a tactic to garner power."

"In all fairness," Juliette said quietly, "that part was not a lie."

She blamed Rosalind for falling prey. She pitied Rosalind for falling prey. The Scarlet Gang dealt in violence day by day too. When you were raised in such a climate—loved ones telling you that blood could spill so long as it was in loyalty—how were you to know when to draw the line once you loved someone outside family?

"And the insects," Benedikt continued. "They burrowed into the hosts?"

Juliette leaned forward, her hands braced hard on the table. It had been the same with Qi Ren. One host insect, occupying his body. Giving him the ability to transform into a monster.

"Latched onto their necks and dug right in," Rosalind whispered.

"How did they turn afterward?" The question they needed answered the most. "How did they trigger the transformation?"

All of Rosalind's bindings fell to the floor. Her arms and legs were now free to move, yet she remained on the chair, her elbows resting on her knees, her head dropped in her hands. For several seconds, she remained like that, as still as a statue.

Then Rosalind looked up suddenly. "Ethanol."

Juliette blinked. "*Ethanol?* Is that . . . alcohol?"

Rosalind nodded gingerly. "It's what the insects were first found floating in, so it's what brings them out. Alcohol was what the Frenchmen used the most. A few drops was enough—it didn't have to be concentrated."

Benedikt spun around, seeking Juliette's gaze. "How are we supposed to find enough alcohol? How are we supposed to find alcohol at all?"

Restaurants were closed. Cabarets were closed. The places that weren't locked by iron and chain were already ransacked and robbed.

"We don't need to," Juliette said. She looked out the window, to that one section she had freed, letting in the street outside. "A car's gasoline has the same effect."

A sudden shriek came from afar, and Juliette jumped, her hand coming to her heart. Rosalind, too, leaped to her feet, but then the sound faded just as quickly as it came, and Rosalind looked unsure what to do, hovering by the chair. She was too proud to give voice to the pain in her eyes. She was not quite cold enough to avoid Juliette's eyes completely and let her believe otherwise.

"Go, Rosalind," Juliette said quietly. "There will be more chaos on the streets in a few hours."

Rosalind thinned her lips. Slowly, she reached around her neck and unclasped the necklace she had been wearing, setting it upon the table. It looked dull in the weak light. Nothing more than a slab of metal.

"Did you tell the Scarlets?" Rosalind asked. Her voice was feather-soft. "Did you tell them that I am responsible for the new monsters?"

Juliette should have. She had had the time and the opportunity. If she had offered Dimitri's name as Rosalind's lover, then revealed Dimitri as the blackmailer, Rosalind's crimes against the Scarlet Gang would be far more severe than mere blood-feud spying.

"No."

Rosalind's face was unreadable. "Why not?"

Because she didn't want to. Because she didn't want to accept it. Because she had made such a habit out of lying and withholding, what was one more?

Out of the corner of her eye, Juliette knew that Benedikt was watching her. "Go, Rosalind," she said again.

At last, Rosalind took the cue and walked to the door. Her hand was already upon it when she faltered, when she looked over her shoulder and swallowed hard.

"Is this the last time I'll see you?"

There was too much in that one, quiet question. Would Rosalind go home? After everything she had done, after everything they had done to *her*, could she return?

And if she did, would *Juliette* ever return home?

"I don't know," Juliette replied honestly.

Rosalind watched her for a moment longer. Her eyes might have filled up. Or perhaps that was wishful thinking on Juliette's part. Perhaps it was just Juliette's own eyes that had grown slick with moisture.

Rosalind walked out without another word.

The rain slowed, then stopped, its last few droplets coming down on the bodies with a dull finality. Hands with the pallor of death were collapsed atop one another, the rot and stink of their shriveling skin shrouding the air.

Celia wasn't sure if she was dead or alive. She was buried beneath so much suffering, cloistered under unmoving corpses. Pain throbbed down her torso, but her thoughts were so fragmented that she almost wasn't sure if it was from a bullet wound or merely a physical manifestation of her internal agony; deep down, she had foolishly thought she was safe from slaughter, that violence only came for the masses. At last, it seemed she had succeeded in becoming one of them. A Scarlet would never be suffering like this. A Scarlet would have made it quick, like Mr. Ping taking one of the first bullets, or stayed far away from such tumult.

What is there now? Celia wondered.

Then someone was grabbing at her. "I've got you. I've got you."

Celia turned her head, opening her eyes from the darkness of her burial to a sudden flash of light: a streetlamp, burning above her. Before her vision cleared, she guessed the silhouette pulling at her to be an angel, some hazy being come to ease the horrors of war. Then a fresh wave of pain erupted down her side, and her mind snapped back in place, her chin jerking up. It was no angel come to save her.

It was her sister.

"How are you here?" Celia gasped.

Rosalind already had wet streaks down her cheeks, glinting under the light, but when she paused, having freed Celia from the bodies, she burst into fresh tears, hands tapping around Celia's shoulders, checking for immediate wounds. There was only one: the growing stain at her side.

"How can you ask that?" she said, sniffling. "I ran for the street that everyone said had suffered a massacre. I came looking for you."

Celia bit down on her gasp of pain, complying when Rosalind tried to pull her to her feet. She swayed, unable to set any weight down, but Rosalind's arms were accommodating, taking the brunt of her balance. Though Celia's head spun, she still sighted red marks along Rosalind's wrists, vivid and angry.

"Can you walk?" Rosalind asked. "Come on. Any longer and you'll bleed out."

Celia put one foot in front of the other. It was a staggering, exhausting effort, but it was an effort, nonetheless.

"Thank you, jiějiě." When the breeze blew into her face, Celia wasn't sure if she felt coldness because there was blood smeared on her cheeks or if she had started crying too. "Thank you for coming back for me."

Rosalind tightened her grip. She kept pushing them forward even while Celia swayed, phasing in and out of consciousness.

"I want you to think of Paris," Rosalind ordered. It was an attempt to keep Celia awake, to keep her focused even as her senses grew weak. "Think of the speakeasies, the lights in the distance. Think about seeing them once more, when the world is no longer so dark."

"Will there ever come a day?" Celia whispered. Her vision blurred. Her surroundings tunneled, colors bleeding into monochrome.

A stifled noise came from Rosalind. Up ahead, the silver of a building flashed, and Rosalind stumbled them forward, step by step by step. This was Rosalind's silent promise into the world. She would have her sister see another day. She would have her sister see all the days and more, each and every one of them rising from the horizon.

"I ruined us all for a love not true," Rosalind whispered. "At the very least, I can still save you."

Forty-Seven

The sun was setting.

In Zhabei, the streets were starting to fill with people again, so Juliette and Benedikt found no trouble hurrying through, passing soldiers without a second glance. The Nationalists could try as they wanted to keep this city under lock and key, but it was always too full, brimming with activity, and at the slightest whisper of a commotion, the people came out to seek it. Whispers were flying about the public execution. Word traveled fast among the workers, among the civilians who wanted a show, never mind where the political tide in this city turned. The only question was whether the Kuomintang had caught wind too. As nice as it would be if Dimitri Voronin was arrested and hauled in, Juliette had to hope that the Nationalists didn't show up. Because then the Montagovs would be arrested alongside Dimitri, or simply shot.

"He gave you just *one*?" Benedikt asked now, his breath coming fast.

In sync, they swerved around a fallen rickshaw, Juliette circling left and Benedikt circling right, before meeting again and continuing onward on the street. There was a glow of light up ahead. The intersection of a street with a crowd gathered in thick.

"Only one," Juliette replied, her hand patting her pocket to confirm. "I suspect he couldn't produce more fast enough."

"Damn Lourens for giving us *something* but not giving us *enough*," Benedikt muttered begrudgingly. He sighted the scene up ahead too. "It does beg the question of us. We make use of the monsters for chaos . . . but what if they release their insects? In such proximity, it will be immediate death."

That was the question Juliette had been mulling on since leaving the safe house, but slowly, something was beginning to formulate into shape. She looked up at the clouds once more and found them hazed with purple, dark and bruised. The deeper they walked into Zhabei, the more the storefronts around them changed, looking shabbier, less well kept. The foreign influence faded, the glamour receded.

"I have an idea," Juliette said. "But can we hurry first? The fire station is some few streets away."

They moved fast. When the station came into sight—its red tiled roof muted under the setting darkness and its smooth entrance lined with four gate-like arches—it was almost a surprise that the building was abandoned, given the supplies that sat awaiting inside. Perhaps the soldiers who had been asked to stand guard around the public facilities had all been redirected elsewhere, tending to the chaos around the city like a dozen little fires. They were in civil war. Communists popping up like moles from their hiding places and Nationalists desperately trying to thwack them back down so they could hold on to governance.

Juliette skidded into the station, immediately searching for what they needed. Her footsteps echoed loudly on the linoleum floor. Benedikt was making slower work, eyeing the labeled shelves while Juliette climbed atop one of the smaller firefighting cars to peruse the second floor. It didn't seem like there was much up there, gauging by what she could see past the banisters.

"I can't find a single damn weapon," Juliette spat. "Not even an axe. In a fire station."

"If this goes well, pray you don't *need* a weapon." Benedikt came around, showing her what he had found. A hose, looped around his arm, and two jugs of what Juliette had to guess was gasoline. "How are we supposed to carry this back there?"

Juliette jumped off the hood of the car. Then she looked at it again. "Can you drive?"

"No," Benedikt answered immediately. "I'm not—"

Juliette was already opening the door into the passenger seat, reaching over and pressing the start button on the dashboard. The ignition came to life. As the night grew darker outside, the headlights flared a high beam, cutting a path ahead of them.

"Put the gasoline in the back," Juliette said. "And drive."

"Your idea is risky."

"It's a good idea. You cannot protest it merely because you have to stay behind."

Benedikt shot her a glare from the driver's seat, his foot on the pedal as the car inched down the road. They were almost at the intersection where the crowd had gathered. Now it was proper nightfall, the sky dark and the streets lit by gas lamps and torches, hot orange embers dotted among the people.

"It will guarantee their safety," Juliette maintained. "You said it yourself—this whole execution business is symbolic. Dimitri is after Roma. He gains no extra points with Alisa. No extra points with Marshall. Second to Roma, there's—stop here, stop here. We cannot go any closer."

Benedikt pressed down on the brake, halting the car. A few steps forward, and they would be within view of the crowd.

"Second to Roma," Juliette resumed quietly, "there's only me."

Gangster royalty, dead by his hands. The two empires of Shanghai's underground—the heirs of families that had kept this city rumbling on capital and foreign trade, on hierarchy and nepotism—both fallen and executed under his bullet. It was too good to pass up. Too good for Dimitri to decline. Juliette was counting on it.

"He will sense a trick."

"He will," Juliette said. "But by then it will be too late."

She would offer to trade herself for Marshall and Alisa. Once Marshall and Alisa were away from the scene, Benedikt would activate the monsters, Juliette would give Roma the vaccine from Lourens, and even if all the insects came out, they would be safe, and they would leave, and that was that.

Easy as pie.

Juliette pulled off her coat, tossing it to the floor of the vehicle. When she reached for the door, Benedikt's arm shot out suddenly, closing around her wrist.

"He'll be safe," Juliette promised before Benedikt could say anything. "Marshall and Alisa are the first order of priority."

Benedikt shook his head. "I was only going to say be careful." He let go, casting a look into the back of the car, where the hose sat awaiting.

Juliette took a deep breath and got out. The street was on a decline. When she started forward, the angle immediately gave Juliette a perfect view of the small crowd and a perfect view of what they were clustered around: Roma, being tied to a wooden pole, his hands behind his back, rope secured around his waist.

All she could do was put one foot in front of the other and keep walking, eyes pinned to the scene, to the armed workers under Dimitri's command who were moving to finish up their final knot on Alisa next. Juliette wondered where the wooden poles had come from. It was that which her mind wandered to, of all places—whether the poles were nailed into the ground or wedged into the tram lines running down the middle of the road.

Her eyes scanned the waiting crowd. There weren't many here—there couldn't be, or the noise would stir trouble with the soldiers nearby. Twenty, maybe more, but twenty was all you needed for word to spread about Dimitri's good deed. They appeared curious, unbothered as the armed workers walked their outer edges, rifles at the ready in case soldiers approached.

At the periphery of the crowd, Juliette sighted the man who had followed them onto the train. The French White Flower. Her blood started to run hot, pumping adrenaline into her body, keeping her warm even as the cold breeze blew on her sleeveless dress.

Juliette had shed her coat intentionally. She wanted immediate recognition in her bright and beaded getup the moment she approached the crowd.

And she got it.

Benedikt needed to work fast, but it was hard when his palms were slick with sweat. He pulled the end of the hose taut, then adjusted it on the roof edge, aimed at the scene beneath him. They had stolen dozens of gallons of gasoline. They could afford to be liberal. But it had to work. It had to flow properly through a very, very long tube, and he couldn't screw this up.

Too much was riding on it.

"Okay," Benedikt muttered. It looked set. On the street below, Juliette had reached the crowd, her arms held up, ignoring the whispers as her name echoed through like a chant.

"I come unarmed," she called.

Benedikt stepped away from the rooftop, hurrying through the building and back to the gasoline in the car. He hadn't prayed to God in years, but today he was going to start.

"Is that—"

Slowly, Juliette put up her hands, showing herself to be weaponless. "I come unarmed," she called. The crowd had fallen silent.

Whatever Dimitri might have been in the midst of saying was cut off as he stared at her, eyes steely with consideration. To his side, Roma looked aghast. He did not speak, did not yell her name in horror. He knew that Juliette was up to something.

"Somehow, I find that hard to believe," Dimitri said. He waved his hand. The nearest armed worker leveled his rifle at her.

"Pat me down and you'll see I bring nothing. Only my life. In trade."

Dimitri hooted with laughter. He threw his head back with the sound, drowning out the gasp that Roma made and the muttered confusion coming from Marshall.

"Miss Cai, what makes you think you have any trading power?" Dimitri demanded when he turned his attention back to her. "I can have you shot—"

"And then what?" Juliette asked. "*Juliette Cai, Princess of Shanghai, killed by random worker.* The textbooks on the revolution will be sure to mention it. I come to you, offering you my life side by side with my husband, and you throw it away?"

Dimitri tilted his head now. Her words registered.

"You mean to say—"

"I'm not trading my life for Roma's," she confirmed. "For Marshall Seo and Alisa Montagova. Let them go. They didn't need to be dragged into this fight."

"*What?*" Marshall exclaimed. "Juliette, you're out of your mind—"

The nearest worker pressed his rifle into Marshall's neck, shutting him up. Dimitri's gaze, meanwhile, swiveled to his captured subjects, a notch appearing in his brow as he tried to consider the matter. He didn't look like he was entirely buying it. Perhaps Juliette was not acting this right.

She met Roma's gaze. He didn't believe her either.

Perhaps the only way to convince Dimitri was to convince Roma first.

"I made a vow to you, Roma." She took a step forward. No one stopped her. "Where you go, I go. I will not bear a day parted. I will take a dagger to my own heart if I must."

Her shoes clicked down on the ground—on gravel, on tram-line metal, on a drain covering. With every step, the crowd continued to part and shuffle. There was confusion, hearing her words spoken to Roma, to her enemy. There was panic, not wanting to be caught in her path, fearful of her even when her hands were in the air, even with rifles pointed at her head from three different directions. It was as if she were partaking in the most bizarre wedding march, if the groom waiting on the other end of the aisle was Roma tied and bound for death.

"No," Roma whispered.

"This city has been taken," Juliette went on. The hitch in her voice was not feigned. The tears that rose to her eyes were not feigned. "All that is good is gone, or perhaps it never existed. The blood feud kept us apart, forced us onto different sides. I will not allow death to do the same."

By then Juliette had come to a stop right before Roma. She could have tried to break him out in that moment, snatch a rifle and slash the sharp part over his rope bindings.

Instead, she leaned in and kissed him.

And from under her tongue, she pushed the vaccine into his mouth.

"Bite down," she whispered, just before two of the armed workers yanked her away. The crowd around them murmured in utter bewilderment. This had been a public execution, and now it was appearing more like a ground for scandal.

Juliette whipped her hand out, closing her fingers around one of the rifle ends and pointing it straight at Dimitri. The workers scrambled to stop her, but Juliette wasn't doing anything except keeping her hand near the barrel. She was nowhere near the trigger.

The rest of the rifle remained strapped to the poor worker, who had frozen in confusion.

"You don't know what I am capable of," she said, her voice ringing loud in the night. "But I am honorable. Let them go. And I will not resist."

The scene was still for a long moment. Then:

"I tire of these dramatics," Dimitri announced. "Just tie her up. Let go of the other two."

Alisa cried out softly in protest, her eyes drawn wide. Marshall, meanwhile, leaned forward with a vicious curse. His face would have been red with exertion if the light were better, wanting to fight Dimitri himself and put a stop to this.

"You cannot be serious. Juliette, you cannot *trade* your life. What's wrong with you—"

Juliette said nothing. She said nothing as they untied Alisa and let her stumble away. She said nothing as Marshall was released from his bindings too, his expression utterly rattled, looking up at Juliette as they dragged her to the pole and looped her tightly to it. He was bouncing on his toes—a second away from lunging at Dimitri, all the armed workers be damned.

"You cannot be serious," he said again. "You absolutely cannot—"

"Go, Marshall," Roma said roughly. He didn't know what he had swallowed, but he had to know now that it meant there was a plan. "Don't make this all for nothing. Take Alisa and go."

Go, Juliette wanted to add. *Go, and Benedikt can explain everything.*

Marshall visibly hesitated. Then he took Alisa's hand and hurried away with her, charging through the crowd as if afraid that they would shoot him in the back as soon as he turned around. Juliette let out a breath when they disappeared from view.

She had almost been afraid they *would* shoot.

"And so this is how it ends." A click of a pistol. Dimitri was loading in his bullets. "It shall truly be a new era."

"Marshall!"

Marshall jolted, stopping dead in his tracks. He was breathing hard, the sound audible even before Benedikt tumbled out from the car. Marshall had never looked so horrified in his life. His expression flashed with surprise, then relief in sighting Benedikt, but it didn't last long.

"Ben," Marshall gasped. He hurried to him, clasping on to his hand. "Ben, Ben, we have to go help them. Roma and Juliette—"

"It's okay, it's okay," Benedikt reassured him, smoothing his other hand against Marshall's neck. "I'll explain. Alisa, get in the car. We need to be ready."

"Freed from Scarlets. Freed from White Flowers," Dimitri continued.

Juliette started to count, wondering when Benedikt would make his move. Surely, soon. Surely, very soon.

"Instead," Roma said, "it is a city ruled by monsters."

One of the workers nudged his rifle hard into Roma's head, shutting him up. Dimitri maintained a neutral stare. He was still pretending.

"What convenience that you bring it up," Dimitri said. He looked the picture of innocence. "Then I shall reveal to the city that I present to it *two* gifts. The end of gangster tyranny, and—" He gestured to several bags on the ground by his feet. Juliette hadn't noticed them before, but they looked like the sort used to store flour or rice, found in multitudes at the food markets. These were tied up at the ends with string, the cotton fabric looking like it would fray at any second to give way for whatever was bulging inside.

"—a vaccine, distributed to all who are loyal to me."

A murmur spread through the crowd, and Juliette's gaze flickered up with surprise. So that was how he was going to play it. Exactly as the Larkspur had done: set ruin on the people with one hand and offer salvation with the other.

The wind blew cold against Juliette's cheek, and she let it—she let the seconds draw long, squirming against the rope around her waist. They hadn't bothered securing it very tightly because she was supposed to be dead in seconds. Her hands were still freed. Within reaching distance of the worker to her right, his rifle in line with her face.

Dimitri raised his gun. "The history books will mark today momentously."

"Yes," Juliette said. "They will."

A gurgling noise came from above. That was the only warning that rang into the night. In the next second, a rain of gasoline was showering down, covering the crowd, the workers, the entire street side. It stung her eyes dreadfully, but Juliette had the advantage of knowing what was coming. The worker keeping guard next to her screamed out and covered his eyes with his hands, leaving his rifle free for the snatching. Juliette spared no time in yanking it from him and turning the point down, slashing the sharp end on the rope around her waist. Her hip stung; it had caught a cut, running fresh blood, but Juliette didn't pay it any mind. She coughed hard against what had trickled into her mouth and turned to Roma.

"Open your eyes, my love. You'll need to see if we're going to escape."

Roma's eyes flew open just as Juliette sawed through the rope on his arms.

"What *is* this?" he demanded, shaking the slickness off his arms.

482

Juliette nodded out into the crowd. She cut through his waist bindings too. "Look."

Before their very eyes, five monsters burst into shape. The screaming was immediate—the chaos that Juliette had expected. The civilians scattered in all directions; the workers abandoned their posts as monsters roared up into the night. With a brutal curse, Dimitri finally forced his eyes open just as the gasoline came to a stop, screaming, *"Release!"*

It was too late. Dimitri was too late. Even as the insects poured out, Juliette dropped the rifle and reached for Roma's hand, tugging him forward, searching for a good pathway. Just as she started to move, there was a *click* from behind them, and faster than Juliette could react, Roma yanked her down, narrowly avoiding a bullet that skimmed the concrete ground.

They turned around. Dimitri was holding his pistol out. "You should be dead," he seethed at Roma. A clump of black ran over his shoe. "The insects should be killing you."

"It would take more than that to kill me," Roma replied.

Dimitri tightened his grip on the pistol. Destruction tore through the scene before he could shoot: a bloodbath, infecting those who hadn't run fast enough. Juliette's eyes swiveled to the side. A woman: dropping to her knees, fingers sinking into her neck and pulling without any hesitation. A scream—a figure, running to her. Her husband: cradled over her corpse and keening a loud, desolate noise. Then he too gouged at his own throat and fell to the ground.

It was utter confusion and pandemonium. Dimitri kept swiveling around, trying to push away the workers who came to dive in front of him. They were all begging, using their last gasp of control to entreat Dimitri to save them, before he shoved them out of the way and they gouged themselves to death.

"Roma," Juliette whispered. "I thought I was rescuing you, but I don't know if we can walk away from this."

Chaos. Complete chaos. Save for Dimitri, only Roma and Juliette stood immune, the three of them like combatant gods in the midst of primordial chaos, and wasn't this *exactly* what was wrong with this place? Deciding who deserved to be saved and who deserved to be abandoned. Letting the whole place rot and fester so long as the top was not touched, so long as there was no inconvenience within sight.

Juliette glanced at Roma. He was already watching her.

They could walk away in the physical sense. Could bolt while Dimitri was distracted, take a bullet or two in carelessness and still live to tell the tale. But for as long as Dimitri was alive and these monsters moved under his thumb, how could they ever be *free*? She would always be thinking about this city, these people—*her* people—suffering from something she could have stopped.

"Together or not at all, dorogaya," Roma whispered back. "I'm with you if we run. I'm with you if we fight."

Dimitri gave a vicious shout and fired on a worker with his pistol, killing the woman before she could prostrate herself at his feet a moment longer. The screams around them were fading. This was one small crowd infected with madness. In days, weeks, months, there could be more crowds in other cities, across the whole country, across the whole world. In the end, the only ones who would ever pay for such destruction, in blood and in guts, were the people.

Keep fighting for love.

Juliette had wanted to be selfish, had wanted to run. But *this* was their love—violent and bloody. This *city* was their love. They couldn't deny their upbringing as the heirs of Shanghai, as two pieces of a throne. What was left of their love if they rejected that? How could they live with themselves, look at each other, knowing they had been presented a choice and gone against who they were at their core?

They couldn't. And Juliette knew—the Roma she loved wouldn't *let* her leave like this.

"We must move fast." Juliette brought out her lighter from her pocket. "Do you understand me?"

It wasn't just Dimitri who needed to die. That was the easy part. That only required picking up one of the fallen rifles.

It was the monsters that needed to be destroyed.

A split second passed. Roma looked to the scene around them. The workers in front of Dimitri had at last all collapsed.

"Always, Juliette."

In a flash, Roma lunged at Dimitri. Before Dimitri could gather his bearings and recover from the pleas of the workers, Roma was distracting him again by turning his pistol skyward, the trigger squeezing and shooting a bullet right up into the air. Juliette, taking the chance, raced forward and tore open one of the bags near Dimitri's feet. She turned it upside down, scattering the clumps of blue all across the other bags, spread evenly upon every single one of them.

A heavy grunt. Dimitri—writhing out of Roma's hold. In the tussle, the pistol flew three feet away, clattering into a pool of blood, but instead of chasing after it, Dimitri only spun around, heaving with his hatred. He pushed Roma hard, almost slamming him to the ground. Then, before Juliette could get out of the way, he sighted her with the bags, and his boot collided with her stomach.

Juliette landed sharply on the gravel, wincing when it tore scratches into her elbows. The gasoline on the ground soaked into the wounds. Roma hurried to her aid and hauled her upright again, but it was no matter. The scene was set. Behind Dimitri, the monsters started to lumber near.

They needed to come closer. Just a little closer.

Roma reached for Juliette's hand. Something about it felt entirely natural even as the world stuttered to a halt around them. It would always be that same feeling as when they were fifteen: invincible, untouchable, as long as they were together. His fingers, solid and steady while they were entwined with hers.

With her other hand, Juliette flipped open the lighter. She met Roma's eyes, asked him in silence one last time if they were truly to do this. He showed no fear. He was gazing at her as one would gaze out into the sea, like she was this vast, momentous wonder that he was glad simply to bear witness upon.

"To have and to hold, where even death cannot part us," Juliette whispered.

The monsters howled into the night. Loomed closer.

"In this life and the next," Roma returned, "for however long our souls remain, mine will always find yours."

Juliette squeezed his hand. In that action, she tried to communicate everything she couldn't put into words, everything that didn't have a spoken form other than *I love you. I love you. I love you.*

When Dimitri stepped forward, when the monsters finally approached within good range, Juliette turned the spark wheel on her lighter.

"Don't miss," Roma said.

"I never do," Juliette replied.

And with Roma's nod, she threw the burning flame onto the bags of highly flammable vaccine.

"What could be taking so long?" Benedikt demanded. He had his foot on the pedal. They needed to be ready to go the very second Roma and Juliette appeared.

Alisa whimpered from the back seat. Marshall strained against the rear window, waiting to see if anyone was coming up the street and within sight.

The ground beneath them seemed to shudder. One thump. Another.

Then Marshall turned around, swearing so loudly his voice cracked. "Go, Benedikt, go!"

"What? But—"

"Drive!"

Benedikt pressed down on the accelerator, the car tearing through the street so suddenly that its wheels shrieked into the night.

Behind them, with gasoline drenched into every square inch of the pavement, the explosion rang so loud and hot that all of Shanghai rocked with the blow.

Epilogue

There is scarcely any movement around this part of Zhouzhuang, scarcely any sound at all to disturb Alisa Montagova as she kneels by the canal, folding yuánbǎo out of silver paper. She doesn't think that they much resemble the ingots they are supposed to look like, but she is trying her best.

Today is the Qingming festival: Tomb-Sweeping Day. A day of veneration for ancestors who have passed away, for gravesite cleaning and praying and burning false money into the afterlife for the dead to use. Alisa has no ancestor to pray for in Shanghai. In Shanghai, there are only gravestones, laid side by side over empty graves.

Nobody had argued against it. With the explosion twelve months ago, the papers the next day had gotten ahold of a marriage certificate that sent the city into an uproar. A certificate that showed Roma Montagov and Juliette Cai married, bound together this whole time while the blood feud tore the streets apart.

Alisa adds another yuánbǎo to her pile. In truth, the certificate never existed. But Alisa heard their vows that night, eavesdropping instead of going to sleep. She had forged the document and sent it to the press. The blood feud may not have fallen apart immediately, but that was the first moment it started to fragment. If their heirs did

488

not believe in the feud, why should the common people? If the heirs had died for each other, what was the basis for their people to keep fighting?

They had buried them together. There were no ashes, no bones. Kept apart in life, allowed together in death.

At the thought, Alisa sniffles suddenly, finding her nose to be running. She didn't believe it. The first time she saw their gravesite, she had dived at the headstones, trying to carve the engravings right out.

"They're not dead!" she screamed. "If you can't find their bodies, they're not dead!"

They said the explosion had been too hot. That they found the monsters because of how tough their skins were, that they found Dimitri Voronin body because of his distance from the blast. But no Roma and no Juliette.

Benedikt had to pull her off. He had to throw her over his shoulder so she wouldn't dig the grave up, but even as he walked her away, her eyes remained pinned on the stones.

Roman Nikolaevich Montagov	Cai Junli
Роман Николаевич Монтагов	蔡珺丽
1907–1927	1908–1927

"They're gone, Alisa," Benedikt whispered. "I'm sorry. They're gone."

"How can they be gone?" She clutched her cousin, burying her face in his shoulder. "They were once the mightiest people in this city. How can they just be gone?"

"I'm sorry." That was all Benedikt could say. Marshall crouched down beside them, offering his presence. "I'm sorry. I'm sorry. I'm sorry."

Those aren't even their names, Alisa wanted to scream. *Those headstones have the wrong names.*

Now, she finishes her little pile of false money and gathers them into a tight circle. Twilight creeps deeper against the horizon, bathing the sky in orange. Alisa is here because she cannot stand the insincere gestures in Shanghai, cannot bear to join the crowds at the cemeteries, all the sobbing faces who didn't even know her brother. Benedikt and Marshall had fled the city a month after the explosion. They wanted to take her with them to Moscow, where no one knew who they were, where no one had heard of the Montagovs and their legacy, where Kuomintang generals wouldn't be on the hunt for them. Alisa refused. She wanted to know what happened to her father. She wanted to see what would happen to her city.

She hasn't gotten any good answers. Her father remains missing, and the city slowly returns to normal. War rages through the country with no sign of ceasing, but Shanghai has always been a city in a bubble. War rages on, and the city tells the tale of Roma and Juliette like some folk song passed between rickshaw runners on their breaks. They speak of Roma Montagov and Juliette Cai as the ones who had dared to dream. And for that, in a city consumed by nightmares, they were cut down without mercy.

"Alisa Montagova, it is starting to get cold."

Alisa turns around, squinting into the dark. "I'm almost done. I would have been faster if you had helped me fold."

A grumble. "I will stay here. Don't fall into the water."

Alisa strikes a match, bringing it to the false money. She cups the flame so that the soft wind does not blow it away, her hand steady until an ember catches and flares to life.

Today, of all days, there will be crowds upon crowds tending to Roma and Juliette's gravesite. Which is why Alisa has come here instead, to Zhouzhuang, where Roma once said he wanted to go. If the human soul has an afterlife, has a will, then his would be here for rest, and Alisa has no doubt that Juliette's would follow.

It had been absolute hell trying to find a way out to this little township. Alisa no longer lives at White Flower headquarters. Head-quarters doesn't *exist* anymore, taken over by Nationalists and soldiers once the White Flowers were run out. Benedikt was immensely worried when he was leaving with Marshall, wondering what Alisa was going to do, where Alisa was going to go. She already had an answer for him. He hadn't liked it, but he couldn't stop her.

She became a Communist spy.

It isn't that she cares all that much for the cause. It isn't even that she likes the people very much, short of her superiors who decide her tasks, and on the occasion, drive her out into the countryside when she pouts for long enough. But she sees the city trying to revert to its old ways. She sees the lines and cracks growing and growing, and she wonders what it was all for, why her brother made such a sacrifice if nothing is going to change. The White Flowers are fractured beyond repair; the Scarlets have disintegrated. Lord Cai joined the ranks of the Kuomintang; the government sits steady. And yet this city hums with injustice. No true law, no true rule. Foreigners, lurking at the seams, waiting for the moment the Kuomintang missteps. Imperialists in other parts of the country, their armies at the ready, simply biding their time. Alisa is no expert in politics, but she is quick and nimble. She crawls in and out of hiding spaces before anyone can see her. She hears the reports of the Japanese taking land in the north. She hears the British and French plotting to consume what they can. For as long as the country is kept in chaos, the people fear the fates that they mourn in Roma and Juliette. For as long as hatred lurks in the waters, the story of Roma and Juliette starts anew.

And Alisa just wants them to have *peace*.

The sun sets over the horizon at last. Alisa watches the papers burn, letting the darkness fall around her. Soon it is only the burning fire that illuminates the canal. The flames reflect back in her dark eyes, warms the breeze that swirls about.

"I wish you could see it," Alisa whispers into the night. "They find hope in your union. They wish not to fight anymore."

The canal trembles with the wind. Its water sloshes, the only sound in the clearing. Most people in this small township have already retired for the evening, shuttering their windows and laying their heads to sleep.

"Alisa. I am growing wrinkles."

"Don't be *dramatic*, Celia."

The fire has finally finished burning, so Alisa nudges at the ashes with her foot and turns to leave. Her superior is a few steps away, looking as if she is guarding the canal, but there is no one nearby to guard from, and besides, there is nothing in Zhouzhuang to worry about. She uses the term "superior" lightly—the others are far older, but Celia can't be any more than nineteen, the only one who will put up with Alisa's annoying requests. There has always been something familiar about Celia, as if Alisa has met her briefly before. But she can't quite put her finger on how or when, at least in a way that makes sense.

Alisa bounds over. Even when she comes to a stop, Celia is watching the canal, her eyes scanning the darkness.

"You come into Zhouzhuang *all* the time on solo mission runs," Alisa says, trying to sight what has taken up so much of Celia's attention. "Are you afraid your contacts will spot me? Maybe they'll want to work with me instead."

Celia jerks her eyes to Alisa, taken aback. "How did you know that I come here?"

"You bring back buns with shop labels on them. Stop feeding me if you don't want me to know where you're going."

A long exhale. Celia points a warning finger at Alisa. "Don't tell. It's off the record."

Alisa mocks a salute. She doesn't protest as Celia turns her around by the shoulders and pushes her to start walking. Their car is parked outside the township.

"It's not a contact, then? Should we worry about being sighted?"

"Don't even get me started on being sighted. Remember what I told you last month? My own sister started working for the top command within the Nationalists. We could get"—she imitates a pistol with her hands and makes a shooting noise—"sniped at any moment."

Alisa giggles, but it trails off quickly, feeling out of place. Celia is trying to amuse her, but there was pain in that joke, still raw, still baffled. Celia has said nothing about who her sister is; she barely even shares any information about herself. All the same, Alisa feels her heart twist.

"Thanks for bringing me out here," she says quietly. "I needed to do this."

The canal makes a splash from behind them.

"He's proud of you, you know."

Alisa casts Celia a sidelong glance. "You didn't even know Roma."

"I just have a feeling. Come on. It's going to take us forever to get back into the city."

Without waiting, Celia rushes ahead, ducking under the waving branches of the trees and sidestepping the various herbs laid out to dry on the sidewalk. Alisa doesn't know what it is in that moment— perhaps the moonlight as it grows brighter overhead, perhaps some movement sensed by the hairs at the back of her neck—but she turns around, glancing at the canal again.

There is just enough illumination to catch a fishing boat as it passes by, lighting the profiles of two people. Alisa catches a glimpse. A glimpse of a girl in a dress too nice, leaning over to kiss a boy with a face familiar. Then laughter—a light, airy laughter that echoes across the clearing. In seconds, the boat has drifted away, under the cover of a willow tree that sweeps over the canal, deeper into the maze of waterways that make up this quiet township.

Alisa turns back around.

For a second she only stands in stillness, staring into the night, not knowing what to do. Then she is crying—tears running down her cheeks too fast to bother catching. It is not sadness that strikes her but *hope*, hope that overwhelms her with such ferocity she remains rooted to the spot, unable to move a muscle in fear that this feeling will pass. She could run after them. She could chase along the canal, keep going and going until she finds the fishing boat. See them with her own two eyes and *know*.

Alisa doesn't move. The wind dances around her, blows her hair into her eyes, making the strands stick to her wet cheeks. She would chase politicians until she understood their every move, she would chase top officials until she knew every last piece of their classified plan, but she would not chase this. She would rather hold this hope so close to her chest that it feels like a fire on its own, flickering against the darkness, flickering even where other embers burn out.

There will be hatred. There will be war. The country will fight itself to pieces. It will starve its people, ravage its land, poison its breath. Shanghai will fall and break and cry. But alongside everything, there has to be love—eternal, undying, enduring. Burn through vengeance and terror and warfare. Burn through everything that fuels the human heart and sears it red, burn through everything that covers the outside with hard muscle and tough sinew. Cut down deep and grab what beats beneath, and it is love that will survive after everything else has perished.

Alisa wipes her face with her sleeve. She takes a steadying breath.

"Don't worry," Alisa whispers. "We will be okay."

And she hurries forward, away from the canal, returning to Shanghai once more.

Acknowledgments

Writing the second book of a duology is like the great evil in a YA novel emerging once again, except more is at risk because the protagonist has everything at stake. In this case, the evil is book-writing, and the stakes are my dignity to make sure the second book fights as hard as the first book. Since we made it to the end, I'm counting this as a victory, and of course, the victory wouldn't be possible without the people accompanying me on the battlefield.

Thank you to Laura Crockett, the fiercest advocate that any writer could have. You are my publishing lifeline, and I am so eternally grateful for your brilliance. Thank you also to Uwe Stender and Brent Taylor for the marvelous, tireless work at TriadaUS.

Thank you to Sarah McCabe, who I'm so happy to have in my corner. This book thrived under your editorial eye, and I await so much more thriving to come. Thank you to my glorious publicists Cassie Malmo and Jenny Lu, and Mackenzie Croft over on the Canada team. Thank you to Justin Chanda and everyone at Margaret K. McElderry, to Karen Wojtyla, Anne Zafian, Bridget Madsen, Elizabeth Blake-Lin, Greg Stadnyk, Caitlin Sweeny, Lisa Quach, Chrissy Noh, Devin MacDonald, Karen Masnica, Cassandra Fernandez, Brian Murray, Anna Jarzab, Emily Ritter, Annika Voss, Lauren Hoffman, Lisa Morelda, Christina Pecorale and her sales team, as well as Michelle Leo and her team. Thank you to Katt Phatt for the cover art. Thank you to Molly Powell, Kate Keehan, Maddy Marshall, and the UK Hodderscape team. Thank you to the team at Hachette Aotearoa New Zealand for championing this book at home. And thank you to Tricia Lin, where this book all started.

Thank you to Māma and Bàba, to whom this book is dedicated, because I wouldn't be the writer I am today otherwise. Thank you to Eugene and Oriana too, of course. And over in my eternal corner, thank you to Hawa Lee, Aniket Chawla, Sherry Zhang, Emily Ting, and Vivian Qiu.

Thank you to the cheering crowd who keep me sane at school: Kushal Modi, Jackie Sussman, Ryan Foo, João Campos, Andrew Noh, Rebecca Jiang, and Ennie Gantulga. Thank you also to Professor D. Brian Kim, for answering all my questions about Russian duels.

Thank you to the friends in publishing who always make me *soft emoji*. To Tashie Bhuiyan, for our bestie (and now roomie!!!) goals. To the Gen Z D.A.C.U squad for our absolute chaos: Christina Li, Racquel Marie, Zoe Hana Mikuta (and Tashie again). To the "let's get dinner" group chat for our cutest brunches: Daisy Hsu and CW (and Xiaolong!). To all the friends whose virtual (and sometimes real) company I always enjoy: Rachel Kellis, Alina Khawaja, Eunice Kim, Miranda Sun, Tori Bovalino, Heather Walter, Alex Aster, Meha, and Sara.

Thank you to the authors who were kind enough to blurb These Violent Delights: Natasha Ngan, Amélie Wen Zhao, Joan He, Tessa Gratton, and June Hur. Thank you to the cheerleaders of These Violent Delights as it released, including but certainly not limited to Shealea and Caffeine Book Tours, Michelle, Skye, Lauren, Lili, Kate, Tiffany, Alexandra, and Subtle Asian Book Club.

Thank you to the booksellers who have cheered for these stories and pushed them into readers' hands. Thank you to the librarians who have loved these stories and placed them onto the shelves. And, always, thank you to the readers. Thank you to everyone who has a These Violent Delights-related username on the socials, to those who have drawn fan art or written fan fiction, to those who make currently reading threads on Twitter or fan edits on Instagram or excited videos on TikTok. Books move and rise by the power of word-of-mouth, and I couldn't be more grateful to have your excitement and support.

Author's Note

As promised, the author's note at the back of the sequel is a continuation of where we left off with the first book's author's note. Like *These Violent Delights*, *Our Violent Ends* works with true history, but the characters (and monsters) are invented. With the exception of Chiang Kai-shek, the real life Commander in chief of the National Revolutionary Army, other figures who play a part in the city's politics are a figment of my imagination. Whether they are mentioned in brief or appear on page as characters, they are only loosely based on players who may have been active at the time and cannot stand as parallels to any true historical figure.

However, while I wanted to tell a story of fiction, I attempt to depict the climate in 1927 Shanghai as truthfully as I could manage. The Shanghai Massacre you see in Chapter Forty and Chapter Forty-Three was the first event that kicked off the Chinese Civil War, after the Nationalists and Communists finally broke apart as allies. Chiang Kai-shek, the foreigners, and the Green Gang entered an informal alliance to launch a surprise attack on the dawn of April 12 to eradicate Communists from the Kuomintang. The events that I portray are true—with a swap of the Green Gang for the invented Scarlet Gang, and an insertion of the White Flowers among the purged—but timelines have been hastened for the sake of the story. In history, the purge's initial surprise attacks occurred at dawn on the 12th, while the union workers marched to the 2nd Division headquarters in protest on the 13th. In *Our Violent Ends*, the protest occurs more quickly, unfolding later that same day of the purges. Despite the timeline change, the real students and workers were indeed fired on despite being unarmed, and there remains no confirmed source as to how many were killed in the purges or the massacre. The White Terror in Shanghai erupted soon after to continue arresting and executing any Communists who hadn't fled the city, and while *Our Violent Ends* implies the name had some relation to the White Flowers, it was called the White Terror in actuality because of the anti-Communist violence. The textbooks will do a better job at explaining the details than a fictionalized account, and if you are interested in the events that are depicted in the book, non-fiction resources are the place to go. At the end of the day, this is only a novel that works with real history, and it aims to be as messy and nuanced as the way we piece together accounts of what happened in the past. There is no good faction; there is no bad faction. Power changes hands in the blink of an eye, and real people in history make decisions that go on to alter the whole course of a nation. Other events that are condensed for timeline include the takeover in Chapter Thirty-One, where the seizure of Shanghai came as a result of the workers' armed uprising. When this happened on March 21, this was already their third armed uprising, which *Our Violent Ends* omits given the first uprising was the altered version seen at the end of *These Violent Delights* and the second uprising occurred in February which was excluded for the sake of story coherency.

Other small historical adjustments include the appearances of buildings that actually didn't exist yet. The Grand Theatre, which the book opens with, was not constructed until 1928. Then it went bankrupt and was redesigned in 1932, officially opening again with its Art Deco architecture in 1933. The Paramount dance hall—otherwise known as Bailemen (literally translated for "gate of 100 pleasures")—was also not built until 1932, opening to the public in 1933. However, because these sites became critical focal points of Shanghai's glimmering golden era, they needed their shining time in this book despite being a few years ahead of schedule. At the very least, the scene is now set for the 1930s, which is soon to come....

WANT MORE?

If you enjoyed this and would like to find out about similar books we publish, we'd love you to join our online Sci-Fi, Fantasy and Horror community, Hodderscape.

Visit hodderscape.co.uk for exclusive content form our authors, news, competitions and general musings, and feel free to comment, contribute or just keep an eye on what we are up to.

See you there!

HODDERSCAPE
NEVER AFRAID TO BE OUT OF THIS WORLD

 @Hodderscape 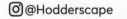 @Hodderscape 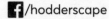 /hodderscape